DEATH
ON THE
BEACH

OTHER TITLES BY ANNA JOHANNSEN

The Island Mysteries

The Body on the Beach

DEATH ON THE BEACH

AN ISLAND MYSTERY

ANNA JOHANNSEN

TRANSLATED BY JOZEF VAN DER VOORT

THOMAS & MERCER

Text copyright © 2018 by Anna Johannsen
Translation copyright © 2020 by Jozef van der Voort
All rights reserved.

Previously published as *Das Mädchen am Strand* by Edition M in Luxembourg in 2018. Translated from German by Jozef van der Voort. First published in English by Thomas & Mercer in collaboration with Amazon Crossing in 2020.

Published by Thomas & Mercer, in collaboration with Amazon Crossing, Seattle

www.apub.com

Amazon, the Amazon logo, Thomas & Mercer and Amazon Crossing are trademarks of Amazon.com, Inc., or its affiliates.

ISBN-13: 9781542018975
ISBN-10: 1542018978

Cover design by @blacksheep-uk.com

Printed in the United States of America

First edition

DEATH
ON THE
BEACH

Prologue

Sunday 17 July

I can't hate them. I don't want to hate them.
And I don't want to turn my back on God.
If only I knew why this is so difficult.
Is there really just one way? God created us all.

Nobody should pass judgement over their neighbour.
Everyone has the right to live.

Including me.

1

Lena Lorenzen stood alone at the railing, braving the September gusts. The ferry was minutes away from the dock in Wittdün. After a tiring few days at the Schleswig-Holstein CID in Kiel, she had clocked off late in the afternoon and only just made it in time to catch the boat to Amrum. She now had six whole days to spend with Erck. Sleeping, going for walks, cooking and – as he had hinted over the phone – talking.

Over the last eight weeks they had rekindled their relationship – though Lena inwardly avoided that word since she felt it didn't adequately describe the current situation. After fourteen years away from the island, she had been assigned a case on Amrum at the beginning of summer and had crossed paths with Erck on the very first day. During the days that followed, something had happened that she had thought impossible: after fourteen years of absence, it seemed she had fallen in love with him again. Or had he always been there, in the distant background? Over the last couple of months, she had enjoyed leaving her work behind in Kiel and immersing herself once more in this different but deeply familiar world. A few weeks ago, Erck had surprised her by whisking her away to the lighthouse for an evening of champagne and romance. Lena grinned. She wouldn't forget that night in a hurry. But she also knew that, at some point, the question of the future would rear its head. The ferry slowed and Lena breathed in deeply, savouring the salty North Sea air, before sighing and heading back to her VW Passat.

A short while later, she was steering her car through Wittdün. The wind had dropped and the temperature was around twenty degrees – remarkably mild for the beginning of September. As the last of the houses disappeared behind her, the red-and-white lighthouse came into view on the horizon. In the light of the setting sun, the landscape spread out before her looked like something from a picture book.

She drove slowly through Nebel, the village in the middle of the island. Many of the old Frisian houses with their steep gables had been built in the eighteenth and nineteenth centuries by sea captains returning home, and today they lent the village its picturesque charm. Before long she arrived in Norddorf, where Erck lived in an old house that he'd renovated himself. After Wittdün, Norddorf was the main centre for tourists on the island, with hotels, holiday apartments, restaurants and cafés.

Lena pulled up in front of the house and got out of her car. The ground floor was brightly lit and the faint sound of soul music reached her through the open window as she threw her duffel bag over her shoulder and walked up to the front door. Erck had offered her a key weeks ago, but she had turned it down, pointing out that the door was never locked anyway. From the corridor, she caught the aroma of cooked fish. She put down her bag and opened the kitchen door. Erck was standing in front of the hob, wearing a checked apron and stirring something in a small saucepan.

She wrapped her arms around him, pressing her face into his back. 'Why do you always go to so much trouble?' she asked, laughing. 'We could have gone out for dinner.'

He turned round and kissed her tenderly. 'It helps me pass the time until you're with me. Besides, it's much nicer here than being surrounded by chattering tourists.'

Lena stroked his cheek. 'I'll just freshen up a little and then I'll be right back. Do I have time?'

'Sure, as long as you're sitting at the table in ten minutes ready to praise my cooking to the skies.'

Lena laughed. 'Only your cooking?'

'I'll leave that up to you. Now get out of my kitchen, I need to concentrate on dinner.'

As Lena emerged from the bathroom, her work phone rang. She glanced at the screen and gave a quiet groan. 'Good evening, Detective Superintendent,' she greeted her boss. 'I'm sorry, but I've taken a few days off and I'm not in Kiel right now.'

'Good evening, Detective Inspector,' Warnke replied in a honeyed tone.

Lena was instantly on her guard. Although she and her boss had negotiated a ceasefire of sorts after the case on Amrum, their relationship was still strained. If Warnke was cooing at her like this, there had to be a reason for it.

'Of course I'm aware that you're on holiday. All the same, may I ask where you're staying?'

'I'm on Amrum.'

After a slight pause, he continued. 'A fourteen-year-old girl was reported missing this morning on Föhr. The local police conducted a search for her today with the help of the fire brigade and a few volunteers, but to no avail. Around two hundred officers are ready to resume the hunt first thing tomorrow, and I need a capable colleague who knows the island and the people who live on it.'

Lena held her breath. A young girl – still a child, really. She hated cases that involved children. 'I'm really sorry, but I—'

'You'd be doing me a big favour if you could look into the matter. The girl might well turn up tomorrow, and then you can just tack an extra day or two on to your holiday. You'd really be helping me out . . .'

Lena cursed herself for not switching off her phone, but she was loath to invent an excuse. And why shouldn't she help out with the search effort, since she was in the area? After all, Föhr was just an hour on the ferry from Amrum. Erck was self-employed and could manage his own hours as he saw fit. Besides, the case might drag on, which meant she could stay near him for longer than originally planned. 'Are you personally involved in this?' asked Lena on a hunch.

DSU Warnke hesitated. Eventually, he answered, 'No, of course not. But I have an interest in someone from our team being on the scene, in case . . .' He broke off mid-sentence.

Lena pricked up her ears. It was far from normal for a CID officer to be assigned to a missing-person investigation as a pre-cautionary measure. Most cases involving missing teenagers soon turned out to be a false alarm. If Warnke was asking her personally, it suggested there was more at stake here than he was willing or able to tell her.

'Trust me,' he added.

'A little more information might be useful.'

Lena heard him give a quiet sigh. 'The girl's parents belong to a free church. A deeply devout free church – I think that's how she'd put it.'

'She?'

'My wife. She's in contact with this community. Only very loosely.' The words *for now* hovered unspoken at the end of the sentence. 'She – my wife – asked me . . . She thinks it extremely unlikely that this girl would have run away from home. As I say, my wife and I don't know this family personally.' Warnke sighed again. 'All the same, you'd be doing me a huge favour if you . . .'

Lena noticed that Warnke's voice had changed during the conversation. At first, he had addressed her as a detective superintendent, but now it was Warnke the man who was speaking. She owed him nothing in his official capacity, but on a human level, she couldn't refuse a request like this.

'OK. I'll take the first ferry tomorrow. Please let the officers on Föhr know.'

'Thank you. And sorry again for disturbing you.' DSU Warnke ended the call.

Lena sighed and went back to Erck in the kitchen.

'You're just in time,' he called as he took the fish out of the oven. 'Sit down and dig in!'

A freshly poured glass of white wine was already waiting for her. Erck placed the casserole dish on the table and reached for his glass. '*Prost*. Here's to a few days' peace and quiet, with no death or criminality.'

Lena gave a strained smile as she clinked her glass against his. He looked at her enquiringly. 'That was my boss. A girl has gone missing on Föhr, and he wants me to . . .'

Erck briefly furrowed his brow, but his smile soon returned to his face. 'I get the impression there's only one capable policewoman in the whole of Schleswig-Holstein.'

Lena felt a wave of relief. 'So it seems.'

'When do you need to go?'

'Tomorrow, on the first ferry.'

Erck picked up her plate. 'Can I dish up?' She nodded, and he served her a piece of rose fish and a steamed leek, along with a side of aromatic basmati rice. 'Sauce?'

'Yes, please,' she answered. He handed the plate back. 'Smells amazing.'

'That's the aged Gouda and the herbs.' He looked up. '*Guten Appetit.*'

Softly, Lena asked, 'Are you annoyed that I have to work tomorrow?'

He shrugged. 'I expect I'll have to get used to the fact that you don't have a normal office job. And no, of course I'm not annoyed. Hey – it's your work, and you're really good at it. Let's just pretend that phone call never happened.' He raised his glass again. 'I don't think I've told you today how crazy I am about you.'

Lena smiled as she lifted her glass to his. 'How crazy?'

He took a sip of wine, slowly replaced his glass, and grew serious. 'Enough to make me start googling Kiel.'

Lena swallowed. 'Oh! I don't think you'd like it there. And who'll take over your work if you move?'

Erck managed a portfolio of holiday homes; as well as taking care of the guests, he fixed broken washing machines and showers where necessary and also ran the website. 'An all-round service', he called it.

'Aren't there any holiday homes in Kiel?'

'I don't know. Definitely not as many.'

'Then I'll just have to find another job.' Erck forced another smile. 'But for now, let's eat. It'll go cold otherwise.'

Lena gently stroked Erck's bare chest. After dinner, they had tidied up the kitchen together before making themselves comfortable on the sofa in his cosy living room. So far, they had deliberately avoided the subject of Kiel and her assignment on Föhr.

'It's wonderful spending time with you,' Lena whispered. 'So familiar, and yet still so new.' She kissed him tenderly on the lips. 'Let's just enjoy it. I don't want to think about the future right now – about any contrived arrangements for how we can live together like a normal couple.'

After a short silence, Erck quietly asked, 'And you think that'll work out? Just enjoy it and don't think about anything? We aren't eighteen any more. And even when we were, it didn't work.'

Lena's thoughts turned to her Aunt Beke, who had spent her entire life on Amrum and had never been able to contemplate leaving the island. Lena's mother – Beke's sister – had also loved Amrum. She had died in a car accident shortly after having a row with Lena's father.

Lena had been eighteen years old.

A few months after that, Lena had turned her back on Amrum and on her father. And with a heavy heart, Erck had decided to remain on the island instead of joining her on the mainland.

'That was another life back then,' said Lena. '*I* was another person. And I had no other choice.'

Erck drew her towards him and kissed her. 'I know all that. But I'm afraid of losing you again. There's nothing to keep you on Amrum, apart from Beke.'

'Are *you* nothing? But you're right, I still haven't spoken to my father. Let alone his new wife.'

'New? They've been married for nearly thirteen years now.'

'To me, she's still the new one. Always will be.' Lena pronounced the word *new* with all the contempt she could muster. She would never shake that woman's hand. And her father had already been dead to her long before he remarried. Her family consisted of Aunt Beke, and nobody else.

'You know, I happened to run into your dad two weeks ago. He struck up a conversation and—'

Lena placed her finger on his lips and simply shook her head.

2

Lena entered the unassuming two-and-a-half-storey brick building that served as Föhr's police station, which stood in the harbour close to the ferry terminal. Even at this early hour of the morning, it was bustling with activity. An advance party for the search team from the mainland had evidently just arrived. Lena asked for directions, and soon found herself face to face with the officer in charge. As she showed him her warrant card, she sensed Sergeant Arno Brandt's guard go up.

He handed her pass back to her. 'CID? To what do we owe the pleasure? I thought you only got involved in the toughest cases.' Brandt took a half step back and regarded her coolly, almost stand-offishly, as if he wanted nothing to do with her. Lena guessed he must have heard about her last case on Amrum, where there had been difficulties with the local police.

'I happened to be in the area, and I've been asked to lend my support to the team here.'

Arno Brandt blinked. 'No problem! We can use all the help we can get, of course. I was just on my way to the briefing. Would you like to join me?'

Lena nodded and followed her colleague.

It was clear as they stepped through the door that the station's small recreation room had been turned into an incident room. Two policemen were standing in front of a large map, and Brandt introduced them as the leaders of the search team. Then he turned to Lena. 'I guess you'll be running things from here on in?'

'Like I said, think of me as a reinforcement. I reckon it's best if we just get started. Everything else will become clear in due course. What's happened so far?'

Brandt took a deep breath and walked over to the map. There were also three photos pinned to a bulletin board, all depicting a young girl with long dark hair. 'Maria Logener hasn't been seen since Monday afternoon – the day before yesterday. When her sister reported her missing yesterday morning, we immediately checked the ferries. Nobody has seen her buying a ticket, and she hasn't been spotted on the ferry itself. We've examined the CCTV footage from Monday and have been keeping an eye on it since she was reported missing yesterday, but there's been no sign of her. She hasn't left the island on a plane either, so she must still be here on Föhr.' He marked a point on the map. 'She lives with her parents in Oldsum. We started with a sweep of the immediate surroundings before putting together a small search party.' He gestured at the map. 'One team is heading north, while the other is working its way west. Put simply, we haven't found a thing so far.'

One of the officers from the mainland – a man named Jakob Meier – approached Brandt. 'A couple of hundred people will be arriving on the ferry in just over half an hour to help with the search. What do you suggest? Should we start again from scratch, or leave out the area you searched yesterday?'

'Good question. I think it's more important to expand the radius of the search. The colleagues working on the case yesterday may not have any experience in this area, but I doubt they would have missed anything.'

Meier pointed to the map. 'What about this canal? Has it been thoroughly searched?'

'Not with boats,' Brandt replied. 'But I've requested a RIB boat for the day from the marine police.' He looked at his watch. 'They'll cover that whole area, and they should be starting very soon.'

'OK – in that case, we should focus on the land. My team will cover the area up to Utersum. Heino' – he turned briefly to his colleague – 'will strike out in the other direction. We should be done by the early afternoon, and then we'll both head south.'

Heino nodded. 'The supply unit should be getting here in three hours. Is everything in hand with the sports hall?' he asked.

'Yep,' Brandt confirmed. 'It's being prepared as we speak. The beds for the search party can go up around midday at the latest, along with everything else that's needed.'

'Perfect!' Meier turned to Lena. 'What do you think?'

'Did the interviews with the parents or with other people close to Maria give us any clues about her likes and dislikes? Where does she hang out in her free time? What do her friends have to say? Where was she last seen on Monday?'

Brandt looked at her with a pained expression. 'The parents aren't exactly cooperative.'

'What do you mean by that?' Lena probed.

'They belong to a cult that seems to reject government authority. The father didn't even help out with the search. He just stayed at home with his wife and prayed. In the end, all our information came from Maria's adult sister, who's actually only visiting the island and doesn't seem to know very much about her life any more. She was the one who reported Maria missing.'

'OK,' Lena replied. 'Give me the interview notes and I'll look into it.'

Jakob Meier cleared his throat. 'Are we done here? We'd like to take a look at the area before our people move in.'

'Of course. I'll be on the scene in an hour to coordinate the search, as we agreed,' said Arno Brandt. 'The equipment ought to be in place already. Good luck.'

As the two policemen left the room, Brandt turned back to Lena. 'Let's see if we can find those notes for you now.'

◆ ◆ ◆

Lena drove out of Wyk with the folder of notes on her passenger seat. Keeping left just before Oevenum, she passed through Alkersum and gradually approached Oldsum. Broad fields and meadows filled with grazing cattle stretched out on both sides of the road. Lena had almost forgotten that the island quickly began to look very rural as soon as you left the 'capital' of Wyk.

Lena turned right towards Oldsum, following a sign pointing to the Wadden Sea Conservation Centre. A few yards after the sign marking the edge of the village, she turned right again and found herself in front of an old farmhouse. She parked her car and approached the building. Only now did she notice that it had brand-new wooden windows, and that the roof must have been renovated fairly recently too. The front garden was remarkably well maintained: the lawn was neatly mown, the flowers planted in a straight line, and the path to the front door looked as though it had been swept that very morning. After two rings of the bell, the door opened a crack and a woman in her early fifties stared coldly out at her. Lena recognised her from one of the photos hanging on the bulletin board at the police station: Rosa Logener, Maria's mother.

'We aren't interested in buying anything,' said the woman, and was about to shut the door when Lena held up her warrant card. 'Lena Lorenzen from Schleswig-Holstein CID. I'm here about Maria. Could we have a quick chat?'

Slowly, Maria's mother opened the door. 'My husband is out. Could you come back in an hour?'

'I'm afraid not, Frau Logener. I need to speak with you now. It's really important.'

Hesitantly, Maria's mother stood aside and let Lena in. Then she walked down the corridor, opened a door and gestured for Lena to go through it. 'Please.'

Lena found herself in a large, open-plan living room and kitchen. To her right was a kitchen counter with a cooker, fridge and sink. Opposite it stood a table with four chairs. It looked as though Frau Logener had just finished cleaning and tidying up.

'Would you like some tea?'

'Yes, please, if it's not too much trouble, Frau Logener.'

'Of course not.' Maria's mother turned away and set a pan of water on the hob. Lena examined her carefully. The woman was a head shorter than her and wore her hair pinned up into a bun. She didn't have any make-up on, and her dark-blue gingham dress resembled a tabard.

Once she had poured the tea, she approached Lena at the table with their cups.

'Please, sit with me,' Lena urged her.

Maria's mother hesitated briefly before pulling out a chair and sitting down.

'You – or rather your daughter, Johanna – reported Maria missing yesterday. As you know, a large police unit is coming from the mainland today to continue the hunt.'

'My husband told me.'

'The search is one thing, Frau Logener, but it's just as important for us to learn as much as possible about your daughter in order to find her more quickly.'

Rosa Logener nodded imperceptibly. 'My husband—'

'I'm sure you can help me too, though,' Lena interrupted her gently. 'When did you last see Maria?'

Maria's mother looked at her hands. Lena feared that she would refer her to her husband again, but then she began to speak in a quiet voice. 'On Monday. Maria went to school in the morning. She took the bus to Wyk, just like every day.'

'Was that the last time you saw her?'

Once again, Rosa Logener took her time answering. 'She came home for lunch.'

'And what happened after that?'

'She told me she had homework to do and went up to her room.'

'What time was that?'

Rosa Logener seemed to think for a moment. 'Just before two o'clock. We always finish eating around then.'

'Were your husband and your daughter Johanna here for lunch too?'

'Walther was on the mainland.'

'And Johanna?'

'She's . . . she wasn't here.'

'So you were alone with Maria. What happened next?'

'I don't know. When I went up to check on her, her room was empty. I looked all over the house for her but she wasn't here.'

'Does Maria have a mobile phone?'

Rosa Logener shook her head.

'She doesn't have one at all? Or is it broken?'

'Only my husband has a telephone. He needs it for work.'

Lena made a note on her pad. 'Your daughter Johanna reported Maria missing to the police the following morning. Why did your daughter do that, and not you or your husband?'

Frau Logener said nothing.

'Where is Johanna right now?'

Once again, Lena didn't get a reply. She pressed on. 'My colleague told me that Johanna doesn't live with you any more, but that she's visiting at the moment. Is that right?'

'Johanna is at university. She didn't want to stay with her family.'

'Where is she studying, and what course?'

'Kiel. She wants to be a pharmacist.'

'So she's studying pharmacy in Kiel and is presumably on her summer holiday at the moment. How long will she stay on Föhr?'

'I don't know.'

Lena groaned inwardly. Did this woman really know so little about her daughter, or did she just not want to say anything? She didn't seem at all concerned about Maria either. Lena had known parents of missing children who could scarcely utter a word and had sat before her in a state of complete anguish, as well as others who had paced anxiously up and down the room and bombarded her with endless questions. But she had never encountered a mother who seemed so placid and uninvolved before.

'May I see Maria's room?' Lena finally asked.

Rosa Logener got haltingly to her feet. 'My husband should be back any minute now. Can't we wait for him?'

Lena forced herself to remain calm. 'No – I'm sorry, but time is of the essence in a missing-person case. I'm sure you understand that. Where is Maria's room?'

Frau Logener stood uncertainly before her and seemed to be wondering what to do. Eventually, she led Lena along the corridor and up the stairs. Maria's room was fairly large – big enough for a couple of double beds. There was a small desk beside the bed, along with a wardrobe, an armchair and a bookcase on the opposite side of the room. The walls had no posters on them; nor were there any other objects that would suggest it was home to a fourteen-year-old girl. Everything seemed oddly sterile.

Lena walked up to the bookcase and pulled out a few books. She found a Bible, along with various treatises on religion and some classic novels that had been borrowed from the library. 'Does Maria keep a diary?'

Rosa Logener gave a start. She looked at Lena with wide eyes. 'Our Maria is a good girl.'

'I didn't mean to doubt it – we just need more information in order to find your daughter.'

'Maria doesn't have anything like that.'

'Does she own a computer or a laptop?'

'No.'

Lena could see how much Rosa Logener was struggling to answer her questions, but she found her reaction hard to understand. Wasn't this woman interested in her daughter being found? So far, Lena had only a few pieces of the puzzle, and none of them fitted together. That was no surprise at this early stage, but Maria's disappearance seemed particularly mysterious to her. There was no evidence so far that the girl had left Föhr. Maria hadn't been spotted at the ferry terminal or aboard a boat; nor had she been seen anywhere else on the island during the period in question, as far as they knew. What was more, Rosa Logener's behaviour invited suspicion, although Lena baulked at that thought.

'Would you have any objection to my carrying out a detailed search of this room?' asked Lena, as nonchalantly as possible.

Just as Rosa Logener was about to reply, a deep male voice thundered from behind her. 'What's going on here? What are you doing in there?'

Lena spun around. In the doorway stood a powerfully built fifty-year-old man who glared at her with steel-blue eyes. 'Herr

Logener?' asked Lena, showing him her warrant card. 'Detective Inspector Lorenzen from the CID. I'm leading the search for your daughter Maria.'

'So what are you doing in her room?'

'I'm looking for clues that might help us. A diary, files on a laptop, that sort of thing.'

'You won't find anything like that here,' answered Maria's father with a stony expression. He stepped to one side and unambiguously gestured for Lena to leave the room. 'Let's go into the parlour,' he said in a tone that brooked no refusal.

Lena nodded to Rosa Logener and followed her husband.

The Logeners' sitting room was at least twice as big as the spacious kitchen. There was a small three-piece suite in the corner, as well as a long table surrounded by numerous chairs. Walther pointed at one of these and then took a seat at the table himself once Lena had sat down. His wife stood in the doorway and seemed to wait for instructions, but quickly disappeared when her husband paid her no further attention.

'As I said, I'm leading the search for your daughter and I need more information about her home environment. Your wife has already told me you were on the mainland on Monday. When did you get back?'

'How is that relevant? Look for Maria, and don't poke around in our private lives!'

By now, Lena was seething with anger, but she managed to retain her composure. 'Herr Logener, you have to trust us. It doesn't look as though your daughter has just got lost somewhere, and right now, every second counts. So – you were on the mainland?'

For a moment, Lena thought the man was about to throw her out of the house, but then he replied in a calm voice, 'Yes. I came back on the last ferry.'

'What did you do after that to find Maria, and did you notice anything unusual? Even the tiniest detail might prove important.'

'I made some phone calls around the congregation, but nobody had seen her.'

'Congregation?'

Walther Logener raised his eyebrows. 'The Brethren in Jesus Christ.' When Lena looked at him quizzically, he continued. 'We're an evangelical free church . . .'

'On Föhr?'

'Not just here – on Amrum too, and on the mainland,' he went on. 'We're a large congregation.'

Lena looked around the 'parlour', as Herr Logener had called it. 'I assume you meet here for your . . . gatherings?'

'I don't know what this has to do with Maria, but yes, we regularly welcome members of the congregation here at our home.'

'And you called these congregation members on the phone?'

Walther Logener took a deep breath. 'Didn't I just say that?'

'And nobody had seen Maria that afternoon or evening?'

'No. Nobody.' Logener suddenly grew serious. He closed his eyes for a moment and his right hand trembled slightly. 'It's as if she's vanished from the face of the earth.' In a quiet voice, he added, 'None of my brethren have seen her. Nobody has.'

'Why was Maria reported missing by your daughter Johanna?' asked Lena abruptly. 'Shouldn't that have been up to you?'

Walther Logener fell silent. Lena wondered why neither he nor his wife had asked her about the imminent search operation. 'Where is Johanna at the moment?' she asked.

'She's elsewhere,' said Logener in a determined tone.

'On the island?'

He looked at Lena with no perceptible emotion. 'Do you have any other questions?'

'Yes, I do. When did you last see Maria?'

'On Monday at six o'clock, over breakfast, like every morning.'

'Did she seem different from her usual self at all? Was she perhaps excitable, or particularly quiet?'

'No, she behaved the way she always does. She was completely normal.'

On a hunch, Lena asked, 'Did you go out with the search team yesterday?'

'No. I stayed here and prayed with my wife.'

3

Lena slumped exhaustedly into the driver's seat. Her interview with Maria's father hadn't got her anywhere. She reached for her phone and dialled a number.

'Johann Grasmann,' answered her young colleague from Flensburg. She had worked with him during her last case on Amrum.

'*Moin*, Johann. It's Lena. I need your help. Can you do some research for me?'

After a slight pause, Johann answered, 'I reckon so. What case are you working on?'

'Have you heard about the missing girl on Föhr?'

'One of my teammates was talking about that just a moment ago. Are you there right now?'

'Yes, and I've just spoken to the girl's parents. They're both very odd characters – members of some dubious free church.' She caught herself. Wasn't DSU Warnke's wife a member of this community? Perhaps even Warnke himself?

'A cult?'

'I don't really know very much about these things. It's called the Brethren in Jesus Christ. Could you look into them?'

'Of course, I'll get on it right away. Should I call you back?'

'I don't have very good reception up here. If you can't get hold of me then send me a quick email to tell me what you've found.'

'Will do.'

'One more thing, Johann. DSU Warnke's wife is also a member of this church, or is about to join it. So be careful. Don't mention it to anyone else for now. I'm not sure what Warnke expects from me.'

'Understood. Look after yourself, Lena.'

Her next call was to Leon, a hacker who occasionally helped her out with certain, not entirely official, inquiries ever since she had saved him from prosecution a few years back. He only picked up after the tenth ring.

'Are you out of your mind? Do you even know what time it is? I was asleep!'

'I'm sorry, Leon. It's important.'

'Oh, of course it is – everything's always super-important and urgent with you.'

'I'll make it up to you.'

Leon laughed. 'Do you have any idea how many favours you owe me by now? Am I on the police payroll these days or what?'

Lena waited a moment until she heard Leon sigh and say, 'All right, fine. What's up?'

She told him she was looking for a missing girl whose parents hadn't proven very helpful.

'I can hardly help you with that though, can I?' answered Leon, who was still in a grump.

'They told me the girl doesn't have a mobile phone or a computer, but I can't imagine that's true.' She gave him the names of the four family members. 'Can you search for smartphones or other devices? The sister is a student in Kiel and she's bound to have an Internet connection. And a phone.'

Leon groaned. 'Are you the police officer here or am I? Can't you put in a formal request? That'd be much quicker.'

'Not really. I wouldn't be asking you otherwise.'

'Ah Christ,' he swore, and hung up.

As Lena was putting on her seatbelt, she heard a knock on the car window. A young woman was staring at her impassively. Lena wound the window down.

'Are you from the police?'

'DI Lorenzen, CID. Who are you?'

'Johanna Logener. I'm Maria's sister. Have you found her?'

Lena got out of the car and shook her hand. 'Not yet, I'm afraid. But the two search teams will be heading out any moment now.'

Johanna sighed in relief.

'I've just been to speak with your parents, but—'

'Oh, I'm sure that must have been a lot of fun for you,' Johanna said bitterly. 'If I hadn't gone to the police, they'd still be sitting there waiting for Maria and praying.' She cast a glance at her parents' home.

'Should we find somewhere else to talk?' Lena asked. 'There must be a café open in Utersum by now.'

Johanna nodded, walked around the car and got in.

Lena knew Utersum from her schooldays. The seaside resort on the west of the island was well known for its wide beach, and there was also a large sanatorium on the southern edge of the village with views over the sea.

From the corner of her eye, Lena examined the young woman sitting beside her. The feminine face with its pale complexion contrasted sharply with the dark, almost black hair that Johanna had casually tied back over her shoulder. She was wearing purple trousers with a white tight-fitting sweater that drew attention to her slim figure, along with matching clip-on earrings and a subtle layer of lipstick. After talking to her parents, Lena could well imagine that Johanna's appearance alone would be a source of provocation. 'Do you visit your family often?'

'No. If it weren't for Maria, I'd just stay in Kiel. I'm studying pharmacy.'

'Your relationship with your parents is . . . not a harmonious one?'

Johanna shrugged. 'If you want to put it like that. You could also say that I'm the black sheep of the family – the rebellious daughter who desperately wanted to get out into the big wide world.'

'What could they have against you going to university?'

'Ask my father that. He'll tell you what's good for women. And a degree in pharmaceutical science definitely doesn't fall into that category.'

By now, they had reached the first houses in Utersum. Lena remembered that there had been two cafés in the village back when she was at school. 'Any preference as to where we go?' she asked, glancing across at the girl beside her.

Johanna pointed at an old Frisian house with a 'Café' sign hanging over the entrance. 'That one's nice.'

Lena parked the car and the two of them got out and walked up to the building.

'Do you think Maria is still alive?' Fear was now written all over Johanna's face.

'There's no reason to think otherwise at the moment. Most missing teenagers turn up within forty-eight hours. So let's hope for the best.'

Lena held the door open and waited for Johanna to go inside. The customer-facing areas of the building had been lovingly refurbished and offered a pleasantly calm atmosphere. They found a table by one of the small casement windows and ordered some coffee.

'Could you tell me a little about your sister? What she's like, her hobbies, any problems she's been having?'

'Maria is . . . she's very fragile, you should know. Ever since I moved to Kiel two years ago, she's been – how should I put this? – the sole focus of my parents' attention. She's their last hope, since I've been such a disappointment to them across the board.'

'The sole focus of their attention? What do you mean by that?'

'You know my parents belong to this cult?'

'I know that they're active members of a free church.'

'Church! Don't make me laugh. It's like something from a horror movie. Nothing but Bible, Bible, Bible. As for children – there's no playing or running around allowed. I had to be a good and obedient little girl. Wear my neat little dress and look at the floor while the adults handed down their pearls of wisdom to me. Finally I couldn't take it any more, so I was glad to get a place on my course.' She gave a contemptuous laugh. 'I expect my father had long since chosen a husband for me. He probably wanted to marry me off while I was still a child. It's like something from the Dark Ages. They're a bunch of complete zombies.'

'Are your parents devoutly religious?'

'It really doesn't have anything to do with religion. They're just sick, plain and simple. Obsessed with their holy family. The two of them don't have any other children, so they've basically smothered Maria with all their so-called love. And of course anyone who loves their child like that is entitled to beat them too. Can you imagine? Oh wait, I'm sorry, I should have said "guide them back to the path of righteousness", or . . .' By now, there were tears running down Johanna's cheeks. Lena handed her a tissue, which Johanna took, but didn't use.

'Please, try to stay calm,' said Lena. 'I'm sure this isn't an easy situation for you, but if you want to help your sister then tell me about her. How does she deal with the pressure from your parents? Does she have friends who might be hiding her, or even a boyfriend? Where would she go if she did want to run away from home?'

Johanna took a deep breath and wiped the tears from her face with the palm of her hand. 'She doesn't have any real friends. The kids at school blank her, and she doesn't get on with the other teenagers in the Brethren either. If it weren't for me . . .' Johanna shook her head. 'I shouldn't have gone away. It's my fault.'

'I can understand why you might want to blame yourself, but you aren't responsible for your sister. That's your parents' job.' Lena gently stroked Johanna's hand. 'So you don't know of any places where Maria spends a lot of time?'

'This is a small island. There aren't many options. Plus she's under constant surveillance. I know she likes to walk on the beach near Utersum whenever she has a free period at school – though she always has to make sure she gets home on time afterwards.'

'The beach, then. I expect you don't know exactly where?'

When Johanna shook her head, Lena reached for her phone. Standing up and moving away from the table, she asked Arno Brandt to send a few officers to the coast.

'That's a little tricky right now,' he demurred once she explained the situation to him. 'But that area is scheduled for this afternoon or tomorrow, anyway.'

'We can't wait that long. Please send eight colleagues there immediately. Six of them should head south along the dyke and the other two should go north.'

'Frau Lorenzen, that will completely mess up our—'

'Do you need to be told by my superiors? I'd be happy to arrange that, but it'll only cost us both a lot of time and stress.'

'I have to say I don't like your tone one bit,' Brandt snorted. 'I'm the one leading the search operation, and I'll—'

'I don't think we need to discuss this any further right now,' Lena cut him off and ended the call.

A few seconds later, she had DSU Warnke on the line and was explaining the situation to him.

'Give me ten minutes,' he answered.

Back at the table, Lena smiled at Johanna. 'Apologies, I had to make a quick call to the station.'

'Sergeant Brandt?' asked Johanna.

'Yes – do you know him?'

'I spoke to him briefly yesterday – otherwise, no. But his son Enno is in Maria's class at school. Enno is one of the handful of kids who've been tormenting her over the last few years.'

'I see. Do you know any of the other students involved?'

Johanna gave another name, before adding, 'Maria didn't like to talk about it. As crazy as it sounds, she didn't want to get anybody into trouble.'

'And why do they bully Maria?' Lena asked.

'Those dirtbags are well aware that our parents belong to a cult. I came in for some of it too when I was at school, but I stood up for myself. Maria is completely different. She'd rather turn the other cheek.'

'Do you think this might have anything to do with Maria's disappearance?'

Johanna shrugged. 'I have no idea. None at all. But Maria definitely suffered a lot from all the teasing.'

'Your father told me that Maria doesn't have a mobile phone or a computer. How do you manage to stay in touch with her?'

Johanna hesitated. 'You're on our side, right? If I tell you something then my parents won't hear about it, will they?'

'No, of course not. I'll do all I can to avoid that happening. Did you give her a mobile phone?'

'Not a phone, but a second-hand tablet with a SIM card. If Maria made phone calls at home, my parents would get wind of it straight away. You know Skype?' Lena nodded, and Johanna continued. 'With a tablet, she can write to me whenever she wants, and we can call each other too when she's out of the house. With video and everything.'

'I'm sure you've tried to get in touch with her?'

'She hasn't been online since Monday. I keep checking, but . . . nothing.'

'Could you give me the name of her Skype account and the number of her SIM card? I'll need your mobile number too.'

Johanna reached for her phone and noted the details down on a serviette. Once she was done, Lena texted the information to Leon. 'I've sent it to my colleague. He'll deal with this professionally. Please leave your Skype account logged in – it could be important.'

'Of course.' Johanna gave Lena an imploring look. 'What else can I do? If there's anything, just tell me – whatever it is.'

'I understand you're visiting your parents. When did you arrive?'

'As a matter of fact, I'm not actually visiting them at all. I only got here yesterday, on the first ferry, and I went straight to the police when I arrived. Maria hasn't been in touch at all since last Thursday, and eventually I got so anxious that I called the house on Monday evening. Luckily my father was out, as I probably wouldn't have found out what was happening otherwise. I last spoke to my mother at about half seven, and then I left very early the next morning.'

'Did you stay at your parents' house last night?'

'No. My father was furious that I'd reported Maria missing without asking him first. I'm staying with an old schoolfriend in Wyk.'

Lena was slowly starting to understand what it must have meant to Johanna to grow up in such an extremely religious household. 'Is there anything else I should know about your family?' she asked cautiously.

Johanna looked at her hands and shook her head.

4

Lena knocked on the window of the Mercedes van and opened the door. Inside, Arno Brandt was sitting with two other policemen, staring at screens. The head of the police station on Föhr took off his earphones and gave her a sullen look. 'Any news?' asked Lena.

Brandt got out and closed the sliding door behind him. 'If we'd found the girl, you would naturally have been the first to know, Inspector.' He virtually spat that last word at her.

Lena smiled at him. 'I would have expected no less. How is the search on the beach coming along?'

He made a show of looking at his watch. 'They ought to be leaving about now.'

'Excellent. Oh, and one other question: who spoke to the missing girl's sister yesterday? I couldn't make out the signature on the interview notes.'

'What's this about? Was something wrong?'

'Sergeant Brandt, we aren't playing paperchase here. This is police work. I hardly need to explain to you how important it is to carry out thorough background research.'

Brandt stared at her with a surly expression. 'I can't tell you off the top of my head who conducted the interview – I'd need to look it up first. But I think the search for the missing girl should take priority right now. Or have I got that wrong? Of course, we could always ask for advice from our superiors, since you seem to know your way around the upper echelons.'

'That won't be necessary in this case,' said Lena, choosing not to rise to his bait. 'I'll be at Maria's school, if you need me.' She gave him a nod and headed back to her car.

◆ ◆ ◆

In the car park of the *Eilun Feer Skuul* – the single complex that housed the island's grammar and comprehensive schools – Lena looked up Johann's number on her phone.

'How are you getting on?' she asked, once they had exchanged greetings.

'It's all rather complicated. The Brethren are an offshoot from the Mennonites, who are mostly found in the USA, but also have a presence in northern Europe. I couldn't find out how many members the church has in Schleswig-Holstein, but it's been estimated at fifty to eighty families, which would amount to three or four hundred people. The Föhr congregation appears to be a relatively large one, but like I said, there's no way to get an exact membership number.'

'Did you find any specifics about the views of these congregations?'

'That's also tricky. Of course I found a few things online, but they were all highly subjective assessments – generally from people who had left the church. I also called the cults and sects commissioner at the regional assembly to ask her opinion. Strictly speaking, the Brethren don't fall under the scope of her monitoring, but she was still able to give me some information. I can sum that up in a few key points: extremely conservative; almost entirely literal in their interpretation of the Bible; the man is the head of the family, with traditional domestic roles for the women, just like two hundred years ago; and children generally marry within the community. In fact, the commissioner suspects they sometimes even have their marriages arranged for them during childhood. There have been complaints about kids being subjected to corporal punishment, but those are presumably exceptional cases – one of the hallmarks of the Mennonites is actually their pacifism. All in all, the community goes to a lot of trouble to avoid negative press. But I couldn't find out if that means certain things get swept under the carpet.' He paused briefly, then asked, 'Do you really think DSU Warnke has something to do with this club?'

'They're a free church, or a sect – not a club. And to answer your question: not directly. But his wife seems to be very religious and I suspect she's in contact with the community.'

'Truth be told, I find fundamentalists of any stripe completely abhorrent.' He gave a loud snort. 'Anyway. Is that enough for now? Like I said, there isn't much information publicly available. I'll spare you the history of the Mennonites for the time being, as I can't imagine it'd be particularly relevant to the case.'

'That's great, Johann. You've been a big help.' She paused. 'It might be that I need some assistance on the ground here too. And of course I thought of you. Would you have any objections?'

'I can pack my bag in five minutes.'

'I thought you might like to get out into the fresh air! I'll call you back. Say hi to everyone in Flensburg for me.'

'Anybody in particular?'

Lena smiled. He'd obviously heard that she'd got to know his colleague Ben at a conference. For Lena, it had been a one-night stand – but she wasn't sure Ben felt the same way.

'No – nobody in particular, DS Grasmann.'

They said their goodbyes, and Lena got out of her car. Before her stood a typical 1970s school building: white-fronted, with plenty of concrete and glass and a flat roof. At first glance, it didn't look like much had changed since Lena had taken her *Abitur* exams here more than fourteen years ago.

The memories came flooding back as she made her way to the headmaster's office. After attending the comprehensive on Amrum until the age of sixteen, she had switched to the grammar school on Föhr for a further two years in order to complete her *Abitur* qualification. Like most students from Amrum, Lena had lived on Föhr, staying in a dedicated hall of residence and travelling back at weekends. Yet after six months, she had increasingly begun heading back to Amrum to see her mother during the week too. At that time, her mother had been struggling with her marriage, a problem that had grown more intense with each passing month.

Lena knocked on the headmaster's door and entered. A short, balding man was sitting behind a desk reading a book. Only when Lena cleared her throat did he look up.

'Good morning, Herr Schröder.'

The man sized her up and tilted his head back slightly as if trying to remember something. Then he smiled. 'Lorenzen. Lena Lorenzen. Am I right?'

'Absolutely.'

He raised his hand to stop her from saying anything more. 'You started here just after the fiftieth anniversary of the school. That must have been in 2000. You were one of the students from Amrum. And you did very well in your *Abitur*.' He beamed at her. 'So what are you up to now?'

Lena took her warrant card out of her pocket and handed it to him over the desk. 'I'm afraid I'm here in a professional capacity. It's about Maria Logener. I'm sure you're already aware that she's been missing since Monday.'

Schröder's expression grew serious. 'Of course. We've given the sixth-formers the day off so they can help with the search effort. Has she still not been found?'

'I'm afraid not. I'm here to speak with Maria's teachers and fellow students. Who is her form tutor?'

'Herr Weissdorn. He joined us fairly recently.' Herr Schröder got to his feet and walked over to the timetable, before turning back to face Lena. 'He's currently teaching class 8b, but there's a break starting in ten minutes.'

'OK, in that case I'll wait outside the classroom for him. Will I still be able to get hold of you later?'

'I don't have any teaching until this afternoon. If I'm not here, ask the secretaries – they always know where I am.'

Lena gave him a nod. 'I'll be on my way, then.'

A few minutes later, she was standing to one side of an open door as a pack of chattering adolescents trampled past her. Once the last student had left the classroom, she stepped inside and approached a man who was roughly her own age. 'Lena Lorenzen, CID Kiel.' She showed him her warrant card. 'Are you Maria Logener's form tutor?'

He held out his hand. 'Lars Weissdorn. I did think it was odd that nobody from the police had come to the school yet.' He went over to the door and closed it. 'Would you like to sit down?'

'That won't be necessary – I only have a few questions. After that I'd like to speak to Maria's classmates.'

'Understood. Ask away.'

'I'm looking for clues that might help us find Maria. How would you describe her and her background?'

Lars Weissdorn took a deep breath before he began to speak. 'Academically, she's top of the class. People do say that left-handers are meant to be more intelligent. Goethe, Newton, Einstein, Leonardo da Vinci . . . perhaps there's something to it. I mean, in terms of her performance she's truly one of our best students, if not the best outright. At first glance she seems fairly reserved – almost shy. But that's understandable. Her parents . . .'

Lena nodded. 'Yeah, I know.'

'And Maria's classmates know it too. You always get one or two kids who pick on the weak, or on those they assume to be weak. Of course, we do our best to nip that sort of thing in the bud, but we can't monitor every aspect of our students' social lives. Nor would we want to, to be quite honest.'

'Maria gets bullied – is that what you're telling me?'

'*Bullied* – that's a little strong. Teasing might be the right word for it. She isn't exactly one of the popular kids, but I wouldn't call her an outcast either.'

'Who is her closest friend?'

Lars Weissdorn shrugged. 'That's a difficult question. I don't think she's very close to anyone in her class. But I've often seen her together with Lisa Behrens from the other class in her year.' He stood up and went over to the window. 'She ought to be down there somewhere, now I come to think of it.' Lena followed him and looked down on her old school playground. Some of the younger students were playing football, but most of them were standing in small groups, huddled over their phones. 'Or apparently not,' he added. 'Yes, I think Lisa is who you want to talk to. If I understand correctly, her parents are also members of the same . . . community. But she lives with her grandmother here on Föhr, while her parents live on Amrum.'

'Thanks for the info – I'll make sure I talk to Lisa. You mentioned just now that Maria *seems* reserved, almost shy. Does that mean she isn't really those things?'

'No, I think that's more of a cover. Her father is . . . have you met him already?'

'Yes, I spoke to her parents earlier today.' As she spoke, Lena cast a glance at her mobile phone. The search team on the beach must be halfway through by now.

'Did you meet her mother too?' Weissdorn asked. Lena nodded, and he went on. 'Well, you're ahead of me there. Maria's mother has never set foot in this school, as far as I'm aware. I've only ever had any contact with her father, and he came across as highly authoritarian to me. He doesn't seem to have much faith in our school system either. But you were asking if Maria really is shy. No, I think she's a very clever and independent girl who hides behind a facade to make herself less vulnerable to attack. Like I say, that's perfectly understandable, given the conditions that she lives under. But at the same time, she's highly sensitive. I can't imagine it's easy to reconcile those two things.'

Lena made a few notes. Lars Weissdorn seemed to know his students well and clearly wasn't solely interested in their academic performance. 'So in your view, there might be a very different Maria hiding behind that facade?'

'I'm not a social worker, let alone a psychologist. But yes, there's another Maria; a highly confident girl who knows what she wants, or is at least searching for it – which is perfectly normal at her age. I really can't tell you any more than that, though. I'm sticking my neck a long way out as it is. Under normal circumstances I would never share information like this with anyone, as a lot of it is based on speculation. After all, she's one of twenty-five students in my class, and there's plenty I don't know about them, if you see what I mean.'

'Absolutely. Thanks all the same for telling me.' Lena's phone buzzed. She grabbed it and looked at the screen. It wasn't a message from Arno Brandt; instead, Erck had sent her a sunshine emoji followed by a number of dots. Lena smiled, then instantly shifted her focus back to the conversation at hand. 'Sorry about that. Message from the team. Thank you once again – you've been a very big help to me so far.'

'You're welcome. Every single one of the children is very important to me. What else would you like to know?'

'As far as I'm aware, there are quite a few families in this religious community. Do you know of any other children from that background?'

'In Maria's year, there's only her friend Lisa. I don't really know about the other year groups, but I can ask around among my colleagues. We share this building with the comprehensive school.'

'Yes, I know – I went to school here myself.'

'Oh!' Lars Weissdorn looked at her in surprise. 'And now you're . . . I see. But I was about to say that I think the other school also has a few boys from this . . . religious community. I just don't know their names, I'm afraid.'

'Could Maria's disappearance have anything to do with the school? She got good marks, you said. She isn't the most popular girl in the year, but she muddles along. Have I understood all that correctly?'

'Yes, you have. And naturally I've already been racking my brains to figure out how it all might fit together. I mean, this is only a school, of course – but even so, we still get wind of certain things. And yet I haven't come to any conclusions. I have no way of knowing what happened to Maria at home.'

'Does she have a boyfriend?'

'No, I don't think so. At least, I've never seen her hanging around boys, and I haven't noticed a particular boy pay her any special attention, so to speak. Admittedly, she's a very pretty girl – but like I said, it's hardly a surprise when you consider her religious background.'

Lena's phone rang. When she saw Arno Brandt's name on the display, she apologised again to Lars Weissdorn and stepped away from him before taking the call.

'We've found her,' he yelled down the line. She could hear the wind rushing in the background. 'She's dead.'

'Where exactly?'

'On the beach. Just up from the Goting Kliff. Drive down Wikingwai and then head north on foot.'

'Are you on the scene?'

'Yep. Got here two minutes ago.'

'You're certain?'

'I've only seen the photos. But it's her. I'm pretty sure of that.'

'I'll be there in ten minutes. Cordon off that whole section of beach. Nobody is to touch anything. Do you understand?'

'I'm not an amateur,' Brandt growled and abruptly ended the call.

'Has something happened?' asked Lars Weissdorn from across the room.

'Thank you for your help – I'll be back to continue this conversation another time.' She spun on her heel and hurried down the corridor.

5

Lena drove at high speed down the L214 towards Nieblum, her blue lights flashing. She raced through the village and turned down a side road just outside Goting, where a bridleway behind the houses led directly to the beach. There were already two police cars parked where the road turned into a path, with one of the island policemen standing beside them. Lena leapt out of her car, greeting him hurriedly as she ran past, and sprinted onwards.

An entire section of the beach had been cordoned off, with a policeman stationed at each end. Without breaking her stride, Lena held up her warrant card to her colleague, who nodded and lifted the police tape for her. Arno Brandt and three officers from the search team were standing beside the body. The scene looked oddly peaceful: the girl was sitting propped up, leaning slightly to one side, in a depression on the edge of the beach. Her eyes were closed and her arms rested on her lap.

Brandt walked up to meet Lena. 'Looks like suicide. She slit her wrist.' He held up a box cutter inside a transparent plastic bag.

Lena suppressed a critical remark and hoped that Arno Brandt had taken a photo of the position of the knife before moving it.

Over the years, Lena had had to get used to looking at dead bodies — but she still found it extremely difficult when the body belonged to a child. She slowly approached the scene, taking in her surroundings. Before her sat the girl, whom she recognised from her photograph. Maria's torso was resting on the gentle slope of the sand dune, her head fallen to one side. Her coat and skirt were caked in dried blood that had flowed from her forearm. Lena took a small digital camera out of her pocket and asked her colleagues to step back. Then she photographed the body from all sides.

'I've sent for a doctor from Wyk. He should be here any minute,' announced Arno Brandt.

'We won't need him,' Lena answered.

'But . . .' Brandt began, but stopped when he noticed her expression. 'OK, I'll tell him not to come.'

Lena nodded and turned back to the body. She'd bled to death, that much was clear. Yet there was still some small detail nagging at Lena. She cast her gaze over the girl and the beach, but nothing caught her eye. Maria's long checked skirt had ridden up slightly, and the left sleeve of her cream-coloured coat was rolled up to the top of her forearm. 'Have you notified the crime-scene investigators?'

Brandt coughed. 'Do you think that's necessary? It looks like an obvious case of suicide.'

Lena carefully stepped back from the girl. From the looks of the ground around the corpse, her colleagues had already destroyed plenty of evidence. 'Set up a ten-foot perimeter around the body. Nobody is to come near her until CSI have got here.' She walked a few yards off to one side and called DSU Warnke to explain the situation, adding, 'I'm not at all sure that this is a suicide. I need a qualified CSI team and I also want a post-mortem to be carried out in Kiel.'

'I'll try to have our team flown in by helicopter. Ask your colleagues to send me the coordinates and secure a landing site.'

'I need Dr Stahnke here.'

Luise Stahnke was a pathologist based in Kiel whom Lena had been friends with for many years. She trusted her with her life.

'I'll see what can be done.'

'I'll also need Johann Grasmann – along with a few other colleagues from Flensburg too, if my suspicions prove correct. We can decide how many further down the line.'

'OK. I'll talk to Flensburg. Grasmann should make it over to you today, with any luck.' After a brief pause, he added, 'Did the girl have problems at school or with her friends?'

'That's not how it looks to me right now, but I haven't managed to speak to many people who were close to Maria yet.'

'Rumours will start to circulate very quickly. I hope you realise that?'

'You mean, because of the parents' religious views?'

'The media will have a field day over that. Don't get me wrong: if the parents have anything to do with her death, I'd be the last person to cover it up. But if they don't, we need to make sure their daughter's death doesn't turn into a witch hunt. Do you understand?'

'I'm with you on that.'

'From now on you're in charge on the ground. I'll take care of the formalities. Can I count on you?'

'As long as you have my back.'

'Of course.' He paused for a moment. 'It's starting to look like we might make a good team after all.'

Lena wasn't sure what to make of his remark. They had called a ceasefire after the Amrum case and managed to work together without butting heads for the most part, but Lena still had little faith that the peace would last. 'I'll call you tomorrow with my first report. Please let me know when the CSI team and Dr Stahnke are on their way.'

'I'll be in touch,' said Warnke, before ending the call.

She walked back over to Arno Brandt. 'I need a landing site for a helicopter.'

'Here on the beach?' he asked incredulously. 'Are they collecting the body?'

'The CSI team is being flown in from Kiel.' She looked at her watch. 'Hopefully they'll be here in less than two hours. Where can they land?'

Brandt looked around. 'There's a meadow up by the road. I'll have it closed off and marked out.'

'Good. No information gets out about this – not a word. I'm holding you responsible for that.' Arno Brandt gulped and seemed about to reply, but Lena was already issuing her next instructions. 'And call off the search operation. I need a team here to sweep this entire section of beach and the path back up to the main road. Plus a dog to track the girl's scent. I don't think she would have travelled very far on foot, but it's worth a try. I want you to stay here and supervise things.' She explained to him which areas needed to be searched. 'I'm going to drive over to visit the parents now. Please arrange transport to take the body to Kiel. The van has to leave today, but Maria's parents need to identify her first.'

'Here on the beach?' Brandt asked a second time, visibly irritated by now.

'Of course not. Once CSI are done, we'll need to find a place where her parents can see her.'

Arno Brandt sighed. 'I'll get on to it.'

On the way to her car, Lena called Johann and quickly brought him up to speed. 'So pack your bags – I need you. Warnke is talking to your boss. When can you get here?'

'I'll be on my way as soon as I get the go-ahead. Right now it's . . . just a second . . . exactly five past two. I'll let you know when I'm on the ferry.'

'I'll ask the local police to find a room for you. One more thing: we'll probably need at least another two officers from Flensburg – more likely four. Tomorrow or the day after, at the latest. Could you pass that on to your boss? Warnke already knows and will be in touch with him.'

'You think there was foul play?'

'Let's wait for the autopsy report – we'll know more then. You should plan to be here for at least a week, by the way.'

'Understood. See you later.'

Lena pulled up in front of the Logeners' house, turned off her engine and leaned back in her seat. As much as she loved her job, she hated having to break the news about the death of a family member to the next of kin. Every time it happened, she pictured herself standing in her own doorway while a uniformed officer informed her of her mother's death.

Slowly, she approached the house. The curtains twitched behind one of the windows; a screeching seagull circled over the house. When the door opened, she found herself facing a man she scarcely recognised. Maria's father seemed to have aged by years. He was stooping slightly, as if he were carrying a heavy weight on his back. His formerly bright eyes were now dull, his right hand trembled gently and his face was ashen. Wordlessly, he stepped aside and beckoned Lena into the house. Then he led her to the kitchen and offered her a seat.

'My wife is resting,' he said, before sitting down with her at the table. 'A member of the congregation called me. You've found Maria?'

'Yes, I think it's safe to assume so. Unfortunately we were too late – I'm afraid she was dead when we found her. Judging by the photos, it's definitely Maria. I'm so sorry, Herr Logener.'

He stared at Lena as if he didn't understand what she'd just told him. Eventually, he spoke. 'Was she . . .?'

'I'm afraid I can't say anything yet. We need to wait for the results of the examination.' In situations like these, Lena avoided the word 'post-mortem' in order to spare the feelings of the relatives.

'Was it an accident?'

'I can't tell you that yet, either. But I'm afraid I need to ask you to identify your daughter before she—'

'What's going to happen to her?' Walther Logener interrupted her.

'As I said, we need to get to the bottom of the circumstances behind Maria's death, so she'll be examined in Kiel. I expect she'll be back here on Föhr in a few days' time.' Lena found it hard to talk about the young girl like this, as if she was still alive.

'I don't want that,' he said, with his last strength. 'You can't do that without our permission.'

'In this case, I'm afraid we can – in fact, the authorities are legally required to investigate the cause of death. I'm truly sorry, but there's no way around it.'

'Maria is my daughter.'

'I understand your concern, Herr Logener, but . . .' Lena stood up. 'I'll let you know as soon as you can see her. That'll probably be in a few hours.'

Walther Logener nodded resignedly.

'I'll show myself out,' said Lena, before leaving the kitchen.

Outside the house, she encountered three women and two men wearing similar clothes to the Logeners. Judging by their appearance, they were also members of the Brethren. Lena greeted them and kept walking.

Back in the car, her phone rang. She picked up instantly. 'Hi, Leon. Do you have anything for me?'

'The tablet was briefly online half an hour ago. I got in, but I didn't have time to do anything.'

'Do you know where it was logged in?'

'I can't pinpoint the location. But it's somewhere on . . . that island.'

'Föhr – the island is called Föhr.'

'Whatever. I'll call you back.'

Before Lena could ask another question, Leon hung up.

The knowledge that the tablet had been online galvanised Lena. Had the culprit taken it? She called DSU Warnke, briefly explained the situation to him and asked him to put in a request to locate the device.

'I'll get hold of a court order and set the ball rolling,' he said. 'By the way, Dr Stahnke and the CSI team are on their way to the airfield. They should be with you in an hour.'

'OK. I've just notified the parents. I'll get back to you tonight with a brief report.'

Warnke thanked her and ended the call.

Lena toyed indecisively with her phone. On the way to Maria's parents, she had resolved to tell Johanna personally about her sister's death. She'd assumed that the news wouldn't spread all that quickly – yet the fact that Maria's father had already been informed suggested that the island's grapevine was shorter than anticipated. She looked up Johanna's number and hit the call button.

'Johanna speaking,' said a timid voice.

'This is Lena Lorenzen. Where are you? I'd like to talk to you again.' She tried to sound as nonchalant as she could, but there was no fooling Johanna.

'What's happened?' she asked in a voice filled with dismay. 'Have you—'

'Where are you?' cut in Lena.

Johanna Logener gave the address of her friend in Wyk.

'I'll be there in ten minutes,' she said, and ended the call.

Lena started her engine and drove across to the other side of the island. Johanna's schoolfriend, Nina Grote, lived in a block of six flats on the edge of the village. Lena ran up the stairs to the attic apartment. Just as she was about to ring the bell, the door swung open.

'What's happened?' asked a near-hysterical Johanna.

'Can I come in?'

Johanna nodded anxiously and stood to one side. She led Lena into a cramped living room with a sofa and two armchairs.

'Please, have a seat first,' Lena suggested, and waited until Johanna was sitting safely in one of the armchairs.

'Have you found Maria?'

Lena took a seat opposite her. 'It looks like it, yes. We've found the body of a girl on—' The rest of her words were lost amid Johanna's loud, piercing shrieks. She pitched forward on to the floor, gasping for breath. Just then, a young woman dashed into the room and knelt beside her, taking her into her arms and comforting her until the wailing subsided into a quiet whimper.

Lena nodded to Johanna's friend and placed her card on the small side table. 'I'll come back tomorrow,' she said quietly. 'Will you look after her?'

'Yes, of course,' answered the young woman.

Johanna lay silent in her arms, as if she had fallen asleep.

6

As she got out of her car by the beach under Goting Kliff, Lena heard the distant sound of the helicopter. The local police had used traffic cones to mark out a clearly visible landing site on the meadow. Lena waited until the chopper landed and the team from Kiel had disembarked, including Luise Stahnke. She went over and welcomed the group, leading them to the spot where Maria Logener had been found.

'Another island assignment, then?' asked Luise as she and Lena walked towards the beach.

'I happened to be on Amrum.'

'Happened to be? You've been spending an awful lot of time out here lately. Are things more serious than you were letting on?'

Three weeks ago, Lena and Luise had gone on one of their girls' nights out. After her third cocktail, she had finally broken her strict silence and told Luise about Erck.

'He thinks so, at any rate.'

'What about you?'

Lena shrugged. 'I don't have time to think about it right now. There's a fourteen-year-old girl lying dead on the beach over there, and I can't believe it was suicide. I wanted you to take a look at the scene for yourself.'

'Hey – a helicopter ride over our beautiful countryside is nothing to be sniffed at.' Luise paused, before quickly adding, 'Even if the occasion is a tragic one.'

By now, they had reached the perimeter. Lena hung back and watched from a distance as her colleagues got to work. Luise would conduct an initial superficial examination before determining the time of death by taking the temperature of the body and gauging the onset of rigor mortis, as well as applying various other methods that would lead to a more-or-less accurate result. Scientifically speaking, it was only possible to narrow the time of death down to a four-hour window, but Luise usually gave Lena a shorter unofficial timeframe.

An hour or so later, Luise walked back over to Lena while the two men from CSI continued to meticulously scour the scene. 'Such a pretty girl,' said Luise with a sigh. 'It's always tough when they're so young.'

'What's your initial impression?'

'You know I can't say anything until after the autopsy—'

'I know,' Lena interrupted. 'Off the record, though. What do you think?'

'She has light bruising on both her forearms. I don't want to pre-empt the post-mortem, but your suspicions aren't completely far-fetched. Right now I really couldn't tell you when the bruising occurred, though. The cuts on the wrist look different from those I've seen in other cases too.'

'Could you—?'

'Basically, most people cut across the wrist. The blood flows more slowly that way, and it often isn't enough to cause death. An incision along the arm is more dangerous – if it's long and deep enough then you'll bleed to death in no time.'

'And she has a cut along the arm?'

'Yes – and as far as I can judge right now, a very deep one. Which means the incision opened not only the veins, but the underlying artery too – and then it's all over pretty quickly. I've rarely seen such deep and accurate cuts before in a case of suicide. But I still need to examine everything in detail.'

'Sure. What about the time of death?'

'I'd need to pin down certain factors more precisely, but the information I've managed to enter into my software so far suggests a time between ten and fourteen hours ago. Rigor mortis hasn't fully set in, there was no response to stimulation of the facial muscles, and the pupils responded minimally to eye drops.'

Lena looked at her watch. 'It's now just after five, so that means she died between three o'clock and seven o'clock in the morning. Can you narrow that down any further?'

'You know the rules. Not officially. Besides, I need to go over the data again in the lab and look a few things up. Here on the beach, with all this wind, the body will have cooled down more quickly than if it had been found on a street corner.'

'Off the record, though – what's your best guess right now?'

'Eleven to twelve hours. But like I said—'

'I get it. So we're talking about five or six o'clock this morning. That's something to go on for now. Hopefully I can get the girl to you in Kiel by the end of the day. I'd like the parents to identify her here to spare them the trip to the mainland.'

'That's not best practice, as you know.'

'I'll make sure they stay at least two feet away from Maria. The rest I'll answer for.'

Luise nodded, then went back over to continue her examination.

Eventually, one of the forensic technicians waved to Lena. That was the sign that the body was ready for collection by the funeral home. Lena walked over to the two black-clad men waiting near the perimeter. 'You can take the body now, but put these on first, please.' Lena handed the men two pairs of latex gloves. 'I'll follow you in my car. Wait for me before you unload her at the other end.'

The older of the two men nodded and walked over to the corpse with his young colleague. With practised movements, they placed the young girl inside the CSI body bag.

Lena said her goodbyes to Luise. 'Thanks for coming. Will you call me as soon as you've finished the autopsy?'

'Of course. And Lena . . .'

'Yes?'

'Don't let this case get under your skin. You need to keep a professional distance.'

Luise knew her all too well – Lena had always found it very difficult to deal with child victims of violence. She needed to keep a clear head to stop her emotions from clouding her judgement. 'I'll be careful, Luise. Johann Grasmann is on his way here.' She grinned. 'He'll keep me in line if I get carried away.'

Luise gave her a farewell hug. Just before she reached the path, Lena looked back over her shoulder and waved at her.

It took only a few minutes for her to drive to the funeral parlour. Once there, she called the officer who was waiting with the Logeners at their home and asked him to bring them in to identify the body.

Walther Logener had to support his wife as they got out of the police car, and they walked slowly into the funeral home together and stood before their younger daughter in silence. Eventually, Herr Logener nodded and led his wife back out to the car.

It was early evening by the time Lena met Johann Grasmann on the quayside. They both looked out at the departing ferry, which was carrying the hearse and the accompanying police officer towards

Kiel. The boat would dock in Dagebüll in an hour and a half, and from there it would be another eighty-five miles to the state capital.

'That's one thing out of the way,' she said. For the first time that day, she realised how much strain she'd been under. She threw her head back and stretched. 'Do you have somewhere to stay?' Lena asked the young DS.

'The local police found me a small bed and breakfast. I booked two rooms, just in case you miss the last ferry.'

'Always thinking ahead,' said Lena. She looked at her watch and, as she did so, Erck flashed through her mind. 'The last ferry today leaves just before nine, so we still have a few hours.' Johann had been assigned to her from the Flensburg police force during her investigation on Amrum over the summer. Although he was only twenty-five years old, they had quickly developed into an effective team. Lena had to apply the brakes on his impetuousness from time to time, but she was 100 per cent certain she could count on his loyalty.

'Have you eaten anything today?' Johann asked.

'Not really. I haven't had time.'

'Let's go for a working dinner then. I'm sure you still know your way around here. Where should we go?'

'That was a long time ago. And to be honest, when I was at school I didn't have the money to eat out anywhere.'

Johann took his tablet out of his messenger bag and spent a few moments tapping the screen. 'Zum Walfisch looks good. Apparently they have outdoor seating too.' He swiped his finger over the display. 'If the food tastes only half as good as it looks, it'll be ideal.'

'You do know we aren't here on holiday, right?'

'Of course, Detective Inspector.' He glanced back at the tablet and then pointed towards the pedestrian zone. 'Down there. About five minutes' walk, I reckon.'

A little later, they found themselves standing in front of the restaurant – a modern building with a small portico over the entrance. The outdoor tables were already occupied, so they found a quiet spot inside. Once they had ordered, Lena asked, 'Have you found out anything more about this religious association?'

Johann nodded. 'I've done a little background reading. Let's start with some more general facts about the Mennonites. As a movement, they've been around since the sixteenth century. They started up during the Reformation. I don't want to bore you with the details, and I expect they aren't really relevant to our case anyway, so I'll just point out that there's never been a single centralised Mennonite movement. It's sort of a guiding principle. A lot of things are organised at the level of the congregation, and they've always rejected central authority of the kind you see in the Catholic Church, or the Evangelical Church here in Germany – which of course partly explains why the movement has developed in so many different directions. The Mennonite Brethren formed in the late-nineteenth century, and they place a stronger focus on the individual congregation and its autonomy, with lay people playing a more important role. Presumably that all happens through private worship and Bible study groups – but don't ask me exactly how it works. There isn't much information available online. Have I already mentioned that there are also some hardliners who home-school their children?'

'No, I don't think so.'

'It seems there were disputes over that here on Föhr too, but in the end the authorities got their way. That doesn't seem to be the case everywhere, though. Even though home-schooling is illegal in Germany, I've read that some states don't come down on it as harshly, and don't do much beyond issuing a few fines.'

'How long ago were these disputes?'

'I'd need to take another look at my notes, but from memory I'd say it was about fifteen years ago.'

Their drinks arrived. Johann had ordered a beer, while Lena opted for a Coke.

'All in all, the Mennonites seem to have some very conservative views. The men make the decisions, the women look after the home and family, the children have to do as they're told. I even found a video on YouTube where one member of the sect genuinely argued that all women who've had more than one sexual relationship in their life are whores. And this guy wasn't in his eighties – he was the same age as me.' Johann swallowed half his beer in one draught. 'I hardly need to tell you that the congregations are homophobic too. In general, they work a lot with fear: fear of hell, of Satan, of goodness knows what else. It's all about blind obedience to authority figures. In this case, that means the parents – or I guess the father, who decides what the family should and shouldn't do.'

'That all sounds pretty grim,' Lena interjected.

'Depends on your point of view. It definitely wouldn't be the right lifestyle for free-spirited, independent types. But anyone looking for – or in need of – a strong sense of cohesion will find like-minded people in the community and will certainly feel happy there, at least to begin with. These aren't necessarily bad people. Quite the opposite, in fact. A lot of them very consciously put their faith into practice and spend a lot of time thinking about their fellow human beings. I think there's definitely empathy there – just within narrow limits. The whole thing reminds me very strongly of my childhood on the Lower Rhine, which is a deeply Catholic area.'

'I have to admit I don't have much personal experience with all this. I didn't grow up in a very religious family . . .' She paused, and her thoughts turned to her father. Had he ever even been to church? Lena herself had never been christened; nor had she had any contact with organised religion. 'But then I have you for that. Thanks for the info.'

'Any time,' answered Johann, who flashed a broad grin before picking up his glass and taking another huge swig of beer. 'So when do we get the post-mortem results?' Lena had already told him of her doubts about the possibility of suicide on the way to the restaurant.

'We'll definitely get something over the phone tomorrow, but it might be a few days before we have the written version. For the time being we should assume foul play, though.'

Just as Johann was about to take his notebook out of his pocket, the waiter arrived with the main course.

'I believe the sole was for the gentleman?' he asked. Johann nodded, and the waiter deposited the plate in front of him.

Lena had chosen steak with potato wedges. 'Well, *guten Appetit*,' she said, reaching for her cutlery.

A quarter of an hour later, Johann pushed his empty plate aside and pulled out his notebook. 'Back to the case. Where should we start tomorrow?'

Lena wiped her mouth with her napkin and drained her glass. 'Good question. First of all, we should get ourselves settled in at the police station. I'll call Sergeant Brandt later and ask him to arrange an office for us tomorrow. We'll find out at the briefing whether anything turned up during the search of the area around the body. Then we'll hopefully have the initial results from CSI, which will give us a sense of what might have happened.'

'OK. So we're assuming foul play. The girl' – Johann peered at his notes – 'Maria Logener was missing for forty-eight hours. If we take the presumed time of death into account, that leaves us with just under forty hours when we don't know where she was. Even if she spent an hour in her bedroom, that still gives us a fairly long period to investigate.'

'That's right,' said Lena. 'Two whole nights. And it's too cold for her to have slept out on the beach without any kind of shelter. Tomorrow we'll have to check which of Maria's belongings are missing. Did she plan to run away from home? If so, she would have taken a backpack full of clothes with her. Is her ID card still there? Things like that.'

'Do you think the parents will be more cooperative now?' asked Johann. 'Didn't you say that the father basically threw you out of the house this morning?'

'I've been wondering the same thing. But we'll be able to get hold of a search warrant quickly enough if our suspicions of foul play are confirmed. I'll talk to Warnke again later – maybe he can arrange something in advance. I'd prefer not to conduct a compulsory search of the whole house, though. As soon as people on the island find out that Maria didn't kill herself, they'll start to come up with their own theories. I'd be glad if we could keep the parents out of the firing line when that happens.'

'You're right. This could quickly turn into a witch hunt.'

'Have you done a background check on the parents?'

Johann nodded. 'No criminal record. And nothing else worthy of note either. But I'll talk to the local police tomorrow – they might know more.'

'Do that. And then we should hold an in-depth interview with the sister too. I just hope she's fit to talk again tomorrow. She seemed to know Maria better than anyone.'

'What about the friend from the other class? What was her name again?'

Lena took her notepad out of her pocket and briefly flicked through it. 'Lisa Behrens.' She looked at Johann. 'Can you find out where she lives?'

'Sure.'

'Then we have the form tutor. I had to cut our conversation short today, but he seems to be very observant when it comes to his students. And while we're at the school, we should also talk to Maria's classmates – both the boys and the girls. By the way, I've been told that Sergeant Brandt's son was actively involved in bullying Maria.'

'Oof, that sounds like trouble.'

Lena grinned. 'You'll look after me, though, right?'

7

Erck circled his finger around Lena's belly button. She'd arrived an hour ago, taken a shower and crawled into bed beside him. 'Do you have to catch the first boat in the morning?'

'I know it's hardly worth going to sleep, but I didn't want to stay on Föhr.'

'Why not? It's a nice island.'

Lena poked him playfully in the ribs. 'You know exactly what I mean. And yes, I wanted to spend the night with you.'

'Because of my superb mattress?'

'Among other things.'

Erck looked around the bedroom. 'Because of the wonderful ambience?'

Lena sighed and kissed him on the lips. 'Shut up and give me a cuddle. Otherwise I'll swim back to Föhr right now.'

'In the middle of the night?' he asked, feigning dismay. 'I can't be having that.' He took her in his arms, kissed her and whispered, 'I'm glad you came back.'

Erck placed a steaming cup of coffee on the kitchen table in front of her.

'Thanks,' said Lena. 'You really didn't have to get up with me, though.'

'I know I could have stayed in bed, but then I would have had to get up on my own, and I've been doing that for . . .' He pretended to count back. 'Has it been fourteen years now?'

Lena took a large gulp of her coffee and shoved the gun that one of the forensic technicians had brought over from Kiel for her the day before into its holster. 'Could be. I haven't been counting.'

Erck leaned over and kissed her on the forehead. 'It doesn't matter, Detective Inspector. You're here now. Occasionally, anyway. And maybe—'

'Please, Erck. Not today. We can talk about it when I have a clear head, OK?'

He went over to the sink, poured himself a cup of coffee and returned to the table. 'OK,' he finally said. 'Beke asked about you, by the way. We were meant to visit her today.'

'Bugger, I'd completely forgotten. Did you tell her about the case?'

'Yep, she knows already. We can go and see her at some point over the next few days.' He closed his eyes and quietly added, 'Or weeks.'

Lena sighed inwardly. She had evidently underestimated how unhappy Erck was with their long-distance relationship – though did the last couple of months even count as a relationship? 'You know that the first forty-eight hours are crucial. If we don't find any leads now, then . . .' She tailed off. What did Erck want from her?

'I'm sorry,' he said, after a few moments of silence. 'That was really bad timing. You focus on your case. We'll discuss everything else another time. OK?'

Her attempt at a smile fell short. 'Yep, we definitely will. Delayed is not forgotten.'

'I always used to say that too. Do you remember? When you wanted to jump in the North Sea far too early in the year. Just a quick dip, you said, but you swam such a long way out. I felt cold just watching you.'

Lena remembered how she had run from the sea up to Erck on the beach; how he had waited for her with a huge towel in his hands and then taken her into his arms.

'Or when you desperately wanted to sleep on the beach, although it would have been far too cold even with a tent.'

Lena laughed. 'Were you really that much of a wimp? I remember you very differently.'

'How, then?' Erck instantly asked.

'Strong, confident, and yet tender and sensitive.' Lena noticed that her words seemed to make Erck uncomfortable. 'Hey, what's so bad about that? It's just how you were.' She leaned forward, kissed him on the lips and quietly added, 'And how you still are.'

'I don't know . . .' He glanced to one side and his eyes fell on the clock. 'You don't have much time.'

Lena slowly got to her feet. Why couldn't she say the three words that lay on the tip of her tongue? Was she afraid there would be no going back? Three words that meant so much – that were spoken millions of times every day all over the world. Why did she find it so difficult to say them? 'I'll just clean my teeth and then I'll be on my way.'

When she emerged from the bathroom, she found Erck waiting for her in the corridor. 'Will you call me when you get there?'

'Sure. Maybe I can get away a little earlier today.'

'We'll see.' He hugged her. 'Look after yourself.'

She gently stroked his cheek with her palm. 'See you later, Erck.'

As she made her way across Amrum towards Wittdün, the sun began to emerge from behind the horizon. Lena suppressed the urge to turn off just after Nebel and go for a stroll around the small harbour in the village of Steenodde. Her thoughts turned to Beke, with whom she had walked the path along the Wadden Sea countless times. Her mother had often joined them too. They had always stopped in Steenodde for a cup of tea and a slice of cake before walking all the way back to Norddorf. Lena made a mental note to call Beke later that morning.

The first houses in Wittdün appeared in front of her. A few minutes later, she pulled up on the esplanade in front of the jetty and got out of her car. At that time in the morning there were just a handful of tourists waiting at the dock, who presumably had a long journey home ahead of them. Lena breathed in the salty sea air and went over the next few days in her mind. They hadn't gathered much useful information so far. If the autopsy didn't show any clear evidence of third-party involvement, then the case would soon be closed.

Ever since she had seen Maria lying on the beach, the image had haunted her thoughts. She knew from the statistics that more than half of all suicides were by hanging, followed by a handful of desperate individuals who threw themselves off bridges or overdosed on medication. Wrist-cutting was the least common method – partly because victims were often discovered in time, or because they cut in the wrong place. It also took incredible willpower to injure oneself with a knife badly enough to cause death. Had Maria really been capable of that? Had the pressure on her been so great that she'd seen no other way out? What role had her parents' religion played in all this? Lena and Johann would need to look at all these questions over the next few days and, with luck, they'd find some answers.

When the first cars in the queue began to move, Lena walked back to her own car and drove on to the ferry. Soon after that, she was standing in her usual spot by the railing, enjoying the view. The boat would dock in Wyk an hour from now, and her first meeting was at eight o'clock.

During the early stages of a new investigation, Lena avoided trying to come to any hasty conclusions. She found it more important to give free rein to her thoughts – to follow her intuition, note things down as they occurred to her, and gradually draw some initial vague connections before discarding them and coming up with new ones. Only then did the time come to dig deeper. The facts were rarely what they initially seemed to be – that was the real secret to her work. Lies often felt like the truth to the person telling them to the police. Character judgement only got you so far with people like that, and even the best detectives could easily be taken in by them, since they exhibited none of the usual signs shown by a liar.

A few of the other passengers got out of their cars and came to stand by the railing – and as Lena watched them, the various people surrounding Maria Logener positioned themselves in her mind's eye. Sometimes they came close to the victim, before distancing themselves once more. The father, the mother, the sister. The Brethren. The classmates. The best friend. The teacher. Lena felt sure that every new interview would reveal more people in Maria's circle. Each domino knocked over the next one, which would bring down more in turn.

'Hello, Lena,' said a voice behind her.

Only when she turned around did she realise who it was.

'How are you?' asked her father, who took a half step back when he saw her expression.

This was bound to happen at some point, thought Lena with dismay. It had just been a question of time. And yet she still felt completely unprepared. All the ripostes that she had stored up over the years suddenly vanished, as if scattered by the wind. She asked in a sharp tone, 'What are you doing here?'

'I'm off to Sylt for a few days with work.'

Lena suddenly realised how absurd her question was. It was none of her business why her father was travelling wherever he was going, and it didn't interest her either.

'Can we talk?' he asked.

'There's nothing I want to talk to you about,' said Lena, leaning forward slightly as a sign that he should move aside.

'Please. It would mean a lot to me,' said her father gently. 'Please, Lena.'

She was still torn between fight and flight, but she could feel her resistance slipping away. 'Well? What do you want?' she asked angrily.

'Shouldn't we go inside? How about a cup of coffee?'

'I've already had one. So?'

Werner Lorenzen gave an audible sigh. 'I've heard you've been spending more time on Amrum again.'

She shrugged.

'I was hoping we might be able to see each other. Talk to each other. Get some things off our chests, I mean.'

Lena said nothing and stared directly at him.

He looked away and began to speak – hesitantly at first, but then more and more fluidly. 'It must have been . . . a terrible time for you . . . back when Mama . . . yeah, when your mother and I didn't get on so well and we were constantly arguing. I didn't realise at the time how much that affected you. I probably just didn't want to see it, and that was a terrible mistake on my part – I know that now.' Lena's father raised his head and looked her in the eye. 'I can only ask you for forgiveness. Believe me, if I could take everything back, I'd do it right here and now. But I can't.' He sighed heavily and stared at the floor. 'And yes, I expect I'm partly responsible for your mother's accident. I had nightmares about it for years afterwards. Even now, I still wonder whether I could have stopped it from happening if I'd reacted differently that day.'

Lena stood as if in a trance, forcing herself to suppress all sympathy for him. She thought of her mother, of her awful death in a roadside ditch, of the last days she had spent with her, and rage gradually welled up in her once more. 'That's exactly the problem,' Lena snarled at him. 'It can't be taken back. It's your fault, and you can't make up for it with a few fine words.' Her voice grew louder and started to shake. 'Find somebody else to absolve you. I can't do it and I don't want to.' From the corner of her eye, she could see that several people had turned to look at them.

Werner Lorenzen fell into a pained silence. Eventually, in a quiet voice, he said, 'I'm so sorry, but I understand. If you change your mind, then I'd love to find a quiet moment to talk it all over with you. Goodbye, Lena.' With tears in his eyes, he turned and hurried over to the staircase.

Lena stared angrily after him. Why did he have to run into her on the ferry, of all places, where there was no escape? Why couldn't he accept her decision and leave her in peace?

I've got more important things to do than . . . God fucking damn it!

She turned around and stared at the horizon, where the outline of Föhr was just coming into view.

8

In the incident room, Johann was standing by the large map and talking to Arno Brandt and Jakob Meier from the search team. He walked over to Lena as soon as he spotted her. 'Morning. Should we make a start?'

Lena greeted first Johann and then the two policemen. 'Can you bring us up to speed? Did the search of the area around the body turn anything up?'

Brandt nodded to Meier, who circled an area of beach on the map with his finger. 'We went through everything within a radius of five hundred yards with a fine-tooth comb – as far as Goting in the south, and up to the car park and the little wood behind it on Hockstedeweg in the other direction. Aside from the usual litter left by holidaymakers and rubbish washed up by the sea that you would expect to find on a beach like this, we didn't come across anything obviously useful. Here's a list of the items we found.' He handed it to Lena and then pointed to a long green rectangle on the map. 'The wood here is about twelve acres. We didn't find anything we could connect to the victim there either.'

'Any tyre tracks?'

'The CSI team took a few impressions, but they didn't seem to expect much from them.'

Lena scanned through the list and handed it to Johann. 'How far did the dog manage to follow the scent?'

'Only up to the road, unfortunately. So we can assume that she came by car.'

Or another vehicle, Lena inwardly added.

'It was a windy day and the dog had trouble following the trail over the sand. We made several attempts, including further up the path, but with no luck. My men are still here on the island, but I think we can probably withdraw. Or do you have another job for us?'

Lena had already studied the area on Google Earth the night before. There wasn't a shed or any similar structure that Maria could have used as an overnight shelter within a radius of two miles. And they hadn't found a bike, which meant she must have either got there on foot or been driven in a vehicle. Yet there wasn't any conclusive evidence for either of those alternatives. If it was up to Lena, the team would spend the next few days working on an expanded search area, but she knew even DSU Warnke wouldn't give her the go-ahead for that. Even if her suspicions of foul play were confirmed, the effort would be completely disproportionate to the likelihood that they would find anything.

'What about bike tracks?' she asked.

'We found no end of those. Sergeant Brandt tells us that cycling is the most popular way of getting around for tourists on the island. It hasn't rained for at least two weeks, so you can imagine just how many overlaid tracks there are by now.'

Lena sighed. 'All right. In that case, I think you and your team can withdraw.' She shook Jakob Meier's hand. 'Thank you very much for your dedicated support, and have a safe trip back.'

The officer nodded to her and left.

Lena joined Arno Brandt by the map. 'I've had a look at the satellite photos to see if there's any kind of shelter within walking distance.'

'There's nothing,' replied Brandt instantly.

'Could anything new have been built out there over the last few months?'

'No – I'd definitely know if there had.'

'What about beach huts?'

Amrum had a tradition going back many decades of building shelters on the shore out of flotsam and jetsam. It would be perfectly possible to spend a few nights in one of these huts.

'No, that sort of nonsense isn't tolerated on Föhr.'

'Can you completely rule it out?'

Arno Brandt sighed. 'I don't patrol the entire coastline every day, if that's what you mean.'

Lena turned to Johann. 'Can you get in touch with the marine police and ask them to check for us from the sea?'

'Will do.'

'And ask someone from the search team that covered the beach. That way we can rule out any huts to the north, at least.'

Johann nodded. 'What about boats? Are there any moorings on that stretch of coast?'

'No,' Lena answered. 'At best, they can anchor nearby and then come ashore on a smaller boat. So I think that's unlikely, but we should still ask the harbourmaster for a list of everyone who sailed out during the period in question.'

Arno Brandt had been following the conversation with a slightly satirical expression. 'I still think it was probably suicide. Anything else would be absurd. Who would have a reason to murder the girl?'

'Probabilities won't get us anywhere,' replied Lena calmly. 'Maria's family have a right to know what happened to her.'

'If you say so.' He cast a glance at his watch. 'Your office should be ready in half an hour, but we haven't managed to find a solution for your computers yet.'

'I have our laptops here,' said Johann. 'All we need is an Internet connection.'

'If there's anything else I can do for you, then please let me know. In the meantime I'll go back to the escaped herd of cows.' Brandt smiled sourly and left the room.

'He won't make it on to the list,' said Johann with a grin. When he noticed Lena's enquiring look, he added, 'Our Christmas card list.'

'Give him time. I doubt either of us would be thrilled to have a bunch of strangers turn up unannounced in our precinct.'

'OK, I see we're in a good mood today.' Johann's grin widened. 'Let's get to work. Should we talk to the sister first?'

'We should wait for Luise's . . . for Dr Stahnke's initial findings before we interview the relatives again. I want to have another chat with the teacher too. We could get that out of the way first.'

Johann looked up at the building. 'Why do schools always look the same?' he said with a grimace.

Lena ignored him and opened the door. After they had been signed in, she hurried down the main corridor. Johann had called ahead and the headmaster was expecting them.

Johann caught up with her. 'I see you know your way around.'

'I went to school here. Didn't I say?'

'No, you didn't,' murmured Johann as Lena knocked on the headmaster's door.

After a brief chat, Herr Schröder gave them a list of the students in class 10a, as well as the names of the teachers who taught that year group. It didn't include their addresses or any other details.

'We'd like to speak to Herr Weissdorn again, and possibly some of the other teachers too. Plus Maria's classmates.'

'You're obviously very welcome to talk to the staff whenever you like, but I'm not sure about the students. I'd prefer it if they could be accompanied by their parents.'

'We won't be interrogating them, Herr Schröder, simply asking them a few questions. We're just making inquiries. Would it be all right if we gave the students our phone numbers?'

'That's perfectly fine, of course. Herr Weissdorn is currently on a free period. You can find him in the chemistry lab – he's preparing a lesson there.' He sighed. 'This isn't easy for us either, you know. After all, we're partly responsible when a student . . . leaves us like this. We've been asking ourselves what we did wrong, or what we didn't see. I would ask you to take that into account.'

Lena and Johann thanked the headmaster and continued on their way.

When Lena opened the door to the chemistry lab, she found Lars Weissdorn standing in front of a long workbench arranging test tubes. He looked up. 'Good morning.'

Lena returned his greeting and introduced Johann. 'I expect you've already heard the latest news by now.'

He placed a test tube in its box and folded his hands. 'Yes, of course. We're all completely devastated and desperately wondering how it could have happened. I've told the students in Maria's class and had a long chat with them. Frau Braasch is with them now. Eva teaches religious studies and music. Regular teaching is out of the question today, but we didn't want to send the students home either. We think it's best if they stay here, with other people around, so we can look after them.'

'We'd like to talk to you again about Maria,' said Lena.

'Certainly.' He pointed to a large desk with four chairs. 'Should we sit down?'

They took a seat. Lena flicked through her notes. 'Our first conversation was interrupted, as I'm sure you remember. You told me that you thought Maria was a very confident girl, even if she didn't always seem that way to everyone.'

'Yes – and now this. Suicide. To be honest, I just can't believe it. I can't imagine Maria doing something like that at all.'

Lena deliberately didn't mention that they suspected foul play and asked, 'Did you notice any changes in Maria over the last few weeks?'

'I've been racking my brains over that question all day. Naturally, I can't keep every single student under continuous observation in a class of twenty-five. Not least because I only spend a handful of hours each week in the classroom. But the short answer is yes. Maria was having . . . yesterday I would have said a difficult few days, perhaps even weeks. Though that happens to every student from time to time.'

'Can you be any more specific than that?' asked Lena.

'She wasn't taking part in lessons as actively as usual. In hindsight, I'd even say she almost seemed lost in her own thoughts. Like I said, most students will have off days once in a while, so I didn't pay it much notice.'

'So she wasn't participating in class like she normally did?'

'She seemed exhausted, even at the beginning of the day. She was pale and . . .' For a moment, he seemed to be searching for the right expression. 'Yes, sad. Her eyes . . . but it's hard to tell you all this from memory. If only I'd known . . .' He broke off and closed his eyes for a moment.

'Could you describe your relationship with Maria Logener?' asked Johann.

Lars Weissdorn hesitated before he replied. 'I try to treat every student equally, but I'm not always successful. We teachers are only human. But by and large, we have to manage it somehow if we want to be fair to everybody.'

'So Maria Logener was just like any other student to you?' Johann probed.

'As a teacher, you have twenty-five or more little personalities sitting in front of you, and all of them are special. Maybe one or two of them stand out from the crowd slightly, and yes, Maria is' – he paused – '*was* perhaps one of those students who stood out. Not at first glance, but once you got to know her a little.'

'Why?'

'I'm sure you can remember your own teenage years. A lot of the kids are . . . a little chaotic, let's say. They don't really know what to do with themselves and tend to rebel against pretty much everything in the adult world. They play at being grown-ups, but mentally they're still just little children who would rather cuddle up to their mothers. Maria wasn't like that. There was a seriousness about her that you rarely encounter in anyone her age. She sometimes seemed much older than she really was.' He shrugged. 'But like I said, we teachers interact with over a hundred children every day. Perhaps my assessment is completely off the mark. Some of the kids are gifted actors too.'

Lena, who had been listening attentively, stood up. 'It should be break time soon. Where can we find your colleague Frau Braasch?'

Lars Weissdorn pointed out the way and shook their hands in farewell.

'What do you make of him?' asked Lena as they walked down the long corridor together.

'A dedicated teacher. He seemed to like Maria.'

Lena stopped outside one of the classrooms. 'Yeah, he seemed to know what he was talking about.' She knocked and opened the door.

A young woman looked over at them in surprise. 'We're in the middle of a lesson here. Please wait outside.'

Lena walked up to the teacher and then surveyed the class. 'We're from the police. Herr Schröder already knows we're here.' She shook the woman's hand. 'Lena Lorenzen. We'd like to say a few words to the class.'

'Oh, OK.' The teacher stepped back from them.

'Would you have a few minutes for us afterwards?' added Lena quietly.

'During the break, certainly,' answered Eva Braasch.

Lena turned to face the class. A few of the children looked back at her with mournful eyes and it was evident that some of them had recently been crying. Others sat indifferently on their chairs, as if they had no interest in what the police had to say to them. 'All of you will have heard by now that your classmate, Maria, has been found dead on the beach. My name is Detective Inspector Lorenzen, and this' – she turned to Johann – 'is my colleague Sergeant Grasmann. We're investigating the case, and we need the help of everybody who knew Maria.' She turned around and wrote her mobile phone number on the board. 'Please make a note of this number. If any of you would like to speak with me, you can call at any time.'

A few of the students nodded, while others stared at their desks. One girl raised her hand.

'Yes, Anna?' said Eva Braasch.

The girl looked anxious and uncertain. She glanced at the girl next to her before reaching for the pen lying on her desk and gripping it with both hands. Eventually she leaned forward slightly. 'I wanted to ask . . . did Maria really . . . I mean, did she kill herself?'

'Our investigation is still ongoing,' answered Lena. 'At the moment we can't say what happened with any certainty. That makes it all the more important that you tell us about anything unusual you might have noticed over the last few weeks. I can guarantee you that nobody will hear about it other than the police. Not the school, not your classmates, and not anybody else either.'

'Does that mean,' asked Anna, 'that Maria might . . .?' She fell silent.

'Like I said, we still don't know exactly what happened.'

The speaker over the door buzzed, announcing the end of the lesson. 'You're all free to go. If anyone wants to speak with us now, you can find us here in the classroom during break.'

The students got to their feet noisily and left the room. Only their teacher remained behind. 'You wanted to speak with me?' she asked, glancing back and forth between Lena and Johann.

Lena took the lead. 'Your colleague, Lars Weissdorn, told us that you knew Maria well.'

'Oh, did he now?'

'You teach the class religious studies?' Lena continued, choosing not to comment on Frau Braasch's remark.

'Yes, and music too. Of course I know Maria. She's . . . she *was* one of my students.'

'Did you notice anything about her over the last few weeks? Any changes?'

'No, I don't think so. I'm sure you already know that her parents belong to an intensely devout free church. That didn't exactly make her life easier.'

'In what respect?'

'The Brethren are reactionary, to put it bluntly. Strict obedience to your parents, no sex outside marriage, demonisation of all other lifestyles . . .' Frau Braasch shuddered slightly as she spoke those last words. 'And all that during her teenage years. How could that not be a recipe for conflict?'

'Maria argued with her parents?'

'I didn't say that, and I don't know any specifics there either. She raised the subject with me from time to time – after all, I'm . . . I was her religious studies teacher.'

'What did she talk about exactly?'

'Really just the usual topics for kids her age. She wasn't sure whether her parents' world view was really correct. We spoke about religion and the Church, and also about Maria's role in the class. She wasn't always very happy here, you should know.'

'So you were very close to her then? Closer than is normal for a teacher?' Johann interjected. He spoke more sharply than he had to Lars Weissdorn, and Eva Braasch gave him a bemused look.

'Excuse me?'

Lena repeated Johann's question, although she felt sure that the teacher had grasped what he meant.

'I don't understand what you're asking me. Maria went to school here, and I'm her teacher. A good teacher always tries to build a close relationship with their students. That's important if we're going to work together.'

'OK, let's go back to our opening question. You didn't notice any changes in Maria over the last few weeks?'

'Off the top of my head – no, there was nothing. Or nothing I registered, in any case. I'm sorry I can't be more help there.'

'I noticed,' said Johann, 'that the other students in the class look older than fourteen. Or have I misjudged that?'

'You're right. Maria was the youngest here. She was moved up a class in primary school. It's true she was younger – and you could tell that by looking at her, of course – but in terms of her personality she was just as advanced as her classmates.'

Lena's phone buzzed and seeing Luise's number on the display, she answered immediately. 'Hang on a second, Luise.' Turning to Eva Braasch, she said, 'Please excuse me for a minute – I'll be right back.'

She left the classroom and continued her conversation with the pathologist.

'I'm obviously not done yet, but I expect this information will be very important for you,' said Luise.

'What information? Tell me!' Lena urged her.

'I'm pretty certain that the girl was raped. Not right before she died, but about two, maybe three weeks beforehand.'

9

Lena and Johann stood huddled together in the school playground. After the pathologist had called, they had hastily made their excuses to Eva Braasch and left the school building.

'Sorry about that, Luise,' said Lena once she had her friend back on the line. 'I've put the phone on speaker so Johann can listen too. So you think Maria Logener was sexually assaulted?'

'Yep, the evidence is unambiguous. But the bruises on the inner thighs and forearms are at least two weeks old. I couldn't find any semen or pubic hair either, which is no surprise given how long ago it happened. Semen disappears after three or four days, and the rest would have been washed away in the shower.'

'But the bruising leaves no room for doubt?'

'None whatsoever. There are also abrasions on her chest and groin that point to clothing being forcibly removed. All classic markers of rape. Her hymen wasn't intact either – though that doesn't necessarily mean much, as it might have broken during sport or other activities. Taken together, however, all signs clearly point towards a sexual assault.'

Lena looked up. A group of five schoolchildren was approaching. She nodded at Johann and stepped away from them before she resumed speaking. 'And it happened at least two weeks ago?'

'Probably a bit longer than that, but I can't pin it down more precisely.'

'This makes suicide seem more likely,' Johann interjected.

'Yes, you could say that – and yet on the other hand, I didn't find any hesitation wounds. Those are shallow incisions with which the individual tests out – in a manner of speaking – how painful it is, or what it actually feels like to cut yourself. I would have expected to find those here. But what's even more suspicious is that the cuts are deep, and that there are at least four separate, individual wounds. These incisions would cause extreme pain, and it's highly unusual for someone to cut themselves like that multiple times without numbing the arm first. Admittedly, it's possible to get hold of topical anaesthetics in the form of sprays and creams, but the CSI team didn't find anything like that near the body. I haven't got around to it yet, but I don't expect to find any residues on the skin either.'

While Luise spoke, Johann fished out his notebook and wrote something down. He held up the page. *Date rape drugs?*

Lena nodded and asked, 'Did you find any evidence of date-rape drugs or anything like that?'

'I can't work miracles, Lena, my love. We'll need to wait a day or two for the lab results first. And before you ask, I don't know if she was pregnant yet either. Now, if you don't have any more questions, I'll get back to work. One of your colleagues should be arriving with the chief prosecutor any minute now, and then I'll be starting on the official autopsy. So I'm afraid you'll have to wait.'

'Of course,' said Lena. She needed a little time to process this unexpected news anyway. 'And thanks for the advance information.'

'I'll call you with more results tomorrow, if not before.' She ended the call.

Just as Lena was putting her phone back in her pocket, it started to ring again. 'Hello, Reiner,' Lena greeted the head of CSI.

'*Moin*, Lena. I thought you might like me to tell you our findings ahead of the first interim report.'

'Please do! I'll put you on speaker so my colleague from Flensburg can hear them too.'

'First off, the photos are ready for download now. But I presume you're mainly interested in whether the girl was alone on the beach.'

'That's right.'

Just then, a turboprop plane flew over their heads. Lena asked Reiner to hold on for a moment while she and Johann walked over to the car.

'So, as I was saying,' Reiner resumed once things had quietened down again, 'the evidence has unfortunately been complicated by our somewhat over-zealous colleagues on the search team, to put it politely. But I'll get straight to the point. I don't think she was alone, but I can't prove it yet. I'll need to identify all the shoeprints layer by layer first. We've taken your colleagues' prints, and yours too of course. In other words, there's still a whole lot of work to be done.'

'But you suspect . . .'

'I've found a few prints that, in my humble opinion, are older than those of your team. But the presence of so many overlaid tracks makes things difficult. You'll need to be patient for a while yet.'

'OK. Thanks all the same. What else is there, apart from the footprints?'

'The knife, of course. The only fingerprints on it definitely belong to the girl – but my suspicions were raised as soon as I analysed it here in the lab. Really the knife ought to be absolutely covered in fingerprints. And yet it isn't. There's just one neat set of prints – a textbook indicator that someone else had to be involved.'

'You suspect they were put there after her death?'

'You saw for yourself what a mess it was there. Yes, I strongly suspect that these prints got on to the knife post-mortem after it had been thoroughly wiped clean.'

'Understood. Did you find anything else?'

'Not in the immediate surroundings of the body. But there were DNA traces in the form of some short dark hairs. Analysis of those is ongoing. In a few days we'll know if there are any skin particles present, or anything like that.'

'Is there any way to speed that up? We're twisting in the wind a bit here.'

'Not really. I've already set it to top priority, but I expect I won't be the only one with an urgent request, as usual. Maybe you'll have more luck if you talk to your superiors. I've heard rumours that you and Warnke—'

'OK, Reiner,' said Lena, unwilling to be drawn on her relationship with her boss. 'So to sum up, it's very likely that Maria Logener wasn't alone on the beach?'

'If you ask me – in a completely personal capacity – then that's exactly what I think. But we'll have to wait and see if I can give you any evidence that would stand up in court. I'm sorry. These things take time.'

'Thanks, Reiner. Call me when you have any news.'

'Will do. And say hi to the man from Flensburg for me.'

'Hello back,' said Johann.

Lena ended the call and Johann shot her an enquiring look. 'Now what?'

'Back to the office. I want to look at those photos. I've had a funny feeling since yesterday that I'm overlooking something. After that, we'll go see Maria's sister.'

◆ ◆ ◆

Johann had printed out the photos on the police station's colour printer and the pile now lay on the table in front of him and Lena. One by one, they pinned the images to a bulletin board and stood before them in silence.

'I can't find anything,' said Johann finally. He took a step back and sat down on one of the two chairs.

Lena examined the photos in turn, concentrating first on the surroundings, then on Maria. When she reached the last picture, she shook her head and murmured, 'How could I have missed that?'

Johann leapt to his feet. 'What have you spotted?'

'She was left-handed. Lars Weissdorn told me that during our first conversation. He didn't say she was ambidextrous – he expressly said . . .'

Johann tapped one of the photos and pointed to the incision on Maria's wrist. 'And that's her left arm. So she didn't do it herself after all.'

Before Johann could even finish his sentence, Lena had called Luise. 'I have another question,' she opened abruptly.

'Shoot.'

'Maria was left-handed. How likely is it that she would have cut her left wrist?'

'It's possible, of course. But as I said, an incision that deep would take a good deal of precision and you'd only be able to achieve that with your dominant hand. Besides, people don't stop to think about this kind of thing – especially not in such an extreme situation. They act instinctively. You wouldn't deliberately use the wrong hand. Although it's not watertight evidence, it definitely suggests third-party involvement.'

'Thanks, Luise – that's exactly what I was thinking. I'll catch you later.'

Johann was already at the board noting down the arguments that suggested foul play in the Maria Logener case. 'Footprints,' he said, writing it down by the first bullet point.

Wrong hand was the next item, followed by *Missing for 48 hours*.

'Do we think the rape speaks in favour of foul play, or against?' he asked next.

'Both. She obviously didn't confide it to anyone and tried to cope with it on her own. That could have been the trigger. But equally, she might have decided to report the incident and was murdered to keep her quiet. We don't know enough about her to be able to say.'

'OK, in that case I'll write it down on both sides.' Under the 'Suicide' heading he also added *Family*. 'If she didn't agree with her parents' religious views, then that could easily have been a contributing factor. So that gives us three against two,' he summed up his list. 'I guess we'll need to look into both alternatives, but there seems to be more evidence suggesting third-party involvement.' Johann wiped his notes away with a sponge and sorted the photos back into a pile. 'Should we ask for reinforcements already?'

'Good question. I'll talk to Warnke later. I reckon he'll give us another two officers.' She reached for her coat, which she had hung over the back of her chair. 'It's time to talk to the sister.'

As they left the station, a ferry was docking on the other side of the harbour. The search team's vehicles were lined up in the car park waiting to be transported back to the mainland.

Shortly after they rang the apartment doorbell, Nina Grote opened the door. Lena introduced her colleague and asked for Johanna.

'She's in the kitchen.'

'How is she?'

'Not good. She's completely beating herself up over everything. But she's capable of conversation, if that's what you mean.'

Johanna didn't get up when they entered the kitchen.

'Hello, Johanna. This is my colleague Johann Grasmann from Flensburg.'

Johanna looked up and a faint smile passed over her face. 'Hello.'

Johann stood rooted to the spot for a moment. Then he suddenly blinked and held his hand out towards her. 'Hi, I'm Johann Grasmann.'

'Hi,' said Johanna softly.

Lena coughed. 'Can we join you?'

Johanna nodded. Nina Grote stood in the doorway and asked, 'Would you like something to drink?'

'No, thank you,' Lena answered, adding, 'We'd like to speak with Johanna in private.'

Nina blushed. 'Yes, of course. I'll be in the next room if you need me.'

Johanna had an air of detachment, seeming to understand neither Lena's request nor her friend's reply. Lena and Johann sat down with her at the table. 'Do you think you could answer a few questions for us?' Lena asked, and waited until Johanna nodded. 'During our first conversation, you told us that your sister had been having problems at home.'

'I heard that Maria' – she gasped for breath – 'that she . . . slit her wrist.'

'That's how we found her on the beach.'

'And do you really think . . .?'

'We're still at the very beginning of our investigation. That's why it's important for us to find out as much about Maria as possible. Her teacher told me that Maria was left-handed.'

'Yes, that's right.'

'Not ambidextrous?'

'No, she's completely useless with her right hand.'

'We heard that from her form tutor, Lars Weissdorn. Do you know him?'

'Yeah, but not very well. He never taught me personally. Maria mentioned him from time to time though. She thought he was very nice.' Johanna shook her head. 'But that's not saying much. She's the kind of person . . . For her, there were no bad people. She accepted everyone for who they are.'

'Did she ever mention her religious studies teacher, Eva Braasch?'

'Religious studies? No, she was a member of Frau Braasch's drama club. She enjoyed that a lot. Maria used to positively gush about her, almost every time she went, but I don't know her personally. She must have joined the school after I left. Then again . . . I'm not actually sure if Maria was still going to drama club. No, she hadn't mentioned it at all lately, even though she'd been back at school for a while. The summer holidays end a lot earlier out here on the islands than on the mainland – I don't know if you knew that?'

Lena nodded. 'I went to school here too. Was Maria in close contact with Frau Braasch?'

'I'm not sure. Maria was always very well disposed towards everybody. But judging by the way she spoke about her, she liked her a lot. Why is that important?'

'At the beginning of an investigation you can never tell what might prove important. That was just one question among many.'

Johanna shrugged. 'If you say so . . .'

Lena decided to ask her more sensitive questions now, before Johanna grew too exhausted. 'Did your sister have difficulties at home?'

'Difficulties. That's a nice way of putting it.' Johanna was now staring at her hands. She spoke quietly but clearly.

'Your parents live and think in a very traditional way . . .'

Johanna looked up. 'Why not tell the truth? They're fanatics. They have Maria's death on their conscience. A pack of murderers.'

Lena deliberately avoided passing comment and instead asked, 'Wasn't your sister religious?'

'What that lot get up to has nothing to do with religion!' Johanna exploded. 'Maria believed in God, if that's what you mean. Perhaps that's something you still need at her age.'

'But she didn't want anything to do with her parents' religion?'

'No way, definitely not! I've never understood why she still believed in all that hocus-pocus.' Johanna now seemed fully alert. Her eyes had grown brighter, her gestures more energetic.

'Did she actively refuse to take part in church activities?'

'How could she have done that? Do you really think our father would have allowed it? No, one black sheep in the family is bad enough. Maria had to conform.'

'Did your father ever resort to violence?'

'When we were little, yes. Disobedience had to be nipped in the bud. He would rap our knuckles and spank us. Later on, he tried to win us over with words – but don't get me wrong, that wasn't about rational argument or discussion. In his view, what we should believe and how we should behave is written in the Bible. Set in stone for all time. And anyone who doesn't abide by the rules will burn in hell. Satan is lurking everywhere – he thinks I've been possessed by him, for instance.' Johanna twisted her face into a grimace and snarled like an animal. 'You see? Satan. I should have got married years ago, popped out some kids . . . with one of the holy Brethren, of course. It makes me sick.'

'What about Maria? How was her relationship with the congregation?'

'She was cleverer than me. I never managed to fool them. Not that Maria was a hypocrite; she just never took the path of confrontation. But she wanted to get away from here too. We talked about her moving out to join me in Kiel in a year or so, when she turned sixteen . . .' Johanna wiped the tears from her eyes. 'I did some research. Any earlier than sixteen and we wouldn't have had a chance against these people. Children belong to their parents. We're their property. Like animals.'

'Did you notice any changes in Maria over the last two or three weeks? I assume you weren't on Föhr during that time?'

'No, of course not. I'm hardly ever here. But we spoke to each other almost every day. That's why I got her the tablet.'

'Was she different to usual?'

'Different? What do you mean? Did something happen three weeks ago?' She ran her hand through her hair and sighed softly. 'I don't think she killed herself. And I think it's even less likely that I wouldn't have noticed anything. People don't just decide out of nowhere that they want to die.' She stared at her hands again, before giving a slight start and looking up at them. 'Why are you investigating this anyway? You don't think she killed herself either, do you?'

'We don't yet know exactly what happened,' said Johann. He had kept quieter than usual so far. From the corner of her eye, Lena had noticed that he'd been studying Johanna intently the whole time.

'What does that mean? Was Maria murdered?'

'That's what we're going to find out,' said Johann.

Johanna stared at him in dismay. 'But who would have done that?'

'If there was a third party involved, we'll find them. You can count on that.'

Lena inwardly gave a start. How could Johann make a rookie mistake like that? Promising a family member that he would find the culprit? 'What my colleague meant to say is that we are investigating every possible scenario,' said Lena, casting a stern glance in Johann's direction. 'Like I said, we're currently at the very beginning of our inquiry. To go back to my question: did you notice anything unusual about Maria over the last three weeks? Did she seem nervous? Did she have any questions she hadn't asked before? Did you speak to her as often as you had over the previous months?'

'I had exams, which meant we weren't Skyping quite so often. But we still spoke to each other every two or three days. And yes, maybe I wasn't quite as focused as usual. But I would still have noticed if Maria . . .' She gave a start. 'She asked me if I'd ever been with a man. We'd never actually talked about anything like that before. Maria hadn't even turned fifteen yet.'

'Was that the only thing she asked?' Lena forced herself to remain calm. 'Did you discuss it for long? What exactly did you talk about?'

Johanna stared into space. It looked as though she was sleeping with her eyes open. Suddenly, she began breathing more rapidly and straightened up in her seat. 'What did you want to know?'

Lena repeated her last question.

'I was frank with her. I have a boyfriend in Kiel, and before him . . . Maria asked if it hurts and how easy it is to get pregnant. I told her she was too young for that sort of thing. We didn't discuss it beyond that.'

'Are you absolutely sure?'

'Why is that so important? It was just a question between sisters.' She threw her head back and thought carefully. 'OK, I also told her she was over the age of consent so she could get the Pill without her father's permission, but she seemed to know that already.'

'Did you talk about going to the doctor?'

'Yes, now that you mention it. She asked me another time whether she could go to the doctor on her own. And then it occurred to me that she has private health insurance. Our father is self-employed and she has to go on his policy, which means he would have found out from the invoice if she'd made an appointment. I told her we could organise it over in Kiel if it ever proved necessary. We would just have had to pay the bill ourselves.'

'So she didn't go to the doctor?'

Johanna's eyes blazed with fury as they met Lena's. 'How should I know?'

'That's all right, Johanna,' Johann interjected in a calm tone. 'Did Maria ask you any other unusual questions?'

Johanna seemed to calm down instantly. She shrugged. 'Maria always had so many questions.' She leaned forward and took a deep breath. 'We talked about alcohol too. She'd never asked me about that before either, and if I remember correctly, it wasn't so long ago.'

'What did she want to know?' Johann asked.

'What it's like to get blackout-drunk, and how much you have to drink for that to happen.' Johanna grew pensive. 'I laughed when she asked that, and I told her to leave the stuff well alone.'

'Did she keep asking questions despite that?'

'Yes – she told me that her friend had had a lot to drink one night and couldn't remember what had happened.'

'Did she have any specific questions, or were they all fairly general?'

'I explained to her what happens in your brain when you have a blackout, and gave her a rough idea of how much she'd have to drink for that to happen. She'd never drunk alcohol before, so it'd be fairly quick. Then she asked whether you'd be able to taste it if you drank something with alcohol in. Of course I said yes, except when the drink is very sweet, as that can sometimes mask the taste.'

'Did she ask you about date-rape drugs too?' asked Lena.

'No – why would she? This is Föhr, not Berlin. I don't understand all these questions. Date-rape drugs? What's that got to do with Maria?'

'We're still at a very early stage of the investigation,' Johann explained again. 'We need to follow all possible leads, and a lot of those will inevitably prove to be dead ends.' He spoke quietly, his voice full of concern. Lena almost had the impression that he knew Johanna Logener personally.

Johanna smiled dully at him. 'I still don't understand, though. What exactly happened to Maria? Where was she all that time?'

'That's what we're going to find out,' Johann promised again. 'You can rely—'

'Will you stay much longer on Föhr?' Lena interrupted her colleague.

Johanna nodded. Now she looked tired and drained, with dark circles around her eyes, her face pale, her posture hunched slightly forwards.

Lena rose to her feet. 'I expect we'll have more questions for you further down the line. Please let me know if you plan to leave the island.'

'I'm staying here,' said Johanna softly. 'I owe it to Maria.'

10

'What was the matter with you just now?' asked Lena once they were in the car.

'What do you mean?'

'Johann, since when do we promise family members that we're going to find the killer? Especially when we don't even know if there is a killer in the first place.'

'I felt bad for her. I'm sorry, it just slipped out.'

'Twice in one interview? That was beyond unprofessional. What's wrong with you?'

Johann sighed quietly. 'I don't know. It won't happen again.'

'OK. Let's forget about it.' She looked at the clock. It was a little after 11 a.m. 'I'll try to get hold of Warnke. After that we can head over to see the parents.'

Lena got out of the car and dialled his number. The detective superintendent only picked up on the sixth ring.

'Is this a bad time?' asked Lena.

'I've just ducked out of the autopsy.'

Lena was surprised to hear that the DSU was personally attending the post-mortem. As far as she knew, that was the first time he'd ever done so. 'Then I guess you're already up to date. In my view, all the evidence suggests foul play.'

'You seem to know more about the autopsy results than I do. But I think you're right. If the chief prosecutor agrees afterwards, we'll launch an official inquiry into her death. What do you need?'

'To start with, at least two more officers from Flensburg.'

'I'll see to that.' He paused for a moment. 'How's the family doing?'

'DS Grasmann and I just spoke to the sister again. She's studying in Kiel and is only visiting the island. She's coping, just about. But she doesn't live with her parents. We're going to visit them next.'

'Be careful,' Warnke warned her, before ending the call.

Lena flopped back into the driver's seat. 'Warnke's attending the autopsy.'

'Is that normal?' asked Johann in surprise.

'It seems he has more of a stake in this than he wants to admit. We're getting our reinforcements anyway. You picked out two people, right?'

'In a manner of speaking. I chatted briefly to two of my colleagues. They'll definitely volunteer.' He gave her a grin. 'Ever since the case on Amrum you're something of a legend in Flensburg. I expect they've all formed a queue already.'

Lena smiled. 'Such a comedian. I thought you weren't into carnival?' she ribbed him. Johann had grown up on the Catholic Lower Rhine, Germany's carnival capital, where stand-up comedy forms part of the annual celebrations. But Johann had never taken much pleasure in the proceedings.

He rolled his eyes. 'Shouldn't we get going?'

Neither of them spoke as they drove across the island. Only when they reached the edge of Oldsum did Johann break the silence. 'You know, I still don't think it's out of the question that Maria committed suicide.' When Lena said nothing, he added,

'I think I've already told you that I come from a deeply religious background.'

'I remember.'

'A hyper-Catholic small town, complete with church visits, confession – the works. Some people might feel safe in an environment like that, but I felt like I couldn't breathe. It seemed like all the people around me were already dead, or were controlled by some external force like puppets. And of course, as a teenager you feel everything even more intensely. There were no alternatives – nobody to talk to.'

'I get it. You're drawing parallels with Maria.'

'In a sense. I can well imagine how it must have been for her. And going by what her sister told us, Maria's situation was a good deal tougher than mine.'

By now, Lena was pulling up outside the Logeners' house. She parked the car and switched off the engine. 'But suicide?' she asked.

Johann hesitated, then began to speak in a quiet voice. 'Absolutely. If you can't see any other way out . . . I considered it myself more than once. If I'm honest, there were a few days when I was on the verge of going through with it. I was doing badly at school and in danger of being held back a year; my friend had moved to Cologne with his parents – and then there was the whole Catholic shit-show.'

'A lot of teenagers have phases where they think about suicide. It doesn't mean they actually end up doing it.'

'That's true, but it was different with me. I'd got hold of some tablets and was planning to . . .' Johann hesitated. 'It was close – very close. Luckily, my old friend happened to come back for a few days to visit his grandparents, and he noticed straight away that there was something wrong. He saved me, so to speak.'

Lena nodded, trying to hide her surprise. 'Maria had her sister.'

'Who was busy thinking about her exams. And if Maria *was* raped, that must have been an extremely traumatic experience for her.'

'It certainly would have been. I'm not ruling suicide out altogether, but right now I just see too many inconsistencies for that to make sense.' Lena paused before she continued. 'Please be careful, Johann. Don't let yourself get too close to the case.'

'I'll try, but aren't we all the products of our own experiences? I'd have to suppress an important part of my own personality if I wanted to tackle this impartially. Can you always do that?'

Lena met Johann's eye. 'Of course not. We aren't robots. But we still need to keep our distance or we won't be able to see the whole picture.' She laid her hand on his shoulder. 'Let's go and talk to the parents, for now.'

As they approached the house, Walther Logener opened the front door. Lena shook his hand and introduced Johann. 'We'd like to speak to you and your wife.'

'My wife isn't here.'

'Can we come in?'

Logener stepped aside. 'You already know the way.'

In the kitchen, he offered the two of them a seat, but remained standing himself.

'Please, come and sit down with us,' Lena urged him.

With a blank expression, he drew a chair back from the table and settled into it. 'So what do you want now?'

Lena decided not to beat around the bush. 'We found your daughter Maria with cuts on her forearm; however—'

'That's a lie!' Walther Logener barked at her angrily. 'Maria would never lay a hand on herself.'

'I understand why you're upset, Herr Logener, but we can't rule out suicide altogether at this stage. That said, there are suspicions that somebody else might have been involved – and that's precisely why we're making inquiries.'

'What do you mean by that?'

'I'm afraid I can't give you any more information just yet.' She paused briefly. 'We'd like to talk to you about Maria. Did you notice anything out of the ordinary over the last three weeks? Did Maria behave any differently to usual?'

'No, of course not. She was completely normal.'

'Please take a moment to think it over. We're interested in even the smallest details: comments, questions, sudden changes to her routine.'

'I've just told you there wasn't anything.'

'OK then, we'll come back to that question later.' Lena opened her notebook and took out a biro. 'How would you describe your daughter?'

'I don't know what you mean,' Walther Logener rumbled indignantly.

'Was she confident or shy? Did she enjoy going to school? What was her relationship like with you and your wife?'

'She's . . .' Herr Logener buried his face in his hands for a moment. 'Maria was a very sweet and well-behaved child. Always was. She never had any problems at school. Just ask her teachers. She was even moved up a year.'

'Did she struggle with the fact that her sister hasn't lived here for over two years?'

'No. She didn't want any contact.'

'You mean with Johanna, your eldest daughter?' asked Johann.

'I just told you they weren't in contact.'

'Why not?' Johann probed. The moment he opened his mouth, Lena realised he was having difficulty keeping himself under control.

'You don't have the faintest idea,' Walther Logener hissed. 'Not a clue!'

'Wasn't she allowed to get in touch with her?' Johann added.

'Maria knew who her family was.'

'Since when is a sister not a member of the family?'

'This is none of your business!' Logener barked at him angrily.

'If you pushed your daughter Johanna away on religious grounds, then that's most definitely our business. How did Maria respond to that? Did she just accept it? Did you demand unquestioning obedience, like you did with Johanna?'

Walther Logener gave Johann a contemptuous look and turned to Lena. 'Do you have any other questions?'

Lena glanced meaningfully at Johann, who stood and briefly held up his phone. 'I have an important call.'

After Johann left the room, Lena and Walther Logener sat together for a while in silence. Eventually, Lena spoke. 'My parents weren't very religious. We only ever went to church at Christmas. But that doesn't mean I have anything against religion or people of faith. In fact, there are Christians I know whom I would trust with my life.'

'Why are you telling me this?' asked Walther Logener warily.

'I can well imagine that your community often comes up against prejudice and mistrust. I'm not here to criticise your religion or your way of life. I'm here for Maria – to find out what happened to her. I'm sure you and your wife want that too.'

'My daughter didn't take her own life,' he murmured.

'No, at this point I don't think that's very likely either. But we're required to investigate every possible scenario. And to do that, we need your help. If you don't have anything to hide – and I assume you don't – then please, help us.'

'Why should I trust you?' Walther Logener spoke through gritted teeth.

'Because you owe it to your daughter.'

Lena heard a noise behind her. 'The inspector is right.' Rosa Logener appeared to have been following their conversation from the corridor. Now she joined them at the table, paying no heed to her husband's indignant expression. 'What would you like to know?'

'Good afternoon.' Lena smiled at her. 'Did Maria change at all over the last three weeks? Did you notice anything different about her?'

Rosa Logener nodded thoughtfully. 'I think so. She spent a lot of time in her room. More so than usual. When she wasn't at school she would often help me around the house, but . . . yes, it must have gone on for around three weeks.'

'Did you talk to her about it?'

'No – I wanted to give her time. Besides, she told me she had a lot of homework.'

'Was Maria ever alone at home over the last four weeks? For a longer period of time, I mean.'

'No, we never leave her . . . left her alone.'

'So she always went with you when you and your husband travelled to the mainland, for example?'

'She still had to go to school. If necessary, she sometimes stayed with Gesa.' In answer to Lena's enquiring look, she added, 'Gesa Behrens. She's a member of our congregation.'

'Is that the grandmother of Maria's schoolfriend Lisa Behrens?'

'Yes. Lisa's parents live on Amrum, but she attends school here during the week. Gesa has a house close to Wyk.'

'Was Maria there for any longer periods over the last month?'

'Only for two days. She stayed overnight too,' Walther Logener interjected.

'When exactly was that?'

Rosa Logener gave her the dates: 15 and 16 August. Lena counted back. That was twenty-three days before Maria's presumed time of death.

'And she stayed just the one night?'

'We picked her up on the evening of the second day,' said Walther Logener. 'That was a Tuesday. Nothing happened there. We can always rely on Gesa.'

Lena thought for a second and then changed the subject. 'Do your church meetings always take place here in your home?'

'No,' answered Rosa Logener instantly. 'We take turns. But not every family has enough space. And sometimes we rent a room if we have visitors.'

'Did you have any larger meetings over the last four weeks?'

'Yes, at Utersum village hall. It overlooks the beach, and we always rent the big room there. That was three days after we got back from the mainland. Friday the nineteenth of August.'

'I'll need a list of the people who attended the meeting,' said Lena. 'You can just—'

'Out of the question,' said Walther Logener. 'We won't give you a single name.'

'I can't force you, but please consider how that will look,' said Lena coolly. 'If you and your community have nothing to hide, then it shouldn't be a problem for us to interview the members individually. The more obstacles you put in my way, the more difficult you make it for me to find the truth. Put yourself in my shoes for a moment. What would you think of me if I acted like this? I can only advise you to cooperate with us.'

'Those are just empty words. None of my brethren have anything to do with Maria's death. Not one of them.'

Lena stood up. 'I'll also need to take a look at Maria's room, please.'

'No,' answered Walther Logener, moving to stand beside Lena. 'Now, if you don't have any more questions . . .'

Rosa Logener had remained seated and was staring sombrely at the table. Only when Lena held out her hand to say farewell did she give a dull smile. 'Goodbye, Frau Lorenzen.'

Her husband accompanied Lena to the front door.

'I'm afraid I won't be able to spare you from having Maria's room searched. It would be better if we didn't need a warrant to do it.'

He opened the door without reacting to her remark. 'Find my daughter's murderer. That's your job – not poking around in Maria's personal things.'

11

Johann was standing by the car waiting for Lena. She unlocked the doors and flopped into the driver's seat. Johann sat down next to her. 'Did you get anything more out of them?' he asked.

Lena described her conversation with Maria's father, adding, 'And now please don't tell me you provoked Herr Logener deliberately.'

'It worked, though,' Johann mumbled.

'What's the matter with you? You need to get a grip on yourself, Johann, or we can't work together. Can I count on that?'

'OK, fine. I'll admit I blew my top. But that guy—'

'That guy is our victim's father, and we treat him with respect. That's all I have to say on the matter. If the case is getting to you—'

'I get the message,' said Johann. 'It won't happen again.'

'All right.' Just as she was inserting the key into the ignition, somebody knocked on the window. Rosa Logener was standing there with a sheet of paper in her hand. Lena lowered the window and took it from her.

'Those are the families who were in Utersum for the meeting. Please don't mention anything to my husband.'

Before Frau Logener could turn back to the house, Lena asked, 'I have another question. Maria was left-handed. Did she ever use her right hand too?'

Rosa Logener shook her head. 'No. I tried to get her to when she started school, but it didn't work. She struggled to do anything with her right hand.'

'Thank you, Frau Logener. I'll get in touch as soon as there's any news. I might also need to speak with you in private again.'

Maria's mother nodded, before turning away and walking back to the house.

Lena unfolded the piece of paper and saw a list of eight surnames, along with their places of residence. From the handwriting, it was obvious that it had been written in a hurry.

Johann raised his eyebrows. 'They're a pretty weird family, aren't they? What would happen if her husband found out?'

'She knows more than she's telling us.'

'Or is allowed to tell us.'

'Johann! We can't focus too closely on just one aspect of the case. We'll soon get to the bottom of why she hasn't told us everything. I also can't imagine that she doesn't have any contact with Johanna.'

'Just because she's her mother? I could give you—'

'Wait and see,' Lena interrupted her young colleague as she started the engine. 'Can you look up Gesa Behrens' address?' She glanced at the clock. 'With any luck, her granddaughter will still be at school.'

The small red-brick chalet bungalow stood on the northern edge of Wyk. A woman in her early eighties opened the door. Like Rosa Logener, her shoulder-length grey hair was pinned up into a bun, and she wore a modestly patterned apron over her dark-blue dress.

'Frau Behrens?' Lena asked. The woman nodded, and Lena held up her warrant card as she introduced herself and Johann. 'We'd like to talk to you about Maria Logener. Can we come in?'

The old lady hesitated briefly before stepping aside. 'The second door on the right, if you please.'

The small living room was furnished with a shelving unit and a desk, along with a sofa, two armchairs and a coffee table. Lena and Johann sat down on the sofa at Frau Behrens' behest.

'Would you like a cup of tea?'

'No, thank you,' Lena answered.

Gesa Behrens looked uncertain for a moment, but then joined them.

'I expect you've already heard that your granddaughter's friend Maria Logener was found dead on the beach.'

The old lady nodded mutely.

'We're investigating the circumstances of her death and interviewing everyone who had any contact with Maria over the last few months. Maria's mother and father told me that she sometimes stayed with you while her parents were on the mainland.'

Another nod.

'When was the last time Maria was here?'

Gesa Behrens stood up and retrieved a heavily annotated calendar from the desk. After studying it carefully, she gave them the dates they had already obtained from Maria's parents.

'She didn't stay here again after that?'

Frau Behrens looked at the calendar again. 'No, Maria didn't come back after that.'

'My grandmother has a calendar like that too. They're very practical,' said Johann with a smile.

'They certainly are. I have more to organise again now that Lisa's come to live with me. At my age it's easy to forget things.'

'My grandma always says that too. Do you still do all the housework for you and your granddaughter?'

'Who else do you think does it? Though Lisa helps me where she can.'

'I've always done the shopping for my grandmother. That's what she finds most difficult.'

Gesa Behrens nodded. 'Lisa does that for me too. What was your name again, young man?'

'Johann Grasmann.'

'That's a very nice name. My late husband was also called Johann.'

'It's the tradition in our family. Father, grandfather, great-grandfather . . .'

'That's good to hear. People nowadays barely spare a thought for their families, and yet family is so important. Are you married, Johann?'

'No, not yet. I'm taking my time with that.' Johann seemed a little bashful, but Lena could tell he was putting on an act. 'I hope you still have time to relax, what with all this housework. My grandma treats herself to a nice long nap every afternoon.'

The old lady smiled. 'You're a kind soul. Do pass on my greetings to your grandma and tell her that she can be very proud of her grandson.'

'I'd be delighted to. I hope we haven't arrived at an inconvenient time for you?'

'Not at all, young man. I only have my afternoon nap once I've had something to eat.' She looked at the clock on the wall. 'Lisa will be here soon, but I was only going to make pancakes today. That won't take long.'

'When I was little, I loved pancakes more than anything,' said Johann. 'With cinnamon and sugar. But I only ever got them when I was a good boy.'

Gesa Behrens laughed. 'My little boy loves eating pancakes too.' She gave a start. 'But that was a long time ago.' An absent look came over her, as if she could see her son standing in front of her.

Lena had followed the conversation between Johann and the old woman attentively. At first, she hadn't understood why Johann was making so much small talk, but gradually, she was beginning to realise what he had presumably noticed from the very beginning. Frau Behrens had made a somewhat confused impression on Lena. Was she just nervous about the interview, or was there more to it than that?

'May I use your bathroom, Frau Behrens?' she asked, getting to her feet.

'Yes, of course. Go ahead. It's the second door.'

Lena went out into the corridor and quietly opened the kitchen door. Next to the fridge was a large pinboard that was covered in countless notes arranged in the order of Frau Behrens' daily routine. Judging by the handwriting, they'd been written by her granddaughter. Various activities such as watering the flowers, making tea, dusting, and collecting the post were listed beside their assigned times. Lena opened the fridge. On the middle shelf she saw a sugar bowl, and there was a pepper mill in the door. Quietly, she left the kitchen and returned to the living room.

'Did you find it all right, Frau . . .?'

'Lena Lorenzen. From the police.'

'You have a nice name too.'

'Thank you. When do you expect Lisa to get back? We'd like to talk to her.'

'I'm sure she'll be here soon. School doesn't end that late, after all. Or maybe you could just come back in a while.'

Just then, they heard the door open. A voice called, '*Oma*, where are you?'

Frau Behrens stood up and went to the door. 'I'm in here, sweetheart! We have visitors.'

Lisa Behrens froze when she saw the two officers. 'What are you doing here?' she asked in an irritated tone.

Lena held up her warrant card. 'Lena Lorenzen, CID Kiel. We're here because of your friend Maria.'

Lisa's long blonde hair was tied up in a loose ponytail. Lena guessed she was shorter than Maria, despite being a year older. She wore an oversized sweatshirt, perhaps in an attempt to conceal her full figure.

Lisa turned to her grandmother. 'Why don't you put the soup on?'

'Soup?' asked Gesa Behrens in surprise.

'Yes – we're having vegetable soup for dinner, remember?'

Her grandmother got up laboriously from her armchair and bid Johann a friendly farewell. 'Get home safe now, young man.'

Once she had left the room, Lisa closed the door.

'Should we sit down again?' asked Lena.

After hesitating briefly, the girl complied. 'I can't tell you anything,' she said defensively.

'When was the last time you saw Maria?' asked Lena.

'On Monday at school, in the playground. Along with everyone else. Maria isn't in my class.'

'But you were close friends with her.'

'Yes, we were friends.'

'Did Maria stay at your house from time to time?'

'Only when her parents were both away. Otherwise, no.'

'Your grandmother knows the Logeners well.'

'They're members of the same . . . church. But I'm sure you know that already.'

'Did anything unusual happen last time Maria spent the night here?'

'I don't know what you mean. We watched a film and then we went to sleep.'

'What about after you got out of school?'

'We came straight back here. My grandma made dinner.'

'Did Maria have any problems with her parents?'

'No, not that I know of.'

'Was Maria romantically involved with anyone?'

'You mean, did she have a boyfriend? No, of course not.'

'Why "of course"?'

Lisa hesitated before she spoke. 'Her parents wouldn't have wanted that.' Another pause. 'And neither would Maria.'

'Did you notice anything unusual about Maria over the last three or four weeks?'

Once again, Lisa took slightly too long to answer. 'No, nothing. She didn't say anything to me either – I mean, about whether there was anything the matter.'

'Was Maria religious?'

Lisa shrugged. 'I think so?'

'You don't know very much about your best friend,' Lena observed, summing up the interview.

Lisa said nothing.

'Your grandmother is ill,' said Johann abruptly.

'Ill? Don't be silly. She's a little unsteady on her feet, that's true. And she can't ride her bike any more. But she isn't ill.'

Johann ignored her remark and continued speaking. 'You don't want anyone to find out. But we aren't from social services – we're here to find out what happened to Maria. It'll be better if you talk to us. There's no way around it.'

Lisa stared defiantly at Johann. 'I don't know what you're talking about. *Oma* is fine. And right now I need to do my homework. And then eat dinner.'

Lena stood up, followed by Johann. She placed her card on the table. 'My colleague is right. We'll be back tomorrow to ask you the same questions again.'

Lisa looked at the floor and repeated, 'I don't know what you mean.'

'Goodbye, Lisa. You can call me whenever you like. No matter how late.'

Lisa didn't say any more as they left the room.

'Everyone here seems to be stonewalling us,' said Johann as they made their way to the car. 'The old lady instantly reminded me of my grandma. I'll bet you anything she's in the early stages of dementia. She definitely had no idea what those two girls got up to.'

Lena told him about the kitchen pinboard and the fridge. 'I think you're right. And by the way, well done for handling Frau Behrens so sensitively.'

'Thanks,' said Johann, glancing away.

Lena couldn't help but smile. Her praise seemed to make him bashful. 'Lisa will talk tomorrow. There would have been no point in prising it out of her just now.'

Once they were inside the car, Lena's phone buzzed. She opened the message. The CSI team had located Maria's tablet ten minutes ago. Lena immediately handed her phone to Johann. 'The tablet is online. Can you enter the coordinates?'

She was pulling out on to the road when Johann cried, 'That has to be the school!'

Lena put her blue light on the roof, turned on the siren and raced through the village towards the school while Johann informed the team in Wyk and requested support. The squad car arrived just after they had pulled up in front of the building. Everyone leapt out of their cars, including Arno Brandt.

'We're looking for a tablet. It was briefly online around twenty minutes ago,' Johann called over to their colleagues.

'It'll be long gone by now,' muttered Brandt.

His teammate nodded in agreement.

'You two patrol the surrounding streets,' said Lena, ignoring Brandt's remark. 'I need a list of all the students you find.'

Arno Brandt seemed on the verge of replying, but then he gestured to his colleague and got back in the car.

'Come on!' said Lena to Johann. 'There can't be many students left in the building at this time.'

They sprinted through the main entrance. Lena headed right while Johann ran up the stairs, calling down to her that he would start on the top floor. Most of the classrooms were locked; only two lessons were still ongoing in the basement. The first class had ten students. Lena introduced herself and asked if anyone had a tablet with them. When everyone answered in the negative, she asked the children to open their bags.

'I'm sorry, but I have to insist,' she said as a murmur passed through the room. Two minutes later, she had searched through every bag. With the words, 'Thank you for your cooperation,' she left the classroom and turned her attention to the next one.

'Nothing!' said Johann when he met her on the stairs half an hour later. 'I only found three classrooms still in use. How about you?'

'Nothing either. I knew it was too good to be true.'

'The headmaster wanted to throw me out,' Johann told her indignantly. 'He held me up for ages. What do they think we're doing here anyway?'

'He's worried about the reputation of his school,' answered Lena. 'That's perfectly normal. We need to speak to him now anyway.'

'All the same, he ought to offer us a little more support. Say, I just passed a whole row of lockers. Did Maria have one of those too?'

'Yep. The local police already searched it on Tuesday night. It was empty.'

'Shouldn't we go back and conduct a forensic analysis? I mean, now that our assumptions have changed.'

'Yeah, the thought had crossed my mind too. If it weren't so far for the team to travel then I would have put in a request.'

'I've got my case in the car, which is inconveniently at the harbour.'

Lena was aware of Johann's little hobby; back when he was still in training, he had completed a lengthy placement in forensics and acquired some equipment of his own. 'That would definitely be the easiest solution, if you reckon you're up to it. Let's see if the others had any luck.' Lena took her phone out of her pocket and called Arno Brandt. 'How are you getting on?' she asked.

'We stopped ten students but we didn't find anything. My colleague is writing up a list for you as we speak.'

'OK. How long are you on duty for today?'

'Strictly speaking, only until six o'clock. But I'll stay on, of course.'

'I'll see you later then,' said Lena, ending the call.

By now, they had reached the headmaster's office. Lena knocked and entered. 'Do you have a moment for us?'

'Come in,' answered Herr Schröder huffily.

They sat down in front of his desk.

'Once again, please accept my apologies for our little raid. But there wasn't a moment to lose. We're looking for Maria Logener's tablet.'

'I would urge you to let me know in advance whenever you plan to do anything in the school. Maria's suicide is of course extremely tragic, but even so, the level of police scrutiny seems somewhat over the top to me.'

'An official inquiry has now been launched into her death. In other words, we can no longer rule out foul play.'

'Murder?' asked a horrified Herr Schröder.

'In the worst-case scenario, yes,' said Lena. 'At any rate, the investigation will last for a while longer, and it'll increase in scope too. And it goes without saying that that will also affect your school.'

'But who could have . . . surely you don't think that someone from our school . . . it's impossible!'

'As I said, we're looking for Maria's tablet. It was online somewhere in the vicinity of the school just under an hour ago.'

'Then one of the students must have stolen it from her. But murder . . .' The headmaster caught himself. He seemed to realise he was making a bit of a leap.

'If I've understood correctly, some of your students would have just been leaving the school around the time in question.'

Herr Schröder nodded.

'I'll need a list of every student from year nine and above. Not just names this time – addresses and phone numbers too.'

'I'm afraid I can't just hand that information over to you.'

'I can get a court order by tomorrow at the latest.'

The headmaster hesitated briefly, but remained firm. 'I'm sorry.'

'As you wish. In any case, we'll need to take another look inside Maria's locker now too. My colleague DS Grasmann will conduct a forensic examination tomorrow.'

Herr Schröder groaned quietly, but he reached for his phone and asked the caretaker to come to his office. 'Anything else?' he asked in a gruff tone.

'Maria's religious studies teacher, Eva Braasch – how long has she been at the school?' asked Johann, taking out his notebook.

'For two years now. Why?'

'And she also runs the drama club?'

'That's right.'

'Was Maria a member? And if so, for how long?'

Herr Schröder turned to his computer and tapped a few buttons on the keyboard. 'Yes, Maria was a member. From the very beginning, as far as I can tell. Although . . .' He took a stack of papers from his desk and leafed through them. 'Yes, I did remember rightly. Maria quit just under three weeks ago. The secretary probably hasn't got around to updating the membership list yet.' The headmaster pushed the papers to one side. 'Why do you want to know?'

The two officers rose to their feet, and Lena said, 'We're gathering all the information we can, but at this stage, we can't tell whether any of it will prove important. We'll be in touch about the list.'

Just then there was a knock at the door. A middle-aged man peered into the office. 'You wanted to speak with me?'

'Herr Ahlers, the officers here would like to have one of the students' lockers opened.'

'No problem. Which one?'

'Maria Logener's. You already opened it on Tuesday, after she was reported missing.'

'Sure thing.'

The headmaster's goodbye was a little frosty, but Lena insisted on shaking his hand. 'Please, don't worry. Like you, I have an interest in making sure no harm comes to the reputation of the school.'

They followed the caretaker down a long corridor to a row of lockers. He pulled his skeleton key out of his pocket and opened one of the doors – but then stood back in surprise when he saw a dark-blue backpack sitting on the shelf.

'What's going on?' he cried in horror. 'She can't have . . .'

'Wasn't this backpack here last time you opened the locker?' asked Lena.

'No! It was empty. Just ask your colleagues.'

'Could Maria have come back into the building after the first time it was opened?'

'Not on that Tuesday night, she couldn't. The school was already locked. If she did, it would have been early on Wednesday morning.'

'And she was dead by then,' muttered Lena under her breath.

Johann pulled on a pair of latex gloves and removed the backpack from the locker. Carefully, he opened it and searched for the tablet. 'It's not here,' he eventually said. He unfolded a large plastic bag and placed the backpack inside it.

'What now?' asked the caretaker, apparently still in a state of shock.

'I'll need you to keep this incident entirely to yourself,' said Lena. 'Not a word to anybody. Do you understand?'

'Yes, of course.'

'We're going to seal the locker now, and we'll be back early tomorrow morning to conduct a forensic examination.' She turned to Johann. 'What time do you want to start?'

'At seven o'clock? Could you let me into the building?'

'Certainly. I'll meet you by the main entrance at seven. No problem at all.'

Johann closed the locker door, turned the key and sealed it shut with a sticker.

12

The two detectives stood indecisively in the school car park.

'Are you hungry?' asked Lena.

Johann shrugged. 'Right now I'm just frustrated at how chaotic everything is. Either everybody stonewalls us, or we suddenly find something that wasn't there before.' He gave a deep sigh. 'Yeah, I guess I could do with a bite to eat.'

'You know what I always used to love when I was at school? Getting a takeaway pizza and eating it on the beach.' Lena glanced upwards. 'It doesn't look like rain. What do you think?'

'Sounds good. Do they sell takeaway beers at the pizza place too?'

Lena grinned. 'If they don't, I'll persuade them.'

Half an hour later, they had rented one of the island's iconic two-seater wicker beach chairs and were sitting with their pizza boxes on their laps.

'*Guten Appetit,*' said Lena.

On the way to the beach, Lena had called DSU Warnke and asked for a court order for the school. He'd told her that the post-mortem was now finished and she could expect more lab results over the next few days.

The two detectives ate their pizzas in silence. It was high tide, and a gentle breeze rippled across the water, ruffling their hair.

Lena breathed in the salty air. The day had been exhausting. First her unexpected encounter with her father on the ferry, and then Brandt's obstinacy once she arrived on Föhr – not to mention the many interviews they had conducted. She had rarely encountered such a dense wall of silence on a case before. Even Frau Braasch hadn't felt it worth mentioning the drama club, which had apparently been so important to Maria. The only glimmer of hope was Rosa Logener, who had decided to break her silence against her husband's will. Lena hoped she would be able to talk to Maria's mother in private the following day and finally learn more about Maria's family background.

'It's pretty convoluted, this case,' said Lena with her mouth full. She picked up her last slice of pizza and put the box to one side.

Johann nodded and took a sip from his water bottle. 'And yet I somehow have a funny feeling that a lot more will come to light over the next few days.'

'Me too,' said Lena, wiping her mouth with her serviette. She sighed. 'Let's try and bring a little order to all the chaos, shall we?'

'Now?' asked Johann. He was leaning back in the chair and holding his face up to the last of the sun. 'Haven't we clocked off for the evening?'

'This is a whole new side to DS Grasmann I'm seeing here.'

'I'm older and wiser now. Saving the world every day gets pretty tiring.'

Lena laughed. 'Hey, we aren't saving the world here – this is Föhr, a tiny island in the North Sea. I reckon we should be able to rescue it from the forces of evil.'

Johann gave a theatrical groan. 'Fine, if we have to.'

'Good. So what do we have so far? A fourteen-year-old girl suddenly disappears and is found dead on the beach forty-eight hours later. Question one: where did she go for those forty-eight hours? And above all, did she go of her own accord, or was she forced?

If we assume that Maria didn't leave the island, that leaves only a limited number of options. I don't think it's likely she would have slept outdoors. So did she visit her friend Lisa? Did Maria have other friends on Föhr who she might have stayed with? Or was she held captive somewhere? Could she have met someone here who abducted her and locked her inside a holiday home, for example?'

'She wasn't a six-year-old,' Johann objected, making himself comfortable in the beach chair. 'Why would she have just gone off with a stranger? Besides, none of the local residents have given us any information that would suggest a kidnapping.'

'I don't think the abduction scenario is very likely either, but we should still launch an appeal for witnesses tomorrow. The *Island Courier* has a good website. Can you get in touch with them? Ask the standard questions. Who saw Maria when and where, that kind of thing.'

Johann sat up and pulled his notebook out of his pocket. 'Will do.' He continued her train of thought. 'Question number two: unless the final post-mortem report tells us otherwise, we have to assume that Maria was sexually assaulted two to three weeks before she disappeared. Where did that happen? Who are the possible suspects? And why didn't Maria mention it to anyone? With any luck, Luise Stahnke might be able to give us a more accurate time – though I don't hold out much hope for that.'

Lena sighed. 'Me neither. We were already very lucky that the bruising and the other injuries were still visible in the first place.' She stood and began pacing up and down in front of the beach chair as she spoke. 'As far as we currently know, Maria wasn't left unsupervised for any meaningful amount of time apart from on two particular occasions – the two days she spent at Gesa Behrens' house and the meeting of the Brethren. Grandma Behrens probably wouldn't have noticed if anything unusual had happened, so we should look into those two days more closely tomorrow. As for the church meeting – all we know is that it took place in Utersum village hall. Was Maria under supervision throughout the whole event, or did the children have their own separate programme? Can you also find out from her form tutor if there were any cancelled lessons over the last few weeks where Maria might have taken the opportunity to go for a walk on the beach, for instance? Maybe that's where she met her killer.'

Johann made a note. 'Sure. I have his phone number.' He patted the seat of the beach chair. 'Would you mind sitting down again? You're making me nervous.'

Lena took a seat and began drawing circles in the sand with her toe. 'In any case, my assumption is that Maria knew her killer. Which of the people in her immediate environment could be a suspect? We urgently need to find out more about her friends and acquaintances. If Lisa Behrens won't talk to us tomorrow then we'll have to get the thumbscrews out. I think she knows a lot more about her best friend than she let on today.'

'Next, we have Maria's parents and her religious background. That seems to be one of the hardest nuts to crack. I can't imagine we'll get any more out of the people on Rosa Logener's list than we did from her husband. He made me feel like some kind of Stasi interrogator, he was so suspicious.'

Lena stood up again, stretched and breathed in a deep draught of sea air. She knew from experience that the early stages of the investigation were the most crucial. They had to make sure they were moving in the right direction. 'Question three: what role did Maria's family and religious background play in her disappearance and death? What did Maria really think of the church? I'm not so sure any more that Johanna's perspective on the situation is entirely accurate. She might be projecting too many of her own conflicts and opinions on to her little sister.'

'I don't think so,' said Johann, leaning back comfortably in the chair once more. 'How could a teenager possibly approve of these old-fashioned views and lifestyles?' When he noticed the look on Lena's face, he immediately back-pedalled. 'All right, fine, we should take an open-minded approach. I get it.'

Lena lay down on the sand in front of the beach chair and continued speaking intently. 'Question four: how did that backpack get into Maria's locker? It obviously wasn't there on Tuesday, and the caretaker swore to us that Maria couldn't have got back into the school afterwards. And even if she did – why would she leave the backpack there? It makes no sense at all. On top of all that: where's the tablet?'

Johann looked pensively out to sea. 'Might the killer have it? But then why would he be dumb enough to switch it on?'

'Maybe he didn't know it has a SIM card and goes online automatically like a smartphone.'

'Perhaps. In that case, we'd need to look for the murderer at the school. Could it be one of the students?'

'We can't rule anything out at the moment,' Lena replied, staring at a line of seagulls flying out to sea. 'We need to find out more about Maria's class. Can you run another background check on the two teachers?'

Johann made another note. 'Will do. Though I don't expect we'll find anything there.'

'Maybe, but we have to be thorough, or we'll regret it later. We have no option but to go through everybody and rule them out one by one.'

'Is there a question five?'

Lena sighed and stretched out her feet. 'I'll think about that on the way back to Amrum.' She looked at her watch. 'With a bit of luck I'll make it in time for the six o'clock ferry. Can you take care of Sergeant Brandt and his list of students?'

Johann closed his notebook. 'No problem. I have to go to the station anyway to drop off the backpack.'

'Yeah – send that off to CSI. If anyone can find anything, it's the team in Kiel. That backpack didn't get into the locker by magic.' Wearily, she sat up and got to her feet. Johann followed her example. Lena pulled down the cover of the beach chair and locked it. It was still summer, which meant the chairs were left out twenty-four hours a day so that customers could use them whenever they liked. She held up the key. 'I think I'll keep hold of this for a while. There are advantages to having our own private little HQ.'

Johann grinned. 'It's just a pity we can't submit it on our expenses claim.'

◆ ◆ ◆

When Lena went to buy her ferry ticket to Amrum, she was told there was no space left on board for her car, so she parked near the harbour and embarked on foot instead. She called Erck and he immediately offered to pick her up from the dock in Wittdün.

By now, the sky was completely overcast and the temperature had dropped to twenty degrees, but her weather app told her that the cloud would lift again soon.

Her favourite spot by the railing was empty. Lena threw back her head, her blonde hair streaming in the wind, and closed her eyes, a feeling of warmth and anticipation rising within her at the thought of returning to Amrum. Although Kiel wasn't far from the Baltic, she had always missed the smell of the North Sea, along with the call of the seagulls. Did they sound different here? Was the wind a different wind? Or was she herself a different person here? All these years, she had missed the place where she grew up, but had never admitted it to herself. Only now, looking out across the water, did she realise how deeply she had been longing for her home. And for Erck too?

The sound of her phone roused her abruptly from her thoughts of the future. She looked at the screen. Leon. He must have gained access to the data on the tablet after it was online. Lena had been resisting the urge to call him. She knew he would get in touch if he found anything. '*Moin*, Leon. Do you have something for me?'

'Why else would I be calling?'

'Who knows? We always have such nice little chats.'

Lena could picture the hacker rolling his eyes and struggling to find the right words. Eventually he gave a grunt. 'The tablet was online. But you know that already.'

By Leon's usual standards, that counted as a detailed explanation. 'Right,' answered Lena. She waited.

'It wasn't online for long.'

'Long enough, though?'

Leon laughed. 'Long enough. But I need more time. It's a complete mess.'

'Can you give me anything concrete?'

'There's a cloud.'

'She saved her files on the Internet?'

Leon didn't seem to think it necessary to answer such a banal question.

'But you haven't got hold of the data yet?' Lena added.

'No.'

'You're working on it, though?'

No reply from Leon.

'Did you find anything else?'

'She spent a lot of time in a chat room.' Leon's voice had a contemptuous note, as if he considered it irredeemably stupid to log into a public chat site.

'Will you send me the address?' Without waiting for a reply, she added, 'Is there anything else?'

'Fragments of the conversation history from her messaging app. But there wasn't enough time.'

'Can we get anything out of these . . . fragments?'

'I'm working on it.'

'Will you call me back when you have more news?'

Instead of replying, Leon hung up without saying goodbye.

'And a lovely evening to you too,' said Lena under her breath as she put her phone back in her pocket. If Leon was right – and Lena didn't doubt him for a second – then Maria didn't seem to have been in contact solely with her sister. With that, Leon had formulated her fifth question: who had Maria been talking to in the chat room? Had she arranged an offline meeting? What did the cloud have to do with that? What files had been so important to Maria that she'd saved them externally? Could it be her diary?

Slowly but surely, the investigation seemed to be gathering pace. They would be able to make quicker progress with their research and their interviews once their reinforcements arrived in the morning.

'Tomorrow is another day,' Lena murmured, looking out over the North Sea once more.

13

Erck embraced Lena warmly and kissed her. 'Have you eaten?'

'I had a pizza on the beach,' answered Lena.

'Wow. The police know how to look after their staff, don't they? Maybe I should have become a civil servant.'

'Too late for that. Besides, I like you just the way you are.' She pictured Erck wearing a tie over a starched collar and couldn't help but smile.

'What's so funny?'

Lena kissed him. 'Just the thought of you in a suit and a freshly ironed shirt.'

'I guess I'll just have to keep dressing like this, then.' He gestured with a grin at his jeans and T-shirt.

'I wouldn't have it any other way. So what now? How about a quick stroll along the shore? We should make the most of the fine autumn weather. And afterwards we could pay a visit to that bar overlooking the beach.'

'Sounds good. Shall we? My Rolls-Royce is parked just over there.'

◆ ◆ ◆

'Stressful day?' asked Erck, breaking the silence.

They had been walking south for some time over the Kniepsand – the enormous sandbar separating Amrum from the open sea. The tide was going out, and they encountered only a handful of holidaymakers. All they could hear was the gentle whisper of the wind, along with the occasional call of a seagull. Lena relished the peace and quiet. 'It doesn't look like suicide. But we don't know much more than that at the moment.'

'You mean this girl was . . .'

'Yes, sadly. In the early stages of this type of investigation you often find yourself blundering in the dark. Unless the culprit turns themselves in, or it turns out that there's only one person who could have done it.'

'Sounds like a jigsaw with thousands of pieces that all look very similar.'

'Pretty much. The next two days will be crucial. If we don't get any clear leads by then, it'll only get tougher with every day that goes by. Those are the cases that eventually end up gathering dust in the archive.'

Erck shrugged uncertainly. 'It sounds like you're under a lot of pressure.'

'I never really notice it at this stage. It's only later, once the case is wrapped up one way or another, that I tend to realise how stressful it all was. But most of the time you get the reward of putting the bad guys behind bars.'

They had stopped and were gazing out together over the Wadden Sea. Erck reached for Lena's hand and held it gently. 'We make a cute couple, don't we?' he murmured.

'You mean, because we're standing here holding hands?'

'For instance.'

'Is that something only seventeen-year-olds are allowed to do?'

He shrugged. 'You tell me!'

She leaned her head against his shoulder. 'To be honest with you, I couldn't give a crap what we should or shouldn't be doing at our age. Things are how they are. I'm just enjoying it, here and now.'

'What about tomorrow?'

'Tomorrow is tomorrow.' She sighed quietly. 'I know what you're thinking – and I've also been asking myself what this is between us, and what it can or should turn into. But I don't have an answer to that. Not right now, anyway. And I'm scared that we're going to ruin everything if we don't give ourselves the time we need.'

Erck said nothing for a while, before picking up a small piece of wood that had been washed on to the beach by the waves and hurling it as far out to sea as he could. 'We've already lost so many years. Half a lifetime.' He gave a deep sigh. 'What if it's the exact opposite? What if we lose each other again precisely because we give ourselves too much time? You're constantly switching between two different worlds. How are they ever going to fit together?'

'Erck, I don't have the answer to our complicated situation either. But lots of couples have long-distance relationships . . .'

'Maybe, but I hate distance. And all this waiting too. Aren't we too old for that kind of thing?'

'We both still have another forty or so years to go, with any luck – and you're asking if we're too old? Too old for what?' Lena felt a jolt. Was Erck talking about kids? But there was still plenty of time left for that too. She was startled by her own thoughts.

Erck must have realised what she was thinking, as he asked, 'Don't you want a family?' He spoke so quietly that at first Lena wasn't sure she'd heard him properly, but his eyes told her that she had.

'I don't know, Erck. I really don't know.'

Erck picked up another piece of wood, but this time held on to it, examining it from all sides. 'It's crazy what the sea does to the wood, isn't it? Like a transformation. The wood isn't just any old piece of wood any more – it gets a special character of its own. Just like the two of us.'

Lena kissed him tenderly. 'Come on, let's keep walking. Or head back.'

'I think I could do with a glass of thirty-year-old whisky.' He grinned. 'Provided the inspector will let me drive home afterwards.'

Lena took his arm. 'The inspector has clocked off for the evening.'

'That's lucky – so has the island odd-job man.'

Erck unlocked his old Volkswagen Golf and fell into the driver's seat.

'Home time?'

'Would it be all right if you dropped me off at Beke's? Just for half an hour?'

'No problem,' said Erck. 'I wanted to fix us a little bite to eat anyway.'

Lena could hear the disappointment in his voice and briefly considered going straight home with him after all, but then she thought better of it. Beke was family, and she'd already cancelled on her twice. Erck wasn't entitled to have her all to himself. That was precisely what she hated about relationships – all the clinginess and guilt-tripping.

'I swear it'll just be half an hour,' said Lena finally. 'Who knows how hectic the next few days will be.'

He nodded and pulled out of the car park, heading towards Norddorf.

◆ ◆ ◆

Beke only opened the door after Lena rang the bell a second time. 'My dear, I wasn't expecting you at all! Come in, I've just made some tea.'

Lena embraced her aunt. 'How are you, Beke?'

'I'm all right, my dear.' She ushered Lena into the house. 'But you look a little pale. Erck already told me that they found a young girl dead on the beach on Föhr, and that you have to work on the case. It's nice of you to stop by and see me despite all that.' Beke took a second cup out of the cupboard and filled it with tea. 'Will you be around for a while yet?'

'That depends on how things develop. But it'll definitely be at least a few days.'

'And you're coming back to Amrum every evening?'

'If work will let me. I was actually planning to spend a few days' holiday here, but I'll tack those on at the end of the assignment. I'll have plenty of time for you then, if not before.'

Lena took a sip of tea and cast her eyes over the kitchen. She had always felt comfortable here. The old sideboard that Beke had inherited from her grandmother – Lena's great-grandmother; the heavy wooden table and cane dining chairs that had been there since Lena was a child; the grandfather clock that rang out the hours through the whole house; the gas cooker that was now showing its age too. On the wall there was a shelf lined with jars of herbs and spices, along with a photo of Beke's late husband. For Lena, this room was still the very essence of comfort and warmth.

'Good,' said Beke. 'I'm sure Erck will be very happy about that. Why didn't he come in with you?'

'We were on the beach just now. I had to stretch my legs. Then we went to the Strandhalle for a drink.'

'And that's why he didn't stop by?' asked Beke in surprise.

'Oh no, not at all. He's already at home – he wanted to make us some dinner. I promised him I'd only drop in for a quick visit. I need to get up early tomorrow to . . . I mean, it makes sense for . . .' She caught herself. Why did she get in such a tangle when she talked about Erck?

Beke raised her eyebrows. 'Is everything all right between you two?'

Lena shrugged. 'In general, yes – but Erck . . . He wants certainty. And I can't give him that. How can I?' She sighed. 'His ideal solution would probably be for me to give up my job and move back to Amrum.'

'Aren't you being a little unfair to Erck there? I don't think he'd ask anything like that of you. Or is that what he told you?'

'No, of course not,' answered Lena sheepishly. 'But if I'm honest, that's what it feels like. And that isn't good. Erck wants to define our relationship once and for all and I can't and don't want to do that right now. One moment I feel so close him, as besotted as a schoolgirl, and the next I want to run away from him and all his nagging and leave everything behind.'

Beke leaned forwards and gently stroked Lena's hand. 'Feelings aren't something you can just suppress. Tell the truth – explain to Erck how you feel. Talk about it. Keeping quiet or making some ill-advised attempt to spare his feelings will get you nowhere.'

'You're right – and yet saying it out loud is a whole other story.' She sighed quietly. 'But I don't want to burden you with my problems. You're—'

'For one thing, you aren't a burden,' Beke interjected, 'and for another, what else is your family there for? You have a job that you love and don't want to give up, while Erck has built a life for himself on Amrum and can't imagine leaving.'

'That doesn't exactly sound like a recipe for a happy future,' Lena objected.

'Whatever's happened to my Lena all of a sudden? The one who isn't afraid of anything, who loves life and always finds a way through. She can't have vanished overnight.' Beke smiled. 'No, she's just hiding herself away – but she's still the same old Lena.'

Lena stood up, gave her aunt a hug and kissed her on the cheek. 'Thank you, Beke. Maybe I really am being too pessimistic about all this. Erck and I will find a solution . . . and now you have to tell me all your news. How's your back doing? Did you go to the doctor in the end?'

◆ ◆ ◆

Erck served the dressed salad on two plates and added a few freshly grilled prawns. Then he handed one of the plates to Lena and sat down with her at the table. 'I've bought a new white wine. Give it a try – I think you'll like it. A Pinot Blanc with low acidity, notes of apple and pear and a smooth mouthfeel.'

Lena took a sip and hummed appreciatively. 'Fantastic! Where did you get it from?'

'Online. The shop's called *Hanseatisches Weinkontor*. They even deliver to Amrum.'

'So you're something of a wine connoisseur these days?'

Erck laughed. 'OK, I confess – I learned that line by heart just to impress you.'

Lena smiled. 'Well, it still worked. I'd have needed to write all that down.' She tried one of the prawns. 'Perfect, as always.'

Erck handed her the bread basket. 'Baked by yours truly.'

'When did you find the time for that?'

He tilted his head. 'I was up early this morning. And since my beloved was off catching bad guys . . .'

Lena was enjoying the crisp salad with its finely balanced balsamic vinaigrette, as well as the perfectly cooked prawns that Erck had served with shallots and a touch of garlic. 'Just what I needed after a day like today,' she said, raising her glass to his. 'What are we drinking to?'

Erck seemed to consider for a moment before answering. 'To us! To our love. To a long life.'

They clinked their glasses. Lena took a sip and then raised her glass once more. 'And to my rediscovered love, who I'd been carrying in my heart all these years.'

Erck's eyes grew moist as she spoke, and his gaze warmed her. She stood up and held out her hand to him. 'Come on – I know a very cosy spot upstairs.'

Later, Erck covered Lena's belly in kisses.

She giggled quietly. 'Hey, I'm ticklish there!'

Erck looked up. 'Really? I had no idea.'

Lena tousled his thick black hair. 'Liar.' She gently pulled him up towards her and kissed him tenderly on the lips.

'I love you,' whispered Erck.

'Me too.'

They lay together in silence for a while, looking into each other's eyes and smiling. Eventually, Lena asked, 'Will we make it, the two of us?'

'I'm not going to let you go a second time.'

'And I wouldn't want to go anywhere.'

'We'll find a way.'

'But what if we don't?'

'Then we'll keep looking,' said Erck, stroking her cheek.

'Do you promise?'

'Cross my heart and hope to die.' He took her in his arms and kissed her again.

◆ ◆ ◆

'It's time you got on the boat,' said Erck to Lena.

They'd been standing on the quayside for the last ten minutes, wrapped in each other's arms. After a few hours' sleep, they had got up at four-thirty in the morning. Erck had made coffee while Lena took a shower, and then they had set off together for Wittdün.

'That stupid ferry,' murmured Lena.

'Will you come back tonight?'

'Hopefully. But I can't make any promises.'

Erck gave her a peck on the lips. 'Off you go, Inspector. Bernd is waving at you.'

'I don't know anyone called Bernd.'

'But I do! Look, there he is.' He pointed to the ferry where the captain was waving down at them. 'Say hi to Johann for me. And let me know if you're coming back or not.'

Reluctantly, Lena let go of Erck, gave him one last kiss, then ran up to the ferry. She waved back at him from the railing. He remained standing at the dock until she could only make him out as a tiny dot. Lena waved one last time, though she knew Erck could no longer see her.

The further the boat got from Amrum, the tighter the knot grew in the pit of Lena's stomach. Had it been right for her to laugh off Erck's questions about their shared future? Should she have talked things over with him instead of leading him off to bed? What was it her mother always used to say? *Delayed is not forgotten.* When the case was over – if not before – she would have to face up to Erck's questions. Lena shivered in the sea breeze and fastened her coat. As a detective, she knew she could solve even the toughest mysteries – and yet her own case left her stumped, time and time again. Was she afraid of what was to come? How could she reconcile the two sides of her own nature? There wouldn't be an easy solution, as much as she wished there was.

14

As Lena left the ferry, her phone rang. 'Morning, Luise. You're up early.'

'There isn't much I wouldn't do for you, Lena. I've sent you the preliminary post-mortem report, and knowing you, you'd have called me as soon as you saw it anyway.'

'What did you find?'

'The very short version is that the suspected sexual assault on Maria Logener has now been fully confirmed. The injuries were barely visible on the surface, but they were clear enough during the autopsy. I'll spare you the details, though. And in answer to the question I'm sure you're about to ask: no, I can't narrow the time down any further. It happened between sixteen and twenty-five days ago. That's the best I can do. Even then I'm sticking my neck a long way out – but I think I can answer for it.'

'Had she taken any sedatives or anything like that?'

'I was just getting to that, Inspector. I found GBL in her urine.'

'Isn't that a date-rape drug?'

'That's right. Also known as gamma-butyrolactone.'

'Are you sure?'

'Lena! Is that a serious question?'

'Sorry, I didn't mean to doubt you. But that means there was definitely foul play – that her wrist and arm was cut by a third party.'

'Yep – especially as the dose was so high that she must have been unconscious at the time.'

'And she couldn't have taken it herself? As a sedative, in order to—'

'I don't think that's likely,' said Luise. 'Besides, we didn't find a bottle anywhere.'

'She might have got rid of it beforehand.'

'That's your department – I can't help you there.'

Lena was still busy processing this new information. From now on, they would be investigating a clear-cut case of murder. Although Lena already had her doubts that Maria had killed herself, Luise's unambiguous verdict still took her by surprise.

'I'm sorry, what did you say?' she eventually asked.

'That I can't do much to help you draw any conclusions from this.'

'Oh yeah, apologies. You're quite right.' Lena focused on her next question. 'What about DNA?'

'I'm getting to that. First off, she wasn't pregnant, and I didn't find any traces of semen or any recent injuries either. Based on that, I don't think she was raped again before she died. As for DNA – I didn't find any obvious samples. There were no particles of skin under her fingernails, which strongly suggests that she didn't defend herself. But we'll have to wait and see if there are any other DNA traces. You already know about the short dark hairs, and we've gone over the rest of her clothing with adhesive tape, but it remains to be seen whether that will turn up any samples. You know how long the analysis can take.'

Lena sighed. 'Up to a week. Can't we speed it up at all?'

'I've already set it to highest priority, but the team can't work miracles. I've had cases before where the results came through in only two days, but that depends on the quality of the evidence and—'

'I'm sorry to cut you off Luise, but I'm just about to arrive at the police station on Föhr, and I have to—'

'No worries, Lena. In that case I'll get straight to the most important point. You remember how we talked about the cuts on her wrist? Well, I took another close look at them last night.'

'Did you find anything new?'

'Yes, and it matches up with the date-rape drug. Based on my findings, Maria Logener couldn't have made the incisions herself. The main force of the blade was clearly directed towards the right, which means the cut must have been made by somebody standing to the victim's left.'

'You're certain about that?'

'You can't compare it to a fingerprint, but in my view it's a clear piece of evidence. Of course, there might be other experts who would disagree with me. I couldn't find any similar cases in the literature, so we're in uncharted territory here. But speaking for myself, I don't have any doubts. In theory it would have been possible for the girl to cut herself like that – but really only in theory. She would never have managed to maintain a steady hand at that angle for the full length of the incision. Besides which, why would she have decided to use her less favoured hand in such a distressing situation? No, we can definitely assume there was foul play here, based on the date-rape drug and the incisions. That's exactly what I'm going to say to the chief prosecutor's office later today too.'

By now, Lena was standing outside the station. 'Thank you for your quick and meticulous work. You've been a huge help.'

'Any time. I'll let you know as soon as I have the results from the ongoing tests.'

'Thanks again, Luise. I'll be in touch this afternoon or tonight, if I can.'

'I'll be at home – just give me a call.'

They said their goodbyes as Lena hurried up the steps. She found Johann in their office, typing something out on his laptop.

'Good morning,' he called good-humouredly. 'Can I get you a coffee?'

'Yes, please – with plenty of milk.' Lena dropped her backpack on to the table and took out her laptop and notebook. By the time Johann came back with the coffee, she had already scanned through Luise's post-mortem report.

Johann put her cup down in front of her and took a seat on the other side of the table. 'Three colleagues from Flensburg will be getting here around lunchtime. I've booked rooms for them and emailed them directions.'

'Brilliant. That means they can get started on the interviews this afternoon. Did you find addresses for all the names on the list Rosa Logener gave us?'

'I've just finished.' He leaned forward, plucked two sheets of paper from the laser printer and handed one to Lena. 'All of them are registered here on Föhr. I've also added Lisa Behrens' parents – I assume we'll need to contact them too.'

'I'll ask Brandt to assign us one of the local officers. That'll give us three teams to work with. I don't think we'll need anyone here to handle the coordination for now.'

'Even if we did, there's only enough space in the incident room. We'll figure it out somehow.' He opened his notebook. 'I did a little background research on Frau Braasch and Herr Weissdorn. Let's start with the form tutor: he's thirty-five years old and was born in Lüneburg. He studied in Kiel and did his teacher training in Schleswig, where he also worked for two years before coming to the school on Föhr five years ago. All pretty normal. Then we have

'Frau Eva Braasch: twenty-six, also studied in Kiel, though after Lars Weissdorn had already left. She trained in Flensburg and came to Föhr as soon as she was qualified. That was two years ago. She grew up in a tiny village in Hesse – I didn't write the name down but I don't think it matters.'

'And?' asked Lena, guessing that this was going somewhere.

'A friend of mine works as a teacher at her old school in Flensburg, and I managed to get hold of him just before you arrived. It seems there were a few rumours.' He paused theatrically.

'Come on, spit it out!' Lena urged him, tapping her finger restlessly on the table.

'Like I said – rumours. But it seems Frau Braasch had a relationship with a female student.'

'How old was she?' Why was she having to drag everything out of Johann today? He seemed to enjoy drip-feeding his information to her.

'A sixth-former aged nineteen. No problem from a legal perspective, of course, but professionally . . . She would probably have found it very difficult to ever qualify as a teacher. Like I said, there were only rumours, and there weren't any consequences at the time. In the end, Frau Braasch applied to another school and the student finished her exams and left, so the whole thing blew over.'

'Rumours. Do you know how many of my colleagues have suggested behind my back that I'm a lesbian? And even if that were true of Frau Braasch, it's none of our business. Besides, Maria Logener was fourteen—'

'Nearly fifteen,' Johann cut in.

'OK – well, we need to talk to Eva Braasch again anyway. Let's keep it in mind.'

'While we're on the subject of interviews – yesterday I went back to see Johanna Logener.' Johann left a slight pause between the first name and surname.

Lena shot him an enquiring look. 'Any particular reason?'

'I had time, and I thought it might prove useful.'

'And?' asked Lena, pulling a sceptical face. Inwardly, she gave a groan. She could guess that Johann hadn't visited Maria's sister purely on a fact-finding mission.

'I chatted with her for a while. I thought I might be able to get more out of her if it didn't feel like an interrogation. In any case, she's completely racked with guilt. She'd been thinking of getting in touch with social services for some time, but she kept putting it off.'

'Why?'

'She was afraid there might be repercussions for Maria – that her parents would isolate her even further. I suppose that's not so far-fetched. Hindsight is twenty-twenty, and maybe it really would have been better if—'

'What else did she say?' said Lena.

'I asked her about her initial interview with the local police and she told me they didn't really take her seriously. The questions only got a little more detailed when Johanna insisted that something bad must have happened.'

'I've looked at the notes, and she's not wrong. Amateurish would be putting it mildly.'

'Our colleagues here on Föhr seem to strongly disapprove of the Logeners' religious community, and it looks like they lumped Johanna in with the church too.'

Lena leaned forward and propped herself up on the table with her arms. 'If there are any issues here that need to be resolved, then we'll do that over the next few days – but right now it doesn't seem like a priority to me.'

'Perhaps. I just wanted to put it out there. Anyway, I obviously also spoke to her about her relationship with Maria. She didn't see very much at all of her little sister over the last two years. At first she would come back now and again to spend the weekend with her parents, but later on the two sisters mainly spoke to each other online. Johanna visited the island maybe once every six months or so. When she did, she'd stay with her friend – like she's doing now – and meet up with Maria outside the family house.'

Lena stood up, went to the window and threw it open. The sky was a radiant blue and the air still smelt of summer. She turned back to Johann. 'Two years is a long time at their age.'

'Definitely, but I got the impression that Johanna still spoke to her sister quite a lot. Though that got trickier over the last few weeks, it seems. Johanna had to retake two exams, and one of those was her last chance to pass, so she had a lot of work to do for it.'

While Johann was speaking, Lena walked back over to the table and stood in front of him. 'Did she say how often she actually talked to her sister?'

'I didn't ask that so directly.' He threw his head back and seemed to think for a moment. 'But it really can only have been a handful of times, and even then only briefly.'

'Did you find out anything else?'

'No, aside from the fact that Johanna has a catastrophic relationship with her mother and father and that she despises her parents and their lifestyle. I can understand where she's coming from.' When Johann saw Lena's expression, he added, 'I know we're unbiased observers and that we shouldn't get personally involved in the case. But I'm not sure we shouldn't be a little less impartial in this instance. I reckon Herr Logener is hiding one or two surprises behind that respectable facade. Johanna told me that her parents actually chose a young man for her to marry. She was only sixteen at the time. He would sit at her table during church meetings and visit the family occasionally. Of course he was older than her, by seven years. Unbelievable, isn't it?'

Lena let a moment pass before she answered. 'We need to keep our distance. And you know that too.'

'I've got it under control. I promise.'

She sat down at the table opposite Johann once more. 'OK. Does Johanna know if her sister faced the same fate?'

'I asked her, of course, but it seems Maria was a closed book on that topic. In other words, if she did, Johanna didn't know about it.'

'We should bear that in mind then. Have you seen Sergeant Brandt's report?'

'Yep. They stopped ten students, took down their details and searched their backpacks. I was planning to talk to Jürgen about it later.'

Lena gave Johann a quizzical look. She'd already noticed how quickly he had struck up a rapport with the local staff. For her own part, Lena preferred to maintain a certain distance – though that didn't always make her work any easier.

'He's the constable who patrolled the area around the school with Arno Brandt. I submitted a request to the network provider yesterday to get the data from their signal masts in the area, which should hopefully be with us this afternoon. But I don't expect it to tell us much, given that every kid aged twelve and up has a mobile phone these days. There'll just be too much information.'

Lena took a sip of her coffee. 'Anything else?' she asked.

'No, that's it for now.'

She nodded, then told him about Luise's call and the latest findings.

'So we can assume it was definitely foul play from here on in. At least that gives us a clear line of inquiry. Things are getting serious,' he said.

'That they are. Did you manage to get hold of Lars Weissdorn yesterday?'

'Yep. He's positive that there were no cancelled lessons over the last few weeks. Certainly nothing more than an hour here and there – but in those cases, the students have to stay in class and get given work to do. He wanted to take another look at the timetables this morning, though, and he said he'd let me know if he'd forgotten about anything.'

'OK. When do the colleagues from Flensburg get here?'

'Hang on a moment.' Johann looked through his emails. 'Quarter-past twelve.'

'We should schedule a meeting for one o'clock then.'

They went through the next steps together and split everyone up into teams. Two of the officers from Flensburg would track down the members of the church, while the second team would interview the students in Maria's class. The court order for the kids' addresses and phone numbers had already arrived. Meanwhile, Lena and Johann planned to speak to Lisa Behrens again before paying the Logeners another visit.

'If we hurry, we might be able to catch Eva Braasch at the school and ask her a few more questions before the ferry arrives,' said Lena, shutting her laptop.

'Murder?' asked Eva Braasch, her eyes open wide. 'You mean, Maria was . . .?'

'Yes – we believe there was foul play involved.'

During the break they had asked the teacher for a second interview, and they had been sitting with her for the last few minutes in an empty classroom.

'But who . . .?' Eva Braasch was dumbstruck.

'We've heard that Maria was a member of your drama club.'

'Yes, that's right, up until a few weeks ago. Is that important?'

'Why did Maria quit?' asked Lena, ignoring her question.

'She wanted some time out. Membership is voluntary, and if – for whatever reason – a student no longer has enough time or energy to devote to acting, then we have to accept that.'

'So you didn't discuss the reasons with her?'

'No. Maybe her parents had a problem with it.'

'You previously told us that you discussed religious topics with Maria outside of class. Where did you meet with her?'

'Here at school, of course. What are you getting at?'

'Please just answer the inspector's question,' Johann cut in sharply.

Eva Braasch shot him an indignant look, but answered, 'We would meet in the classroom while the other students were on their break, or in the playground. We might also have sat down together in the staff room at some point.'

'Did she tell you about the problems in her family too?' asked Lena in a calm voice.

'Yes,' she replied.

'And was Maria picked on in class?'

Eva Braasch tilted her head uncertainly. 'One or two of the boys might have had it in for her.' She shut her eyes briefly. 'Maria was a beauty – that was already plain to see. And she had a highly developed personality for someone her age. The first of those two things makes you an object of desire, while the second is an outright provocation, especially to teenage boys. They generally aren't as mature as the girls their age, but they don't want to admit that. Hence all the superficial macho posturing. But I think you can chalk all that up to game-playing.'

'Maria was a beauty. Nobody has phrased it to us quite like that before,' said Lena.

'Haven't you seen any photos of her? In the flesh, she was even more . . . They say that beautiful people have an easier time of it, but that's only partly true. Maria was never coquettish with her good looks – quite the opposite. She always acted like any other girl.'

Lena noticed that Eva Braasch's voice changed when she spoke of Maria. It was softer, gentler and full of affection. 'But she wasn't just like any other girl?'

The teacher looked at Lena in confusion. 'I didn't say that. Maria was more grown-up, more serious than the other girls in her class – let alone the boys. But beyond that . . .'

'Did she believe in God?' asked Lena.

At first, Eva Braasch looked bemused, but eventually she replied, 'It's difficult to answer such a general question. There are so many different ways of believing in God.' She fell silent for a moment and closed her eyes once more. When she opened them again, Lena could sense just how deeply the conversation was affecting her. 'Yes, I think she believed in God. But that only served to intensify her conflict with her parents. Normally, teenagers instinctively reject their parents' way of life. They don't make distinctions or try to be understanding. Maria was different – she didn't condemn her parents, and she didn't dismiss their beliefs either. She tried to understand them. That's unusual at her age. Very unusual – especially when you consider how radical her parents' church is.'

'So Maria felt sympathy for her parents?' Lena probed further.

Eva Braasch stared blankly through the window. A few seconds ticked by, until she suddenly gave a start and sat upright. Her eyes went to Lena, then Johann, then back to Lena. 'I can't tell you anything more than that.' She stood up. 'I'm afraid I have another meeting. If you don't have any other questions—'

'What was your relationship with Maria Logener?' asked Johann, locking eyes with her.

Slowly, the teacher sank back on to her chair. 'Relationship? Haven't you asked me that already?'

'Yesterday we asked you how close you were to each other.'

'Isn't that the same thing? I was her teacher. Though it's true that I sometimes paid her more attention than I did the other students in her class.'

'Where were you on Tuesday night?' asked Johann, almost as an afterthought.

Eva Braasch didn't react at first. It looked as though she hadn't heard or understood the question. When Johann began to repeat it, she raised her hand. 'During the night? I was asleep.'

'Were you alone?' said Johann.

'I live alone.'

'That doesn't answer my question.'

She sighed quietly. 'There was nobody other than myself in my apartment on Tuesday night. Not during the evening, not overnight, and not on the following morning either. Will that do?'

Johann made a note on his pad and then looked up. 'Of course it will. And your home is on Föhr?'

'Two bedrooms, kitchen, bathroom. Seven hundred square feet, eight hundred euros per month including bills. Rosenstrasse 6, second floor on the left.'

Lena couldn't suppress a smile, but before she could say anything, Johann asked his next question. 'Did Maria ever visit your apartment?'

Eva Braasch took her time answering. 'Yes, she came round once. Not that I invited her. She suddenly appeared at my door and wanted to talk to me, so I asked her inside, of course.'

'When was that?'

'I don't remember exactly, but off the top of my head I'd say it was six, maybe seven weeks ago?'

'What exactly did she want from you?'

'It was . . . the usual. Problems with her parents, with her classmates.'

'How long did she stay?'

'I couldn't tell you exactly. I made us a cup of tea and we sat in the kitchen. Maybe an hour or so.'

'Was there a specific reason why she came over? If I understand you correctly, it's not normal for students to consort with you outside your working hours.'

'Of course it's not normal. I don't know what you're insinuating here.' Eva Braasch had raised her voice and it was plain to see that she was annoyed.

Johann went on impassively. 'I'm not insinuating anything. Was there a particular reason for her visit?'

'No!' The teacher folded her arms over her chest and stared at him defiantly.

Lena cleared her throat. 'I have two more questions. We still don't know where Maria went after she disappeared on Monday. Do you think she was capable of running away from home?'

Eva Braasch rubbed her hands together as if she was cold. Eventually, she answered, 'That's a tricky question. I don't think she would have just taken off after having a row with her parents, for example. That wouldn't have been like her. If she did run away, that means something very serious must have happened to her. And even then, she would still have planned everything. She would have known where she was going, or who she would stay with.'

'Thank you for that assessment. My second question concerns Maria's friend Lisa Behrens. How would you describe the two girls' relationship?'

This time, Eva Braasch replied straight away. 'They were friends, I'd say. But Lisa is a very different person to Maria. She's wilder, more spontaneous. She doesn't mull anything over for long – she dives straight in. That makes her very impulsive, but she has strong social skills too. Her parents are also members of this . . . sect, but they live on Amrum, which is why Lisa lives with her grandmother. Maybe that's why she and Maria got on so well. Shared experiences and . . .' Eva Braasch briefly seemed to be elsewhere with her thoughts. 'Yes, the two of them complemented each other well.'

Lena stood up and shook the teacher's hand. 'Thank you for speaking so openly. We'll be in touch if we have any further questions.'

Johann nodded to Eva Braasch and left the classroom with Lena. 'Shouldn't we have—?' he began.

'Not here on the corridor,' Lena instantly cut him off.

Once out in the car park, one of the local constables walked over and handed them the court order. Lena and Johann headed back inside and found the headmaster in his office.

'Good morning, Herr Schröder,' said Lena, handing him the document.

'So much fuss,' he murmured once he had given it a cursory examination.

'We currently believe that there was a third party involved in Maria's death. I think the fuss is more than justified.'

'But . . . they said earlier that she . . .' The headmaster struggled for breath. 'And at our school too. I can't believe it.'

'Could you please give us all your class registers, along with a list of every teacher at the school?'

Herr Schröder got to his feet. 'I'll be right back.'

'We should have put that Braasch woman under more pressure,' Johann blurted once they were back in the car.

'Why, exactly?'

'How come she only gradually admitted to us that she was more than just a teacher to Maria?'

'Because she's afraid of unfounded accusations?' Lena started the engine and backed out of her parking space.

'Since when are you such a bleeding-heart liberal? She didn't tell us the truth – or not all of it, anyway. I'm sorry, but that woman seems suspicious to me. Why didn't we ask her for an alibi? Isn't it possible that she might have let Maria stay in her apartment? And then when she got scared . . .' He left his sentence hanging in the air.

Before Lena reached the exit from the school car park, she stopped the car and turned to look at Johann. 'So you think she took Maria to the beach, sedated her and sliced her wrist open, just because she was afraid somebody might find out that a student spent the night in her apartment?'

Johann didn't reply until Lena had turned on to the road and begun driving towards the centre of the village. 'I know that sounds a little far-fetched, but it might have been more than one night. Why did Maria quit the drama club? What if they'd already grown closer to each other at that point, and it all escalated later on?'

Lena shook her head. 'That all seems too vague to me. Even if Eva Braasch had fallen in love with Maria, it doesn't mean she then got too close to the girl. We can't even say with any certainty that Frau Braasch is gay. What you heard were just rumours.'

'That's right. Rumours – nothing more than that, but nothing less either.'

Lena stopped at a red light. 'All right, fine. You talk to your friend again, and if you still think there might be some truth to these rumours, we'll ask a colleague in Flensburg to look into it. Does Eva Braasch have a car?'

'There isn't one registered in her name. But she could have hired one, of course.'

'I absolutely don't want to feed the rumour mill here on Föhr and cause any fresh difficulties for Frau Braasch. This subject is every bit as sensitive as that of the parents' religious community, if not more so.'

Johann was on the verge of replying, but then he fell back in his seat and ran his hand through his hair. 'You're right – we should move slowly and carefully.'

15

'The Flensburg contingent is here already,' said Arno Brandt as Lena and Johann entered the police station. 'They're waiting in the incident room.'

'Then we should get started right away,' Lena answered.

Brandt walked ahead of them, opened the door and stepped aside with a theatrical gesture to let Lena and Johann go in first. Lena rolled her eyes and entered the room.

A constable and three men in plain clothes were standing by the large map of Föhr and talking among themselves. They turned to face Lena when she approached, and she stopped for a moment when she saw Ben. With some effort, she managed to conceal her surprise at seeing her one-night stand from her last conference suddenly turn up here on Föhr. He had hardly changed at all – he still had the same soft, youthful smile, radiant blue eyes and blond hair, which he wore casually combed back. He was wearing a faded pair of jeans, a V-neck sweater and red trainers.

'Hi, Lena,' he said with a meaningful smile.

'Hi, Ben,' she replied, before walking up to the group.

'Allow me to introduce you to the team,' said Ben, turning to the young man on his right. 'This is Jochen Frank from Burglary and Theft, and next to him is my colleague Franz Weinbach, who works with me in the Violent Crime Division.'

Lena shook both of their hands. 'Welcome to Föhr. Should we take a seat?'

She briefly summarised the investigation so far, answered their questions and assigned them their jobs for the day. Then she asked Johann to report on the results of his examination of the locker.

'As expected, there were a lot of fingerprints on the door, both on the outside and the inside,' he began. 'I managed to identify three different sets, and I also took a reference sample from the neighbouring lockers, where I found similar numbers of prints – so we can't necessarily assume that any of the fingerprints belong to the person who put the backpack in the locker. There was no useful evidence on the inside. Obviously I took a close look at the lock too. The door definitely wasn't forced open, but there were scratches suggesting that it might have been opened with a lock-pick, so I took some photos and sent them to the experts in Kiel. In my view, the lock would be easy to pick, even for an amateur. The backpack should have reached the forensics team early this morning, and I've asked them to make it their top priority.'

'Thank you.' Lena was just about to end the meeting when a uniformed colleague entered the room and handed her a sheet of paper. She quickly scanned through it and announced, 'I've just been given the location data for Maria Logener's tablet. As we all know, the last time it was used was in the vicinity of the school. It seems the device was also online in various places around Wyk on Monday afternoon, with the last time being eight o'clock that evening. After that, it was offline until Wednesday, when it was online briefly, and then it was offline again until yesterday.'

Johann had been taking notes. 'That doesn't get us anywhere for now. Maria might have logged in on Wi-Fi overnight, but we have no way of tracing that as we can only track devices via mobile data.' He took the sheet of paper from Lena. 'I'll pin down the exact locations to give us an accurate movement profile for the Monday at least.'

'OK,' said Lena. 'Let's meet again here at five o'clock and collate our findings. Thanks, everyone.'

The officers rose to their feet and filed out of the room. When Lena then went to fetch a coffee from the vending machine on the corridor, Ben appeared beside her. Johann had gone back to the office to check his emails and draw up the movement profile, while Franz Weinbach – Ben's teammate for the afternoon – had nipped off to the toilets.

'You were surprised to see me?' asked Ben, pouring milk into his coffee.

'Was I?'

Ben grinned. 'I think so. We may only have been close for those couple of days, but—'

'Can we just drop the subject?' she interrupted him.

'The subject? That's an odd way to put it, isn't it?'

'You know what I mean. Call it what you like. I'd like to focus on the case and leave everything else to one side.'

Ben took a sip from his cup before putting it down and shrugging. 'If that's what you want. I'm happy to see you again, all the same.'

Franz Weinbach, a short, stocky man with a thick beard, emerged from the lavatory and walked up to them. 'Shall we?'

Ben handed him the car key. 'You go ahead, I'll be right behind you.'

Weinbach nodded to Lena and departed.

'Nice guy,' said Ben. 'We've been working together ever since he came to Flensburg. You can count on him one hundred per cent.' Their eyes met. 'You aren't very happy to see me here. I'm sorry about that, but I couldn't say no. The other divisions are all understaffed and—'

'That's all right, Ben. I expect I overreacted. Let's just forget about it, OK?'

'Sure, let's do that.' He smiled at her. 'And I swear on my mother's life that I—'

Lena laughed. 'Stop it! And don't keep your teammate waiting. Please tread carefully, by the way. I'm afraid this church isn't very keen on government authority. If the rest of them turn out to be as suspicious as the victim's parents were, it'll be very difficult to get any information.'

Ben nodded and was about to follow his colleague, but Lena wasn't done yet. 'Oh, and Ben? Please keep things very discreet. I don't want to stoke any more rumours on the island.'

Ben looked at her in surprise. 'Is there something we should know about?'

'Orders from on high,' she said.

'Warnke? Since when are you two so buddied up?'

Lena shrugged. 'I don't bear grudges. Besides, I completely agree with him. We should proceed very carefully – this investigation could easily come off the rails otherwise.'

Ben nodded again and turned to leave. After a few steps, he looked back at her. 'Will I be seeing you tonight?'

Lena put down her cup. 'I'm planning to catch the last ferry back to Amrum.'

He shrugged again. 'Well, if you don't make it, you have my number.'

Lena watched him go. Why was it so difficult for most men to accept a red light? Hadn't she made it clear enough to him that she wasn't interested in continuing their brief affair? On the other hand, he hadn't made any attempt to get close to her – he hadn't hugged her or touched her hand or her shoulder. Why shouldn't they remain friends?

She heard somebody approaching from behind and turned around.

'I'm done upstairs. Shall we head over to see Lisa Behrens? School finishes early on a Friday, so she should be at home,' Johann suggested. 'She might be more talkative today.'

'Did the movement profile get us anywhere?'

'Not really. Maria logged on to one of the mobile exchanges five times, but I can't directly link that to anyone she knew.' He showed her a sketched-out map of the island with the different locations marked on it. 'Look, this one is out towards the Behrens' house. That might be an indicator that she was visiting Lisa.'

'Well, let's see what Lisa has to tell us.'

Gesa Behrens opened the door.

'Good afternoon, Frau Behrens. We need to speak to Lisa again.'

The old lady gave her a sceptical look. 'Why?'

'Let them in, *Oma*!' her granddaughter called from upstairs. 'I'll be right down.'

As Lisa descended the creaky staircase, Lena's breath caught for a moment. The sound reminded her of her own parents' house and her mother's familiar tread. Lena's melancholy thoughts were only dispelled when Lisa invited them to come in.

'Hello, Lisa,' she said, stepping through the front door.

A few moments later, the three of them were sitting in the living room. Lisa had accompanied her grandmother into one of the bedrooms and returned via the kitchen, bringing a bottle of water and two glasses. 'Would you like something to drink?' she asked with strained politeness.

'No, thank you. Not right now,' answered Lena. Once Lisa had sat down, Lena asked, 'How is your grandmother?'

'Good,' Lisa murmured, before drawing herself up in her chair and adding in a louder voice, 'Is that what you came to ask?'

'No, that was just a friendly enquiry. We're here because of your late friend Maria. We don't think you told us everything yesterday. But first of all, you should know that we no longer believe Maria committed suicide.'

Lisa gulped. 'So what did happen?'

'We have reasons to suspect foul play. That makes it all the more important for us to find out where Maria stayed on Monday and Tuesday nights. We already asked you about that yesterday, but we—'

'And I gave you an answer,' said Lisa defiantly.

'That's right, you did. All the same, I'd like to ask you the same question again.' When Lisa opened her mouth to reply, Lena held up her hand as a sign that she should listen. 'Sooner or later, we're going to find somebody who saw Maria during the time she was missing. Maybe outside on the street, or together with you. When that happens, things will get very difficult for you.' Lena paused briefly. 'You'll be taken in for questioning, your parents will have to come over from Amrum, and we'll have to search the house. You know what that could mean for you and your grandmother.'

Lisa said nothing and stared at the floor.

'Maria was your best friend. Do you really not care what happened to her?'

'Of course I do,' answered Lisa quietly.

'Was Maria here with you on those two nights?'

Lisa clenched her jaw and shut her eyes. 'I didn't have anything to do with any of it,' she said finally.

'Was Maria here?' Lena repeated her question.

Lisa looked at the door as if she was afraid her grandmother might be listening. Eventually, she glanced at Johann, before turning back to face Lena. 'Can we talk in private?'

Johann stood up. 'I'll be outside making a few calls.'

Lena gave him a nod. Once he had closed the door behind him, she leaned forward slightly and asked, 'What do you want to tell me?'

'Do you promise,' Lisa began after a few moments, 'that you'll leave us alone after this? *Oma* is doing well – I'm looking after her.'

'I already told you yesterday that we aren't from social services. So far, I haven't seen any evidence that you aren't being looked after properly here. But I can't make you any promises – I need to hear what happened and what you know first. You'll have to trust me on that.'

Lisa got up, walked over to the window and threw it open. She took a deep breath of fresh air before closing it again and coming back to Lena. 'Yes, Maria was here.'

'Did she come directly from her house?'

'I don't think so. She turned up here just after eight in the evening on Monday– she threw some gravel at my window and I let her in.'

'What did she have with her?'

'Her backpack and a duffel bag.'

'A duffel bag? How big was it and what did it look like?'

'It was her usual bag – the one she always brought with her whenever she stayed here. Small and black.'

Lena wrote the details down in her notebook. 'What did she say? Where was she planning to go?'

'I couldn't get anything out of her at first, but eventually she told me she'd run away from home.'

'Where did she want to go?'

'I asked her that, but she didn't answer. I told her she was being ridiculous – that we might as well be in prison here on the island. You can't just jump on a train and travel to Hamburg.'

'What did she say then?'

'Not a lot. She already knew that, of course. But she seemed very confused – completely distraught – as if she didn't quite know what to do next.'

'What happened then? Did she spend the night here?'

'Yes, of course. That was what she came for. She was afraid of getting caught. Besides, it gets very cold at night. And where else could she have gone?'

'Is that what she said to you?'

Lisa seemed to think carefully before she replied. 'No, I guess not. I must have assumed all that. But she had to find somewhere to sleep if she didn't want to go back home.'

'Did you go to school the following day?'

Lisa nodded.

'Was Maria still here when you came back?'

'Yes, to my surprise. I thought she wanted to leave.'

'Was she waiting for somebody to pick her up?'

'I kept asking her how she planned to get away from Föhr and where she wanted to go. At first, I thought she was on her way to Johanna's.'

'Did Maria mention that?'

'No, I don't think so. That was just my assumption.'

'Do you have a computer or a laptop?'

'Yes, *Oma* gave me one as a present last year.'

'Do you have Wi-Fi here in the house?'

Lisa paused before she replied. 'I added an Internet connection to the phone line last year. But please don't tell my parents that.'

'Did you know Maria had a tablet?'

'From her sister, yeah. But she was always very secretive with it.'

150

'Did you give her the Wi-Fi password?'

Lisa nodded.

'When was the last time you saw Maria?'

Lisa fell silent and stared at her hands.

'This is really important, Lisa. You've helped me a lot already, but the time just before Maria's death is very, very important.'

'We had a fight,' said Lisa softly. 'I was so mad at her. I found out at school that the police were looking for her, and it was only a matter of time before they came knocking on my door. But Maria wasn't interested in any of that. She didn't care what happened to me and *Oma*. She couldn't give a shit.'

'Did you throw her out?'

'No, I didn't. She left on her own.' Lisa groaned. 'Fuck!' She gave a start, seeming surprised at how loud she had spoken – or perhaps she was afraid that her grandmother would hear her. 'I guess I . . . shouted at her and . . . said some awful things. She ran out of the house and . . .' Lisa tailed off.

'She left her backpack behind, didn't she?'

'I noticed it too late. What was I supposed to do? I didn't know where she was, otherwise I would have—'

'When exactly was that?'

'Late in the afternoon on Tuesday. Around five, maybe even six.'

'Did you put the backpack in her locker?' Without waiting for Lisa's reply, Lena added, 'Where did you get the key from?'

'I thought Maria had run away. If somebody had found her things here . . . my parents would have taken me out of school straight away, and I . . .' Lisa was now gasping for breath. 'I'm such a coward! Why didn't I say something? Maria would have been all right if I had.' She paused to collect herself. 'The key was in the front pocket of the bag. On Wednesday morning, when Maria didn't come back, I put her backpack inside mine and took it to school. I put it in her locker during a free period that afternoon.'

'Was Maria's tablet inside the backpack?'

'Yeah, it was.'

'Did you switch it on?'

Lisa nodded. 'More by accident than anything. I don't know exactly how long it was on for. As soon as I noticed, I turned it off again and quickly zipped up the bag.'

Lena thought carefully. That meant somebody must have taken the tablet out of the bag later on, and would have had to open the locker in order to do so. 'Did anybody see you put the backpack into the locker?'

Lisa shrugged. 'How should I know? I was so nervous that I didn't really pay any attention. Once I'd locked it up again, I had the feeling that somebody was looking around the corner and I got scared – but there was nobody there when I went back up the corridor.'

'Did you see anybody near the locker later on?'

'No, definitely not. But I was very worked up. Maybe—'

'OK. This next question is very important.' Lena waited until Lisa looked her in the eye before she continued. 'Maria spent the night with you around three weeks ago while her parents were on the mainland.'

Lisa nodded, but Lena sensed that she found this subject uncomfortable.

'I'm under the impression,' Lena went on, 'that something happened during those two days. Were you with Maria the whole time?'

Lisa took her time replying. 'That was a long time ago. I don't really remember.'

Lena stared at Lisa. 'I don't believe you. What happened?' Until now, she had been using a sympathetic, almost friendly tone of voice – but she now abandoned that, speaking louder and more forcefully.

'I really don't know what happened,' Lisa answered, examining her hands.

'Lisa! What I'm asking you is very important. This isn't about you or your *Oma* – this is about Maria. Do you understand?' She leaned forwards and laid her hand on Lisa's arm. 'I won't leave until you tell me everything you know.'

'Maria . . . there was someone she wanted to—' Lisa fell silent.

'To meet?'

'Yeah – that's what she told me, anyway. I didn't want her to go. I thought it sounded dodgy.'

'What time did Maria leave here to go and meet this person?'

'In the evening. Around seven o'clock – maybe a bit earlier.'

'Where was she going?'

'I really don't know – I swear it.'

Lena was unsure whether Lisa was telling her the truth. If she was lying, she was a remarkably gifted actor. Or had she simply practised this reply so often that she had come to believe it herself?

'She didn't tell you anything? Not even a tiny clue?'

'No, I don't know where she met this person.'

'It's difficult to find a spot on the island to meet with somebody in secret. Even on an isolated beach you'll come across walkers. Where would you go if it were you?'

'She definitely didn't tell me. Please believe me. I didn't want to know either. It was all just . . .'

'And when did she come back?'

Lisa shrugged. She was now hunched up in front of Lena, close to tears. 'I really don't know. At some point in the night. She had a key. I wanted to wait up for her, but I fell asleep, and when I woke up in the morning I found her lying next to me in bed.'

'How was she the next day?'

'She overslept – it was hard to wake her up. After that . . . she didn't say a word over breakfast. Of course I asked her what had happened. Nothing, she eventually said – everything was fine.'

'What sort of impression did she make on you?'

'A really strange one. I couldn't make any sense of it.'

'What do you mean exactly?'

'It looked as though she had a really bad hangover – but Maria never drank alcohol. Not even a tiny sip.'

'Did you ask her who she met, or who she wanted to meet?'

'I might have done. But I was really angry with her. If her parents had found out about it . . .'

'Did you ask her?'

'I really don't remember. But it wouldn't have made any difference if I had asked her. She hardly made a peep. She didn't want to tell me anything.'

'So you have absolutely no idea who she met?'

'No.' Tears were now trickling down her cheeks. 'I swear I don't know.'

'It's OK, Lisa. I believe you.' Lena handed her a tissue. 'Take a few moments to compose yourself and then I'll call my colleague back in.'

A short while later she sent a text message to Johann, who soon joined them in the living room again. If he noticed the state Lisa was in, he showed no sign of it.

Lena resumed the interview. 'Lisa, I'm sure you would know whether Maria had a boyfriend.'

'Here on the island? No, I would have noticed that.'

'We've heard that she was bullied by a few boys in her class. She must have mentioned that to you.'

'Yeah, of course. That meathead Enno kept egging on the others in Maria's class. He was always slagging her off – about her parents, their cult, that sort of thing. Asking whether they drove around in a horse and cart and rubbish like that.'

'How did Maria respond?'

'She didn't pay him any attention. Though there was one time where she properly smacked him one. That was in the playground – I was standing next to her. He'd just insulted her mother. Enno stopped for a few days after that, but then it just got even worse. He started to stalk her really badly – he'd lurk around waiting for her. I told Maria she should talk to Herr Weissdorn but she didn't want to. She even felt guilty for having hit him.'

'Did Enno ever get physical with her?' asked Johann.

'I wouldn't put it past him. He thinks that just because his dad is a pig . . .' She gave a start. 'A policeman, I mean. That's why he thinks he's untouchable.'

Johann moved on to the next question. 'Why did Maria run away from home, in your view?'

'Why do you think? I'm so glad I can stay here with my grandma. I wouldn't be able to stand it for long on Amrum. And Maria's parents are much worse than mine.'

Johann gave a satisfied nod in response to Lisa's answer, but Lena probed further. 'Did she tell you that?'

Lisa shook her head. 'We didn't discuss it very much. It's bad enough as it is, so to then spend all your time talking about it – no, you'd go crazy.'

'Did Maria reject her parents' religion?' Lena asked.

Lisa seemed to find this an uncomfortable subject. She rubbed her hands together and shuffled back and forth on her chair. Eventually, she gave an uncertain shrug. 'Nobody ever really knew what was going on with Maria.'

'Let me put it more simply. Did she believe in God?'

'Maybe, but she definitely didn't want all this hocus-pocus to go with it – living by the Bible and all that. I mean, hello? That thing is two thousand years old!'

'You never really talked about it, did you?'

'Maria is dead, and you're here asking me this. You can't imagine what it's like to have parents like ours.'

'Are you going back to Amrum today?' asked Lena, without responding to Lisa's remark.

'I'm leaving tomorrow afternoon and coming back on Sunday.'

'Please give me a call if you remember anything else.' She stood up. 'We already have your parents' phone number.'

Lisa looked up in horror. 'Please don't call them. Please!'

'The number is just for emergencies, and I can also pass myself off as a teacher at your school. Would that be OK?'

'Thank you!' Lisa murmured. She showed the two officers to the door, where she thanked them a second time.

16

'Amazing!' exclaimed Johann, once Lena had updated him on what Lisa Behrens had told her. 'And who's to say it's the truth?'

Lena was holding her key in her hand ready to unlock the car. She turned back to Johann and said calmly, 'It all sounds credible enough to me. Though the question is, why did Maria turn up at Gesa's house at eight o'clock on Monday night? She had plenty of time to catch a ferry to the mainland. And I hardly think that anybody would have been holding her captive. Why didn't she just leave?'

Johann shrugged. 'Because she was waiting for somebody who didn't show up?'

'That's a possibility. Someone from the island, or from the mainland?'

'The mainland doesn't make much sense. Why would someone come here to collect her? She could have made the crossing on her own.'

Lena leaned against the car. 'So somebody from the island, after all?'

'Or from Amrum. On their way through, so to speak.'

'But in that case she'd have gone to meet the person on board the ferry. No, it must have been somebody from Föhr who stood her up. She suddenly found herself on her own and didn't know where to go, so she went to her friend's house. Maria must have noticed on her previous visits that Lisa's grandmother isn't quite with it – and even if the old lady had noticed her there, she probably wouldn't have said anything.'

'Or maybe somebody came from the mainland to visit her.'

Lena frowned and shook her head. 'But why would she have packed her bags?'

'Maybe the person didn't know that Maria wanted to leave the island. To run away with them, as it were.'

'The other version of events seems more logical to me,' Lena objected, opening the car door.

Johann resumed the discussion once he had sat down beside her. 'What about the next day? Lisa and Maria have an argument, and Maria storms out of the house and forgets her backpack. Then she goes to the beach, where she . . . It all sounds fairly implausible, doesn't it? How far is it from Gesa Behrens' house to the spot where she was found?'

Lena turned on to the main road leading back to the police station by the harbour. 'Depends which way you go. Along the beach, maybe three miles. But we won't get anywhere until we find out who she wanted to meet.'

'Her duffel bag never turned up. That means the culprit must have taken it with them.'

'Or she dropped it off somewhere. Someone should search the route – or routes – from Gesa's house to the beach. Can you organise that? And even if we think she was waiting for someone from the island, we should still take a close look at the ferries. If it was somebody from the mainland, they'll almost certainly have come by car.'

'I'll get on to it,' said Johann, opening the passenger window. Fresh air blew into their faces.

'Did the *Island Courier* publish our appeal?'

'Yep, I saw it this morning. I'll ask them to add the duffel bag to it later on. Small and black, right?'

'That's right.' Lena parked the car directly in front of the police station.

'And what are we going to do about that ominous Monday night in August that Maria spent at Lisa's, when she obviously met up with this unknown person and presumably was assaulted by them?'

'We don't yet know if it was the same person she might have wanted to run away with.'

'It's pretty likely, though, isn't it?'

'Not necessarily. Why would she want to meet the person who assaulted her in order to flee the island with them? I think we're probably talking about two different people here.'

'Two mysterious strangers? That seems a little far-fetched to me,' Johann remarked. 'Or maybe we're missing something.'

'Time will tell. In any case, Maria's behaviour on the following day fits into the picture. Either she really did drink alcohol – whether deliberately or without realising – or she was knocked out with a date-rape drug that night too. The big question is: where on earth did the assault happen? That makes me wonder if she might have been expecting somebody from the mainland after all.'

'Agreed. Did they just hang out in his car? It wouldn't be easy to rape someone in a vehicle. Unless it was a camper van. Though those will be easy enough to check on CCTV. The other vehicles will be trickier.'

'Try your luck for now. We need to follow up on every lead. Last Tuesday night has got me completely stumped too. Maria wasn't wrapped up warmly enough to have slept on a park bench, so where did she go?'

'Back to the killer's car?'

'I'm not sure. Who's to say there even was a car? Even if we assume she really was waiting for this person and planning to leave the island with them – she apparently stormed out of the house after her argument with Lisa, which doesn't suggest that this person was already on the island; if they were, Maria wouldn't have still been at Lisa's – she'd have gone to meet the killer already, wouldn't she?'

'If this person *is* our killer, then that must be true. That said . . . the last ferry docked at eight-thirty in the evening. Assuming that's how he got here.'

Lena sighed. 'This is an awful lot of speculation. Let's rule things out one at a time. You look into the CCTV at the dock and we'll take it from there. As for me, I think I'll try again with Frau Logener. She'll only talk to me in private – if she's even willing to talk, that is. What are your plans for the rest of the day?'

'I still have a few things to cross off my to-do list. I might also head over to see Johanna again.'

Lena concealed her surprise. 'Do you still have questions for her?'

'She must have had some inkling if her sister had a friend on the island – a close-enough friend that she wanted to run away with them.'

'Wouldn't she have already told us that?'

'If it had been obvious, sure. But even if Maria didn't mention it, there might have been signs that Johanna didn't pay any attention to at the time and that she only recognises in hindsight now that she knows the latest facts. You could come with me too, of course . . .'

Lena took the key out of the ignition and opened the car door. 'It's fine. I'll call you when I'm back.'

Johann got out, and Lena dialled the Logeners' number. 'Good afternoon, this is Lena Lorenzen from the police. I'd like to speak to you again in private.'

'I'm sorry, you must have dialled the wrong number.'

Lena immediately changed tack. 'I take it you aren't alone at home right now?'

'Yes, that's our number.'

'What if I come round in an hour's time?'

'Yes, I think you need to go back and check the number with whoever gave it to you. There's no Herr Müller here.'

'OK, then I'll be with you in one hour. If that doesn't work for you, just give me a missed call.'

'Goodbye,' said Frau Logener and hung up.

Lena briefly considered using the time to join Johann in the office, but at the last minute she decided to take another look at the crime scene instead. She drove out of Wyk towards Nieblum, and after passing the small copse on her left, the golf course that separated the road from the beach came into view. Once through Nieblum, she drove straight on, taking a different route to the way she had gone on Wednesday. Half a mile later, she followed the road around a blind corner and passed a farmyard, before pulling into a small car park next to the beach a few hundred yards down the road.

On the way to the scene, she had to cross a narrow bridge over a branch canal, which brought her on to the path she had parked on two days earlier. The sandy beach was up to thirty yards wide at this point. One of the island's two nudist resorts lay a few minutes' walk to the south.

Slowly, Lena walked along the beach, trying to imagine what Maria had gone through that evening. When had she arrived? Who had she waited for, or who had been waiting for her? It must have been unnerving after dark for a fourteen-year-old girl, despite the full moon. Why had she chosen to hide here, of all places? Did this spot have some special meaning for her? Or had she come together with her killer?

Lena sat down on the beach close to the crime scene. How cold had it been that night? Had Maria been planning to sleep out here? The night-time temperature dropped to 13°C at this time of year, sometimes lower.

'What happened here?' asked Lena softly. 'What happened to you? Why did you run away from home? Why now, and not sooner? Who did you want to meet?'

Lena lay back on the fine sand and stared at the sky. The clouds had dispersed over the course of the morning, and the autumn sun was now shining down with full force. She closed her eyes and concentrated on the sounds around her.

The North Sea pushed its water rhythmically against the beach, the seagulls circling above her emitted their shrill calls, and a breeze whipped up the sand and gently rustled the beach grass behind her. 'Why were you here, Maria?' Lena whispered.

In her mind's eye, she saw the girl. It was dark, but Maria seemed unafraid. Her eyes were resolute; a smile played over her lips. Beside her lay the duffel bag, which she held on to with one hand. Maria looked around, stood up and patted the sand from her skirt. Suddenly, she glanced up and looked to one side, seeming to notice somebody. She dropped her bag and ran over to meet the person.

Lena sat up and opened her eyes. Maria hadn't been a shy, reserved little girl any more. Although some of the statements they had heard contradicted each other, an image of a self-confident young woman was gradually emerging – one who engaged more seriously with her environment than was generally the case for her age group.

After glancing at her watch, Lena leapt to her feet and hurried back to the car.

◆　◆　◆

'Do come in,' said Rosa Logener, stepping to one side.

Lena followed her into the kitchen. Maria's mother had made tea and there were two cups standing on the counter, along with some biscuits on a plate.

'Would you like something to drink?'

'Yes, please,' answered Lena, taking a seat on the chair that was offered to her. Rosa Logener poured the tea and sat down with her.

'Did you speak to Johanna?' Frau Logener asked.

'Yes, we've met her a few times now. She's staying with a schoolfriend.'

'How is she?'

'As you might expect, given the circumstances. She's very upset, of course, and she blames herself.'

Rosa Logener nodded. 'When can our little girl come back to us?'

Lena jumped inwardly at the question, which made it sound as though Maria was still alive. 'I'm afraid I can't tell you yet, but I expect the pathologist will be finished with Maria very soon.'

'What's been happening to her over there?'

Lena had attended many autopsies and generally avoided giving any details to the victims' families, but when she saw Rosa Logener's beseeching expression, she decided otherwise in this case. 'Certain examinations needed to be carried out. But I know the pathologist – we're good friends – and she always treats the victim with respect. I'm afraid there will still be some marks left afterwards, however.'

Rosa Logener's eyes grew moist. 'I understand.'

'I'll let you know as soon as I hear anything.'

'Thank you,' she replied quietly.

'Frau Logener, at this stage we're very confident that there was a third party involved in Maria's death. We're currently talking—'

'You mean . . . murder,' Rosa Logener interrupted in a strained voice.

'Yes, that's what we have to assume.'

Frau Logener swallowed heavily.

'I'm sure you'll understand that, in cases like this, our inquiries have to be even more intensive than usual. We're investigating every aspect of Maria's background. By now, we know that Maria very probably intended to leave the island.'

'I know. But I don't understand why.'

'I'm afraid I can't tell you yet either. Do you remember that Maria spent two days at Lisa Behrens' house in August?'

'Yes, of course.'

'And that you picked her up on the evening of the second day?'

'Yes, we came back on the last ferry.'

'Did you notice anything about Maria? Did she seem different in any way?'

'No, everything was completely normal.' Rosa Logener fell silent, seeming to think for a moment, before adding, 'Maybe she was in a bit of a bad mood. I just assumed she'd argued with Lisa.'

'In a bad mood. What do you mean by that, exactly?'

'She was very quiet and she went straight up to her room. But it was also getting late by that point.'

'Did she look pale and tired?'

Once again, Maria's mother seemed to stop and reflect. 'Yes, I think she did. How do you know that?'

'Just a hunch.'

'But she wasn't ill. She went to school the next day, like always.'

Lena made a note on her pad. 'If you remember anything else about that day or the day after, then please call me right away. It's important.'

'If you think . . . Of course, I can do that.'

'I also need to know who Maria was in close contact with. Was there a boy or a young man in your community whom she—'

'No!' Rosa Logener blurted. 'No.'

'Maria would have been turning fifteen next month. At her age, it wouldn't be unusual for—'

'No!' She interrupted Lena once again, this time louder and more forcefully. Her voice trembled slightly but it didn't sound aggressive. She sat hunched in front of Lena, her head lowered, her hands clutching the table.

'Of course, Maria might have met with an unknown person – but in any case, there are clear indications that she met somebody on the beach, or possibly even travelled there with that person. And the fact that she had a duffel bag with her suggests she wanted to run away from home.'

Rosa Logener looked up and met Lena's gaze with mournful eyes.

'Children Maria's age,' Lena continued, 'often rebel against their home environment. That's nothing unusual. Did Maria have any problems with you or your husband? Did she argue with you more often than she used to, for example?'

Tears were running down the woman's cheeks, and she seemed not to notice when Lena handed her a tissue. It took her a few moments to rouse herself from her reverie and wipe her face. 'Maria is . . . was a good child,' she whispered.

'She grew apart from you over the last few months, didn't she?'

'She went very quiet, that's true.'

'Did you talk to her? Ask her what was troubling her?'

'She didn't want to come any more.' Rosa Logener's voice was barely audible. 'To prayers or to church meetings. She only told me that. My husband . . . he's sometimes very strict. He says children should obey their parents.'

'Did Maria continue attending meetings with you then?'

'Yes – my husband . . .' She fumbled for words.

'Did Maria tell you why she didn't want to go any more?'

'Why didn't I just ask her?' She seemed to be talking to herself. 'She was so fragile, our little Maria. It was too early – far too early.'

Lena waited until she was sure that Rosa Logener had finished before she asked, 'What was too early?'

'We only meant the best for her. Martin is such a good worker, my husband says. He's a good boy. We wanted . . .' She fell silent once more.

'Who is Martin?'

'Martin?' Frau Logener looked up in surprise, as if she had only just noticed Lena sitting at the table. 'Martin works with my husband. He helps him out. Not always, but lately . . . He hasn't managed to find a job yet, but my husband says he's glad to have him.'

It gradually began to dawn on Lena what Frau Logener was trying to tell her. 'Martin is a member of your church?'

'Yes, we've known his parents for over thirty years now.'

'How old is he?'

'He turned nineteen two months ago.'

'And what's his surname?'

'Reimers. Martin Reimers. His parents are called Hans and Elfriede. They live in Witsum. They're good, honest people.'

'And you and your husband would have liked to see Maria and Martin start a family one day?'

'That would have been so wonderful. But now . . .'

'Did you ever discuss it with Maria?'

'My husband . . . he wanted to—' She stopped. 'I don't know. We wanted to wait. It was far too early, after all. But once Maria finished school . . .'

'I assume your husband doesn't know you're talking to me right now?'

Rosa Logener looked at her in dismay. 'No! He only gets back this evening.'

'Don't worry, he won't hear about it from me. But let's get back to Maria. Did Martin and Maria often cross paths with each other?'

'Martin didn't do anything to Maria. He would never lift a finger against her.'

'But he knew that you and your husband – how should I put this? – would have liked for him to become your son-in-law?'

Maria's mother gave a long pause before she answered. 'I think Hans spoke to Martin about it. He agreed with us.'

Lena tried to remain calm, but inwardly she was seething. How could a mother be so naive and follow her husband so unconditionally? She must have known that Maria wouldn't simply submit to her fate. Lena now regretted her idle promise not to tell Walther Logener about this conversation.

Lena stood up and gave Frau Logener her hand. 'Thank you for being so honest with me. I'll need to take another look at Maria's room.'

'My husband says—'

'Would you prefer me to obtain a search warrant for the house? Then a whole team would come around and—'

'You can go into Maria's room,' said Rosa Logener, standing up from the table. 'I'll come with you.'

At first glance, it seemed that nothing in the room had changed since her last visit. Lena pulled on a pair of latex gloves, opened the wardrobe and went through the compartments one by one. Maria's clothes lay ironed and neatly folded in piles. The first four shelves revealed nothing unusual, but on the bottom one, which was full of winter clothing, she found a USB stick hidden at the back underneath a thick sweater. Lena placed it into a plastic bag before examining the clothes hanging from the rail, but there was nothing else to be found.

When Lena moved on to the desk, Rosa Logener left the room. She had been standing in the doorway nervously watching the search.

Lena picked up each of the books in turn, leafing through them before putting them back. An exercise book came in for particularly close scrutiny. Maria had written down her homework on the first few pages, while further back there were notes on individual lessons. Lena couldn't remember having ever been so diligent with her own work when she was a schoolgirl. She flicked onwards through the book. Only when she reached the blank pages did she find anything of interest: a sheet had evidently been ripped out here. Lena examined the following page and could just about make out faint impressions of pen marks from the torn-out sheet. She tried to decipher the writing, but soon gave up. CSI would be able to make sense of it. She placed the exercise book inside another plastic bag and sealed it.

The dressing table offered no further clues, and Lena turned her attention to the bookshelf. She picked up the Bible and flicked through it, and as she did so, a number of small pieces of paper fell out. Lena picked them up and laid them out on the desk. There were eight notes, each consisting of just a few words:

HOLY WHORE!

MAY GOD ENLIGHTEN US

IS IT REALLY THAT HOT IN HELL?

DO YOU SHOWER WITH YOUR CLOTHES ON?

HOW LONG ARE SATAN'S HORNS?

IS LAUGHING BANNED IN YOUR CULT?

SATAN'S SLUTS KNOW HOW TO FUCK

HAVE FUN IN HEAVEN!

They had been written out very neatly in block capitals, one letter at a time. The author seemed to have taken great pains not to give much away about themselves.

Lena photographed each of the notes in turn with her phone and placed them inside the plastic bag with the USB stick.

Ten minutes later, she felt sure that she had searched everything thoroughly. She left the room and found Rosa Logener at the kitchen table. 'I'm done for now.'

'Did you find anything?'

'I can't say for sure yet. I found a USB stick, a few notes and something inside Maria's exercise book. I'll need to take all those things with me.' Lena sat down at the table with Frau Logener. 'Is there anything else you can think of that might help me find the culprit?'

'Will you catch him?' Her voice had an imploring note to it.

'I'll do everything I can to find Maria's killer.' Normally, Lena refrained from answering questions like this from the relatives of victims of violence when the facts of the case were still unknown – yet she felt she owed Rosa Logener a reply. The woman had gone against her husband by agreeing to Lena's visit, and Lena didn't like to imagine how he would react if he ever found out about their conversation.

'Thank you for speaking with me and for letting me look at Maria's room.' She stood up and gave Maria's mother her hand. 'I'll be in touch if I have any news.'

17

'I'm dying to know what files are on that USB stick,' said Johann, who had just been brought up to speed by Lena. They were sitting in their makeshift office at the station.

'You do know we really ought to have it examined by CSI first, don't you?'

'Uh-oh – this looks like trouble,' replied Johann with a grin as he watched Lena insert the device into the USB port on her laptop and wait for the system to recognise it.

Eventually, a window opened displaying a list of JPEG files, which suggested they were probably photos. Lena opened the first image. It was a picture of the Logeners that looked as though it had been taken five or six years ago. Maria's parents were smiling at the camera, and Maria herself was holding her big sister's hand and beaming from ear to ear.

'Family photos?' asked Johann in surprise.

Lena clicked on the next file. A small child appeared on screen. Maria and Johanna shared a strong family resemblance, which made it impossible to tell which of the two they were looking at, but Lena suspected that it was Maria as a toddler.

'Does this make any sense to you?' he asked.

Lena opened another file, which showed both sisters at a birthday party. 'Maria used her tablet to take pictures of these photos,' she said, pointing to the edge of the frame. 'They haven't been scanned.'

'But why did she bother? And why did she then store them on a USB stick hidden away in her wardrobe?'

'I expect she wanted to keep the pictures safe in case her tablet broke.' It occurred to Lena that these were probably the same files Maria had saved to the cloud.

'Or in case her father confiscated it. But why did she take these pictures in the first place? There must be family photo albums in the house that she could look at any time she wanted.'

Lena shrugged. 'This way she would always have easy access to the pictures. Maybe her family was more important to her than we thought.'

'Sure, that's one explanation. But not a very logical one.'

'Do you have another?' Lena asked, clicking through the remaining files in quick succession. 'Family photos, every single one.'

'Was she trying to gather evidence of some kind?'

'Evidence for what? Just look at the pictures. A completely normal family.' She paused for thought. 'Did you notice how happy Maria looks in all of these photos, even as a little kid?'

'Maybe she was a good-tempered child.'

'Johann! Happy and good-tempered aren't the same thing. She wanted to bring her past back to life, to remind herself of it. Maybe she felt like her former life was slipping away from her. In that sense, perhaps you weren't so wrong after all. She was gathering evidence all right – evidence of her happy childhood.'

'These are snapshots, though. Everyone smiles for photographs. It doesn't necessarily mean anything.'

'Did you talk to Johanna Logener again?'

'Yes – about this very topic, in fact. Her family. She's convinced her father has something to do with it.' When he noticed Lena's expression, he quickly added, 'I know she's reacting in an extremely emotional way, but now that you tell me Maria was going to be all but forced into marriage—'

'I never said that,' Lena interrupted him. 'Please, let's look at this information objectively. For one thing, her parents were just thinking about who might make a suitable husband for their daughter. Not right now, but further down the line. Of course we'll need to find out more about this Martin, but we have to keep an open mind about him and Maria's parents.'

'OK, forced into marriage was a bit of an exaggeration. But . . .' He left the rest unspoken.

Lena studied him carefully. 'What's going on between you and Johanna Logener? You're too close to the case, Johann. I've never seen you like this before. Weren't you the one who pulled me back down to earth not so long ago when my imagination was running away with me? I'll ask you again: what's going on?'

'Nothing!' answered Johann forcefully; then, after a short pause, he added, 'At least, nothing that will hold me – or us – back from our investigation.'

'Do you like her?'

Johann threw his head back and closed his eyes. 'Like her? Yes, I like her. I feel sorry for her, and you're right, I should keep my distance a little more. In terms of the case, I mean. But at the end of the day, she isn't a suspect, she's a witness.'

Lena groaned. Johann had just admitted to her that he had developed feelings for this woman. 'We need to stay impartial, or we're going to make mistakes,' she said, making one last attempt to get her colleague to see reason. 'I have to ask you not to speak to Johanna Logener again on your own.'

'Isn't that overdoing things slightly? I mean—'

'No, Johann. It definitely isn't.'

'OK,' he replied, as if acknowledging an order. Lena could see how put out he was.

'When are the others coming back?' she asked.

Just as Johann opened his mouth to reply, there came a knock from outside. The door swung open. 'Do you have a moment?' asked Jochen Frank, one of Johann's colleagues from Flensburg.

'Come in,' answered Johann. The rangy sergeant stepped through the door and closed it behind him.

'I realise we're about to have a team meeting, but . . . You know Sergeant Brandt's son and the victim were in the same class at school?'

'Yeah, of course,' replied Johann.

'That means he's on our list. But when Jan Ottenga and I wanted to go and interview him earlier, Brandt said it wouldn't be necessary. I didn't say anything at the time and we just went to visit the next candidate instead.'

'But?' asked Lena, guessing there was more to it than that.

'Well, one way or another we got talking about yesterday, when the two officers from Föhr patrolled the streets around the school. Arno Brandt told us about it this morning.'

Lena had to force herself to remain calm. 'And?'

'Let's just say that Sergeant Brandt seems to have a few quirks when it comes to his own family. Basically, Ottenga mentioned to me in passing that Brandt's son was near the school yesterday, but the two of them didn't stop and search him. Though from the way Ottenga phrased it, I don't think he brought it up by accident. I'd say he was deliberately trying to tip me off.'

'Interesting,' said Johann. 'Brandt's son and heir was one of Maria's main bullies at school. Probably even the ringleader. Well, well, well.'

'You definitely did the right thing coming to us with this, at any rate,' said Lena. 'Johann and I will talk to Enno Brandt.'

The sergeant looked relieved. He nodded and turned to leave, but just as he was reaching for the handle, the door opened and Ben peered into the room. 'A secret meeting?' he asked.

Lena stood up. 'You've got us there – a top-secret secret meeting.'

Ben's grin grew even broader. 'I didn't realise you'd switched to the intelligence services?'

'No comment, Inspector.'

Johann had followed this little exchange with interest. 'Shall we, guys?' he eventually asked.

Ben threw the door open and gave a slight bow. 'But of course!'

Ten minutes later, once everyone had made themselves a cup of coffee, Lena gave a brief summary of her two interviews with Lisa Behrens and Rosa Logener and her findings from her search of Maria Logener's room – though she instinctively refrained from mentioning the eight notes she had found. It seemed unwise to discuss that subject in front of Arno Brandt in case his son turned out to be involved.

'Now, I don't need to tell you that none of this information should leave this room.'

'Of course not, Detective Inspector,' said Arno Brandt in a jovial tone, appointing himself as the spokesman for the group. 'Shall we move things along, then?'

'Certainly, Sergeant.' She turned to Ben and asked him for an update.

'We visited four of the families today and interviewed the adults we found.' He looked at his notepad. 'Let's start with the Grote family. We spoke to Elena Grote – her husband was still at work in the ferry port.'

'What's his job there?' Lena instantly asked.

Another glance at the pad. 'I think he works on the . . . what's that thing called again? The thing you use to get off the boat?'

'The gangway,' Lena prompted him.

'That's the one. He checks the tickets and is responsible for safety while passengers board and disembark. Oddly enough, that seems to be a popular career choice for the Brethren, as the father of the next family on our list – the Reimers – works there too. Though he's more on the administrative side.' Ben's eyes went back to his notepad. 'Ticket sales, among other things.' Ben seemed to notice that Lena found that detail interesting. 'Why is that important?'

'Based on everything we know so far, it seems likely that Maria Logener was waiting for somebody, either from the island or from the mainland. The question was – why? She could easily have taken the ferry herself. However, if she knew that at least two of the men from her church worked at the ferry terminal – and we have to assume that she did know – then things suddenly look very different. She might have thought they'd stop her from leaving, or that they would at least tell her parents. Maybe that was why she planned to flee the island more or less in secret.'

'Surely you don't mean in the boot of a car?' Ben asked.

'It's perfectly possible,' said Lena.

'Yeah – maybe you're right,' Ben conceded. 'It does sound pretty far-fetched, and only yesterday I would have laughed at the idea. But now that I've met a few of these people, I have to admit it's not beyond the realm of possibility.'

Ben gave a brief account of the interviews, all of which had followed a similar pattern: the individuals had refused to talk to the police at first, and had only answered the two officers' questions once they'd been informed that the evidence gathered so far suggested Maria Logener had died a violent death. Even so, their responses had been very vague. All of them knew the victim from the regular meetings of the church, but none of them had been keen to respond to any further questions from the detectives. Nobody could imagine that Maria would have left her family of her own free will, and two of the interviewees accused her sister, Johanna, of putting her up to it.

'In short, we heard the same empty phrases wherever we went. When the women were on their own, they referred us to their husbands, and when we spoke to the men, they told their wives to leave the room. One of them even tried to convert us. All in all, it was a complete wall of silence.'

'So you didn't get anything useful,' Lena summarised. 'And what was your personal impression?'

'You mean, behind the facade? If I take a very broad interpretation of what was said and also think about what wasn't said – the gestures and facial expressions – then I'd say the Logeners were under a good deal of scrutiny. The parents are more or less openly blamed for the fact that their elder daughter left the church. And if I didn't think the idea was completely absurd, I almost got the impression that they view Maria's death as a punishment from God. But like I say, that's reading between the lines.' He turned to his colleague. 'What do you think, Franz?'

'I'd second all that. It wouldn't stand up in court, of course, but my impressions were the same as Ben's.'

'Did you talk to Martin Reimers?' asked Lena.

Ben shook his head. 'If we'd known he'd been working with Logener and was viewed as a future son-in-law, then we wouldn't have taken no for an answer. As it was, they told us he was out – however, when I checked the registration number of the old Vauxhall Astra parked on the Reimers' drive just now, I found out that it's licensed under Martin Reimers' name. So I assume he was in the house after all.'

'Well, he won't get away from us. I'll issue a summons. That ought to help him realise the seriousness of the situation.'

'But that depends on the young man actually putting in an appearance here,' Johann objected. 'I strongly suspect these gentlemen know their rights and are aware they only need to obey a summons if it's issued by the chief prosecutor.'

'We'll see,' said Lena, who didn't like Johann's tone. She turned to Arno Brandt. 'Could you send one of your colleagues to visit the Reimers? Ten o'clock tomorrow would be good.'

'Tomorrow is Saturday. I'm afraid—'

'I'm sure Herr Reimers will understand that we want to track down Maria's murderer as soon as possible. Perhaps you could even go yourself?'

Arno Brandt hesitated a moment too long for it not to be obvious to everyone in the room how reluctant he was to accept the assignment. 'Certainly – I'll drop by when I head home tonight. It's on my way anyway.'

'Thank you, Sergeant.' Lena turned back to the group. 'Now let's hear what the other team has to report.'

Jochen Frank cleared his throat. 'We were on babysitting duty, as you know. Interviewing Maria's classmates.' He grinned. 'Made us feel about twenty years older than we actually are.' He leafed through his notepad until he found the right page. 'We managed seven out of the twenty-four. There were also four others who weren't in, but we made appointments with their parents for tomorrow.' He took a deep breath. 'I used the same opening questions every time: what was the individual's relationship with Maria Logener? What did they have to do with her? When was the last time they saw Maria? And did they know about Maria's problems? The next stage was more personalised, so to speak. The boys – who made up four of the seven interviewees – were very reticent. That was to be expected, of course, since we already know about the bullying and that the boys were the driving force behind it. I knew that even the ones who weren't personally involved would refuse to cooperate out of some mistaken sense of solidarity, so we took a slightly harder line on that particular topic. You know the drill – I played the good cop, Ottenga was the bad cop.'

Everyone's eyes went to Constable Jan Ottenga, who looked bashfully at the floor and said, 'The boys all caved quickly enough. It was no big deal.'

'Don't be so modest, Jan,' said Jochen Frank. 'Anyway, it seems Maria Logener was something of a lust object for the boys in the class. Even on the photos we have, you can see what a beauty she was. In brief, most of the boys had tried it on with her and they'd all been turned down, to put it politely. Maria Logener doesn't appear to have had the slightest bit of interest in boys her own age. The upshot was that some of the boys began to express their interest in a more perverse way. None of the kids we interviewed were personally involved, of course, and they don't know exactly who was. But I assume they all at least watched it happen and did nothing to intervene. And since that isn't a crime and we aren't here to find out who Maria's bullies were, I gave them a few words of warning and left it at that.'

'What about the girls? How did they react?' asked Johann.

Before Jochen Frank could reply, Arno Brandt jumped in. Lena had already noticed that he clearly couldn't see the point in interviewing Maria's classmates. He'd spent the meeting doodling on his notebook and staring out of the window with a bored expression. 'Personally speaking, I don't think we should set too much score by these childish games. That's just how teenagers are. The kids have no sense of proportion and still have a lot to learn, but that's all perfectly normal. What does it have to do with our investigation? We're looking for a cold-blooded killer here. Or have I misunderstood something?'

'We can only decide what facts are relevant to our case once we know what the facts are,' said Lena, striving to remain calm.

'I'm sure Sergeant Frank's inquiries went beyond just the issue of bullying.'

'Absolutely. I'll pick up where I left off then,' added Jochen Frank. He flicked through his notes, finding the right page only on the second try. 'Right, the girls. They don't seem to have really noticed the boys' bullying. Like I said, we only managed to interview three of them, so I can't leap to any conclusions yet. But I reckon they viewed Maria as competition. The girls also – or maybe I should say, especially – noticed that the boys couldn't tear their eyes away from her, and it goes without saying that that annoyed the young ladies. But I think there was more to it than that. Maria wasn't only beautiful, she was also top of the class, and yet nobody – not even the boys – described her as a swot. Essentially, the three girls didn't like Maria, but they didn't want to state their reasons openly. They seem to have felt a general sense of unease about her. Envy, resentment, a lack of empathy – take your pick. They definitely blanked her, but I don't think they did anything more than that. As for the boys, however, I'm not so sure. They gave me too many vague answers, and in response to the wrong questions too. Hopefully I can find out more tomorrow. I haven't written my report yet either' – he grinned – 'but after a quick night shift you should have everything in black and white in the morning.'

'Thank you, Sergeant.' Lena took the floor again and summarised the results of the day's work. The interviews would continue on Saturday, and another meeting was scheduled for the late afternoon.

After glancing at the clock, Lena rose to her feet. 'Thank you for all your work so far. I'll see you all tomorrow.'

One by one, the group dispersed and left the room. Just as Arno Brandt was heading towards the door, Lena stopped him. 'I'd like a quick word, please. Can we go to your office?'

'What's this about?' asked Brandt once they had sat down at the small conference table.

'Your son, Enno, is one of Maria's classmates, as you know. I don't want to bring Constable Ottenga into a conflict of interest, so I'd like to interview Enno myself. How would tomorrow afternoon suit you? Perhaps around two o'clock?'

'I think that's completely unnecessary.'

'Because he's your son?'

Brandt held his breath briefly before exhaling audibly and drawing himself up in his chair. 'Yes, obviously. Quite apart from the fact that I think interviewing the children is completely pointless, I can assure you that Enno had nothing to do with the bullying.'

'Your son has the same rights as any other citizen of our country, of course. And if you refuse my request in your capacity as his father, I'll be forced to go down the official route. I'm sure I don't need to explain to you what that will involve.'

Arno Brandt glowered at her darkly. For a moment, Lena thought he was about to throw her out of his office, but then an intent look suddenly came over his face. 'Fine, if you absolutely have to. I'll tell him to come here tomorrow afternoon. That way I can be present for the conversation.'

'As his father?'

'What do you think?' Once again, Brandt seemed to be having difficulty suppressing his anger at Lena. His right hand trembled, his ears turned red.

'I can't prevent you from doing so, of course, and I wouldn't want to either, but it would mean I'd have to exclude you from the rest of the investigation. I think it would be better if I spoke to Enno alone, or if his mother accompanied him instead.'

Arno Brandt leapt to his feet and shook his head in disbelief, as if he thought Lena's suggestion was a bad joke. 'Are you serious?' The next moment, however, he had himself back under control. 'All right, I'll ask my wife and Enno to be here at two o'clock. I hardly expect it'll take long.'

Lena stood up from her chair. 'I think we'll be done fairly quickly too. Especially if Enno had nothing to do with the bullying.'

Arno Brandt gave an exasperated groan. 'Is there anything else? It's late, and I still need to call at the Reimers', as you know.'

'Thank you, Sergeant, that'll be all. I think the investigation is slowly starting to come together. With any luck, you'll be rid of us before long.' She shook his hand. 'Please pass on my regards to your wife.'

18

Lena was standing indecisively outside the police station and looking over at the ferry terminal across the road. The last boat to Amrum would depart in an hour, but she couldn't see herself leaving on it. Her thoughts were too firmly wrapped up in the case and she needed time to make sense of a few details. Would Erck misinterpret it if she cancelled? On the other hand, did she really want to arrange her schedule around him? With any luck, she'd be able to head over earlier the following day. That made much more sense than taking the last ferry tonight and at best exchanging a few words with Erck before they both fell asleep.

She reached for her phone and dialled his number.

'Hey,' said Erck. 'Everything OK over there?'

'I wouldn't say that, exactly. We're just treading water, despite the reinforcements from Flensburg. And right now I don't see any light at the end of the tunnel.'

'So you're staying on Föhr tonight?'

'Would you be mad at me? I still need to—'

'Hey, Lena – it's OK. I know how important your work is to you.'

'Are you sure?' She could tell from his voice how disappointed he was.

'Maybe if you came a little earlier tomorrow to make up for it.'

Now she could almost feel the grin on his face. 'I was thinking the same thing. I can't promise anything, but I'll try.'

'Sounds good. I'll make us something nice for dinner and we can have a cosy night in.'

'I really will try. And if I don't manage it tomorrow, I definitely will on Sunday.'

'Is the case so complicated?'

'More than you can imagine. I haven't found the right angle yet. It sounds crazy, but I think it's right in front of me, only I can't see it. And I'm sure I don't need to tell you how much it's eating away at me.'

'Hey, didn't you tell me once that some cases drag on for months before the critical clue finally comes along?'

'That's more time than I have here. If I don't find a clear lead in the next few days . . .' She left her sentence unfinished, as she didn't know herself what would happen then. DSU Warnke might even prefer an unsolved case over any negative consequences for the Brethren.

'Sounds like a lot of pressure.'

'For me, at least.'

'That reminds me of the old days. Lena versus the rest of the world. You never gave up, come what may.'

I'm not so sure about that, thought Lena. *I definitely gave up on my family and ran away from them.* 'I may be a lot of things, but I'm no hero,' she said finally.

'To me you are. And now you have to promise that you'll think about me from time to time, and not just about murderers and other criminals.'

'I promise.' She paused for a moment. 'I have to go now, Erck. I'll call you again tonight, if it's at all possible.'

'I'll be up until eleven. Don't work too hard.'

'Speak soon, Erck.'

They remained silent for a while, without ending the call. Eventually, Erck whispered, 'I love you.'

'I know,' answered Lena softly.

'Look after yourself. I don't want to lose you.'

'I always do. Goodbye, Erck.'

Lena held her phone as she stood in front of the police station, unsure what to do next. Johann had given her the address of the bed and breakfast and a set of keys, but she had absolutely no desire to hang out in a small stuffy bedroom right now. She sauntered over to her car, pulled a thick jumper out of her duffel bag and grabbed a blanket from the back seat before wandering north along the promenade. Ten minutes later, she arrived at her 'private' beach chair and took a final glance at the sky before unlocking the cover. The temperature had now dropped below twenty degrees, but she could stick it out for a while yet thanks to her warm layers.

She sat down, wrapped herself in the blanket, took her laptop out of its bag and started it up. First, she looked at the photos she had copied from Maria's USB drive, and her initial impressions seemed confirmed: Maria's smile was unfeigned. Lena could see how happy she must have been within her own family circle. In one picture she was resting her head on her mother's shoulder; in another she was hugging her sister. In every photo, she seemed to be striving to get as close to her family as possible. There didn't even appear to be any distance between her and her stern father – she beamed at him just as much as at Johanna and her mother.

'Were you really so happy?' Lena murmured. 'When did it all fall apart? And why?'

Had she realised that her idea of religion – of nearness to God – was different to that practised by her parents? Her sister had made a complete break with her parents' values. Was there any other way to escape such a strictly religious family? Had Maria been afraid there would be no going back?

Lena tried to recall her own final years on Amrum. Although her situation had been nowhere near as complicated as Maria's, there were still similarities: the dominant father heedlessly pursuing his own interests and failing to notice his own daughter growing apart from him; the mother too afraid to stand up to her husband and striving to keep her family together; the tiny island that exacerbated both the feeling of imprisonment and the need to run away. Those things had all gradually intensified for Lena – and presumably for Maria too – over the course of many months, or even years. The older she got, the more Lena had felt abandoned to the situation. How often she had begged her mother to defend herself, only to receive the same reply: 'He isn't what you think he is. We'll make it through. We're a family, after all.'

Had Maria had the courage to talk to her mother? Did she know her daughter had been raped? Or had Maria realised from the outset that her mother would never stand up to her father?

So far, they hadn't found anybody who had even the slightest idea why Maria might have run away. Why hadn't she turned to her sister for help? Or to Eva Braasch? Maybe even Maria herself hadn't grasped what was happening to her.

Yet the crucial question was: who had Maria been waiting for? Who was supposed to take her off the island? And how did the events of three weeks earlier fit into the picture? Who had she wanted to meet with that afternoon or evening? Was that when she'd been raped? And what influence did that terrible experience have on the weeks that followed?

Lena went through all the available documents once more before leaning back exhausted in the beach chair and closing her eyes. Only the ringing of her phone roused her from her state of inertia. She looked at the display and sighed before accepting the call.

'Good evening, Detective Superintendent.'

'Good evening, Inspector Lorenzen. I'd been expecting you to provide a report.'

'I was just about to call you. The case is much more complicated than it first appeared.' She gave Warnke a brief summary and took the opportunity to put in a request for Martin Reimers' phone records. Warnke wasn't happy about that, but he soon relented.

'I hope we'll be able to get you some results over the next few days,' she said eventually.

'Do you need more people?'

Lena was surprised by the question. She'd been expecting Warnke to threaten to withdraw the support from Flensburg if there were no results soon. 'I think we'll manage with what we've got. I don't want to create too much of a commotion either. Word has already got around that we're here, as you might expect.'

'You're right. Let's stick with the current team then. I assume you've been talking to the relatives yourself and that the interviews with the members of the church are being handled discreetly and carefully.'

Lena was on the verge of giving a sharp retort, but decided in favour of a tactical alternative. 'I may use unconventional methods from time to time, but when I promise you something, you can rest assured I'll deliver without you having to check up on me. I thought we'd established at least that much.'

Warnke sighed quietly. 'I didn't mean to doubt your competence. I'm sorry if that's how it came across.'

'That's OK. We're both under pressure.'

'You aren't wrong there. Call me if you have any news or if you need my help. You have my personal number, don't you?'

'It's saved to my phone. I'll be in touch.'

Warnke said goodbye and ended the call.

Lena was amazed by his apology. Had she misjudged the detective superintendent so badly? If she wasn't careful, she might end up liking him. On the other hand, her experiences with him when they first started working together still weighed on her mind. She didn't believe that people were capable of changing radically in such a short space of time.

Suddenly, Lena realised she was long overdue a call from Leon. He normally let her know if there was nothing more to be done. She looked up his number.

'What do you want?' growled an ill-tempered Leon.

'Do you have anything for me?'

'Did I call you?'

'Can we drop the games? I don't have much time.'

'Me neither. If all goes well, I can get something to you tomorrow. But don't expect too much. They're just fragments. Some bigger, some smaller.'

'Whatever you've got, I'm happy. I'll wait until tomorrow then.'

Leon hung up without saying goodbye, as usual.

Just as Lena was about to lean back in her beach chair again, she heard a noise. She turned around and saw Ben.

'Good evening, Detective Inspector! How about a glass of wine?' Ben was holding a bottle of white and two glasses and beaming at her. 'I thought I might find you here.'

Lena rolled her eyes. 'Did Johann blab?'

'Not exactly. I'm just a superb detective who always gets to the bottom of everything.' He nodded at the space beside her. 'May I?'

Lena shuffled to one side. 'If you have to. Strictly speaking, I'm—'

'You aren't going to tell me you're still working, are you?' Ben laughed, handing her a half-full glass. 'Give it a try. I spent nearly an hour looking for this bottle. Painstaking detective work, you might say.'

Lena took a sip and nodded. 'It was worth the effort.'

'I'm glad to hear it,' answered Ben, raising his glass. 'To us!'

When Lena didn't react, he quickly added, 'For the second time: I didn't push for this assignment. But I'm here now, and I can't pretend that we're just your average colleagues.'

'It's OK.' She took another sip of her wine. 'I just wasn't expecting you.'

'Is it really so awful to see me again?'

'Don't be daft, of course it isn't.'

He gave a cheeky grin. 'Well, that's a weight off my shoulders.'

'You're ridiculous!' Lena laughed. Then she grew serious. 'How's your family?'

Ben fell silent for a moment. 'You mean, have I patched things up with my wife?'

'Last I heard, you were making another go of it.'

'That didn't last long, unfortunately. I've moved out, for now at least. What do they call it again?' He sighed. 'A time out? That's a strange name for it, don't you think?'

'Where are you living?'

'I've got a small one-bed apartment to tide me over. A friend of mine has gone travelling in Australia and he's letting me stay at his place while he's out there.'

'What about the kids?'

'You know how it is in our job. No way of planning anything. We do things together whenever I'm free.' He cast his eyes over the beach. 'I've racked up some overtime, so I should be able to take a few days off once this assignment is finished. Maybe I'll go away with them in the autumn half-term holiday.'

'It sounds like you're planning for the long term.'

He shrugged. 'This is the first time out I've ever had. I have no idea how long it's supposed to last. Don't these things normally end in divorce anyway?'

'I'm not sure I'm the right person to come to with these questions.'

'You asked, I answered.' He leaned back in the beach chair and stared out at the rising tide.

'So you didn't want to take a break?' Lena asked after a while.

'I expect it's for the best. For the kids, for Birgit, and probably for me too.' He closed his eyes and added in a quiet voice, 'No, if I'm honest, I didn't want to. What man would be happy with the break-up of his family? Not me, anyway.' He turned to look at Lena. 'And before you ask: no, I'm not coping with it.' He poured himself another glass of wine and took a large gulp. 'I feel like I'm climbing the walls in that flat, and I can't focus at work. My appetite's gone and I never feel like doing anything.'

'That doesn't sound good.'

'No, it sounds completely fucked up. But let's drop the subject. At least things are going well for you, if I've understood Johann correctly?'

Lena sighed. 'That guy seems to—'

'Don't worry, he isn't running around telling stories about you. We know each other well – you might even call us friends – and while he was telling me about your spectacular case on Amrum, he also mentioned that you'd run into your childhood sweetheart out there. I just filled in the gaps myself when I heard you spent the night on Amrum. Or am I wrong?'

Lena hesitated briefly before replying. 'No, we've been seeing a lot of each other.'

'A long-distance relationship?'

'If you like.'

'Not easy, is it?'

She didn't reply. What *was* easy in life? Had she ever had a straightforward relationship with a man before? It sometimes felt as though she went out of her way to find the complicated ones.

'What does he do for a living?' Ben continued.

'He manages holiday homes. Plus everything that goes with that.'

Ben raised his eyebrows. 'I presume there aren't so many of those in Kiel.'

'You presume correctly,' answered Lena laconically. She wondered why she was finding it so difficult to talk about her situation. Then again, she had once come very close to Ben – closer than she had planned, even.

'That's a tricky one,' Ben murmured. He topped up both their glasses. 'To us two lucky devils!'

Lena tried to smile, but fell short. She drained her glass in one draught. 'You haven't given up, though, have you?'

'No idea. What I'd like more than anything would be to get in my car and head south. Down to Sicily, or beyond. All the way across Africa. That'd be perfect. Only my car would never make it, and I don't have the money for a properly fancy four-by-four. So I'll just stay here. Simple as that. I'll stay here and keep catching bad guys who end up getting away with a suspended sentence. Yeah, I know, we're meant to be the heroes. Great. What has it brought us? Low pay, endless work and a broken family.' Ben seemed to be speaking more to himself at this point. Only now did he take his eyes off the horizon and turn to look at Lena. 'Why me, anyway?'

'What do you mean?'

'That time at the conference – why did we end up in bed together? I keep asking myself that question and I still haven't come up with an answer. Was I just in the right place at the right time? Could it just as easily have been any other man?'

'And what if it could?'

Ben winced. 'That would hurt like hell.'

'So why do you ask?'

'You mean I'd be better off maintaining the illusion? Maybe I'd do that with any other woman. But I can't do it with you.' He ran his hand through his hair. 'Will you tell me why?'

'And then what? That won't get you anywhere, Ben. Two nights, plus a few hours during the day – what does that amount to? It was what it was. And it was good for what it was. Let's leave it at that.'

Ben said nothing for a while, drawing circles in the sand with his shoe. Eventually, he began to speak again in a quiet voice. 'I've been to a whole series of conferences with plenty of attractive women in attendance and I never once felt the need to get to know any of them. Not even just for the night. It was different with you.' He looked at her. 'Don't worry, I'm not about to declare my undying love for you. And no, this has nothing to do with my marital problems either. Our little encounter didn't cause those, or make them any worse either.'

'What made it different with me?' asked Lena. Strictly speaking, she had meant to keep her distance, having resolved to close the chapter on Ben months beforehand. It had been easy to stick to that resolution while he wasn't sitting in front of her – but now, in this situation, she wasn't so sure.

'Everything was so easy and so normal with you. I felt like you didn't see me primarily as a man, but as a person. I suddenly didn't have to contort myself, to pretend to be . . . somebody else. It all felt so natural when we went up to your room afterwards. Do you know what I mean?'

Lena smiled. 'Then I was probably the right woman in the right place at the right time.'

'Maybe . . .'

'I know what you mean. I felt the same.' Lena put her glass to one side and drew Ben towards her. 'Just as friends,' she said, and gave him a kiss on the cheek.

He rested his head on her shoulder. 'That feels good,' he said quietly. 'Just as friends.'

191

19

Lena came to a halt, panting hard. She'd got up early to go jogging and had run through the village down to the beachfront before heading out west to the island's small airfield and back. *I really need to start training again*, she said to herself as she sat down on one of the white wooden benches beside the road.

Her second conversation with Erck the previous evening had been short. She hadn't been able to find the right words and Erck had been unusually taciturn. After that, she'd spoken briefly to Luise and arranged to go on a girls' night out with her once she was back in Kiel.

That night, she'd dreamt about Ben – but on waking, she couldn't remember how the dream had ended. For a moment she'd thought her colleague from Flensburg might be lying beside her and had been relieved to find her bed was empty.

Her phone rang, and she glanced at the display and answered the call. '*Moin*, Reiner. Do you normally work on a Saturday?'

'Always, when justice needs to be done. No, in all seriousness, I'm calling you from home right now. I worked late last night and I didn't want to blather on at you about footprints in the early hours of the morning.'

'What have you found?'

'Good question – ask another. It's all rather complicated. I took photos of the whole area surrounding the body and merged them together into one big picture on my PC. After that, the real work of identifying the footprints began. I took reference samples from you and the others on the team, as you know, and I've more or less managed to isolate a set of footprints that don't belong to any of our people.'

'So the victim definitely wasn't alone?'

'Assuming that nobody walked along the beach immediately beforehand – by which I mean no more than ten to twenty hours earlier – and then hung around for a while in the exact spot where Maria was found. Plus, I'm very confident that somebody tried to erase the tracks. They were only partly successful, of course, as otherwise the ground around the victim would have been completely blank. Basically, I've managed to consolidate several partial prints into one complete print and also come up with a movement profile – though not one that would necessarily stand up in court. I emailed you the documents a few minutes ago. If you have any questions about them, then I suppose I'll let you interrupt my precious weekend, just this once.'

'That sounds like an awful lot of work,' said Lena in a decidedly cheerful tone. 'Thanks for pulling a night shift. I'll be sure to take a look at everything.'

'Please do. I hope you catch the bastard soon.'

Lena wished Reiner a restful weekend and ended the call. Feeling reinvigorated, she ran back to the bed and breakfast, took a shower and walked to the station with Johann.

'I spoke to my contact in Flensburg again yesterday about the rumours at Eva Braasch's last school,' he told her. 'He didn't want to come out with it at first, but when I applied a bit of pressure, he told me that he personally saw Eva in town with the schoolgirl in question. It also seems that Eva didn't make any secret of her sexuality.'

'Why shouldn't a teacher be seen around town with one of her students?'

'Holding hands?'

'All right, fine. Let's take these rumours at face value. And let's even assume that Frau Braasch developed feelings for Maria. Why would she then go on to murder her? And who raped Maria? It just doesn't add up.'

'Perhaps,' Johann replied. 'All the same, that woman seems suspicious to me. I'm sorry to put it so bluntly, but I have the feeling she isn't telling us the truth. At least, not the whole truth.'

They had reached the harbour and were approaching the police station when Lena's phone rang. She made a gesture to Johann and stopped to take the call. 'Hi, Leon. You're up early.'

'Funny. I haven't been to bed.'

'You should get some rest.'

'The messaging app logs are total junk. I'll send them to you in a second. I haven't cracked the cloud yet.'

'I'll take a look at them. Thanks anyway. Do you think you'll manage the cloud?' She pressed her phone to her ear. 'Are you still there?'

Once again, Leon had ended the call without saying goodbye. Lena sighed and hurried after Johann.

'Good morning!' said Lena to the meeting room once everyone had arrived. 'We've had some news from CSI.' She told them about the footprints at the scene of the crime and showed them Reiner's photo on the projector. 'That gives us further confirmation that we're dealing with a murder case here. With any luck, we should have the results of the DNA analysis soon, at which point we can start comparing the samples with suspects.'

'Assuming we have some suspects by then,' interrupted Arno Brandt, who was leaning against the wall with his arms folded.

Lena ignored his comment and moved on to the messaging app fragments, which she had managed to take a look at before the meeting. 'Unfortunately, the logs are incomplete – or rather, they're just snippets of conversations. I'll let you all know as soon as I get anything useful out of them.'

'How did we get hold of them?' one of the officers from Flensburg asked with interest.

'That doesn't matter,' said Johann. 'During your interviews today, please remember to ask whether anyone saw Maria with an unknown person, either at the start of this week or on the fifteenth or sixteenth of August. Maria was staying with a friend back then, and we believe she was sexually assaulted during those two days. Other than that, you've already been assigned your jobs. We'll meet here for debrief at four o'clock, and you can also call me at any time.'

Ben said nothing throughout the brief meeting, but his eyes met Lena's occasionally. Each time, she quickly looked away at one of the other officers and hoped nobody would notice.

Back in their small office, Johann asked her, 'What was up with Ben?'

'How do you mean?' asked Lena, feigning nonchalance.

'I don't know, he just looked so distracted. You know he—'

'Yeah, he told me he's renting his own place for now. If that's what you mean.'

'I'm sure they'll work things out. They have two young children, after all.'

'Martin Reimers is coming at ten. Before that, I'm going to take another look at the fragments from the messaging app conversations.'

'And I have some tip-offs here from members of the public responding to the appeal in the *Island Courier* – all from people who think they saw Maria on Monday. Two volunteers from the fire brigade have also come forward to say they're willing to drive along the routes Maria might have taken from the Behrens' house to the beach and look for her duffel bag.'

Lena nodded and opened her laptop. Even on a second viewing, Leon's snippets made no sense. They could have been taken from the message history of any other teenager. Lena wrote a few fragments down on a sheet of paper and tried to draw links between them:

but I love them   life is   she's my   why did you

can't do it   when are you coming   for all of us, God is

we have to talk   there's no other   difficult

from Johanna   now! I can't   it's easy to

I need you to   there are lots of   I've thought and thought about it   you have to   I'll wait for you and I'm responsible and

Lena added words to fill the blanks and crossed them out again, trying to elicit some meaning from these scraps of conversation. There were plenty of signs that it must have been a serious discussion, with talk of God and responsibility, life and love, Maria's sister Johanna, and a 'them' who somebody loved. After an hour, Lena gave up. There were just too many gaps to get any useful clues. The IT specialists back in Kiel hadn't given her much hope that the American firm behind the platform would release the data either. Software companies took months to respond, even in significantly more serious cases than this one. A judge in the USA would have to issue a court order, and that had happened only five times in the last few years.

'Tell me you got somewhere at least,' Lena said to Johann, who had spent the last half hour conducting phone interviews with a series of witnesses.

'It's hard to say. You know as well as I do that whenever we run an appeal like this the world and his wife always phone in to tell us they've seen something. If I leave the obvious time-wasters to one side, I end up with this.' He handed her a sketched-out map of the island with five red dots, each numbered in sequence and with times noted down beside them. 'Somebody saw Maria here, halfway between Oldsum and Wyk. After that she disappeared for a while until a woman spotted her near the Behrens' house. As you can see from the date, that was on Monday, around the same time Lisa Behrens mentioned to us. Then we have three more sightings the following day.' He pointed to the three locations with his biro.

'This one here isn't far from Eva Braasch's apartment,' said Lena, pointing at the last of the dots. 'On the other hand, she might just have been on her way to the promenade. She could have walked up the beach from there.'

'That would be a bit of an odd detour,' remarked Johann. 'For one thing, she would have been a lot more noticeable there, and for another, the direct route would have been quicker.'

'Maybe she was so worked up that she didn't stop to think about any of that. Or maybe at that point she still didn't know that was where she needed to go. Besides, Wyk is so small that she could have been heading almost anywhere in the village.'

'You already know what I think. We should bring the teacher in for another interview at the station. Record everything, take notes, spell everything out to her. Then we'll see what happens.'

Lena nodded, but replied, 'All in good time. What about the CCTV footage from the ferry terminal?'

'There's over twelve hours of material in total. One of the officers from Föhr is already working on it and I'm going to give him a hand later on. If one of the teams gets back early, they can help out too.'

'Good. I didn't get anywhere with these message fragments.'

'Even so, it's clear enough that Maria was chatting with *somebody*. It's just a question of who. He could be anywhere in Germany, or even abroad.'

'*If* this unknown person who was supposed to pick Maria up really exists, then Maria must have been in contact with them. And she was clearly a very serious-minded girl for someone her age, so she'll have spent a while communicating with this individual before agreeing to meet them.'

'That sounds about right.'

'And it seems obvious that this contact would have taken place online. But you're right – Maria's chat partner could be anywhere in the world. They don't necessarily have any connection with the person who was planning to come and collect her, either.'

'So that brings us back to the real people in Maria's day-to-day life,' Johann summed up. 'And of those, there's one particularly obvious candidate who is about to turn up at the station. Maybe Martin Reimers didn't want to wait several years for his promised bride, so he—'

'Johann!' Lena cut him off. 'That's not how we're going to tackle this. All that'll leave us with is an official complaint and an interview that gets us precisely nowhere.'

'So what questions *will* get us somewhere?' asked Johann indignantly. 'Or will I have to leave the room again when things get interesting?'

Lena shook her head. What had happened to the Johann she'd worked with on Amrum? Had she been too harsh when she'd banned him from all personal contact with Johanna Logener? Or was he just operating under the influence of his childhood experiences? 'All right. I realise it's awkward when interviewees prefer to speak with a particular person in private, or when they only want to talk to a woman, but I thought you were OK with that. After all, I don't withhold any information from you. Quite the opposite, in fact. It wasn't a coincidence that you were the first person I asked to be sent here as backup.'

'Maybe I did cross the line a bit there,' said Johann contritely. He ran his hands through his hair. 'So what are we going to do with Martin Reimers?'

'We'll start off by asking him about his relationship with Maria and then very slowly and cautiously bring up the subject of Walther Logener's marriage offer. Martin isn't fifteen like Lisa Behrens, where we were on thin ice conducting interviews without her parents or any other adults present. If we have any questions that still need answering, Martin Reimers will have to answer them. And if the situation calls for it, we'll have to apply some pressure too.'

'OK. That sounds reasonable. Which of us will be the bad cop?'

Lena laughed. 'I think it should be you, in this instance. If I've judged him correctly, I don't think he'll be willing to take orders from a woman. He's probably used to us playing a more submissive role. But if I'm wrong, we'll just have to improvise.'

'I'm sure we'll muddle through,' said Johann with a grin.

20

Lena placed the recording device on the table in front of Martin Reimers, who had arrived punctually at the police station a few minutes beforehand. Lena guessed he was around six foot three. His black hair was combed severely back and he was wearing brown corduroys, a checked shirt and black work boots. He had a firm handshake, but he looked at the floor as if he didn't dare to meet Lena's eye. His entire body language made it clear how uncomfortable he found the situation. He sat leaning slightly forwards, kneading his hands anxiously, his back hunched.

'First of all, thank you very much for coming in to see us,' Lena began the conversation. She leaned over and turned on the recorder. 'Interview with Martin Reimers in connection with the investigation into the death of Maria Logener.' She stated the date and time before asking her first question. 'Herr Reimers, could you please describe your relationship with the Logener family, and in particular with their daughter Maria?'

Martin Reimers glanced at Johann and then back at Lena. 'Relationship? How do you mean?'

'Do you work for Herr Logener?' Lena helped him out.

'Yes, I help Walther out sometimes. I haven't done any formal training – not yet anyway – but I'm looking for a placement.' He seemed to grow more confident with every word he spoke. 'It isn't very easy to find an apprenticeship in a manual trade on the island.'

'How long have you known the Logeners?'

'All my life,' replied Martin Reimers, looking bemused. 'My parents are friends of the Logeners, and we often meet them together with—' He broke off.

'You see each other at the meetings of the Brethren?'

'Yes, that's right. The families always come along too.'

'In that case, I'm sure you also know Johanna Logener,' said Johann, joining the conversation for the first time. He spoke calmly and without any discernible emotion.

'Yes, I know her.'

'She's no longer part of the church?' Johann added.

'No, she's studying in Kiel and she doesn't visit the island any more.'

'Does she reject your religion?'

Martin Reimers gave a slight shrug. 'I don't know what you mean.'

'When was the last time you were in contact with Maria?'

'With Maria? That was a while ago now.'

'So long ago that you can't remember exactly when?'

'No, no, of course I can. It was in Utersum. At the last gathering.'

'Did you meet with Maria there?'

'Me? No. We – I mean the families . . . it was our . . .'

'It was a meeting for your religious community. Herr Logener told me about it. I believe families are also invited from Amrum and from the mainland?'

Martin Reimers nodded. 'Yes, that's right. Walther says we're all one big family and that we should never forget that.'

'So Maria was also there that day?'

He smiled to himself. 'Yes, she was always there when Walther and his family . . . I mean . . .'

'Did you talk to Maria?'

'We all talk to each other.'

'I meant more in private. Was everybody together in one room for the whole of the meeting?'

'There are several rooms there.'

'Are all of them used during these meetings?'

'We younger members of the church have a separate programme.'

'And you count as a younger member?'

'Yes, along with everyone else under thirty who isn't married yet.'

'The village hall is close to the beach, so I assume that, during the breaks, you . . . There are breaks, aren't there?'

'We don't call them breaks, but yes, we sometimes go outside. Even on to the beach, if the weather is good.'

'Was the weather good on the nineteenth of August? I can't remember.'

'It was very warm. Almost thirty degrees.'

'And did you talk to Maria on the beach?' asked Johann abruptly. His voice was louder and more clipped than before.

'I . . . Yes, I think so,' Martin Reimers stammered. He looked as though he'd been caught off-guard.

'What did you talk about?' Johann immediately followed up, staring at him. 'The weather? Maria's school? The future?'

Reimers gave a long pause before he spoke again. 'I don't remember any more. It might have been that.'

'How was Maria that day?' Lena resumed.

'The same as always, I think.'

'Was she in a good mood? Sad? Tired?'

'Good, everything was good.'

'So you spoke about the future?' asked Johann.

When Martin Reimers didn't reply, Johann added in a more insistent tone, 'You just said you discussed the future. What did you talk about exactly?'

'What do you mean?' Reimers glanced uncertainly back and forth between Lena and Johann.

'The fact that you want to get married at some point, for example. And marriage obviously involves two people.' Johann spoke in a casual tone, but then he suddenly leaned forward across the table and stared at Martin Reimers once more. 'And you got your hopes up, didn't you?'

'Got my hopes up? What do you mean? Maria . . . no, there was nothing between us,' the young man stumbled.

Lena put her hand on Martin Reimers' arm. 'My colleague is referring to the fact that you were in love with Maria. We did understand that correctly, didn't we? From Herr Logener?' She spoke in a quiet and friendly tone of voice, smiling as she did so.

'Did Walther say that?'

'You were in love with Maria. Weren't you?'

For a moment, Reimers seemed to fall into a state of shock. He stared at his fingers, breathing rapidly.

'Did you love Maria?' Lena repeated in a warm, empathetic voice.

Eventually, Martin Reimers nodded, without looking up.

'Did you discuss that with Maria that afternoon?' Lena quickly added.

'Yes,' the young man answered quietly.

'The two of you were alone?'

'Maria . . . we . . . walked along the beach.'

'What did you talk about exactly?'

Martin Reimers pursed his lips. When he didn't reply, Lena repeated her question. More silence. 'Was it you who suggested that you go for a walk?'

He shrugged.

'How long were you together on the beach?'

'I don't know,' said Reimers after what felt like an eternity.

As if from nowhere, Johann slammed the palm of his hand down on to the table. The loud bang made Martin Reimers jump in his seat. Before he could react, Johann snarled, 'What *do* you know then, man? What happened that Friday on the beach? Tell us!' He practically yelled the last two words.

The boy stared at Johann with wide eyes, but didn't reply.

Lena gently cleared her throat. 'Did Maria tell you that there would never be anything between you two?'

The young man answered with only a nod.

'How long were you on the beach for?' Johann asked. 'An hour? Two hours, even three?'

Once again, Martin Reimers didn't reply.

'Herr Reimers,' said Lena. She waited until he looked at her. 'This is an official interview. If you don't answer our questions, that makes you seem suspicious. Do you understand?'

'Yes,' he answered after a slight hesitation.

'We need to know what happened that day. What did you talk about with Maria? Who instigated the conversation? How long were you both on the beach for?'

'I don't have to tell you that,' said Martin Reimers in a strained voice.

'No, you're right – you don't have to answer our questions if you want to incriminate yourself. Do you want to incriminate yourself?'

A sudden jolt passed through Reimers' body. He drew himself upright and took a deep breath. 'Why do you want to know all this?'

'We're currently conducting a murder investigation,' said Lena, deciding not to beat around the bush. 'As such, we're interviewing everybody who had any contact with Maria during the weeks before she died. We already know that the Logener family saw you as a future husband for Maria. You were in contact with her, and you've just admitted that you were in love with her. We need to know what happened during the days leading up to Maria's death.'

'I didn't . . .' He was evidently lost for words.

Johann took the conversation in a new direction. 'Where were you on Tuesday night this week – let's say from seven o'clock until the following morning?'

Martin Reimers wrung his hands as he spoke. 'At home. I was at home.'

'Are there any witnesses?'

'My . . . parents.'

'What did you do that evening?'

'The same as always. We . . . had dinner. Then we watched TV.'

'What time do you eat dinner?'

'At six o'clock every evening.'

Lena sensed that the young man was finding his feet again and growing more confident with every reply.

'I suppose you'd be done after half an hour or so. Is that right?'

Martin Reimers nodded. 'Yes, roughly speaking. Sometimes we finish quicker than that, but there are also days where we sit together for a while afterwards.'

'How many siblings do you have?' Lena asked.

'Five. Two brothers and three sisters.'

'Are you the eldest child?'

'No, my sister Anna is three years older than me. I came second.'

'But you're the eldest son,' Johann jumped back in. 'That comes with a certain burden of responsibility. The family needs to be kept together – right?'

'Yes,' answered Martin Reimers, growing uncertain once more. Lena wondered whether that was down to Johann's sharp tone, or if there was another reason for it.

'Your sister is around the same age as Johanna Logener. Do they know each other?' Johann continued.

'Of course. Our families have been friends for a long time. We often—'

'What does your sister think of Johanna?' Johann interrupted him.

'Why? What do you mean?'

'Don't pretend to be any dumber than you are!' Johann bellowed at him out of nowhere. 'What does she think of her? Were they friends? Are they still in touch?' Johann lifted his hand before answering his own question. 'No, I don't think so. I'm sure there's a strict ban on anyone talking to such a terrible person. Am I right?'

Martin Reimers said nothing.

'Am I right?' Johann roared at him.

'She abandoned the God-fearing ways of our community,' Reimers eventually replied. His words sounded like he was reading them out loud or had learned them by heart. 'We don't have any contact with her.'

'She, her – are you not even allowed to speak Johanna's name any more? What is she to you? Possessed by the devil? Were you scared that Maria would follow the same path? Leave the island? And not in two or three years, when she finished school, but right now? Today or tomorrow? Were you afraid of that happening?'

Martin Reimers' furious expression spoke for itself. 'I don't know what you mean.'

'Oh, yes you do! You know exactly what I mean! Maria had been promised to you. She was going to be your wife.' Johann paused briefly, then yelled, '*Your* wife!' He glared at Martin Reimers. 'And that was exactly what Maria didn't want. Not now, not ever. She wanted nothing to do with you. Nothing! She was done with you. All this hocus-pocus your so-called Brethren come out with made her sick to her stomach. She'd turned her back on it, once and for all.'

'No!' the young man shrieked, leaping to his feet. 'That's not true!'

'Calm yourself,' said Lena, rushing to stand beside him. 'And sit back down.'

Martin Reimers was breathing heavily and looked as though he hadn't understood a word she'd said. For a moment, Lena was afraid he would hurl himself at Johann, but eventually he took a seat once more. When he had calmed down, Lena asked, 'Did you talk to Maria about possibly getting married in the future?'

He gave a hesitant shrug.

'Could you say that out loud, please? We need it for our records. Once again: did you talk to Maria about your shared future?'

'Yes.'

'What did she say in reply?'

'Maria was a good girl,' said Martin Reimers.

'That's not what I asked you. Do you need me to repeat the question?'

'No. What Maria said is private.'

'I understand that, under normal circumstances, you wouldn't want to tell anyone about a conversation like this. And ordinarily, you'd be perfectly within your rights. But this is a police investigation into the death of Maria Logener. As I've already said, it doesn't make a good impression if you refuse to answer our questions.'

'I've already said everything there is to say.' He folded his arms over his chest. 'Do you want to ask me anything else?'

Lena retrieved a plastic sleeve from the drawer of the desk, pulled out a cotton-wool bud and said, 'We need to take a DNA sample. I'm sure you'll have seen this before in the movies. Please open your mouth.'

At first, the young man was too surprised to resist. Almost mechanically, he opened his mouth and allowed Lena to briefly scrape the cotton-wool bud against the inside of his cheek.

'Thank you,' she said, inserting the stick back into its plastic sleeve.

'Actually . . .' he began, but then he stopped and fell silent.

'I have one more question,' said Johann. 'Maria's autopsy revealed that she was sexually assaulted two to three weeks before her death.' Johann waited until his words had fully sunk in. Reimers was visibly shocked and was on the verge of saying something when he added, 'Did you do it?'

Martin Reimers glowered at him, incandescent with fury. Lena could clearly see how much effort it was costing him to remain calm. 'No, I didn't do it,' he eventually replied.

21

The rest of the interview with Martin Reimers produced no further results. When Lena asked him to let them take prints from the soles of his shoes, he stubbornly refused.

'At least we have his DNA,' said Johann once Reimers had left the office. 'Do you think he did it?'

Lena stood up and checked whether Reimers had closed the door properly. 'My gut feeling is that he wouldn't be capable of something like that. All the same, he admitted he was alone with Maria at the church assembly.' She sat back down at the desk beside Johann. 'And the rape might have happened around that time, of course. Maria couldn't find anybody to confide in – her parents wouldn't have believed her; she couldn't get hold of her sister; her best friend wouldn't have been able to help her because she wanted to avoid drawing attention to her grandmother's condition; her teacher was afraid of getting too close to her; and she couldn't go to the police because that would have led to an irreparable breach with her parents and exposed her family to the judgement of the Brethren.'

'Maybe Martin Reimers got scared that Maria would talk after all, or maybe he somehow got wind of the fact that she wanted to leave the island. So he went looking for her and abducted her off the street somewhere.'

Lena tilted her head from side to side. 'There's no evidence that she defended herself. Would she have let someone just lead her to her death, like a lamb to the slaughter?'

'What about the date-rape drugs? Maybe he dosed her up in the car so she was powerless to resist. A few more drops on the beach, and then . . .'

'Martin Reimers with date-rape drugs? I find that very hard to imagine, to be frank with you.'

Johann ruffled his hair. 'Perhaps he's just acting the part of the naive, kind-hearted teddy bear. You saw for yourself how angry he got just now. He was on the point of attacking me.'

'But he didn't. At the critical moment, he kept himself under control. An interview like that would push anybody to their limits. The girl he wanted to start a family with is dead. It's hardly a surprise that he'd nearly blow his top when we go on to accuse him of having something to do with her death. I think we should wait for the results of the DNA comparison with the hair we found. The colour matches, at least.'

'Can you speed that up at all? If he really did do it, he'll be thinking of making a run for it about now. We hardly have enough evidence to take him into custody.'

'We can forget about custody. DNA analysis takes time.' She looked at the clock. 'Another two hours before Brandt junior gets here with his mother. You're going to look at the CCTV from the ferry port now, right?'

Johann stood up. 'They've set things up in the incident room so we can project the footage on to the wall. One of us will control the recording and the other will note down any suspicious registration numbers. I only hope the video will be high-enough quality for us to identify the people in the vehicles afterwards.'

'That depends on where the light is coming from. You won't be able to see a thing if the cars are backlit,' said Lena. She got to her feet too. 'I'm going to use the time to pay another visit to Eva Braasch.'

'Ah, so you think she might have something to do with the whole affair after all?'

Lena grinned. 'Is that the detective in you finally coming back out of hiding?'

◆ ◆ ◆

Eva Braasch opened the door in her pyjamas. After a slight hesitation, she invited Lena into the kitchen. 'Would you like a coffee?' she asked. 'I've just brewed some.'

'Yes, please.' Lena took a seat at the small dining table and waited while the teacher poured two cups and then sat down beside her.

'I take it you have some more questions about Maria?'

Lena added some milk to her coffee and took a sip. 'Among other things. I'll get straight to the point: we know about the rumours at your old school in Flensburg.'

Eva Braasch sighed quietly. 'Will that never end?'

'I like to put my cards on the table, and I imagine you prefer that too.'

The woman gave a shrug.

'All right,' Lena continued. 'Am I right in thinking you had a closer relationship with Maria than with the other students in her class?'

'Relationship! You make it sound as if . . . I've never made any secret of the fact that I thought Maria was special. If that's what you're getting at, then you're right.'

'You developed feelings for her,' said Lena. She didn't phrase it as a question.

'What is this? Are you trying to accuse me of something?' She drew herself up and looked Lena directly in the eye. 'I didn't have an intimate relationship with Maria. Will that do?'

'It's a clear statement. All the same, I have to ask you: how exactly would you describe your relationship with Maria? She was something special, I've understood that much. But what was she to you?'

'A student whom I was very attached to.'

'How did that play out in practice?'

'I've already told you all that. Maria saw me as a confidante – somebody she could talk to about her problems with her parents, her faith, even her classmates. I was no more than that, but no less either.'

'Why did she leave the drama club?'

'I don't know. She didn't tell me. We didn't talk much over the last three weeks before her . . . her death.'

'I don't believe you,' said Lena in a cool, detached tone.

'I'm sorry?' Eva Braasch looked at her in astonishment.

'I don't believe you. Why would Maria suddenly start keeping her distance from you for no reason? Did she tell you she'd met a man on the Internet?'

'I don't know anything about that!'

Lena watched her carefully while she answered that last question. If she wasn't misreading her, it seemed that the teacher was genuinely unaware of Maria's online contacts. 'Did you reject Maria?' she said, venturing a new line of inquiry. This time, Frau Braasch reacted by blinking nervously. She held her breath for a moment too long. 'Reject her? First you tell me Maria met a man on the Internet, and now . . . You need to pick a story here.'

'There are lots of ways to reject a person. You should know that, as a teacher.'

Eva Braasch said nothing.

'You were afraid of your feelings – afraid of being dragged into a whirlpool that you would never escape from. Embarking on a relationship with a schoolgirl under eighteen is no trifling matter. A few more-or-less credible rumours could put an end to your teaching career.'

'I don't know what you're talking about.' She folded her arms over her chest.

'I think you do know. Why are you being so obstructive? If you did reject Maria, you were doing the right thing. Even if it didn't feel like it at the time.'

Eva Braasch kept looking out of the window, as if she was expecting someone. Lena waited in silence until she eventually began to speak.

'You have no idea how hard it is to be a teacher. Being responsible for all those adolescents – it's just a nightmare. Whatever happens, it's always your fault.' She added quietly, 'I had nothing to do with Maria's death. I hope you know that.'

'What I think is one thing. Hard evidence, clues and statements are quite another. Believe me, it would be better for you to cooperate with us. I'll have to keep asking questions, regardless of whether it harms your professional reputation.'

'I didn't do anything to Maria. Nothing at all.'

'What happened? When was the last time you saw Maria, really?'

Eva Braasch hesitated, opening her mouth several times as if to speak, before she finally asked, 'Can we keep this just between us?'

'That depends. I'm not from the school board. I'm looking for Maria's murderer.'

'If you tell this to anyone else, I'll lose my job and nobody will ever hire me again.'

'Like I said, I'm not from the school board. If it won't harm the investigation, then I'll treat the information in confidence.'

Eva Braasch tipped her head back and took a deep breath. 'Maria was here. On the Tuesday evening. She begged me to let her stay. Just one night, she said.'

'You knew she'd run away from home.'

'No, I didn't. I'd been ill for the past two days and hadn't left the house. I truly had no idea.'

Lena watched her intently as she spoke, but she neither hesitated nor displayed any other suspicious reactions. 'What were you ill with?'

'Lumbago. I went to the doctor for an injection on the Monday and then . . . I honestly didn't know she'd run away on Monday. I thought it was just a spontaneous decision she'd made that Tuesday evening. She promised me that her parents hadn't noticed anything. It was late – nearly nine o'clock at night. At first I wanted to talk to her and take her home afterwards, but she asked me if she could stay and . . .'

'What happened next?' Lena gave her no time to think about her replies.

'She was gone. When I got up, she was gone.'

'What time was that?'

'It must have been around five in the morning. I went to wake her up, but . . . she'd slept on the sofa. My bed . . . that just wasn't an option. You understand that, don't you?'

'What did you do next?'

'I got dressed. Then I went to the ferry terminal. I was still signed off sick that day. I wanted to stop her, but she wasn't there.' Eva Braasch nodded distractedly and went on, 'I went back for every outgoing ferry, right up until the last boat.'

'You didn't hear in the meantime that Maria had been reported missing?'

'No, I went straight back to my flat each time. I never even dreamed of anything like that. You have to believe me. In the end,

I just assumed she'd gone back home. Yes, I should have bundled her straight into my car on Tuesday night and taken her back to her parents. But I didn't.' Tears were running down her cheeks. 'I've been blaming myself ever since. I wanted to tell you . . . when we spoke on Thursday . . .'

Lena handed her a tissue. 'You mentioned that you and Maria talked when she came here on Tuesday evening?'

Eva Braasch wiped the tears from her face. 'Yes, that's right. I wanted to know what had happened. I've been racking my brains ever since, wondering whether there were any clues I might have missed at the time. Whether she was trying to tell me something and I simply didn't listen.'

'What did you talk about?'

'She was in a foul mood when she got here.' Eva Braasch drew herself up. 'That's why I immediately assumed she'd come straight from home. I made her a cup of tea and waited for her to calm down a bit. At first I couldn't understand what she was trying to tell me. She was ranting about everything – her friends, her family, her faith.'

'Did she mention her friend Lisa Behrens?'

'Yes – she called her a traitor. I couldn't believe the way Maria was suddenly speaking. It sounded so obscene and . . . that wasn't her. She mentioned someone called Martin, but I couldn't make out what the deal was with him. Her parents also came up, though she'd mostly calmed down by then and she suddenly started standing up for them again. At that point I thought she must have left home because of them. Later on, she told me she couldn't ever go back home. I asked her if she wanted to move to Kiel to be with her sister, but she was cagey about that. At some point during the conversation I just assumed that was what she was planning, and that reassured me a little, of course. Not that I intended to let her go there on her own.'

215

'So what did you intend?' Lena interjected.

Eva Braasch hesitated and bowed her head. 'I have to admit I didn't have any specific ideas on that front. It was late – long after midnight – when we both went to bed.'

'What exactly did she tell you about Martin?'

'Like I said, it was all very confused and emotionally charged. From what she told me, he was a boy from her religious community who had taken a shine to her. Her parents kept coming into the picture too. Maria simply couldn't understand why she had to adhere so – how can I put it? – so rigidly to this exact mode of belief. More than anything, she couldn't understand her mother – why she would agree to such a radically conservative model of marital roles. The man in charge, the woman keeping quiet.'

'Please think carefully. This Martin is very important to our investigation. Did Maria talk about the last time she saw him or met with him?'

Eva Braasch leaned back on her chair in exhaustion. 'No, I can't tell you anything there. Or rather, I was too preoccupied with how to handle the situation – what I ought to do with Maria. Maybe I didn't listen to certain things, or maybe I even failed to take them seriously enough.' She held her hand up to her forehead and sighed gently. 'Martin. Yes, there was something else. I suppose you want to know if he was the reason why Maria ran away from home. I had the impression – though I really do mean just a gut feeling – that she felt threatened by him.' She gave a start as if shocked by her own words. 'Of course, I don't know if he had anything to do with . . . with Maria's death. I don't mean to make any accusations. That's the last thing I'd want.'

'You don't need to worry – I can put all this into context. So you also had a feeling that Martin was a threat to Maria?'

'Yes – I think so.'

'Did you have the impression that Maria – and let's leave to one side for a moment the question of who might have done this – did you have the impression that Maria had been sexually harassed, or even worse, assaulted?'

Eva Braasch stared at Lena in shock. 'No! Is that what happened? On the beach, before she . . .?'

'I'm afraid I can't share any details of our investigation with you, but let's not dwell on the timing here. Did you see any signs? Either on that evening or during the previous few weeks?'

Maria's teacher seemed to think carefully before she replied. 'That evening . . . she mentioned that her trust had been abused. But of course I interpreted that differently and thought she was talking about the strict rules she had to follow in her sect. She said . . .' Eva Braasch swallowed. 'She said no one would help her. That she was all alone. Nobody would understand. But those are stock phrases every teenager comes out with.' She was breathing rapidly and staring into space. 'I couldn't see what really lay behind her words – I was too deeply preoccupied with my own fears. But the right thing to do would have been to try and put myself in her shoes. She needed me.'

Lena handed Eva Braasch a second tissue, which she used to wipe her face. 'I'm sorry,' she sobbed. 'It's just so horrible, what happened to Maria. And I could have done something to stop it.'

'It's possible that Maria might still be alive if you'd taken her back to her parents that evening. But she wasn't murdered because you didn't do that. The killer had a motive, and would probably have tried again further down the line.'

'That's not much consolation. She trusted me, and I wasn't there for her. Why was I so bloody scared? I wasn't prepared to take what she was saying seriously. She must have sensed that. Why would she have vanished from my flat otherwise, without saying a word?'

'Did Maria make any phone calls while she was here? Or could she have got online?'

'I don't have a landline, if that's what you mean. I do have a mobile phone, but I always keep it in my room at night. As for the Internet – well, my laptop will have been lying around somewhere. Either here or in the living room.'

'Is it password-protected?'

'No.'

'I'm afraid I'll have to take the device away to be examined. Is that all right?'

'Yes, of course. You mean . . . Oh God, that's all I need.' She closed her eyes for a moment. 'What's going to happen to me?'

'I can understand why you didn't tell us the whole truth at first, but I don't know if I'll be able to keep this information secret. I'll have to write a report. Whether that ends up in the case file will depend on how the investigation progresses. It's very possible that you might be called upon to make a statement in court.'

'I know that I . . . that I let everyone down, no question about it. Somehow I'm going to have to find a way to come to terms with that. Please believe me.'

22

'So you're asking me to check someone's browser history now?' Leon grumbled. Lena hadn't dragged him out of bed, for once. She'd called him from her car, which was still parked outside Eva Braasch's apartment.

'Even I can manage that, believe it or not. But I didn't get very far, unfortunately. The history must have been cleared.'

'These things happen. I'll send out an email. Where to?'

Lena gave him Eva Braasch's email address.

'Just open the message and click on the link,' said Leon.

'I need the results quickly.'

'Ugh,' Leon answered and hung up.

A few moments later, Lena opened Eva Braasch's inbox, clicked the malware link in Leon's email and left the computer running. She knew Leon would remove all evidence of his activity and that nobody would be able to trace anything back to him.

After that, she returned to the station and got to work on writing up her interview with Eva Braasch. Once she was done, she printed the report out and locked it in her desk.

Eventually she felt her stomach begin to rumble, so she left the office, bought a bite to eat near the ferry terminal and sat down on a bench overlooking the marina. The sailing boats rocked gently back and forth in the wind, and the typical odour of salt and algae filled the air. It was sunny and would remain so until the evening, according to the forecast.

She bit into her fish burger – the remoulade tasted just like Beke's own recipe and the fish was fresh and flavoursome. As she ate, she began to mentally sort through the new information she had obtained. After arguing with Lisa and storming out of the house on Tuesday, Maria had evidently spent a while wandering the streets before deciding to knock on her teacher's door. But for some reason, she had decided to leave Eva Braasch's flat in the middle of the night or in the early hours of Wednesday morning. Had she already arranged to meet someone before she got there, or had she organised the rendezvous from her teacher's apartment? Either way, the unknown person must have already been on the island. That pointed to Martin Reimers – yet Lena couldn't fathom why Maria would arrange to meet him in the middle of the night when she had only just been complaining about him to Eva Braasch. Unless she was planning to force him to take her off the island . . .

Lena's phone buzzed. It was Leon.

'The same messaging app as before, at the time you suspected. Nothing else, though. I'm already out. Laters.'

Lena smiled. He hadn't said goodbye to her for a long time. 'Goodbye then,' she replied to the disconnect tone.

Although Leon hadn't found much, it was clear now that Maria had used Eva Braasch's laptop to get in touch with somebody – or had at least tried to. Had she arranged a meeting, or was there another reason for her early departure? Maybe once she'd calmed down, she'd realised that her teacher would only offer her a brief respite until the following morning and then take her back to her parents. Or had she decided to head back home on her own and run into her murderer along the way? In any case, the net was finally starting to close in. With any luck, her colleagues would stumble across some additional evidence, or more witnesses might come forward in response to the appeal in the *Island Courier*. Lena was also pinning her hopes on the review of the CCTV footage. She felt certain that the killer must have had a vehicle. Either the recordings would provide them with a new lead, or their inquiry into an unknown person from the mainland would run completely cold. For the time being, Lena had all but given up on the idea of enlisting the help of the American software company to identify the person Maria had been messaging. DSU Warnke had promised to do everything in his power, but even he held out little hope of getting any reply from the States within the next few weeks. If the investigation eventually hit a dead end, the trail leading to Maria's correspondent might be their last hope.

Lena looked at her watch. Enno Brandt would be arriving at the police station with his mother in fifteen minutes. Although she couldn't imagine that the boy had anything to do with Maria's death, she still didn't want to abandon this line of inquiry. All too often she had seen over-confident colleagues focus exclusively on one lead, only to wind up empty-handed and have to start their investigation again from scratch. At the same time, she didn't think this Enno Brandt was all that innocent either. Her intuition told her that he had something to do with the abusive notes she had found – that he might even have written them himself. She knew that the interview would be extremely delicate and could easily upset the morale of the team if it emerged that the son of a policeman was embroiled in the investigation. Arno Brandt was clearly a prickly individual, in any case.

When she saw a woman with a boy around Enno's age entering the station, she finished her lunch break and followed them inside.

'May I call you Enno?' Lena asked once the boy and his mother were sitting in front of her in the office.

'Whatever,' he answered curtly.

The tall young man resembled his father – the same eyes, those thin lips, the slightly oversized nose. Despite his strongly masculine features, he looked awkward and uncertain. He hadn't once met Lena's eye and his smile looked forced. When he sat down, he didn't seem to know what to do with his hands and clasped them together nervously.

'I'm sure you've already heard about Maria Logener and what happened to her.' When Enno nodded, Lena went on, 'We're currently talking to as many people who had contact with her as we can, and we've already spoken to a lot of your classmates.'

'I know,' murmured Enno.

'Can you describe your relationship with Maria?'

He swallowed. 'She's . . . she was in my class. That's all.'

'You never spoke to her?'

'Not really. Not at all, in fact.'

'I've heard you didn't like her.'

'Huh, who said that then? Nobody liked her!' The boy suddenly broke out of his defensive posture and looked at Lena defiantly.

Until now, his mother had been sitting quietly beside him, following the conversation attentively, but now she laid her hand on his shoulder. Lena suspected that her husband had given her clear instructions and was unsurprised when she said, 'My son is right. All his classmates thought the girl was . . . well, she was an outsider. My son—'

'Frau Brandt,' Lena cut her off. 'If I have a question for you, I'll address it to you. Right now, I want to talk to your son. Can we agree on that?'

Enno's mother glared at her furiously. 'I don't want Enno to be—'

'Please, Frau Brandt. It's perfectly all right for you to accompany your son. But he needs to speak for himself.'

222

The woman lapsed into an indignant silence and Lena resumed the interview. Slowly, she opened her file and placed the copies of the notes in front of Enno, one by one. 'Why did you write these?'

His mother leaned forwards and opened her mouth to protest, but Lena cut her short with an abrupt gesture.

The boy glanced uncertainly at his mother, then back at the notes. 'I didn't write them.'

'The block capitals were a good idea, but not quite good enough, I'm afraid. It won't take long for us to prove you wrote them with the help of a handwriting sample. We might even find fingerprints on the paper. Or were you wearing gloves?'

Lena knew she was on very thin ice here. She could only hope the boy would get cold feet and quickly confess to being the author.

'I didn't do it,' he said quietly, his head lowered.

'These notes on their own aren't a crime. You can admit you wrote them.'

Once again, Enno's mother leaned forwards. Before she could say anything, Lena pushed two of the pieces of paper towards her and asked, 'What would you say if your daughter received notes like these? Would you be OK with it?'

Enno's mother scanned through the texts. Her cheeks flushed and she began to breathe more quickly. 'No, of course I wouldn't.' She turned to Enno. 'You didn't have anything to do with this, did you?'

He sat in pained silence.

'Did you?' she said again, more sharply than before, but he simply sat there, staring at the table and saying nothing. 'I can't believe it, Enno!' she hissed at him.

'The others . . .' he began to defend himself, close to tears. 'They all joined in.'

'Did you write the notes?' Lena asked him in a calm maternal tone.

Enno shrugged.

'Is that a yes?' asked Lena.

'So what if it is? She deserved it—'

'Enno!' his mother snapped at him.

'What about it? That bitch treated us all like crap, and you expect me to be all sweet and nice to her afterwards? What a joke!'

'Did you write the notes?' Lena repeated her question.

'Yes, and?'

Lena opted for a full-frontal assault. 'What did you do with Maria's tablet?' She glared at Enno and her tone left him in no doubt that she expected an answer.

'How did you know . . .?'

Lena could clearly see his resistance crumble away. His eyelids fluttered and he sank in on himself, slumping slightly and gripping the desk with his hands.

'Where is it?' asked Lena dispassionately.

Enno's mother observed the conversation with a horror-struck expression.

'Enno, this is important! *Where is the tablet?*' Lena barked at him.

'In the bin,' he whispered in a barely audible voice.

'At your house?'

Enno nodded and Lena leapt to her feet. 'When does your rubbish get collected, Frau Brandt?'

'Today,' she said weakly.

'What time today?'

'Soon. Around three or four o'clock.'

'What's your address?'

In a trembling voice, Enno's mother gave Lena her street and house number.

'I think we're done here,' said Lena, signalling that the interview was over with her hand.

224

At the door, she instructed the two of them to wait at the station until she got back. Then she dashed through to the incident room to find Johann. 'Come on! We need to get to the Brandts' house before their bins are collected.'

Johann sprang to his feet and hurried after Lena. Only when they were sitting in her car and hurtling towards the house did he ask, 'So what are we looking for?'

'The tablet! Maria's tablet.'

When they turned on to the Brandts' road, they saw the rubbish truck around a hundred yards ahead of them. Two men in orange overalls were walking alongside it collecting the black bins from outside each house. Lena beeped her horn, raced up to the lorry and came to a screeching halt beside one of the bin men.

'What the hell are you doing?' he asked indignantly.

'Leave that bin alone!' Lena cried. 'Stop everything!'

'Why?'

Johann jumped out of the car and held up his warrant card. 'Police. Stand aside, please.'

'What house number is this?' asked Lena, who couldn't see any numbers on either side of the street.

The driver of the lorry climbed out of the cabin and asked, 'Which one are you looking for?' He was older than his two colleagues and seemed to realise the gravity of the situation.

'Number forty-five. The Brandts' house.'

'Arno Brandt lives just here,' the man said, pointing at the house that the truck was parked outside.

'Have you already emptied their bins?' Johann asked.

The driver glanced at one of the two workers, who shook his head and gestured to the container standing beside him. 'No, I was just about to start.'

'OK,' Lena responded instantly. 'I'm afraid you'll need to stop your work until we've searched through the contents.'

The driver gave a shrug and told his men to sit inside the vehicle. 'Will it take long?'

'We don't know,' replied Johann, who had already pulled on a pair of protective gloves. 'With any luck, we'll be done fairly quickly.'

The driver nodded and followed his colleagues.

Turning to Lena, Johann asked, 'Shall we tip it over?'

She put on a pair of latex gloves and opened the bin. As expected, the tablet wasn't resting on top. She nodded, and working together, they slowly lifted the bin over on to its side. Lena took a deep breath before bravely plunging her arms into the contents. Bit by bit, the Brandts' rubbish landed on the road until every bag had been ripped open and thoroughly searched.

'Nothing!' exclaimed Johann disappointedly, giving the now empty container a kick. 'The bins further up are already in the truck.'

Lena pointed down the road. 'Those ones aren't, though.'

Johann groaned.

Fifteen minutes later, they had scattered the contents of two more bins across the pavement, but found nothing.

'Should we carry on?' asked Johann.

'Do you have a better idea?'

'We could bring that little shit out here and make him do it.'

Lena had told Johann about her interview with Enno Brandt and his mother while they were up to their elbows in rubbish, and Johann's temper was at boiling point.

She made a decision. 'OK – you stay here, and I'll go get the boy.'

Lena peeled off her gloves on the way back to the car and dropped them on to the passenger seat. A few minutes later, she pulled up in front of the police station and jumped out of her car.

Enno was sitting beside his mother in the corridor, staring at the floor. Lena explained the situation to her, and after a moment's hesitation, she agreed and followed Lena outside with her son.

By the time they turned back on to the Brandts' road, a handful of neighbours had emerged from their houses and were gathered behind the stationary rubbish truck.

Lena told Frau Brandt and her son to wait in the car and then teamed up with Johann to order the onlookers off the road. Only once they had dispersed, grumbling to themselves, did she go back and fetch Enno and his mother. 'Enno, you told me you threw the tablet in the bin,' said Lena. 'Do you remember which one?'

At that moment, a squad car raced down the road towards them. Lena could guess who was behind the wheel and started walking briskly towards the vehicle. Arno Brandt braked sharply, leapt out of the car and confronted Lena, his face red with fury. 'Are you totally—?'

'Stop right there!' Lena barked at him, before continuing in a calmer voice, 'Your wife has agreed to let Enno show us which bin he used to dispose of the tablet.'

Arno Brandt was thrown for a moment, but he soon exploded once more. 'Bullshit! You've engineered this whole thing just to undermine me. First you make my son believe some ridiculous story, and then—'

'Don't make things any worse than they already are, Sergeant Brandt,' Lena interrupted him, looking him dead in the eye. 'You're going to go back to your car now and allow us to conclude our search. Do you understand?'

'There'll be consequences to this,' Arno Brandt hissed, but he withdrew all the same, muttering to himself as he did so.

Lena waited for him to get back in his car before returning to Frau Brandt and Enno, who by now looked completely distraught.

'Everything is OK,' she said to Frau Brandt. 'Your husband is waiting in his car.' She put her hand on Enno's shoulder. 'Enno, we really need to find that bin.'

'I don't remember which one it was,' he whined.

'Think, then! You came out of the house and you were wondering what to do with the tablet. Which way did you turn?'

Enno raised his hand and pointed down the road. Lena exhaled. The bins at that end hadn't been emptied yet. 'OK! How far did you go?'

He shrugged.

'Were all the bins on the road at the time?'

'No.'

'So you had to find one that was easily accessible.'

'Yeah, I guess.'

'We're going to walk down the road together now, and I want you to think about which house it might have been.'

Slowly, the four of them walked along the row of houses, stopping at each in turn and waiting until Enno shook his head. Just as Lena was about to call off the operation, Enno came to a halt at the end of the street and pointed at a now empty square of paving immediately behind a garden fence. 'It was here, I think.'

Johann hauled the bin belonging to the house out on to the pavement and tipped it over. After a brief search, he retrieved a small parcel wrapped in newspaper from the pile of rubbish and held it up. 'Got it!'

23

DSU Warnke agreed with Lena's suggestion that they ask Arno Brandt to take a few days' leave.

'Our only other course of action is to suspend him,' Lena added.

'I'll talk to his head office in Husum. If the son turns out to be more deeply involved than he currently seems, then we won't have any other choice. After all, there's a suspicion that Sergeant Brandt might have obstructed the investigation.'

'I don't think he knew what his son was up to. Neither the bullying nor the stolen tablet.'

'We'll find out in due course,' replied Warnke, before saying goodbye.

Johann, who was sitting beside Lena in the car, gave a sigh. 'Well, this is a right little mess. But I can't imagine Brandt acted with intent. After all, who *would* be happy to search their own child's schoolbag during a police operation?'

'We might have made a lot more progress if he had. All we can do now is hope that his son didn't destroy the data.'

'The tablet doesn't look in very good nick,' said Johann.

They'd unwrapped the device and examined it at the scene. The screen was cracked, and it looked as though it had been held underwater for a while.

'All the same, it never ceases to surprise me what the boffins in IT manage to get out of wrecks like that,' Johann went on.

'It definitely won't be quick, though,' said Lena as she opened the car door.

Enno was already waiting at the station – his father having driven him and his mother over in his squad car. After they'd found the tablet, Arno Brandt had spent a while talking to his wife before coming to Lena to apologise, still in a state of some agitation.

An hour later, Enno Brandt's and his mother's statements had been signed and the family were on their way home. Enno had admitted that he'd watched Lisa put the backpack inside Maria's locker and had then stolen it to make sure there was no evidence of his bullying inside. When he found the tablet, he'd been scared that Maria might have used it to keep a diary, so he'd taken it away with him, gone through the contents and found some files that mentioned his name. As it turned out, Enno hadn't just written the abusive notes – he'd also followed and harassed Maria multiple times, though his confession didn't make clear how far he had gone on those occasions. As for the tablet – not only had he submerged it and smashed the screen, but he'd also reformatted the hard drive beforehand. Yet he could prove that he'd been on the mainland with his tennis club on the days when Maria had stayed with Lisa, and both his parents testified that he'd been at home on Tuesday night and had got up early for practice on Wednesday morning, so once he had signed his statement, he was permitted to go home.

'Brilliant. That got us precisely nowhere,' was Johann's frustrated summary of the day. 'Quite the opposite, in fact. The evidence on the tablet has almost certainly been destroyed, and knowing who stole it doesn't help us with our investigation.'

'Tell me something I don't know,' Lena muttered. 'How are you getting on with the CCTV footage?'

'I'm sorry,' said Johann, visibly irritated by now, 'but I haven't found your mystery person yet. I'll keep on it, though.'

'Hey, Johann! What's the matter with you?'

He shrugged. 'I don't know.'

'You might get away with being sarcastic to your cat or to your dog, but not to me.'

Johann had to grin, despite himself. 'You know I don't have any pets.'

'How about we go for a little stroll?'

'Why not?' replied Johann, getting to his feet.

They left the station and headed towards the marina, which lay a few hundred yards to the north. When they reached the quay lined with numerous small yachts and motorboats, Lena asked her question a second time. 'So, what's the matter?'

Once again, Johann shrugged, briefly reminding Lena of a sulky teenager. 'Nothing important. Or rather, nothing *very* important.'

'Johanna Logener?' she asked.

Johann rolled his eyes. 'Is it really that obvious?'

'Well?'

'She called me this morning. Wanted to meet me. Of course I said no and came up with an excuse. Too much work, et cetera.'

Lena said nothing and waited.

'All right,' Johann went on, his hands buried in his pockets, his eyes fixed on the horizon. 'Maybe I have developed some feelings for her. Has nothing like that ever happened to you?'

'Would it make things any better if it had? I doubt it. Believe me, the best thing you can do is stay away from her for now. Tell her what the situation is. Your boss has banned you from meeting with her alone. She'll understand.'

'Perhaps. I'll call her back later.'

Lena smiled. 'You've really fallen for her, haven't you?'

Johann hesitated, but eventually said, 'Let me put it this way: if Johanna ever became a suspect, you'd have to send me back to Flensburg on the next ferry.' He sighed. 'This has never happened to me before. You find yourself suddenly standing in front of someone and you get the feeling you've known them all your life. I know that sounds clichéd, like something out of a bad novel, but . . . what can I say? It is what it is. Maybe I'm just imagining it all, but . . .' Johann's monologue stumbled to a halt. 'Damn it, I don't know.'

'If I can give you some personal advice: take things slowly, Johann.'

'I'll give it some thought.' A jolt passed through his body and he drew himself upright with renewed energy. 'But what about the case?' He looked at his watch. 'The others will be getting back from their interview tour in an hour. If you don't have anything else for me, I'll go back to watching cars come off the ferry.'

'Sure. I need to call the pathologist anyway. Maybe I can find a way to speed up the DNA comparison with Martin Reimers.'

Once they were back inside the police station, Lena looked up Luise Stahnke's mobile number.

'Hey, Lena. Any news?' she asked.

'I was just about to ask you the same question,' Lena answered, laughing. '*Moin*, first of all. Do you have any information on the DNA comparison?'

'It's taking it's time . . . but I'll have something tomorrow morning, with any luck. Definitely no sooner than that, though. And there's no point in begging now – I can't speed it up.' She drew out the last five words for emphasis.

'OK, I get the picture, Dr Stahnke,' Lena grumbled. 'Do you have anything else for me?'

'You're going to laugh at this, but I've been at the institute for hours already – on my Saturday off, and everything. I just couldn't stop thinking about the incisions on Maria's arm. I asked a colleague in Washington DC about them – a high-level expert – and she sent me a reply last night. In a nutshell, she confirmed my suspicions. It can't have been suicide. More than that, she thinks the culprit must have had at least some basic medical training in order to make incisions like that. I don't know if that's of any help to you, but I'd look into it if you have any likely suspects.'

'Good tip! We do have someone in mind, actually, which is why the DNA comparison is so important. But no matter, we can hang on for one more night.'

'That's the spirit. I'm just going through my documents here again. I'll call you if I notice anything. Otherwise, I'll hopefully get the results of the comparison to you tomorrow morning.'

'Are the other possible DNA samples on the victim's clothing still . . .?'

'Yep, that kind of analysis takes a good deal longer, as you know. It sounds like you're under an awful lot of pressure over there,' said Luise.

'The rumour mill has gone into overdrive – an island like this one is a lot like a remote village. I have a bad feeling about the next few days, or even weeks. The sooner we solve this case, the better.'

'And how are you doing on a personal level? Are you seeing your boyfriend every evening?'

'I am, but . . . well, you know how it is.'

'Are you having problems?' Luise asked, and Lena instantly regretted not having answered with a simple 'yes'.

'The usual.'

'Don't make me drag it out of you. What's going on?'

'Erck and I don't have a helicopter to fly across and see each other every night. And that won't change for the foreseeable future, unfortunately.'

'But you knew that before you got into this, Lena. There won't be any easy solutions, but if you really want to stay together, you'll find a way.'

'That sounds straightforward, but it's damned hard in practice. Basically, I only see one solution: for me to move to Amrum. But I can forget about my career in that case. Would you do it?'

'No idea – I've never been in a situation like that before. And I haven't met a man yet who'd be worth moving for. So . . .'

'I know I need to make a decision. But I don't want to decide. I want everything to stay how it is right now. End of.'

'I presume Erck takes a different view.'

'You presume correctly. Maybe now you understand why I'm so keen to avoid a conversation with him. Right now, it will only cause trouble.'

'You can't put it off for ever, though. And you know that.'

Lena groaned. 'That doesn't really get me anywhere.'

'Sorry, but there aren't any magic cures for matters of the heart. I'd love to help you, but . . .'

'I know, Luise. Let's talk about it another time.'

The two women said their goodbyes. Just as Lena was about to put her phone away, Erck called. 'Hey! I'm just on my way to the supermarket. Do you know if you're coming today?'

Lena gave a start. She should have called Erck hours ago. 'I'm not sure yet . . .'

'Pity. That sounds like you're turning me down.'

'No, I'm not. I was planning to come over on the six-o'clock ferry, but . . .'

'Don't stress. If it doesn't work out, we'll postpone until tomorrow. I'll buy us some beef fillet – that'll keep for a few days in the fridge. And it cooks really quickly too. So I'll just wait to hear from you.'

Lena felt a lump in her throat. 'I promise I'll try, Erck.' How could she have forgotten to phone him? Or had it happened sub-consciously, and really she hadn't wanted to call him at all . . .? 'Is everything all right with you otherwise?' she asked.

'Yep, all good. Beke came round briefly, by the way. Just for a quick chat. You know how she is. But don't worry, we didn't talk about you.'

Lena wondered why Erck was so keen to emphasise that. A quick chat? That didn't sound like Beke. Her aunt always phoned ahead before she stopped by. Was she concerned about them?

'Why would I worry? Anyway, I need to head into my team meeting. I'll call you back.'

'I'm outside the shop now myself. Talk to you later, Lena.'

With a queasy feeling in her stomach, Lena put her phone down on the table. It would be another fifteen minutes before the meeting started. Why had she told him it was starting now? Lena sighed and pushed her thoughts to one side. She stood up and walked over to the incident room, where Johann and one of the officers from Föhr were busy reviewing the vehicles from the ferry. Taking a position behind them, she took a close look at the footage. The registration numbers were clearly legible, but the people inside the cars were only visible in outline. At least it was possible to gauge how many people were inside the vehicles and whether the drivers were male or female.

Johann paused the video. 'We've already gone through four hundred and thirty-three cars, and we've managed to identify a lot of them as belonging to residents on the island. Janik here' – he nodded to his uniformed colleague – 'knows just about everyone on Föhr, thankfully.'

'Have you found anything suspicious?' said Lena.

Johann showed her a handwritten list of registration numbers. 'I wouldn't exactly call them suspicious, but I'll need to run some checks on these ones after our meeting.' He looked at the clock. 'Oh – we need to pack up. The others will be here any second.'

Shortly afterwards, the mini island task force gathered in the incident room. Lena asked everyone to sit down and then took the floor. 'Sergeant Brandt won't be joining us for the next few days, in light of recent events.' She told them about the interview with his son and the discovery of the tablet. Jan Ottenga listened with a glum expression, and Lena made a note to have a word with him in private after the meeting.

'If Brandt's son went about things properly – and I think we can assume he did, looking at the state of the device – then there'll hardly be any data left on it,' said Ben.

'We'll have to wait and see about that,' said Lena. 'The tablet is on its way to Kiel, and CSI have assured me they'll look at it first thing tomorrow morning.'

Franz Weinbach – Ben's teammate – spoke next. 'It's crazy. I'm sure that thing could have told us an awful lot about the victim.' He coughed. 'Well, anyway. Should I go first today?'

'Please, go ahead.'

'Ben and I went to visit the remaining families from this community. But even though we're now focusing our inquiries on Martin Reimers, we didn't think it was advisable or productive to ask the interviewees about him directly. In short, the interviews with the adults were even tougher than the ones we conducted yesterday. Sometimes we even got the impression they'd agreed their answers in advance, they were so similar. But I guess that was to be expected. Because of that, we decided to turn our attention to the younger members of the community – and by younger, I mean sixteen and up. We insisted on talking to the young people in private and we took our time with them. You can find the details in our report, but as a foretaste: it seems there really is a lot of pressure on young people within the community to start a family as soon as possible, or to at least have a partner in mind. And the age gap between our victim and Martin Reimers doesn't appear to be particularly unusual. After all, there isn't much to prevent someone from getting married at sixteen. Like I said, we tried not to go in all guns blazing, so we introduced Martin Reimers to the conversation as casually as possible. But we got the impression that quite a few of our interviewees knew about the deal, if I can call it that.'

'Which would definitely have put a lot more pressure on Martin,' Ben added, 'since he was now partly responsible for making sure Maria didn't step out of line like her sister did.'

'Exactly,' Franz Weinbach continued, before going on to report on each individual interview in turn. Fifteen minutes later, he concluded with the words, 'I've said it before, but it's almost impossible to get any concrete information out of these people. They didn't refuse to talk to us, but they might as well have, for all they actually told us.'

'Did the Behrens family come up in any of your interviews?' asked Lena. 'Specifically Lisa and her grandmother.'

'It doesn't seem like anybody knows about the grandmother's dementia,' said Weinbach.

'But now that you mention it,' Ben interjected, 'we spoke to Martin Reimers' younger sister yesterday. The man himself wasn't there, allegedly. At one point, she mentioned something – I think it slipped out by accident – that makes me think in hindsight that she might have guessed or even known about Gesa Behrens' illness.'

'What was that?' asked Lena with interest.

'Nothing specific. We managed to get her talking, and since she's only slightly older than Lisa Behrens, the conversation turned to the friendship between the two girls. Reimers' sister hinted that she envied Lisa her freedom. But there was something else too. She added that Lisa had a lot on her plate and had to help her *Oma* a lot, and there was something hanging in the air when she said that. I can't think of another way to describe it.'

'Interesting,' Johann piped up. 'That could mean Martin Reimers knew about the grandmother's illness, which would have given him some leverage over Lisa Behrens. And that in turn might have meant she kept him informed. I think we should submit an urgent request for Martin Reimers' mobile phone data. Do you think we'll get that approved?'

'With a little luck, sure,' said Lena. 'I spoke to DSU Warnke last night.' She decided not to mention that he hadn't exactly been enthusiastic about her suggestion – but in the end, she'd managed to convince him that, in the best-case scenario, the data would help to quickly exonerate Martin Reimers. 'But I don't know if he managed to find a judge to issue a court order yesterday.'

'OK,' Franz Weinbach resumed. 'I think that's all the key findings from the interviews. Although maybe one more thing: we don't have any indication that there've been any other dropouts from the church other than Johanna Logener. That means the community must exert constant pressure to make sure nobody steps out of line.'

'Thanks for that,' said Lena, before turning to Jochen Frank. 'Did you find out anything new during the interviews with Maria's classmates?'

Frank sat up in his chair and opened his notebook. 'Our inquiries obviously also focused on Martin Reimers, but apparently none of the kids knew what Maria's parents had in mind. That was for the best, I'd say. Just like in the previous interviews, it soon became clear how badly Maria Logener was picked on by her classmates. Even the kids that weren't personally involved couldn't care less what happened to her. As is often the case in situations like these, somebody else was always to blame. But we still got a sense of how shocked they were when they heard that Maria had killed herself – and you might say they were almost relieved to find out we're now conducting a murder investigation. Enno Brandt' – at this point, Jochen Frank glanced over at Jan Ottenga – 'was named by quite a few of them as a key figure in the bullying. Of course, we already have that on the record from Enno's own statement, so I'll spare you the details. But what might be of interest – and this certainly matches up with Ben's observation – is that although the kids told us Lisa Behrens was Maria's friend, that bond doesn't seem to have been as unshakeable as we assumed. A few of the kids said things that didn't cast Lisa in a very positive light. They described her as very calculating, and one of them even called her a liar. Of course, they're all still teenagers – that much is clear from their behaviour – so their emotions might have been getting the better of them. All the same, not one of them had a good opinion of Lisa Behrens. But I can't say how much that has to do with the fact that she's also a member of the same religious community as Maria.'

Jochen Frank gave a rapid account of their interviews with each of the students before praising Jan Ottenga once more for his good teamwork.

'All right. I suggest we wrap things up there for the day,' Lena said eventually. 'Tomorrow is Sunday, and at the moment I can't see any developments that call for the entire team to be here, so you can all take the next ferry back to the mainland. That way, you'll be in Flensburg by the evening, so you'll have time to rest and recover before you catch the first or second ferry back to Föhr on Monday morning.'

Chattering among themselves, the officers got to their feet and left the room. Lena called Jan Ottenga over and waited until they were alone.

'Is everything OK?' she eventually asked.

'I think so,' he answered hesitantly.

'Are you worried because of your boss?'

'Of course. So are the rest of the officers from Föhr.'

'You did the right thing, telling Jochen that Arno Brandt conducted himself somewhat . . . carelessly when it came to his son.'

'Maybe. It still leaves a nasty taste in my mouth, though. If I'd known Arno was going to get into trouble—'

'No,' Lena cut him off. 'Misconceived loyalty is never the right way. Even your superiors can make mistakes. And what happened was a mistake.'

'So it seems. But that doesn't make things any better for me.'

'You mean, Arno Brandt is the kind of man who bears a grudge?'

Jan Ottenga shrugged.

'I'll see what I can do.'

'Maybe it's better if you don't do anything?' he suggested cautiously.

'I hardly think that's a solution. No, I think Johann Grasmann and I put pressure on you and forced you to admit that Brandt's son hadn't been searched. I'll write an official statement saying so, for the record.'

Jan Ottenga nodded thoughtfully. 'All right. But won't that cause problems for me?'

'We won't be able to avoid a small entry in your personnel file, but we can probably leave it at a warning. Is that OK for you?'

'It'd be galling to have something like that on my record, but if we have to.'

'I think a warning is all we need. That should take you out of the firing line, at any rate.'

'Thank you,' he said, before heading out into the weekend.

24

Lena zipped up her coat and nestled into the back of her beach chair. The wind was blowing in strong gusts from inland, so she'd rotated the chair to face out to sea. She was turning her phone over in her hands and debating when to call Erck. The last ferry would be leaving in an hour and the terminal was only around half a mile away. If she walked quickly, she'd be on the dock within ten minutes. Before she could make a decision, however, there was a knock on the side of the chair and Ben appeared in front of her.

'I see you aren't on your way to Amrum yet,' he said.

'What about you? Are you staying on Föhr?' Lena shuffled to one side and gestured for Ben to sit down next to her.

'It's a nice enough place. And what would I do in Flensburg?' Ben replied.

'See your kids?'

He pulled his phone out of his pocket and held it up. 'Not my weekend, I've already been informed. They've made plans without me. Makes sense. Why wouldn't they?' His voice sounded sad, but Lena thought she could detect a trace of anger too.

'You should hire a bike tomorrow and explore the island. It's worth doing.'

'Yeah, I was thinking about that too.'

'The weather is meant to be good. No rain, reasonably tolerable temperatures.'

Ben looked out at the sea. 'For a reasonably tolerable life?'

Lena said nothing and simply offered him some of her blanket.

'Thanks, Inspector,' he murmured. 'How much does a chair like this cost, anyway? Maybe I'll rent myself one and spend the day here. That ought to work, with enough alcohol.'

'Isn't that a little over the top? For one thing, it's not certain that your wife really wants to break up with you, and for another, there's a life after marriage.'

'Oh really? If you say so . . .'

'Come on, cheer up. Tell me what you want to do with your kids in the autumn holiday instead. Didn't you always love going to the Danish North Sea coast?'

Ben smiled. 'You remember me saying that? I do. I find the landscape there unique. Up in the north, in the nature reserve near Thisted. Have you ever been?'

'No, but I've heard of it.'

He began to describe it to her – his eyes glowing as he talked about the hikes he had gone on with his kids, the camper van they had driven up the coast, the kite that had almost lifted his son into the air and the sunny days on the beach.

'It sounds great,' said Lena. 'You should hire a van and head off. Who knows, maybe your wife will even come with you.'

'I don't think she would.'

'Think positive. You never know what—'

'She sent me an email yesterday. An email! And you'll never guess what's happened. She's met someone – or maybe I should say she found him. Her husband leaves the apartment and the next bloke is already waiting on the stairs outside. A quick substitution. Pity I didn't get to say hi to him. Shake his hand and ask him to look after my wife and kids. After all, you have to be reasonable, keep your cool. Life goes on.'

'I'm sorry,' said Lena after a while. She hadn't realised things were so bad in Ben's marriage. He had already told her more than once how important the kids were to him. 'You didn't know anything about it?'

'She's a free woman. Besides, if you'd asked me back to your room last night, I wouldn't have said no. So I can hardly blame her for it.'

Lena recalled their walk back to the bed and breakfast from the beach. She had stumbled and Ben had just managed to catch her. Then they'd stood facing each other and he'd put his arm around her waist; their eyes had met, and for a moment everything around them had seemed to fall away into silence.

'I never said you should blame her. But maybe you should fight for her, if she's really important to you.'

'Fighting takes strength, and I don't have any – or what I have is only just enough for my kids.' He lapsed into silence for a while. 'You know what I'd like more than anything right now? A double whisky. Or two doubles. Luckily, I don't even have the strength for that. Besides, that stuff only gives you a tiny little boost anyway. Afterwards, everything is the same as it was before. Only worse.'

Lena knew what he was talking about. She herself had had times that she preferred not to remember. After finishing her police training, she had been deployed to various constabularies throughout Germany and had found that a woman with top grades and strong career prospects wasn't always welcome in the tough masculine world of the police. Many of her colleagues had demanded absolute submission, which had sometimes bordered on humiliation. That had been hard for Lena to bear. And when she defended herself, it only made their pack mentality even worse. A bottle of wine in the evening had quickly become a comforting habit.

'Aren't you going to say anything?' Ben asked, breaking the silence.

'I wish I could help you, but if I'm honest, I have no idea if I can, or if I'm even remotely the right person for it.'

Their eyes met. 'I think you are. The mere fact that we've found each other again – that we're sitting here together by the sea, and . . .' He leaned forward and gently kissed her.

Lena was too surprised to react.

But when he kissed her a second time, she did respond, letting herself get carried along on a wave of emotion that washed over her as if from nowhere. Her right arm moved up to rest on his shoulder while her left hand tenderly stroked his hair. It all felt so simple and so right, almost as though she were in a dream. A dream that would end the minute she opened her eyes, but would leave her smiling for the rest of the day.

At first, Lena heard the ringtone from a distance, as if it came from a phone belonging to a passer-by who had nothing to do with her. Yet when the device continued to ring at the same volume, she abruptly sat up and pulled back from Ben slightly. She suddenly felt as though she was standing a few yards away from the beach chair, looking at herself and the man beside her and realising what had happened. She leapt to her feet, did up her coat again – since Ben had already unzipped it – and looked at her watch.

'I need to get to the ferry,' she heard herself say. 'Can you take my blanket back with you?'

Without waiting for a reply, she set off, moving faster with every step until she was running. At the terminal she came to an abrupt halt and bent over, hands on her knees, panting. The last incoming passengers had just disembarked and those waiting to depart were now heading up the gangway on to the ferry. Lena walked the last few yards, showed her warrant card to the ticket inspector and boarded the ferry.

Once the boat set sail, she dialled Erck's number. 'Can you pick me up? I don't have my car with me.'

◆ ◆ ◆

Erck poured milk into the coffee and handed the cup to Lena. 'Still tired?'

'Maybe we should have gone to sleep a little earlier,' answered Lena with a grin. 'But I'll be fine as long as the caffeine kicks in quickly.'

'I wasn't the one who started it last night . . . though that doesn't mean I didn't enjoy it.'

'Well, well, well, so you enjoyed it, did you?' Lena took a large sip from her cup. 'That's the stuff. You make the best coffee this side of the Alps.'

'I know,' answered Erck, leaning back self-assuredly in his chair. 'That's why all the women love me.'

'I'll pretend I didn't hear that. Or are you just trying to wind me up? All the women . . . I should ask Beke to stop by more often.'

Erck laughed. 'I didn't say I love them back. All they get from me is good coffee.' His mood was infectious.

'I should hope so!'

'I'm not going to wait all these years and then risk everything for a stupid mistake.' He winked. 'Or would you rather have a Casanova?'

His words caught Lena completely off-guard. Ever since she had sprinted along the beach the previous evening, she had pushed those intense few moments with Ben to the very back of her mind. On the ferry, she had taken up her usual spot by the railing, despite the cold wind, and forced herself not to think of anything. And from the moment she saw him standing on the dock, she had focused solely on Erck.

'Hey, what's the matter? Do you want a Casanova? Or should I let you wear the trousers?'

She drained her cup, kissed him passionately and stood up. 'Neither. You just stay the way you are. Come on, we need to go.' She reached out her hand and pulled him up from his chair.

At the quayside they stood wrapped in each other's arms once more until the man by the gangway waved at them. Lena let go of Erck, gave him one last kiss and dashed towards the ferry.

◆　◆　◆

'Good morning,' said Lena as she entered the incident room at the police station. Johann was already sitting in front of the projector reviewing the CCTV footage from the ferry terminal. 'Are you on your own today?'

'Janik called in sick. Upset stomach, he claims. But I expect he's just staging a little protest.'

'Not much we can do about that. Why don't you call Ben? He stayed on the island last night.'

'That had occurred to me, but I wanted to let him have a lie-in. If he comes in an hour, that'll be OK. Will you give him a call?'

'Yep . . . can do,' Lena replied, slightly hesitantly, and quickly turned away. 'I'll be in the office.'

On her desk, she found a piece of paper with two names and telephone numbers, along with a message explaining that these were people who had responded to the appeal in the *Island Courier*. The note didn't have a date or time written on it, but Lena suspected that the calls had come in yesterday afternoon and nobody had bothered to write them up until now. 'Jobsworths,' she sighed, putting the notes to one side. She would call the witnesses just before lunch to avoid disrupting their Sunday mornings.

A further message came from the fire brigade search team who had volunteered to go back over the route from the Behrens' house to the beach. They hadn't found Maria's duffel bag, nor any other suspicious items.

In her email inbox there was an update from CSI. They had found two further sets of fingerprints on the backpack, beside Maria's. Enno Brandt's prints had been taken yesterday and sent to Kiel ready for comparison on Monday. The third set of prints presumably belonged to Lisa Behrens, but that still needed to be confirmed. Lena made a note to herself. She had already decided to have another word with Maria's friend anyway.

CSI had also attached another report concerning the exercise book Lena had found in Maria's room. The imprint of her handwriting from the torn-out page suggested that Maria had been researching runaway teenagers on the Internet. She had noted down the URLs of websites where you could find other teens' stories, along with contact details for support organisations. CSI couldn't say when Maria had made the notes, however.

Just as Lena was about to leave the office, her phone rang. It was Luise.

'Good morning,' Lena greeted her friend. 'Did you sleep—'

'We have a match!' Luise interrupted her. 'The hair on the victim's clothing belongs to Martin Reimers.'

'You're completely sure?' Lena was suddenly all ears.

'One hundred per cent. The reference sample is still under analysis, but it's almost certainly a positive result. The official findings will be released this afternoon.'

'Thank you, Luise, thank you!' Lena cried, already on her way to Johann. 'It's Martin Reimers' DNA!' she called to him. 'We need to get going!'

Johann took a moment to grasp the significance of Lena's words. He jumped to his feet, reached for the gun that he had

247

laid on the desk beside him and slid it into his holster. 'Just the two of us?'

'How many other officers are in today?'

'Two, as far as I know.'

They were already running towards the exit. 'Tell one of them to pick Ben up and bring him to the Reimers' house.'

She opened the car door and threw herself into the driver's seat, while Johann did the same on the passenger side.

As Lena drove out of the village, Johann called the station and let Ben know what was happening. 'We should have arrested him after all,' he said.

'On what grounds? It would have just blown up in our face – or do you think Warnke would have been fine with it?'

They had already left Wyk by now. Lena hit the accelerator, racing towards Nieblum. She passed through the village and stopped a few minutes later on the edge of Borgsum. 'We'll wait here for Ben and the other officer.'

'Do you think Reimers is that dangerous?'

'He wasn't exactly a lightweight. This will stop him getting any silly ideas.'

'Is he our man?'

'Whether he is or not, he must have been in contact with Maria just before she died. He'll have to explain that to us.'

'How did he know where to find her?'

'Good question. From Lisa Behrens? She'll also be getting a visit from us today. I've finally had enough of all these lies and half-truths.'

When the squad car pulled up behind them, Lena got out and walked over to Ben's side. He opened the passenger window and gave her a questioning look. 'Martin Reimers. We need to arrest him. The DNA sample was positive.'

248

'OK,' said Ben, whose appearance betrayed the fact that he had only just got out of bed. His hair was dishevelled, his eyes dull. 'We'll lead the way. I know where the house is.'

They drove through Borgsum at normal speed. Shortly before the end of the village, they turned on to a dirt road leading to Witsum. A few hundred yards further on stood the old two-storey brick house belonging to the Reimers.

'His car isn't here,' said Johann, though there was a rusty Fiat Panda parked in the yard beside a VW Camper. 'Looks like somebody's at home, though.' Johann pointed to one of the windows. A curtain twitched and a child's face appeared.

They got out of their vehicles and Ben and the local constable, Klaas Fokke, stood a little to one side so they could intervene more effectively if Reimers decided to flee. Lena walked up to the front door and rang the bell. After what felt like an eternity, a man in his fifties opened the door.

'What do you want?' he asked with a fierce expression.

'First of all, good morning,' Lena replied coolly. 'Are you Martin's father?'

He nodded.

'Is your son at home?'

'No.'

'Do you know where we can find him?'

'No – and now I'd like you to leave, please.'

'I'm sorry, Herr Reimers, but we need to make sure that your son isn't on the premises first.'

'Do you have a search warrant?'

'In this case, we don't need a court order. Please let us in, Herr Reimers.'

The man positioned himself in the middle of the doorway, his arms folded. Lena looked across at Ben and his driver. Klaas Fokke walked up to them, gave a brief nod and stood in front of Martin Reimers' father. 'There's no point in this, Hans. Let my colleagues in. We just want to quickly check if your son is at home and after that we'll be off again.'

Hans Reimers was breathing heavily, and for a moment he seemed to be debating what the right strategy was. Then he slowly moved to one side. Lena quietly asked Johann to check the ferry timetable before following Ben and Klaas Fokke into the house.

A few minutes later, they had searched every room and were standing back outside in front of their vehicles.

'The boat to the mainland left ten minutes ago,' Johann informed them. 'I'm expecting a call any second now to let me know if anyone saw Martin Reimers' car.'

Lena cursed herself for not having sent an officer straight to the ferry terminal. Had Reimers really managed to give them the slip? Despite repeated questioning, his father hadn't given them any more information about his whereabouts. It was painfully obvious that Martin had made a run for it, or was at least hiding somewhere on the island.

Johann's phone rang. He exchanged a few words with someone and then immediately ended the call. 'He's on the ferry!'

Lena had already opened her car door. 'Get in!'

They raced back down the dirt track and on to the road. 'Should I request a helicopter?'

'That'll take too long. Call the marine police instead. I saw one of their boats moored in the harbour.'

Johann hastily grabbed his phone, requested the extension from the switchboard, and before they reached the other end of Nieblum he had the captain of the boat on the line.

'All sorted,' said Johann once he'd finished his call. 'They're waiting for us.'

'We'll need support in Dagebüll. Worst-case scenario, we'll need to search the entire ferry.'

'The nearest station is in Husum. I hope there are enough officers on duty there.'

Lena glanced at the clock. 'We still have over an hour. They'll just have to call everyone in from their weekend off.'

Johann already had his phone at his ear. By the time they pulled up at the dock next to the marine police boat, he had arranged for ten officers to wait at the ferry terminal on the mainland.

25

'So we're looking for a fugitive?' asked Captain Hansen.

'Yes – we just missed him, unfortunately.'

The blue-and-white marine police boat they were on was over sixty feet long and could travel at nearly twenty knots, as Hansen had explained to Lena. It had been moored in Wyk since the previous day and was due to head back to its home port of Husum that afternoon. If all went well, Hansen assured her, they would arrive in Dagebüll a few minutes before the ferry.

'I suppose this has to do with that dead girl on the beach?' he asked.

'Yes. Have you heard much about that?'

'It's all anyone is talking about on the island. I went for a beer with my senior crewman last night and the whole pub was gossiping about it. Is our man on the ferry involved with that cult too?'

'That cult is an evangelical free church, of which the victim was a member.'

'Free church? That's not what it sounded like in the pub yesterday. The people there were openly speculating about which of these – I quote – "madmen" was the killer. Even the victim's family weren't above suspicion. But that's how it goes. People like to pick on minorities – they make great scapegoats.'

'The young man we're looking for belongs to the same free church,' said Lena thoughtfully.

'And he's a suspect? That'll get people talking for sure. Do you think he did it?'

'Right now, the evidence is against him. There are one or two things he needs to explain to us.'

'That doesn't sound like you think he's guilty.'

'We're a long way from that – unless he confesses.' Lena pointed into the distance. 'Is that the ferry?'

Captain Hansen reached for a telescope. 'Affirmative. Should we give it a wide berth? It might be too obvious otherwise.'

'Good idea. Stop him doing anything stupid.'

'It's not like he can go anywhere,' said Captain Hansen with a grin.

'Oh yes, he can,' murmured Lena. She could well imagine what was going through Martin Reimers' mind right now. They definitely couldn't rule out any knee-jerk reactions on his part.

'What was that?' asked Captain Hansen, who was busy changing course.

'Just thinking out loud. When will we get to Dagebüll?'

He briefly studied the map. 'In ten to twelve minutes.'

Lena thanked him and walked over to Johann, who was standing by the railing on the side of the boat and watching the ferry. The wind was whipping his hair into disarray; Lena had tied hers back with a hairband.

'We'll be arriving in ten minutes. Have you been in contact with the officers at the harbour?'

He held up his phone. 'No signal. Should only take me a few seconds, though. What shall we do with him once we've got him? Take him straight to Husum or Kiel?' Johann's phone gave a beep. He quickly dialled his most recently called number, asked if everything was in place and listened carefully. 'OK, let's do that.'

'All set?'

'The officers have made contact with the ferry. They'll keep the bow door closed for now, but the foot passengers will be able to leave the boat, subject to checks. Four officers should be enough for that. The rest of us will look for Reimers. Let's hope he doesn't realise we're searching the boat and just sits in his car waiting to drive off.'

The nervous agitation of the passengers standing beside their vehicles quickly rubbed off on Lena and the other officers, who were following her in single file. She'd spotted the old green Vauxhall Astra from a distance, and as soon as she could make out the registration number, she held up her hand as a signal that she'd found the car. They approached slowly from three sides, simultaneously instructing the surrounding passengers to get back in their vehicles or move away from the Astra. They couldn't see anybody inside, but that didn't mean it was empty. Lena gripped the door handle while Johann and another officer took up position beside her with their guns drawn. She wrenched the door open and Johann leapt forwards, yelling, 'Police! Come out slowly!'

Lena was the first to confirm that there was nobody inside the car. She beckoned the other officers over and split them into two teams, who then stationed themselves by the ramp leading down to the dock. All of the cars were to be checked before they disembarked – including the boot, if anything seemed suspicious. Johann phoned the captain of the ferry, who opened the bow door. One by one, the vehicles drove forwards for inspection before being allowed off the boat. In the meantime, Lena took down the details of the people parked next to Martin Reimers' car and interviewed them. Nobody had noticed the driver of the green Astra.

Half an hour later, the last of the fifty-odd vehicles rolled off the ferry. Martin Reimers hadn't been inside any of them; nor had they found him during the checks on the foot passengers. Lena left two officers on the gangway and conducted a thorough search of the ferry with the rest of the squad.

'Nothing!' Johann exclaimed disappointedly.

'All right,' said Lena in a dull voice. She turned to the colleagues from Husum, thanked them and ended the operation.

'Could he have been hiding inside one of the vehicles after all?' asked Johann, not for the first time. They were on board the ferry heading back to Föhr.

The green Astra had been towed away for safekeeping in Husum, ready for CSI to examine it for traces of Maria Logener. The boat had eventually departed Dagebüll two hours late, which meant the last ferry from Föhr to the mainland would probably be cancelled.

'That's unlikely,' said Lena. They had withdrawn to a quiet corner of the on-board café to discuss their next steps. Before they left Dagebüll, Johann had put in a request for an official nationwide manhunt, which had already been launched by the time they set off back to Föhr.

'He couldn't have known we were looking for him when the ferry set sail,' Johann went on. 'Maybe somebody managed to call him, but then what happened? Do you really think he jumped overboard?' Immediately after concluding the search, Lena had requested a helicopter to fly back over the ferry route.

'Let's wait and see if the helicopter crew find anything.' Just then, they heard the familiar sound of rotor blades. 'There they are already.' They watched the police helicopter through the window.

'As for the possibility that someone might have phoned Reimers,' Lena continued, 'the ferry was much too far from shore for him to have had any signal. Besides, if I were him, I'd have switched my mobile off altogether. It's pretty well known by now that the police can locate missing persons through their phones.'

'But where is he?'

'If he didn't jump overboard, that means either the car was just a red herring, or he changed his mind at the last minute and he's still on the island.'

'A red herring! He could have just parked the thing on some farmyard somewhere. Then we'd have no idea if he was still holed up on Föhr or if he'd taken the ferry to the mainland. And I guess we'd probably have assumed the latter, since it would be crazy for him to stay here. Is he planning to crawl into a hole in the ground? He can't show his face anywhere on the island. If I were him, I'd have made a break for it. Headed abroad, even if just elsewhere in Europe. I assume the church has enough contacts to make him disappear, at least for a short while.'

'None of this is getting us anywhere,' said Lena, frustrated by all the speculation. 'The whole squad will be back tomorrow. When they get here, we'll have to search the houses of the church members.'

'Your boss won't like that.'

'We'll do it on a voluntary basis, and I'll only ask him to arrange a search warrant if anyone refuses.'

'I can't shake the feeling we're being played here. Martin Reimers must have realised after his interview that we would find his DNA on Maria. He's had plenty of time to come up with a plan.'

'Is that how he came across to you? As a cold-blooded schemer? He didn't to me.'

'OK, I'll grant you that. But we still need to find him.'

'All we have so far is the hair. If he matches the other DNA samples too, then things are going to get really tough for him – but for now, we'll just carry on as normal with the investigation. You keep working on the CCTV and I'll concentrate on Martin Reimers. The pathologist told me that the killer must have had some medical training. We have the footprints, which I'm going to compare with Reimers' shoes; we have witnesses who've seen Maria and who I'm going to ask a few more questions. We also have Lisa Behrens, who we suspect of tipping Reimers off after her argument with Maria. I want to go and see Maria's father again too, since he was clearly the driving force behind these marriage fantasies.'

'Lots of work, then. As soon as I'm done with the CCTV footage, I'll be ready to help you out.'

When Lena and Johann arrived back on Föhr that afternoon, the first thing Lena did was to phone the helicopter pilot. Despite searching for an hour, they hadn't found a body in the sea. After that, Lena called Klaas Fokke – the local constable who had fetched Ben from the bed and breakfast – into her office. 'Do you know the Reimers family?' she asked him.

'This is a small island. As a policeman, you soon get to know lots of different people.'

'You addressed Herr Reimers by his first name,' Lena probed.

'Are you trying to accuse me of something?' the young officer blurted.

'I'm not accusing anyone of anything. Not you, and not Sergeant Brandt either. I asked you a question and I expect an answer.'

'If you really must know, he was my football coach.' Klaas Fokke looked at Lena defiantly. 'Are you going to suspend me now too?'

'Hang on. Sergeant Brandt hasn't been suspended; he's taken a few days' holiday. Everything will be settled in due course, and personally speaking, I don't think there'll be any serious repercussions. Is that clear?'

Klaas Fokke hesitated. 'I didn't know that.'

'Firstly, I assume you didn't warn the Reimers family when we went to arrest Martin.'

'Of course not!' said the young officer indignantly.

'OK, I believe you. Do you also know Martin Reimers personally?'

'We aren't – or weren't – friends, if that's what you mean. He came along to football practice from time to time, though he was still a few years too young to join the team. That's where I know him from, anyway. Other than that we would cross paths every now and then and exchange a few words, but nothing more.'

'Do you know if he had any medical knowledge?'

'Not that I . . .' He caught himself. 'Actually, he's a member of the Red Cross, or at least he used to be. I'd often see him at events here on the island. He drove the van. But I don't know if he had any formal training.'

Lena noted the information down. 'I'd like you to come with me to visit the Reimers. Would that be OK with you?'

'Of course. When?' His answer was abrupt, but Lena had the impression that Klaas Fokke meant what he said.

'In around fifteen minutes. I'll let you know.'

Once he had left her office, Lena took out the note listing the phone numbers of the two witnesses who had responded to the appeal in the *Island Courier*. Judging by the voice of the person who picked up, her first call was to an older gentleman. He claimed to have seen a young girl on Tuesday evening, but after asking a few questions, Lena realised that it couldn't have been Maria. She thanked him for the information and dialled the second number.

'Meta Gerdes,' answered a female voice.

'Good afternoon, Frau Gerdes. This is Detective Inspector Lena Lorenzen from the police. I believe you called us earlier.'

'That's right. I'm sorry I didn't get in touch until yesterday, but I was staying with my sister in Husum.'

'That's perfectly all right, Frau Gerdes. Would you like to tell me exactly what you saw?'

'Certainly, I'd be happy to. It was on Tuesday evening. I'd just watched the eight o'clock news and then gone outside. I always do that – a little stroll around that time helps me fall asleep.'

'So it was after quarter-past eight.'

'That's right. I wasn't far from my house in Wyk when I saw the two of them arguing on the pavement.'

'Can you describe them to me?'

'One of them was a young girl wearing a checked skirt and a cream-coloured coat. She was holding a duffel bag too. Her hair was dark – maybe black, but I can't be certain about that now. The other one was a young man. He said something to her and the girl started yelling at him.'

'What did the man look like?'

'He was tall and burly, and he was wearing dark trousers and a jumper.'

'Can you remember what colour hair he had?'

'Black, or very dark. Very neatly trimmed too.'

'You mean he had short hair?'

'Yes, exactly.'

'Could you hear what they were talking about?'

'I've given that some thought, but I have to admit I didn't really listen properly. It didn't look very serious, you know. Otherwise, I'd have gone to the girl's aid, obviously. But I had the impression that the two of them knew each other well. Young people do argue from time to time – at least, that's what I thought when I walked past them. Do you really think the girl I saw was that poor child they found on the beach?'

'I'm afraid I can't say, Frau Gerdes. Did you happen to notice a car nearby that wouldn't normally be parked there? You mentioned that you like to go for a walk every evening.'

'A car? Now that's a very tricky question.'

'Maybe a vehicle with an unusual colour?' Lena tried to jog her memory without influencing her too strongly.

'I would need to give that some thought, Inspector.'

'One of my colleagues will come round today or tomorrow morning at the latest to take a statement. He'll have some photos of a young man and woman with him, so perhaps you'll be able to recognise them. Would that be OK for you?'

'I'd be very happy to help.'

'Thank you, Frau Gerdes. We'll be in touch.'

26

Lena slid her gun into her holster. Just as she reached for the handle of her office door, there was a knock. On opening it, she found Ben smiling at her. 'Back from the hunt?' he said.

'Empty-handed, unfortunately.'

'So I heard from Johann. Do you need my help?'

'Maybe you could give Johann a hand. Going through all those cars on the CCTV footage is like searching for a needle in a haystack.'

'Do we still need to do that?' said Ben. 'I reckon we've identified the culprit. But I'd be happy to help him out if you want.'

'You could also pay a visit to Frau Gerdes.' Lena told him about her phone call.

'Do we have a photo of Martin Reimers?'

'Not yet, but I was just on my way to see his family. With any luck I can get one there.'

'I'll come with you,' Ben suggested.

'Klaas Fokke was going to—'

'Please. He's just a constable – he normally spends his time tracking down chicken rustlers. OK, so he seems to know the family. In that case, I'm sure he'll do a good job opening the door for you.'

'All right, you can come with us,' said Lena, before walking past him and heading down the corridor to fetch Klaas Fokke.

When they arrived at the Reimers' house, the young constable asked for permission to speak to Martin's father alone first. After a brief hesitation, Lena gave him the go-ahead. Fokke got out of the car and rang the bell.

'How long shall we give him?' asked Ben once Klaas had disappeared inside.

'As long as he needs. You've seen for yourself how secretive these people are.'

'Is that any surprise? Would you want to hand your own son over to the police? And then there's the constant distrust of the authorities. I don't think we're going to get anywhere here. You should just apply for a search warrant and issue a summons to the adults in the family. That would have more of an impact.'

'Let's wait and see.'

They sat inside the car, saying nothing. Minutes ticked by.

'So what was that about yesterday?' Ben asked eventually, breaking the silence.

'Sentimentality,' answered Lena after a brief pause.

'Sentimentality? But that means over-the-top emotion. Passion. Longing. Doesn't sound all that far off the mark, come to think of it.'

'Ben . . . I like you. You know that. But everything else is in the past. I have a boyfriend.'

'Weren't you on your way to see him when we crossed paths yesterday?'

Lena fell silent. Ben had touched a nerve. If he hadn't kissed her, she would have stayed on Föhr.

'What happened yesterday wasn't planned,' Ben went on quietly. 'It just happened. I didn't mean to—'

'It's OK, Ben. I'm big enough to look after myself.'

'One word from you, and I would have—'

'I know,' she interrupted him a second time. 'I kissed you back. Let's just forget it, all right?'

'What choice do I have? I'll try – I can't promise more than that.'

Just as Lena was about to reply, Klaas Fokke emerged from the house and waved to them.

'Here we go,' said Ben, already opening the car door.

Fokke led them into the kitchen, where they found Hans Reimers sitting at the table waiting for them. He stood up and nodded to the two detectives. 'Please,' he said, gesturing at the chairs. 'Have a seat.'

'I believe you already know my colleague,' Lena opened the conversation. 'Constable Fokke has probably told you that we found Martin's Vauxhall Astra on the ferry, but that Martin himself has vanished without trace.'

She received a brief nod in reply.

'There are reasons to believe that Martin was directly connected to Maria Logener's death. We need to speak with him urgently.'

'Why not just come out and say it? You want to arrest him. But he's innocent. Do you really think my son would do anything to Walther's daughter? He'd cut his own arm off rather than so much as touch her. I'd lay my life on it. He didn't do anything to Maria. He never would.'

'We're obliged to follow up on every piece of evidence, every lead. If your son is innocent, we'll confirm that quickly enough. But he's inviting suspicion by running away.'

'What do you want me to do? Hand over my own flesh and blood? Even if I knew where he was, I would never betray him. Never!'

'You don't know where he is?'

'I just told you I didn't.'

'If you want to help your son—'

'Do *you* want to help him?' he interrupted her. 'You despise us, just like everyone else. And why? Because we practise a different form of faith? Isn't that protected by the German constitution? Do you know how often my brothers and sisters have had to flee for their lives over the centuries? From intolerance, stupidity and violence? Do we frighten you people so much that you have to condemn us? We all believe in the same God. Give us the freedom to live how we want. That's our right.'

'I completely agree that you're free to decide for yourself how to practise your religion. And I don't despise your community. The only thing I want is to find Maria's murderer. If your son had nothing to do with her death, then he should hand himself in as soon as possible. He could even prove to be an important witness. That would be better for him, and for your community too.'

'Are you trying to threaten us?'

'No, quite the opposite. Please tell Martin that we're investigating all possible leads. If he's innocent, the truth will out.'

Hans Reimers didn't reply, but he no longer seemed as certain as he was before.

'We'll need all Martin's shoes that he's worn recently,' Lena continued. 'And I'll also need a photo of him.'

'So you can publish it in the papers?' asked Martin's father suspiciously.

'No, we can't do that without the permission of the chief prosecutor. We need the photo to show witnesses. It could prove Martin innocent.'

'What else do you want?'

'I'd like to search his room,' said Lena. 'That might also exonerate him.'

'Or it might do the opposite,' replied Hans Reimers, stony-faced.

'If you're certain that your son is innocent, it shouldn't be a problem, should it?'

'But if you're planning to frame him . . .'

'Hans, I don't think the inspector has that in mind,' said Klaas Fokke, joining the conversation for the first time. 'If Martin has nothing to do with all this, then nothing will happen to him.'

Martin's father sat for a while in silence. Eventually, he stood up, left the kitchen and returned holding a picture of his son.

Soon afterwards, Lena took photos of the soles of four pairs of shoes and searched Martin's room with Ben. They found no evidence to confirm their suspicions – neither date-rape drugs nor any letters or other messages from Maria. There was no computer or laptop, and Martin presumably had his phone with him. Lena had asked for it to be tracked while she was still in Dagebüll and to be informed as soon as he went online.

Hans Reimers stood wordlessly in the doorway while they searched his son's room. Lena could see how much it pained him to know that his son was suspected of such a serious crime. He seemed to have aged years since that morning. As much as Lena tried to put her emotions to one side, she couldn't help but feel sorry for him. Right now, everything seemed to be focused on Martin, and for his father's sake at least, she hoped the investigation would soon shed some light on his son's role – if any.

By the time they got back into the car it was already half past five, so Lena decided to head straight back to the police station.

'How are you getting on, Johann?' asked Lena as she entered the incident room.

'I'm done with the CCTV footage,' he replied, 'and I've already checked some of the suspicious number plates. I was planning to do the rest tomorrow.'

'No matches then?' asked Ben, who had followed Lena into the room.

'Hard to say at this stage. I'm concentrating on male drivers who were alone in their cars – though the footage generally wasn't clear enough to identify the people or to make any visual comparisons.' He pointed to a list. 'Those are the vehicles that arrived on the island during both of the periods we're interested in, the middle of August and earlier this week, and these' – he pulled out another list – 'are the ones that were only here for one of the periods.'

'That all sounds very methodical,' said Ben. 'Good work.'

'I'll second that,' Lena added. 'Is the manhunt for Martin Reimers under way?'

'Yep, for now.' He pointed at the photograph in Lena's hand. 'Should I send that off too? Martin's passport photo is a few years old.'

'I'm afraid we can't. I promised the father we wouldn't use it for the manhunt.'

'What kind of weird deal is that?'

'It's all right, Johann,' Ben cut in. 'We wouldn't have got the photo at all otherwise.'

Johann rolled his eyes before turning away and switching off the projector. 'Does anyone fancy a beer?' When neither Ben nor Lena replied, he gave a shrug. 'Then I'll wish you both a pleasant evening.'

'Are you heading to Amrum?' Ben asked once they were alone.

'Ben – what happened yesterday, that was—'

'I know what it was. We're friends, and that's all we're ever going to be. I get it. Given where the investigation is, I think we three Flensburgers will only be here for another couple of nights at most. So I was just going to invite you out to dinner.' When he saw her expression, he held up his hands disarmingly. 'I swear on my mother's life that I won't make any indecent proposals. No gazing into your eyes, no kisses, nothing like that.'

'I wanted to take another look at the files and I haven't decided yet whether I'm going to Amrum or not. Thanks for the invitation, but—'

'Think about it. You have my number.' He got up. 'I'll see you later – or tomorrow.'

Lena watched him go. It wasn't so easy to find a restaurant table on a Sunday evening. Had he made a reservation? She had to smile, despite herself. What a crazy guy. And yet he seemed to be serious. Friendship. Was that even possible, given that they'd already ended up in bed together? Then again, why not? She didn't want to lose him either. All the same, turning him down still seemed the right thing to do. She was sure they would cross paths often enough in future thanks to their jobs – especially as she visited Flensburg regularly for work.

Lena dialled Erck's number and he picked up after the first ring. She told him about her hectic day – the young fugitive, their meeting with his father and the review of the CCTV footage. Erck was understanding when she said she wanted to spend the next few hours going through the case files, and he hoped she'd be able to come the next day. Yet despite his relaxed tone, Lena could sense his disappointment, and she came close to dropping everything to catch the last ferry.

After ending the call, she stood up with a sigh, wheeled the whiteboard over and used a marker pen to write down the various names connected to the case. Then she started drawing links between them with arrows. Maria stood at the very centre, close to her parents on one side and her sister on the other. Arrows went from Maria's mother and father to Martin Reimers' parents, who were positioned next to Martin. Beyond the Reimers stood the other members of the church. Lena spent a long while debating where to place Lisa Behrens. At first she put her close to Maria, but soon moved her to a position halfway between Martin and Maria.

Eva Braasch seemed to have been an important person to Maria, as did her form tutor Lars Weissdorn, so Lena initially placed Frau Braasch very close to Maria – but then she rubbed her out and moved her further down. Herr Weissdorn landed between Maria and her classmates, including Enno Brandt.

Lena stopped to examine her work, before starting to cross out the connections between the names on the board.

Maria had grown distant from her parents. Lena drew a cross over that arrow, paused a moment to think, and added a second cross.

Johanna's close bond with Maria had remained intact until the very end, but for the last few weeks before her death there had largely been radio silence between them. From Maria's perspective, after all the serious difficulties and uncertainties she had faced, that might have felt like a loss. What was more, Johanna had projected her own experiences on to Maria, leaving little room for her sister's true feelings. Lena therefore decided to draw a cross over the line between the two sisters.

Maria had never really had any ties to Martin. To her, he had been just one of many teenagers and young adults within the church, and Maria had only begun arguing with him after she found out what her parents had in mind. Lena rubbed out the arrow between them and drew a new, fainter line with a gap halfway along.

Lars Weissdorn had tried to protect Maria from her classmates' bullying and seemed to be one of the few people who knew that Maria was stronger than she appeared. But he hadn't been someone she could confide her inner conflicts to. Lena drew a dotted line between the two of them.

Maria had trusted Eva Braasch and told her about her problems at home, as well as how she was bullied by the boys in her class and blanked by the girls. Her teacher had become a substitute mother figure to her – but at the crucial moment she had refused to help her. Had Maria told Frau Braasch about the rape – or at least hinted at it – and then been disappointed when Eva kept her at arm's length? Did she interpret that as a rejection? Lena drew a thick cross over the line connecting them both.

Next, Lena's eyes fell on Lisa Behrens, who had moved further and further away from Maria as Lena worked on her diagram. Maria must have been disappointed by Lisa – so disappointed that she may not have had any qualms about blackmailing her over her grandmother's illness. Had Maria found out that Lisa had betrayed her in some way? Perhaps because Lisa was Martin's informant? Lena added three crosses to the line between Maria and Lisa.

When Lena stepped back and looked at her relationship diagram, she suddenly realised that Maria had been completely alone. Lena returned to the whiteboard and added one final, unnamed person, who was positioned a long way away from Maria but was connected to her by a clear line. Maria had chatted with this unknown person online, unburdening herself and growing ever closer to them as the people she trusted on the island drifted away from her. She had projected all her love and affection on to this person – had trusted them and viewed them as her saviour. Could that be what had happened? Had the virtual world become increasingly real to Maria? Could she even have been in love with this stranger on the Internet?

Lena went through all her notes again before comparing the photos of Martin Reimers' shoes with the footprints found on the scene – yet she couldn't find a match.

After that, she looked up the website of the German Red Cross and found a phone number, which she called. A few minutes later, she had confirmation that Martin Reimers had completed an assistant paramedic's training course. She made an official note and added it to the file.

Eventually, her eyes wandered back to the web of relationships on the whiteboard. She was particularly struck by the large gap between Maria and Lisa, as well as the three crosses on the line between them. Lena got up and fetched herself a coffee from the machine. Was Lisa the key to the puzzle? Might she even have been involved in Maria's death?

Lena baulked at the idea that the girl might be a suspect – and yet she had a motive, as well as the means. Lisa was terrified of anyone finding out about her grandmother's illness. You could find a knife in any household, and date-rape drugs could be ordered online. Had she followed Maria to the beach, struck up a conversation with her friend, offered her something to drink and then murdered her?

Eva Braasch had a motive too, for that matter. Lena underlined Lisa's and Eva's names with a red marker pen, but when she got to Martin Reimers, she hesitated. Initially she decided against highlighting his name, but in the end she drew a faint red line beneath it after all. And then there was this mysterious unknown person who – if they really existed and had visited the island – might have been in closer contact with Maria than anyone else. They too received a red mark.

However Lena looked at it, it was obvious that Lisa Behrens' role in all this was unclear at best. Yet there was little point in pressuring her again, like in their last interview. Besides, they'd been sailing close to the wind when they interviewed the girl unaccompanied by her parents or a lawyer. Lena pondered what Lisa might have been most worried about. She certainly wouldn't have wanted her mother or father there during the interview. On a spontaneous hunch, Lena reached for the phone on her desk, looked up Lisa's parents on the list they had obtained from the school and dialled their number.

'Behrens,' answered a male voice.

'This is Lena Lorenzen from CID Kiel. I'm sure you've already heard about Maria Logener's death?'

'Yes, of course. We're friends of the family.'

'Are you Lisa's father?'

'That I am. What can I do for you?'

'Is your daughter still on Amrum?'

'No, she's on her way to my mother's. She's probably there already, in fact.'

'Did Lisa tell you that we spoke to her?'

'I'm aware of that, yes.'

'I'm afraid I'll need to ask you or your wife to come to Föhr early tomorrow morning. We need to question Lisa again.'

'Question her? What do you mean by that? It sounds as though . . .' Lisa's father stopped mid-sentence.

'Because she's only fifteen years old, we'll need one of her parents to be present for the interview. Is there any chance you could come tomorrow morning?' When Lena received no reply, she asked, 'Are you still there, Herr Behrens?'

'Yes, of course. I . . . I'll need to discuss it with my wife – but we'll certainly come if you need us. What does Lisa stand accused of?'

'The first ferry gets here at around eight in the morning. Would that be doable for you? Perhaps you could pick Lisa up and bring her to the police station. It's right on the harbour.'

'I know.'

'In that case I'll expect you around eight-thirty. Don't worry if you're a few minutes late. Will you let your daughter know?'

'Yes . . . I'll call her . . . right away.'

'Thank you very much, Herr Behrens. I'll see you tomorrow then.' Lena hung up before he could ask any more questions. At almost the same moment, her mobile phone rang. She glanced at the display, gave a quiet groan and picked up. 'Good evening, Detective Superintendent.'

'Are you absolutely certain?' Warnke didn't beat around the bush.

'I assume you're referring to the manhunt for Martin Reimers.'

'What else would I be talking about?'

'We found traces of his DNA on the victim's clothing, and a witness has described seeing a man matching Martin's description arguing with Maria shortly before her death. He's also had medical training and is evidently on the run. What would you have done in my shoes?'

'All right. Have you told the chief prosecutor's office?'

'Of course. I arranged everything with Dr Wolf.'

'You know what I think: if this young man really is the killer, he needs to face the full force of the law. We aren't talking about a minor offence here. But if there's any doubt whatsoever . . .'

'We need to speak with him urgently – there's no way around that. Of course, I'm continuing the investigation in the meantime.' She glanced over at her diagram. 'There are still plenty of other leads.'

'I wouldn't have expected anything else from you. But be careful – you know how quickly the mood can shift in a small community like Föhr.'

'I'll do my very best, Detective Superintendent.'

'Good,' he replied, before bidding her farewell.

Lena put her phone on the desk and suddenly realised how exhausted she was. Her back was aching, her eyes burning, her stomach growling. When was the last time she'd eaten anything? On a whim, she gave Ben a call and asked him which restaurant they should meet at.

27

'Are you sure we shouldn't order some wine?' asked Ben.

They had been sitting for the past hour inside a cosy fish restaurant in Wyk. The starter – an avocado and salmon tartare – had been superb, and they were now waiting for their mains.

At the very start of the meal, Lena had insisted that they both avoid alcohol. 'Let's do without tonight,' she said with a smile.

'Trying to keep a clear head?'

She grinned. 'Maybe.'

Ben gave a shrug and raised his wine glass, which was full of mineral water. 'Then I'll have to make do with this. To our friendship!'

They laughed as they clinked their glasses together. The moment Lena had stepped into the restaurant, she had felt the weight of the investigation fall from her shoulders. Ben had given an enthusiastic account of a trip he had taken across Canada as a younger man and they had both roared with laughter as Lena shared anecdotes from her training. Ben seemed to feel good in her presence too. For the first time since his arrival on the island, a spark had returned to his eyes, replacing his often morose expression.

The waiter served their meals. Ben had insisted that Lena choose for both of them. She'd opted for grilled bream with fennel and was excited to find out how the combination would taste.

'It certainly looks good,' said Ben, studying the arrangement on his plate. '*Guten Appetit.*'

They ate in silence, only occasionally looking up to praise the food or pour themselves some more mineral water. Eventually, Ben laid his cutlery down on the plate and leaned back in satisfaction. 'Good choice,' he said.

'It was you who picked the restaurant,' she said, returning the compliment.

The waiter reappeared at the table and asked if everything had been to their satisfaction. When Lena nodded, he took away their empty plates and returned with the dessert menu.

'Would you like anything else?' asked Lena.

'How about a lemon sorbet? Followed by a nice espresso.'

'Why not?'

Ben placed the order. 'Well, it's been a wonderful evening.'

'So it has. Thanks for inviting me.'

'You're welcome,' he said with a serious expression.

Lena couldn't help but laugh. 'All right, enough with the formalities now.'

Ben laughed along with her. 'OK, let me rephrase it: that was a fucking awesome meal with one of my favourite friends.'

'Now that I can agree with. We'll have to do it again sometime. Maybe in Flensburg? Or do you ever visit our beautiful state capital?'

'That's the first two dinners sorted. First Flensburg, then Kiel. We can arrange the third one halfway between the two. How about Schleswig? It's almost as nice as Flensburg.'

'Don't get ahead of yourself, young man,' answered Lena with a grin. 'We can definitely put Flensburg in the diary for now, though.'

'Perfect. I guess weekends won't be any good for you, but I don't work nights very often so we should be able to find a time during the week.'

Lena was about to reply that she could meet on a Saturday or Sunday too, but then she swallowed hard, shocked at herself. For a moment, she'd forgotten who her weekends belonged to. 'Yeah, sure. We'll find a time,' she said eventually.

Her reaction didn't escape Ben, who murmured, 'I'm sorry. That was thoughtless of me.'

'It's OK,' Lena replied hurriedly – but she caught herself and quietly added, 'Actually, that's bullshit. Nothing is OK. Why should I try and convince you otherwise?'

'Forget it, Lena,' said Ben, making one last attempt.

'Didn't you once tell me I was born to be a policewoman and that you couldn't imagine me in any other job?'

'Maybe. I don't really remember.'

'But I do. And you were right. So what am I supposed to do on Amrum? Apply to be the village sheriff?'

'Then your boyfriend will just have to come to Kiel, or wherever you both decide to live. This kind of thing happens to millions of other people. You'll find a way somehow.'

'Erck would wilt like a flower in the desert if he moved. Great prospects, huh? Either he'll waste away, or I'll mutate into some mild-mannered housewife running around after a gaggle of children. All I need to do now is decide which option I prefer. Have you got any advice for me? Maybe I should just toss a coin. Yeah, that'd suit me – quick, radical, no looking back. Sometimes you just have to grab the bull by the horns.' She paused for breath and looked at Ben. 'Well, aren't you going to say anything?'

Lena put her hands over her face and sighed. What had got into her? She felt as if she had no control over what she was saying. 'Shit, I've done it again, haven't I?' she swore. 'I really didn't want to spoil the mood between us tonight.'

'What are friends for?' Ben tried to console her. 'Besides, you're right – what use is it spouting platitudes like *you'll find a way somehow*? Do you know how often I've heard that phrase myself?'

'Ten times? A hundred? Even more?'

'I've stopped counting. Not least because *I've* said it so many times too. To myself, to my wife, to my parents. I'll probably start saying it to my kids too, before long.'

'Do you think I'm being over-dramatic?' Lena asked.

'I don't know your boyfriend, but if you say he isn't a city person and that he couldn't live on the mainland, then I doubt you're wrong. Did he suggest moving to Kiel?'

'I never would have dared to suggest it myself. Yes, it was him. He's wanted us to have a serious talk about the future for a while now. And I keep putting him off. Sometimes I'm too tired, or there isn't enough time. I'm great at finding excuses. Almost as good as I am at running away.'

Ben shrugged. 'You're not wrong about the running-away part. I was on the verge of filing a missing person's report for you yesterday.'

'That's not a bad idea! Maybe it'd help me find myself. A poster in every police station in Germany, along with a photo and a description. Plus a warning not to approach me, since I'm armed.'

Ben grinned. 'Well, it's worth a try. Let's get to work on it first thing tomorrow. We'll need to come up with some good text and . . .' Ben fell silent when he noticed Lena's expression. 'Not funny?'

'Let's go,' said Lena. 'I need some fresh air. Do you want to come to the beach with me?'

'I'd love to.' He stood up. 'Let me get the bill. You go ahead.'

◆ ◆ ◆

Ben and Lena had been walking on the sand for a while when the sun began to set. The wind had also dropped.

'I ran into my father on the ferry,' she said.

'Oh!'

'All of a sudden he appeared behind me and started talking to me. He wanted to patch things up – asked me to forgive him.'

'And you rebuffed him?'

'What would you have done? I've told you what happened back then. Just because a few years have passed . . .'

'How did you feel about it?'

'I don't know. I couldn't care less. I've coped without him for half my life. He was never at home – always busy with something. Who knows how many times he cheated on my mother? And please don't tell me that he's still my father and that blood is thicker than water.'

'I wasn't going to. If you're done with him – for good, I mean – then there's nothing wrong with how you're handling it. But if you aren't sure, then I'd take him up on his offer. Maybe not right now, but later on, perhaps.'

'Did you notice how convinced Martin Reimers' father was that his son is innocent?'

'Yeah. That was pretty impressive.'

'He'd walk over burning coals for Martin. And yet he can't possibly know whether he did it or not. That made a huge impression on me.'

'It could still have been the son, though. There's plenty of evidence pointing that way at the moment.'

'You're right, it really does look that way. But does that even matter? Even if he did do it, I think his father would still stand by him.'

'I'm not so sure about that.'

'I am.'

'What made you bring this up anyway?'

'Maria's father reminded me of my own,' said Lena thoughtfully.

'And Maria reminded you of yourself?'

'I wasn't as vulnerable as Maria. I had friends, a mother who defended me, my Aunt Beke. There's no comparison, really. But I can understand the pressure Maria was exposed to.'

'So she reminds you of your situation as a teenager.'

'If you really want to put it that way, sure. Only I don't think Maria begrudged her parents. The family photos she saved on her USB stick send a clear message there.' She paused. 'I only have a handful of photos of my mother, and my father is in most of those. Should I cut him out of them? That's the sort of thing that only happens in bad films.' She sighed. 'Do you have any old photos?'

'Of course – a whole shoebox full of them. I kept meaning to put them in an album, but in the end I decided to just leave them in the box. That way, they're just as disorganised and chaotic as my parents were. They were a pair of crazy hippies.'

'You should show them to me some time. Didn't we just arrange a date in Flensburg?'

Ben grinned. 'A date? We certainly did. And if you bring your old photos, I'll let you look at mine. That seems like a fair deal.'

Lena stopped in her tracks. 'But didn't we agree to be friends?'

'I've heard of cases where it isn't always so easy to draw the line.'

'Shall we go back?' asked Lena, ignoring his comment. 'It's getting cold, and tomorrow will be a tough day.'

They walked together in silence for a while, before Lena stopped once again and asked, 'Have you never run away from anything?'

'Honestly? It depends who you ask. My wife could come up with endless examples, but speaking for myself, I never thought I was afraid of anyone or anything. As for my kids . . . I'll ask them when they're older. Maybe they're the best ones to judge.'

'But we're trained to weigh up the pros and cons, evaluate evidence and draw the right conclusions.'

'You can't be your own detective, Lena. Life isn't something you can plan. Everyone who tries it fails sooner or later. And that goes for me too.'

'So I should switch off my rational brain? Is that what you really think?'

'At least the part of your rational brain you use to solve crimes. Would you really spend all this time thinking about your father if you couldn't care less about him?'

'If I hadn't met him, I would—'

'No! Don't say any more,' Ben interrupted her. 'Let's talk about it again in a year's time. Or in two years. OK?'

'How about ten?'

'Sure, if you like.'

They had now arrived at Lena's bed and breakfast. Ben gave a small bow. 'Thanks for a wonderful evening. Sleep well.'

Lena stood in front of Ben and hesitated. For a moment, she wasn't sure what she should do.

'Hey, what's up?' he asked.

She sighed, took a step forward and kissed Ben gently on both cheeks. 'Thank you for a wonderful evening.'

28

Lisa Behrens was sitting next to her mother while her father had taken a third chair positioned slightly to one side. Johann placed the recorder on the table and pressed the start button. 'Interview with Lisa Behrens in the presence of both her parents.' Lena stated the time and date, as well as the reason why they had brought the girl in for questioning.

Lisa had undergone a dramatic transformation. Her self-confidence seemed to have vanished – her eyes flitted back and forth uncertainly, her hands moved restlessly and her back was slightly hunched as if she were carrying a heavy load. Aside from a curt greeting, she hadn't spoken a word since she arrived.

'Lisa, do you know Martin Reimers?' Lena opened the interview.

'Of course we know the Reimers family,' Lisa's father answered for her. 'We see them regularly at church events.'

'Thank you, Herr Behrens – but I was asking your daughter.'

'I know him,' Lisa eventually replied.

'When was the last time you spoke to him?'

'I've never actually talked to him that much. We know each other more by sight.'

'Maria visited your grandmother's house on the fifteenth of last month and stayed the night. Could you tell me again what happened that day?'

'Nothing much. Maria wanted to go out on her own as she was planning to meet somebody. I didn't go with her. At some point she came back.'

Lisa's father looked at his daughter in astonishment, but said nothing.

'Who did she want to meet?' Lena asked.

'I don't know.'

'Somebody from the island?'

Lisa shrugged and said nothing.

'Do you ever speak to Martin Reimers on the phone?'

'No, I don't.'

'So you didn't speak to him on the phone recently?'

Once again, Lisa fell silent. Her mother shuffled nervously on her chair and shot an uncertain glance at her husband.

'Do you know Martin Reimers' mobile number?'

Another shrug.

Lena took a piece of paper out of a folder and placed it in front of her. 'I have here the call records for your grandmother's landline. Over the last four weeks, there were five connections between that phone and Martin Reimers' mobile, each lasting several minutes. I assume we don't need to ask your *Oma* about this and that you were the one who spoke to him.'

Lisa said nothing.

'One of the calls was last Tuesday. You were on the line for three minutes and fifteen seconds. Do you remember that?'

Lena had requested the call data after her second interview with Lisa, and the information had arrived the previous day – just in the nick of time. When Lena arrived at the police station early that morning, Johann had immediately approached her holding the printout.

'Why shouldn't my daughter speak to another member of our church on the phone?' said Lisa's father, attempting to explain the calls.

Lena ignored him and continued her interview. 'Lisa, could you answer my question, please?'

'I don't remember.'

'This was less than a week ago, and you claim to have forgotten it? That doesn't sound very plausible. We have a witness who saw Martin Reimers together with your friend Maria not long after your phone conversation with him. They were arguing.'

'That's nothing to do with me.'

Lena could sense Lisa's resistance gradually crumbling away. 'Let's go back to the fifteenth of August. You were at home that afternoon?'

'Yes, I was.'

'My colleagues are going to speak to your grandmother's neighbours today, so I assume we'll find somebody who saw you there. Perhaps even together with your grandmother.'

The first tears started to trickle down Lisa's face. Lena inwardly breathed a sigh of relief. At long last, she seemed to be breaking through the wall of lies. Early that morning, under the shower, the scales had fallen from her eyes and she had realised the truth. How could she have let this girl lead her in circles for so long?

'You were the one who left the house on the fifteenth of August, not Maria. She met somebody in your room. Didn't she?'

Lisa Behrens nodded.

'Please answer out loud.'

'Yes, she did,' said Lisa tearfully.

'How long were you out of the house?'

'A few hours. Two or three. Maybe longer.'

'And Maria was asleep in bed when you came back?'

'Yes. She was out for the count.'

'Who came to see her? Martin Reimers?'

'I don't know! She didn't tell me anything – not a word. I honestly have no idea.'

'Why did you call Martin Reimers on Tuesday?'

'I was worried about *Oma*. He was threatening to tell everyone about her illness unless I told him what Maria was up to. And I also thought . . .'

'Yes? What did you think?' asked Lena when the girl fell silent.

'That he might . . . He might be able to bring Maria to her senses. Maria was threatening to . . .' Lisa tailed off.

'She was going to give away your secret too?'

'She was so angry.'

'What secret?' asked Lisa's father, who had been following the conversation in disbelief. Angrily, he added, 'What's going on here anyway? I can't believe what I'm hearing.'

By contrast, Lisa's mother didn't seem as surprised at the course of the interview as her father was. She placed her hand over his to calm him.

Lena switched off the recording device. 'I suggest that Lisa and your wife go to another room with my colleague now so he can take a statement. In the meantime I'd like to have a word with you separately.'

Before Lisa's father could reply, Lisa, her mother and Johann had already stood up and left the room.

'Herr Behrens, nothing Lisa has told us so far will have any legal consequences for her. She got into this situation partly because she wanted to protect her grandmother.'

'Protect her?' asked Lisa's father, who relaxed somewhat after hearing Lena's explanation.

'Your mother is evidently unwell. All the signs suggest she's suffering from dementia. I think Lisa was terrified of anyone finding out, as that might result in her *Oma* being sent to a home and Lisa herself going back to Amrum.'

Herr Behrens gulped. 'Dementia? That's absurd. My mother might be a little scatty sometimes, but dementia?'

'I'm not a doctor, so this is only conjecture on my part. But whatever the true state of your mother's health, Lisa is certainly very alarmed by it. Maria Logener and Martin Reimers also seem to have known about it and used it against Lisa, in a manner of speaking. Lisa needs you now more than she ever has before. And so does your mother.'

Lisa's father slowly got to his feet. He still seemed to be processing what Lena had just told him.

'You can wait for Lisa and your wife in the corridor. They won't be long.'

◆　◆　◆

The two detectives from Flensburg came in on the second ferry from Dagebüll, and shortly after their arrival, Lena called them to a meeting along with Jan Ottenga and Klaas Fokke.

Lena asked Johann to give a summary of the previous day's events and he quickly updated them on the new evidence, Martin Reimers' flight and the ongoing manhunt, as well as the results from the latest interview with Lisa Behrens.

Franz Weinbach was the first to speak. 'I guess that means we have a prime suspect. How do we proceed from here?'

All eyes went to Lena, who was having difficulty concentrating on his question. After Lisa's father had left her office, she had spent a while standing by the open window and reflecting on the case. Time and again, her gaze had wandered to the relationship diagram she had drawn on the whiteboard. For Lena, it all boiled down to the question of whether Martin Reimers could be the killer.

'Lena!' Johann roused her from her thoughts.

'Things do seem to be centring on Martin Reimers, but even so, we can't give up on our other leads. Besides, I hardly think Reimers will stay on the run – if that's what he's doing – for very long. So we should use this time to push on with our investigation. We need more evidence and witness statements in order to build a case against him, or to provide us with new leads. Ben and Franz will look into where Martin Reimers was on the fifteenth of August. We need to find out if he was our unknown visitor. The second team can visit the families belonging to the church. I want to make sure Martin isn't hiding with any of them. If anyone refuses to let us in, we'll get a search warrant – but I think word has already got round that Martin's father chose to help us. Constable Fokke can visit Frau Gerdes to take a witness statement, and I assume she'll be able to identify Martin from the photo. Let's meet back here at two o'clock.'

After the group had dispersed, Johann handed a thick folder to Lena. 'This has the details of everyone matching our criteria who brought a vehicle on to the island on the fifteenth and sixteenth of August and during the forty-eight hours before Maria's death.'

'Any hits?' she said.

'In a word, no. That doesn't mean it wasn't someone on this list, mind you. But I haven't found any obvious candidates so far. I've phoned up a few of the drivers and asked them some questions. Given there were over three thousand vehicles, it was the best I could do.'

'Thanks, Johann. Did everything go all right with Lisa's statement?'

'All good. Now we just have to hope that we've finally got the whole truth and that the girl wasn't personally involved in Maria's murder somehow.'

'I've had the same thought myself. So far, she's only admitted to things that we already knew or suspected. All the same, I don't think she has enough of a motive to have actively abetted the killer. But we'll see about that once we track down Martin Reimers.'

'Do you think we'll get the rest of the results today from the DNA tests on the samples found on Maria's body?' Johann asked.

'If not today, then tomorrow.'

'You don't seem quite convinced by the current direction of our investigation.'

'You saw Martin Reimers for yourself. Is he really capable of such a brutal and premeditated crime?'

'You have more experience than I do with the psychology of murderers. Don't they say that almost anyone could commit murder under the right circumstances?'

'A crime of passion? Sure, that's a possibility. On the other hand, we don't know how much pressure he was under. If he really did rape Maria, it would have been crucial for him to conceal the crime – which is why that's the key question for me. Did he assault her?'

'He isn't exactly a smooth operator,' Johann considered. 'I doubt the girls would have been chasing after him.'

'If that was motive enough for rape, then hardly any woman in this country could call herself safe. Of course, he might have serious psychological problems that we can't even guess at right now.'

'Which is why we need to track him down urgently. He can't have just vanished into thin air. But anyway, I'm going back to my paperwork. It sounds like you need me to get cracking on that.'

'Yes, please,' said Lena. 'As for me, I'm debating whether I should go back to see the Logeners. Strictly speaking, Maria's father ought to have an interest in Reimers being found quickly. And he knows Martin well.'

'You're the boss. But I doubt you'll get anywhere.' Johann opened his laptop and started drafting a report about the previous day's events.

Lena grabbed her car key and left the police station. As she made her way to the Logeners, she forced herself to push all thoughts of the case to one side; yet she didn't want to be reminded of last night either – and not because she felt guilty at having betrayed Erck, but because she was scared to acknowledge why she didn't feel any guilt at all.

Walther Logener opened the door. He looked heartbroken – dark rings around his eyes, sunken cheeks, unkempt hair.

'What do you want from us now?'

'I need your help.'

'For what? To put an innocent man behind bars? I won't help you do that. I've known Martin since he was a baby. He would never have done anything to Maria.'

'Then help me prove it. Right now, all the evidence is against him – and I'm not just talking about the fact he's run away.'

'Me, help you! That's a joke. You were suspicious of my brethren from the word go – you just needed someone to take the blame. And you expect me to help you?'

'I'm not convinced that Martin is the culprit either. But I won't be able to prove it unless I find the real killer,' said Lena.

'Why should I believe you?'

'Because you're a good judge of character and a man of faith.'

Walther Logener glowered at her. 'Are you making fun of me?'

'I've told you before that I don't have any prejudices against you. I can only repeat that now – along with the fact that I'm here because I need your help.'

After what felt like an eternity, he stepped aside and let Lena into the house. When they reached the kitchen, he offered her a seat. Rosa Logener was standing by the cooker.

'Good morning, Frau Lorenzen,' she said. When Lena returned the greeting, Maria's mother smiled back at her, despite her obvious exhaustion and grief. She sat down with them at the table without waiting for her husband's permission.

Walther Logener cleared his throat. 'What do you want to know?'

'Tell me about Martin Reimers. You work with him. What kind of person is he?'

'Martin is a good man and a devout Christian,' he began. 'I can absolutely rely on him whenever we work together. He's steadfast – he doesn't complain when things get complicated or take longer than planned.'

'Why doesn't he have any formal training?'

'It's not so easy to get that here on the island. But he's only working with me as a stopgap. He's looking for an apprenticeship.'

'Martin didn't have an easy time at school,' said Rosa Logener, without looking at her husband. 'He had a lot of trouble with spelling and grammar. But that doesn't alter the fact that he's a smart and level-headed young man. He never would have harmed a hair on Maria's head.'

'Our religion prohibits violence,' explained Walther Logener.

'That's not what your daughter Johanna told me.'

He bristled with fury and was about to reply when his wife put her hand on his shoulder in a warning gesture. He took a deep breath and leaned back in his chair.

'Johanna,' Rosa Logener began, 'has broken off all contact with us. She keeps accusing us of hitting her when she was a child. We've taken the blame for failing to keep her in the family. That's only right. And my husband did lash out once. I don't want to make any excuses for that; it happened, and it shouldn't have. For us, love stands at the heart of our existence – there's no place for violence. Walther is still tormented by that one moment many years ago when he couldn't control himself. Johanna has a different view of her life with us, and that hurts us very deeply, but we have to accept that she doesn't want to be our daughter any more and has abandoned the way of the Lord. It was her decision, and we pray for her every day.'

Walther Logener had been listening to his wife's words with his head lowered, but now he looked up and nodded. 'Martin has never behaved violently towards anyone in his whole life. He's the most peaceful person I know.'

'When did Maria find out that you wanted her to marry Martin?'

He lowered his eyes. 'We didn't want to tell her until she turned sixteen.'

'Did Martin broach the subject with Maria?'

'He wouldn't have brought it up himself,' said Rosa Logener. 'Maybe she heard me discussing it with my husband.'

'Martin Reimers confirmed to me that he spoke to Maria about their shared future, but he didn't want to go into any detail,' Lena explained. Maria's parents looked aghast.

'He shouldn't have done that!' Walther Logener exclaimed indignantly, but his wife held him back once more.

'Martin was in love with Maria,' she eventually explained. 'He idolised her. You could see it in his eyes. He worried about her. Whenever he was here, he would always ask me about her – how she was getting on. He thought the world of her.'

'What would have happened if Maria had rejected him?'

'There's no marriage without love,' Rosa Logener replied. 'Maria liked Martin, I'm certain of that.'

'And what if Maria told him in no uncertain terms that she couldn't see any future with him?'

'Martin would have accepted that. But he would have waited for her all the same. Love isn't something you can switch off just because it isn't reciprocated. It's there and it never goes away.'

29

Back in the office, Lena turned her attention to Johann's review of the CCTV footage. He had done exceptionally thorough work, conducting background checks on every vehicle owner who had used the ferry during both the periods in question. The majority of them were island residents who had been visiting the mainland, while a second set consisted of businesspeople, all of whom Johann had managed to contact by phone. The third group were holiday-home owners who visited the island regularly. That left just five vehicles, whose owners Johann had spoken to and ruled out as suspects. Lena went through them each in turn and came to the same conclusion.

The second list was limited to people who had only come to Föhr during one of the periods relevant to the case, and contained over two hundred vehicles that matched the investigators' criteria. Johann had cross-referenced the vehicle owners against the records held by the island's tourist board and ruled out all holidaymakers who had remained on Föhr for longer than five days. The remaining twenty vehicle owners were listed separately.

Lena crossed five people off the list who were over seventy years old. Then she went through the other fifteen names one by one. They had each come from different towns and cities across Germany, aside from two, who were based in Hamburg, and two others in Kiel. Lena decided to focus on these two pairs first and called up one of the Hamburg residents.

'Klaus Meier,' she heard somebody say.

'This is Detective Inspector Lorenzen from CID Kiel. I believe one of my colleagues has already called you to ask about your visit to Föhr.'

'That's right.'

'Were you on holiday there?'

The man hesitated for a moment. 'To be quite honest, I don't understand why this is any business of the police. I was there on a personal visit.'

'How long for?'

'Two days.'

'Where did you stay?'

'With a friend.'

'Herr Meier, I understand why you might feel uncomfortable, but you've come to our attention – or rather your vehicle has – during the course of an investigation. We need to establish what you were doing on the island.'

'I just told you I was there for personal reasons.'

'All right. In that case, I'm afraid we'll have to go down the official route. At some point in the next few days you'll receive a written summons from the chief prosecutor calling you to an interview, which I expect will take place in Hamburg.'

'Is that really necessary?' came the indignant reply.

'Or we can settle this right now over the phone if you just tell me where you were staying.'

She heard a quiet sigh. 'This needs to stay between us, though.'

'Certainly, provided it's not relevant to our investigation.'

'I've met a woman – but she's married, and . . . you get the picture. Her husband was away for a few days so we took the opportunity to meet on Föhr.'

'I'll need her name and phone number.'

'This will stay between us, won't it?'

'Like I said, if—'

'Fine,' he cut her off in an exasperated tone, before giving her the information she wanted. A few minutes later, Lena obtained confirmation from the woman in question that Klaus Meier had stayed with her for his entire visit to Föhr.

Next, she phoned the other Hamburg resident, crossing him off the list too after a brief conversation.

The remaining pair of vehicle owners were two men from Kiel aged twenty-three and twenty-five respectively. She called the first of them and introduced herself.

'Really? Again? Can somebody tell me what this nonsense is all about? Are we living in a police state now?' said Linus Fegler in an outraged voice.

'Your vehicle has come to our attention during the course of an investigation. I believe you took the ferry from Dagebüll on Monday the fifteenth of August?'

'And what if I did? I've told you all this already. Was that not enough?'

'Were you visiting Amrum for a holiday?' Lena asked, and then caught herself. What made her say Amrum? She was thinking too much about her personal life. Just as she was about to correct herself and say 'Föhr', the young man answered, 'That's right. Was there anything else?'

Lena gave a start. Had Linus Fegler forgotten which island he was on after only three weeks? Or had she stumbled on something here? 'So you took the ferry from Dagebüll to Wittdün on Amrum?'

'Is that a crime these days?'

'How long were you on Amrum for?'

'I came back the next day. But I've had enough of this. Please don't contact me again.' Linus Fegler hung up without saying another word.

Lena entered his name into the system and compared his data with the other Kiel resident on the list. The two men lived in different parts of the city – but when she dug deeper into their address records, her breath caught. Linus Fegler and Arne Wagner – the second vehicle owner from Kiel – had spent a year at the same address.

A call to the nearest police station in Kiel revealed that the building they'd been living in contained four rental apartments whose occupants hadn't had any run-ins with the law. Lena double-checked Johann's folder and saw that he'd spoken to Arne Wagner over the phone. An apparent outdoor enthusiast, Wagner had arrived on Föhr on 6 September and spent the night wild camping in the nature reserve on the north coast.

Johann wandered into the office with a mug in his hand and instantly sensed that something important must have happened. 'What's up?'

'Do you remember a Linus Fegler from Kiel?'

'Yeah – quite an unpleasant guy. I put two question marks next to his name. At first he didn't want to tell me where he stayed, but when I applied some pressure he said he slept in his car.'

'And what was he doing on Föhr?'

'Apparently, he'd had a row with his girlfriend in Kiel and wanted to get away for a few days – but he couldn't find any accommodation on the island and went back on the first ferry the next day.'

Lena told him how she'd mixed up the two islands and subsequently discovered that Fegler and Arne Wagner had been registered at the same address. Johann whistled. 'Shit, I missed that.'

'I wouldn't have dug any deeper either if he hadn't let the cat out of the bag. It says here that you spoke to Arne Wagner, who also lives in Kiel. What did you think of him? Could there be some connection between the two men?'

Johann joined her at the desk and read through the entry in his folder. 'Right, I remember now. Wagner was cooperative and didn't seem suspicious. Wild camping is against the rules, but he was very apologetic about it and I figured we have bigger fish to fry. And since he was only on Föhr once . . .' Johann stopped short. 'Wait, a connection? Do you think this Fegler wasn't actually driving his car and lent it to Wagner instead? So Wagner came once in his own car and another time in Fegler's?'

'It's certainly a possibility. And it would also explain why Wagner didn't make it on to your shortlist of suspects. It's worth a try, anyway. Can you look them both up on the footage?'

Johann leapt to his feet. 'Sure. Give me twenty minutes.'

Lena used the time to do some more background research on Arne Wagner. He was currently training to be a teacher, with a focus on religious studies and biology. Before that, he had grown up in Bavaria, moving to the north of Germany three years ago. His parents had both died in a car accident, after which he'd been brought up by his mother's half-brother.

'Did you find them, Johann?' Lena asked as she entered the incident room.

'Yep.' He pointed at the monitor. 'This is Arne Wagner's car arriving on the sixth of September.' The registration number was clearly legible, but the person inside the car was nothing more than a vague blur. 'That could be anyone. Male, short hair, average height.'

He switched to a different window and played another video showing Fegler's car arriving on 15 August. This time, the sun briefly shone directly on to the windscreen, offering a glimpse of the driver.

'Stop!' Lena called. 'Can you print that out?'

Johann nodded, entered a few keyboard shortcuts and waited for the sheet of paper to emerge from the printer.

'Let's compare this photo with Fegler's passport,' Lena suggested. Johann had already opened the database and a few seconds later, a photo of a young man appeared on screen.

'Is that him?' Johann asked.

'No. Look at his nose and the shape of the head. There are similarities, but these are two different people.'

'What now?' asked Johann, who was suddenly on the alert. 'This really could be our unknown visitor. Maria's chat partner and . . .' The thought took his breath away.

'Do we have a photo of Arne Wagner too?'

Johann entered his name on the database. Wagner had applied for a new ID card only a year ago and the photo on it was of the person sitting inside Linus Fegler's car on 15 August.

'That's a match,' Johann cried. 'This is unbelievable! What do we do now?'

'Keep calm,' answered Lena, her hands tingling. 'There might be a harmless explanation for all this. I had someone on the phone just now who was having an affair with a woman here on the island.'

'I doubt that. We need to get to Kiel. Right now.'

Lena glanced at the clock. It was nearly one o'clock. 'The ferry's just left and the next one won't get here for another hour and a half. If we catch that, we'll be on the mainland at four o'clock and in Kiel at five. OK. Let's go to the bed and breakfast, pack our bags and come back here for the meeting.'

◆ ◆ ◆

The meeting with their colleagues had been brief. Frau Gerdes had confirmed that the man she'd seen arguing with Maria was Martin Reimers and the families of the Brethren had allowed the officers to search their homes – but Reimers himself was still nowhere to be found.

Now, despite the stiff breeze, Lena and Johann stood at the railing of the ferry to the mainland and watched the port recede into the distance.

'It's insane!' said Johann. 'This guy came within an inch of slipping through our fingers.'

'Steady, Johann,' said Lena, trying for a second time to hold her young colleague's eagerness in check. She knew they couldn't get too excited at this stage of their investigation. If Arne Wagner really was connected to Maria's death, he'd have gone about things very methodically and probably wouldn't have left much evidence, or would have removed it after committing the crime. They almost certainly wouldn't find anything on his computer, and the clothes he had worn that day on Föhr – which might have traces of Maria's DNA on them – were probably now lying on a rubbish tip in Kiel or in a charity collection box. 'We should make it to the station around five o'clock. I've asked my CID colleagues to bring Wagner in for questioning.' She looked at her watch. 'An hour or two's wait in the interrogation room ought to do him some good.'

'How are we going to tackle this? Can I be the bad cop again?'

'If he's our man, he won't fall for that. Let's wait and see what happens. This could be a long night.'

'That's fine. I'm young and in good shape.'

Lena nudged him playfully in the ribs. 'That makes me one lucky old lady.' She grinned. 'If he makes a run for it, you can chase him down. Just so we're clear on that.'

'No problem. I got my athletics badge when I was in the Scouts. Or was it athletics plus? Either way . . .'

Lena laughed. 'Stop it!'

'Fine,' Johann replied with mock seriousness. 'If you don't want to hear about the achievements of your distinguished colleague, then I'll just have to keep my mouth shut. You're welcome.'

The detective inspector smiled and shook her head.

Johann gave a theatrical sigh. 'Why don't I get us something to drink? Coffee OK for you, boss?'

Lena nodded and he headed off, grinning as he went.

In the subsequent silence, Lena's thoughts went back to the night before – to Ben, and to herself, her hopes and fears. She'd come so close to asking Ben back to her room, and she hadn't felt the slightest pang of guilt over it. Didn't she love Erck enough to be able to resist that kind of temptation? Why was she playing with fire? Was it because she wanted to force herself into a decision? On the other hand, it might have let off some of the pressure from her relationship. What if that was the solution to her situation? An open partnership instead of a forced weekend relationship, with no brooding over the future – over marriage and kids? She remembered what her mother always used to tell her: *sometimes in life you have to make a choice.*

Just then, her phone rang. It was Beke – almost as if she could read her niece's thoughts. '*Moin*, Beke, how are you?' Lena asked.

'All good with me.' She hesitated briefly. 'You too, I hope?'

'I'm on my way to the mainland.'

'Already? I thought . . .'

'No, just for a day or two. I'm coming back afterwards.' Lena guessed that Beke was calling for a reason.

'And will you have a bit more time for me then?'

'I'll make sure of it. Family comes first.'

Beke paused for a while before she spoke again. 'Your father was here. He told me he bumped into you on the ferry.'

So that was what this was about. 'Only briefly. We don't have anything to say to each other, as you know.'

'Don't you think—?'

'No, Beke, I don't think. There's no reason for me to talk to him. None whatsoever.'

'He would so dearly love to patch things up with you. Believe me, he's changed. A lot.'

Lena could see Johann coming back towards her. 'Beke, I need to go. I'll call you as soon as I get back – I promise.'

'All right, my dear. Look after yourself.'

'Your coffee!' Johann stood smiling before her with two steaming cups in his hands. 'Any news?'

She took the cup from him. 'That was a personal call. Thanks for the coffee.'

Johann tapped his cup against hers. 'Once more unto the breach! Maybe that really is our culprit waiting for us in Kiel.'

The windowless room was less than twenty feet long and ten feet wide. A square table stood in the middle, with two chairs on one side and a third on the other. Aside from a small microphone, the table was bare. The rest of the recording equipment was next door, behind a large two-way mirror through which you could see into the interrogation room. There was a camera mounted in each of the four corners of the room, all of them pointed at the chair where Arne Wagner was sitting and waiting for the two detectives.

'He doesn't look very nervous,' said Johann.

'No, he really doesn't. Shall we go in?'

Lena carefully sized up the young man. If she saw him on the street, she wouldn't guess him to be any older than twenty. He was of medium height and slim-built, with thick mid-length brown hair, and he was leaning back in his chair with his arms folded and a bored expression on his face.

'Yeah. Why wait any longer?' Johann replied. Just as he turned away from the mirror, Lena's phone rang.

'Ben,' she said after a glance at the display. She answered the call. 'Hi Ben – we were just about to—'

'Martin Reimers has turned himself in,' he said.

'On Föhr?'

'No, he's on Amrum. He handed himself in at the station there and the marine police are currently bringing him over to us. They should be here any minute now.'

'OK. What do you suggest?'

'How long will it take you to get back here?'

Lena glanced at her watch and thought carefully. 'If there's no traffic, we should be able to catch the last ferry. But I don't think that's likely.'

'So tomorrow at the earliest? Wouldn't it be best to question Reimers as soon as he arrives? We shouldn't give him any time to compose himself and come up with a strategy. We need to take a hard line with him – the sooner, the better.'

Lena searched feverishly for a solution. If they let Wagner go again now, they would lose the element of surprise. It would take them at least another day to travel back to Kiel again. 'I'll get right back to you, Ben.'

Johann gave Lena an enquiring look as she put her phone down. She told him what had happened.

'This is a mess,' said Johann, instantly grasping the tricky situation they were in. 'Should we let Ben and Franz tackle Martin while we talk to this guy? Ben can handle it. In Flensburg, he's considered an expert when it comes to this kind of interview. It can't hurt, anyway. Worst-case scenario, he'll just soften Reimers up for when you get there tomorrow.'

Lena nodded – but she still couldn't shake the feeling that she would be making a mistake, whatever she decided. She glanced at Arne Wagner through the mirror. The young man looked untroubled at having to sit there. How long had he been waiting? Shouldn't he at least be angry that they'd left him for so long?

'Let's do the interview here, and Ben can question Reimers on Föhr.'

Lena called Ben to let him know her decision and gestured for Johann to follow her into the interrogation room.

'A little competition,' said Johann with a wink before opening the door.

30

Lena walked over to Arne Wagner and shook his hand. The young man rose to his feet and greeted her politely.

'This is my colleague, Detective Sergeant Grasmann,' said Lena, looking over at Johann. 'Please, have a seat.'

Arne Wagner slowly pulled his chair back, smiled again at Lena and sat down.

'Sorry to have kept you waiting – we had a long journey to get here. Would you like something to drink?'

'No, thank you. But I'd appreciate it if you could tell me what all this is about?'

Lena turned to Johann. 'Could you fetch us some mineral water and three glasses?'

'Certainly,' Johann replied and left the room.

'First of all, I'd like to thank you for agreeing to come in for this interview. We'll try—'

'Agreeing?' the young man interrupted her. 'The two gentlemen who came to fetch me from my apartment didn't look very willing to compromise, to put it mildly.'

'We'll try to keep it as brief as possible so you can get back home sooner. I think that's in all of our interests.'

Johann returned, handed out the glasses and poured some water for himself and for Lena. 'Please, just help yourself if you'd like some,' he said to Arne Wagner.

Wagner seemed increasingly irritated by the slow start, but he eventually nodded.

'All right,' said Lena. She pressed the red record button on her side of the table and began with the formalities, stating the names of the interviewee and the detectives, as well as the date and time. Then she asked her first question. 'Herr Wagner, I believe you took the car ferry from Dagebüll to Wyk auf Föhr on the sixth of September. Is that correct?'

'Absolutely – but one of your colleagues already asked me that over the phone.'

'Had you been to Föhr before?'

'Yes, I'm familiar with the island, if that's what you mean.'

'Did you go there on holiday?'

'Well, as a student, I can't afford to spend much time there. But it's nice to get away once in a while – feel the North Sea breeze on your face and clear your head.'

'Do you live alone?'

'In my apartment? Yes.'

'Do you have a partner?'

Arne Wagner grinned. 'Partner – that almost sounds like you're asking if I'm married. Girlfriend would probably be a better word for it. Though I'm single at the moment.'

Lena's phone buzzed and a message from Ben appeared on the screen. *We're starting now. He wants to talk.*

'So you were on Föhr last week, and you say you were a frequent visitor before that.'

'It's a lovely island. And easy to get to from Kiel.'

'Do you remember the last time you visited before the sixth of September?'

Arne Wagner shrugged. 'I'd have to think about that. I'm under a lot of stress at the moment with exams, you should know. That makes it easy to forget things.'

'Take your time.'

'It must have been a while ago, but I can't give you the exact date. Sorry. I may still have the ferry ticket at home. Though I don't tend to keep hold of things like that. I might have taken some photos too – the files all come with a date and time stamp.'

'Is photography a hobby of yours?'

'Yes. I study biology, so there's an obvious connection there.'

'And you've also practised your hobby on Föhr?'

'Sure – I always take a few pictures whenever I'm there. The flora and fauna on the island are very interesting. Especially by the Wadden Sea. Yeah, I like taking photos.'

Johann spoke up. 'I briefly considered studying biology myself when I finished my *Abitur* – not to train as a teacher, but as a degree in its own right. I changed my mind in the end, though.'

'Why?' asked Arne Wagner, seeming genuinely interested for the first time.

'I can't stand the sight of blood,' Johann replied. 'And when I heard you have to dissect animals . . .'

'That's only a tiny part of it. Ninety per cent of biology is about the plant world,' he said. 'You don't see much blood there. I originally considered studying medicine, but in the end my grades weren't good enough. Oh well – I'm very happy with my course.'

'Medicine,' said Lena. 'That's interesting. Did you do any preparatory study for that?'

'No – that was also part of the problem. I did a basic paramedic training course back when I used to volunteer with the fire brigade, but not one that was officially recognised. Never mind, though. Things worked out fine as they are.'

'You just said you don't remember when you were last on Föhr, but surely you must have a rough idea. Was it this summer?'

'Like I said – I'm sorry, but I'd have to check at home. I really can't remember exactly.' His eyes went to a corner of the room. 'Is this conversation being filmed? I thought that only happened in the movies.'

Lena showed him the printout from the CCTV footage.

'Oh, did I get caught by a speed camera? I didn't even notice.'

'Do you know Linus Fegler?'

'We're good friends. Why do you ask?'

'This is a picture of you driving his car off the ferry in Wyk. Do you remember now?'

'Ah, yes. That's right. I took a day trip to the island a few weeks ago. Now that you mention it . . .'

'Why were you driving Linus's car?'

'My own car unexpectedly had to go into the garage just before I set off and I couldn't reschedule my visit to Föhr, what with my exams. Linus knew I'd been looking forward to the trip so he was kind enough to lend me his car for a couple of days.'

'What did you do on Föhr?'

'Nothing much. I set off on the spur of the moment, hoping I would find a bed in a hostel or something, but in the end I slept in the car and went back on the first ferry.'

'Why would Linus Fegler tell us the same story, but claim that he was the one driving the car?'

For the first time in the interview, Arne Wagner's eyelids twitched nervously. He took his time replying, but eventually drew a deep breath and said, 'Because I asked him to.'

'Why?'

'A little mishap, so to speak. Nothing serious. I bumped into somebody else's car while parking, and instead of stopping and dealing with it, I took off. Of course that was very stupid of me. Eventually, I got scared someone might have seen me and that I might be prosecuted. I'm training to be a religious studies teacher, after all. I was just afraid it might come back to haunt me later on. That's why I asked Linus . . . He wouldn't be all that bothered if he had to go to court.'

'OK,' said Lena. 'We're going to take a break here.' She stated the time, pressed the red button and stood up. Johann followed her.

'He's a tough nut, isn't he?' he said as they stood by the mirror in the next room. 'Or did he really have nothing to do with it?'

'He's had plenty of time to come up with excuses since you first called him.'

'I don't have as much experience with interrogations as you do, but to be frank, he seems honest to me. Arrogant and self-righteous, sure, but that isn't a crime. If he's lying to us, he's an unbelievably good actor.'

'It's all a matter of preparation. If you repeat a version of events to yourself often enough, pepper it with half-truths and have a knack for repressing things, you can make it work.' Lena pulled her phone out of her pocket. 'I'm going to ask what's happening on Föhr.'

Before she could do so, her phone rang. It was Ben. 'How's it going at your end?'

'Slowly, very slowly,' said Lena.

'I'm afraid I can't give you a confession yet either. Reimers is disputing everything. We've just confronted him with the witness statement and the DNA analysis. That was a shock to him. He's keeping quiet for now, but he hasn't asked for a lawyer yet. I'm just leaving him to stew for a bit and then we'll carry on.'

'What do you think?'

'I reckon he did it. He realised on Amrum that he didn't stand a chance as a fugitive and now he's trying to find another way out of it.'

'Why did he run away?'

'He was afraid we were going to frame him for something. A weak excuse, in my view. He was clearly planning to head for the mainland, only he got cold feet as he thought we might be waiting for him in Dagebüll. So he got off the ferry and jumped on the one heading to Amrum. More fool him.'

'Did he say where he'd been staying?'

'He wanted to visit an old schoolfriend, but he was on holiday. So then he crept into a beach hut somewhere. They're those shacks you find all over the place out there, right? The ones made of flotsam and jetsam?'

'Pretty much,' said Lena. 'I'll explain them to you another time. What's your plan now?'

'He's sitting in there looking like a picture of misery and I don't think he'll hold out for much longer. I'll get the truth out of him soon enough. He doesn't stand a chance.'

'Ben, please be careful. A false—'

'Sure, boss,' he cut her off. 'Everything by the book.'

Lena briefly debated whether she ought to continue the interview with Reimers herself the following day, but decided against it. Ben was an experienced policeman and he would make the right decisions. 'OK, we're going to head back in now. If Martin Reimers confesses, I want to be the first to know.'

'Understood,' said Ben, and hung up.

'The others haven't got anywhere either?' asked Johann as Lena put her phone away.

'No, but Ben feels sure he's the killer.'

'To be honest with you, my money's on Reimers too. But fine – what's our next step?'

Lena rubbed her neck and sighed. 'We'll just have to improvise. He must have a weak point somewhere.'

'Assuming he actually did it . . .'

Back in the interrogation room, Lena switched the microphone on and went through the formalities again. 'Herr Wagner, nobody has come forward to the police on Föhr to report any damage to their vehicle from a hit-and-run driver. What did the car you bumped into look like?'

'Black, it was black. I remember that. A saloon. Not exactly brand new. It might have been a Volkswagen. Or maybe an Audi. I panicked and drove off quickly.'

She placed a small plastic tube on the table. 'We'll need to take a DNA sample.' Slowly, she pulled the cotton-wool bud out of the tube. 'It's very straightforward – I'm sure you've already seen it on TV.'

'Oh come on!' he cried, visibly outraged. 'Why should I have to give a DNA sample just because of a minor hit-and-run incident, which I've just admitted to anyway?'

Lena slid the cotton-wool bud back into the tube. 'This isn't about a hit-and-run incident.' She took a photo of Maria Logener out of her stack of papers and pushed it across the table towards him. 'It's about this young woman.'

Wagner cast a quick glance at the photo. 'Interesting. But I don't know this girl.' One of the sleeves of his sweater had ridden up slightly, and he pulled it back down. 'Can I go now?'

'Tell me where you grew up after your parents died.'

'Sorry, what? Why should I do that? I don't see any reason at all for us to discuss my childhood.'

'Did their deaths have something to do with your choice of degree course?'

Arne Wagner was visibly thrown by the quick change of subject and he hesitated at first, before answering, 'I've always been interested in the natural world, if that's what you mean.'

'And religion too? Your adoptive parents were members of a very conservative religious community and—'

'How do you know that?' he asked her sharply.

Lena inwardly breathed a sigh of relief. Her little feint had been purely speculative, but it had hit home. Now she had a clear line of attack. 'It had a significant impact on you – for better and for worse.'

'That's none of your fucking business,' he snarled at Lena, leaning across the table.

Johann leapt to his feet. 'Sit back down! Right now!'

Slowly, Arne Wagner sank back on to his chair.

'Your adoptive father used to punish you when you were disobedient,' said Lena, sounding him out intuitively. 'He'd lock you up. Beat you. Humiliate you.'

Arne Wagner stared at her furiously but said nothing.

She pushed the photo back towards him. 'How long have you known Maria?'

'I don't know a Maria,' he hissed quietly.

Lena pressed the red button, stood up and gestured to Johann. They left the room wordlessly.

'Shouldn't we have kept up the pressure?' asked Johann bemusedly. 'Just look at the way he's sitting there.' He pointed to the young man behind the mirror; his demeanour had completely transformed since the start of the interview. His shoulders sagged, his body was hunched forwards slightly and sunk in on itself, and his arms dangled awkwardly at his sides. 'A few more minutes and he'd have cracked.'

'No, he would have completely shut down and not said another word.'

'What makes you think that?'

'He's reverted to his childhood behaviour. Shouting in protest, losing his temper, acting all sheepish – and the next step is silent sulking.'

'How long should we wait?'

'Until he pulls himself together.' As she spoke, Arne Wagner sat up slightly, placed his hands on the table and took a deep breath. 'Ten minutes, I reckon.'

'I'll fetch us some coffee.'

'Head right down the hall and turn left along the corridor. You can't miss it. Mine's a latte, please.'

Johann nodded and disappeared. Lena's phone started buzzing. When she saw Luise's number on the display, she picked up. 'Hey, Lena. How are things?'

'I'm in Kiel – we're currently interviewing a suspect.'

'OK, then I'll be brief. The DNA results are in. First off, we've found more traces of the suspect with the black hair.'

'Martin Reimers.'

'That's the one. But we also found some samples belonging to another person. Hopefully that'll be of some help to you.'

'You've called at just the right time. Thanks, Luise.'

'Glad to hear it. Keep in touch.'

Just as Lena was about to put her phone away, a message came in from Ben. *Can I call you?*

Lena dialled his number.

'Wouldn't you know it,' said Ben by way of greeting. 'He's confessed!' His voice sounded euphoric. 'We've taken a break for now, since he's weeping hysterically, but as soon as he's calmed down a little we'll get down to details.'

'Are you sure?'

'That he confessed?' Ben asked with a snide undertone. 'Yeah, I'd say he did.'

'Ben! You've seen enough false confessions in your time. I need to know if—'

'OK, OK. I've already thought of that. Franz is sending the video to Johann as we speak, so you can watch it for yourself. All right?'

'Thanks, Ben. I'll call you back if I have any news.'

She let Johann know and he immediately switched on his laptop to download the email and open the video.

They stared at the screen together. The camera was focused on Martin Reimers, who was sitting at the table with his head lowered. Ben asked him a question and he said nothing in response.

'Let's recap,' they heard Ben's energetic voice say. 'You were in love with Maria and wanted to marry her. Have I got that right?'

Martin Reimers nodded.

'But Maria had absolutely no intention of starting anything with you. Right?'

Reimers nodded once more, then gave a start when a loud bang suddenly filled the room. Ben must have struck the table with the palm of his hand. 'Look at me when I'm talking to you!' he thundered.

Martin Reimers slowly lifted his head.

'You lay in wait for Maria on the evening of Tuesday the sixth of September and had a shouting match with her. We have a witness who saw it happen. Do you understand that? A woman was watching nearby while you were yelling at Maria. What were you arguing about?'

'I . . . I only wanted . . . just to . . . talk to her,' he stammered.

'*Talking* – is that what they call it nowadays?' Ben roared across the room. 'And then what did you do? I'll tell you what you did: you followed her. Am I right?'

Martin Reimers shrugged.

'Am I right?' Ben bellowed at him.

A timid nod.

'Louder! I can't hear you!'

'Yes,' he eventually answered.

'So you followed her. Where did you get hold of the date-rape drugs? Online?' When Reimers didn't reply, he repeated his question even louder than before. 'Did you get the drugs online?'

Martin Reimers looked up in surprise. 'Drugs?'

'Yes, damn it! Date-rape drugs. You've heard of those!'

The young man nodded hesitantly.

'I need you to say it out loud for the record.'

'Yes,' Martin Reimers said audibly. By now, he was once again sitting with a lowered head and sunken torso.

Lena groaned. 'Fast-forward a bit.'

Johann put his hand on the mouse and dragged the slider below the video to the right.

'So you were on the beach?' they heard Ben say aggressively. 'You know the spot, don't you? Spit it out! We've found your DNA on Maria. You don't have a hope of talking your way out of this. Do you realise that?'

'It wasn't me,' said Martin Reimers softly.

'Oh, yes it was. Do you understand that your mother will never want to speak to you again? That your father despises you? Do you have any idea how much Maria's mother is suffering? Nobody from your church will take your side. You're a pariah now. It was murder! You murdered her!' Ben drew those last three words out for emphasis. They heard him stand up and saw him appear behind Martin Reimers' chair. He grabbed Reimers' left arm and wrenched it upwards, pulled his sleeve down and tapped his finger several times on the spot where Maria Logener's arteries had been sliced open. 'Multiple deep cuts. Blood – her blood was everywhere. Red all over the place. The whole beach was drenched in her blood.' He dropped Reimers' arm again and placed his hand on his shoulder. Then he leaned forward and began speaking directly into his ear. 'Blood everywhere. Do you realise what a horrible way that is to die?' Ben straightened up and slammed his fist down on the table. Reimers' whole body flinched. 'I'm going to ask you again! Did you kill her? Did you hurt Maria? Well? Out with it!'

Martin Reimers nodded.

'I need to hear it out loud,' Ben snarled at him. 'Say it!'

For a moment, there was utter silence. Eventually, Reimers raised his head and said, 'Yes. I'm to blame. Nobody else.'

Lena gestured to Johann to switch the video off.

'What on earth has got into Ben?' he said in dismay.

'I don't know. I've never seen him like that before either.'

'What now?'

Lena stood up. 'We carry on.'

'Where were we?' Lena asked, switching the microphone back on. 'Ah yes. So you took the ferry to Föhr on the sixth of September – last Tuesday.'

Arne Wagner said nothing.

'Is that correct, Herr Wagner?' Lena prompted him.

'Yes. I've told you that several times already.'

'When was the first time you spoke to Maria Logener online? Did you realise straight away that you both had similar experiences with your parents?'

'My parents died in a car accident.'

'You didn't notice at first that you were chatting with a four-teen-year-old. You couldn't have, as Maria was a very serious-minded girl.' Lena watched Arne Wagner closely as she spoke. He didn't react, even though Lena had referred to Maria using the past tense. 'When did you realise? Did Maria send you a photo?'

'I don't know what you're talking about,' he replied wearily. 'I don't know this—'

'Or did you ask her at some point? Where did she live, what did she do, how old was she?'

'I don't—'

'She was an intelligent and sensitive young girl. Did you know that you meant a lot to her? More than that – she was in love with you. Did you know that?'

Arne Wagner swallowed heavily.

'Maria was in a difficult situation – her parents, her school, her friends . . . but you know all that already. What did you think when Maria sent you the photo? She looked like an angel. Didn't she? An angel with black hair. Was that what fascinated you?'

'You don't have the faintest idea,' murmured Arne Wagner.

'When did Maria realise you'd abused her?'

He gave a scornful laugh. 'Abused.'

'Yes, abused. I'm sure you know how that feels. You trusted your adoptive parents too. That's only natural. Every child longs for warmth and security. But then? What happened then?'

'Nothing!' he replied listlessly.

'Nothing? Is that how it felt to you as a child? That there was nothing there? No love, no trust?'

He gave an almost imperceptible shrug.

'What do you think Maria felt after you raped her? The fear you felt yourself as a child? When you had to sit on your own in the cellar and reflect on your sins?'

'Leave me alone!' he cried with his last remaining strength. 'I haven't done anything.'

'We won't find anything on your computer, I suppose.'

'No. There's nothing on it.' After a while, he added, 'What would there be, anyway?'

'Did you clean your car too? And I don't mean with a cloth or a vacuum cleaner.' She registered the expression on his face. 'Did you forget that Maria was in your car? We'll find something. You study biology – you ought to know it's impossible to remove every trace. So we'll start there. I can also get a court order by tomorrow that will allow us to take a sample of your saliva. We've found plenty of DNA evidence on Maria's clothing. I think you know what that means.'

'DNA? You're lying. That's impossible.'

'Oh really? Were you wearing a decontamination suit? With a breathing mask and all the works? No? Then I think we ought to drop this little game. It's time you came clean.'

He stared at Lena with a blank expression, as if looking right through her. His face was ashen, his hands trembled, he was breathing quickly. 'It . . . it just happened,' he said quietly. 'I couldn't take her with me. She wanted to . . . reveal everything. Every last thing.'

31

When Lena phoned Ben at around midnight, she learned that Martin Reimers had refused to give any more details after making his confession. Lena informed Ben of the latest developments in Kiel and asked him to keep Martin Reimers under constant watch.

After another three hours of interrogation, Arne Wagner was placed under arrest. He had tearfully confessed to raping Maria Logener after spiking her drink with sedatives, but he swore he couldn't remember any details from that afternoon. At some point, he had fled from the Behrens' house and wandered around the island for hours before finally dozing off in a seaside car park. Personally, Lena felt Wagner had been a lot more calculating than his version of events made him sound – but ultimately, that would be for the courts to decide.

On the morning of 16 August, Wagner had taken the first ferry back to the mainland, nervous that he might be apprehended by the police at any moment – and yet the opposite had happened. Maria got back in touch with him without saying a word about his visit to Föhr. Gradually, he came to realise that she'd assumed she'd been taken ill that afternoon, and that he had undressed her and put her to bed before eventually leaving the house. The more he tried to distance himself from her online, the more urgently Maria had wanted to communicate with him. She began to change, he claimed, saying she could no longer trust anyone and that she wanted to leave the island. Yet he didn't break off contact because he was afraid she would eventually remember that he'd raped her. Finally, on the first Sunday in September, she had insisted that he drive over the following day to take her off the island. She'd told him that she couldn't just get on the ferry herself, as her father's spies were everywhere.

Arne Wagner hadn't gone to Föhr, hoping that Maria would calm down. But on the Monday and Tuesday she had ramped up the pressure, pleading with him to come and get her. In the end, he set off, but once he arrived on Föhr he was too nervous to contact her. Only on the Tuesday night did he respond to her messages appealing for help, and he drove out to meet her at their agreed location. He claimed he wanted to persuade her to go back to her parents, but she refused. In order to avoid discovery, they had parked at the bottom of the dirt track leading to the beach. During the course of their conversation, it had slowly dawned on Maria that the afternoon they'd spent at Lisa Behrens' house hadn't been as innocuous as she'd assumed. Their argument had grown more and more heated until Arne Wagner could see only one way out, so he had drugged her, led her to the beach and murdered her.

'So far, so good,' said Johann. It was the following morning. Arne Wagner had just had his first court hearing and the two detectives were sitting in Lena's car, which was parked in front of the courthouse. Wagner had been remanded in custody, his apartment had already been searched in the early hours of that morning and his car was now at CSI waiting to be examined for evidence. There was little point in questioning Wagner again until the results came in. DSU Warnke had assigned Lena two more colleagues from Kiel, who would spend the next few days investigating the information Arne Wagner had given them in order to generate evidence that would stand up in court in the event that Wagner withdrew his confession.

'I still don't understand why Maria didn't ask anyone around her for help,' Johann continued.

'She couldn't remember what happened that afternoon at the Behrens' house. That's a typical after-effect of date-rape drugs. They cause a blackout, similar to extreme alcohol consumption. Maria tried to tell Eva Braasch about her parents' plans on Tuesday evening, but her teacher was too worried about stoking rumours to listen properly. Her sister didn't have enough time for her, and Maria had probably already realised that she wouldn't respond objectively to her problems.'

'Considering what her parents are like, that's hardly a surprise, is it?' Johann muttered.

'There are reasons and motives behind everything in life – but what presumably counted here is how Maria interpreted everything. Wherever she turned, she must have felt as though the rug was being pulled out from under her. Even Johanna suddenly seemed to have grown distant, at least from Maria's perspective. Her parents let her down – especially her mother, whom Maria still had a very good relationship with. Her best friend Lisa was afraid that Maria might give away her secret about her grandmother's dementia, meaning she'd have to go back to her parents on Amrum, and Martin Reimers – who was probably genuinely worried about her – had become a stalker in her eyes.'

'And I guess all that was intensified by the sexual assault?' asked Johann.

'Exactly. Maria's rape will have played a huge role in the last few weeks of her life. The fact that she couldn't remember anything about those few hours was bad enough – but she must also have sensed that something terrible had happened. It would have turned her entire life upside down. Everything suddenly changed. She probably grew more and more distrustful of everyone and everything. I can't see any other explanation for why she would withdraw from her sister, or why her relationship with Lisa deteriorated so badly. The only way out she could see was to run away – and for that, she turned to Wagner, of all people.'

'Which proved to be a fatal mistake.'

Lena nodded. 'She went to the only person who posed a genuine threat to her. Wagner's fears that Maria would eventually remember being raped certainly weren't unjustified. In cases like these, the victim's memory often returns over the weeks or months following the assault, and Wagner's life would have blown up overnight. His studies and his career prospects as a teacher would have gone out of the window; he would have ended up with a criminal record and would almost certainly have spent time behind bars. Maria was only fourteen, after all.'

'Is Martin Reimers a free man again?'

'I've made sure of it,' said Lena. 'His father had already found a lawyer for him, who immediately announced that Martin was withdrawing his confession.'

'It's crazy. I could have sworn he had something to do with it.'

Lena shrugged. 'I had my doubts about him too. He should have come to us sooner and told us the whole truth from the outset.'

'Will you need me here over the next few days?' Johann asked abruptly.

'You want to go back to Föhr?'

'Just to help out the team – and maybe spend a few hours . . .'

'With Johanna?'

'I spoke to her on the phone this morning. I hope that's OK?' When Lena nodded, he went on. 'Maria's funeral is in three days. She asked me to go with her.'

'That's a good idea,' said Lena. 'I'll try to come too.'

'I'll get the full report to you at some point over the next week,' Lena wrapped up her verbal summary to DSU Warnke. She'd only managed to get hold of him over the phone as he was at a conference in Schleswig.

'Go ahead and take two extra days off,' Warnke replied. 'You've done sterling work. Well done!'

'Thank you.' Lena was surprised at this unaccustomed praise from her boss. She decided to seize the moment and broach a subject that had been preying on her mind over the last few days. 'How's your wife?'

'Thank you for asking.' After a brief pause, he added, 'My wife is devastated by everything that's happened. She's . . . what can I say? I've told her everything I could about the two sisters and the circumstances of the case.' He coughed. 'In my view, the victim's family and community aren't entirely free of blame for what happened.'

'Is that how your wife sees it too?' Lena ventured.

She heard her boss take a deep breath. He took his time replying. 'It's certainly given her pause for thought, if you understand what I mean.'

Lena was on the point of passing comment, but decided against it. 'Yes, I think so.' She hesitated for a moment before adding, 'Please do give her my regards.'

Lena was on her way to the Logeners' house. She had arrived in Wyk an hour ago and met Arno Brandt at the police station. With Warnke's help, she had managed to prevent Brandt from being suspended, and aside from a note in his personnel file he faced no further consequences. Her conversation with him had been brief: he had thanked her for interceding on his behalf, but had offered only a half-hearted apology for his rude and unprofessional behaviour. Lena had wished him all the best before setting off to visit the Logeners.

Maria's funeral was scheduled for eight o'clock the following morning and Lena had arranged to spend the night on Föhr in order to attend.

She parked her car in front of the Logeners' house and walked up to the front door, but it opened before she could ring the bell. Rosa Logener stepped out towards her and shook her hand. 'Please come in, Frau Lorenzen.'

Walther Logener was waiting in the hall. Much like his wife, he bore clear signs of the strain of the last few days. He too shook Lena's hand and asked her into the living room.

Rosa Logener sat down on the sofa beside her husband. 'Your young colleague came to see us yesterday and told us everything.'

Lena nodded. 'Yes, I asked him to do that.'

'Both of us – my husband and I – want to thank you again from the bottom of our hearts. You found the man who did this to our Maria. And you saved Martin from having to go to prison as an innocent man.' She placed her hand on her husband's.

He looked up sheepishly and added, 'We'd like you to join us tomorrow to bid farewell to our beloved daughter.'

'I'd love to,' Lena smiled. 'I've grown very attached to Maria over the last few days, even if I never knew her personally.' She paused briefly, adding, 'I do have one last request, though.'

Rosa Logener gave her a quizzical look.

'Johanna will also be at the funeral tomorrow,' Lena began.

'Yes, your colleague already told us that,' she replied, still clinging on to her husband's hand.

Lena continued, 'I feel sure that Maria would have wanted nothing more than to see you and Johanna reconciled. Maybe tomorrow can be the first step in that process.'

Walther Logener listened to Lena's words in silence, staring straight ahead.

His wife nodded. 'It would be lovely if Johanna could sit in the front row with us. Could you let her know?'

'I'd be delighted to, Frau Logener.' Lena stood up and the Logeners accompanied her to the front door.

'God be with you,' said Rosa Logener in farewell.

In her rear-view mirror, Lena saw the couple stand in front of the house and watch her until she turned back on to the road.

Epilogue

'How are you?' asked Erck.

Lena had rung him while she was standing on the dock in Wyk.

After Maria Logener's funeral, she had assembled the team for one last meeting. Johann's colleagues were heading back to Flensburg that afternoon, though Johann himself was planning to stay on Föhr until the start of the following week.

'I'm waiting for the ferry to Amrum,' Lena replied, without responding to his question.

'How long can you stay?'

'I need to come back here tomorrow to wrap up the case, but after that I'm on leave from the middle of next week until the weekend. Five days.'

'That sounds good.'

'Erck?'

'Yes, Lena?'

'We need to talk. Today.'

'I know.'

'Will you be at home when I arrive?'

'Yeah. I'll wait for you.'

'Good.'

Neither of them said anything for a while.

'The ferry's coming,' Lena eventually spoke into the silence.

'See you soon, Lena. I love you.'

She gnawed at her lip. 'See you soon, Erck.'

ABOUT THE AUTHOR

Anna Johannsen has lived in Northern Friesland since her childhood. She loves the landscape and the people of the region and is especially fond of the North Frisian islands that provide the setting for her Island Mystery novels starring DI Lena Lorenzen.

ABOUT THE TRANSLATOR

Photo © 2014 Jozef van der Voort

Jozef van der Voort is a literary translator working from Dutch, German and French into English. A Dutch–British dual national, he grew up in south-east England and studied literature and languages in Durham and Sheffield. He is an alumnus of the Emerging Translators Programme run by New Books in German and was also named runner-up in the 2014 Harvill Secker Young Translators' Prize.